Pippi's Inn for Wandering Spirits

Erin Ritch

No Wyverns Publishing

First published June 11, 2024

ISBN: 979-8-9903925-0-2

Introduction

Dear valued reader,

Thank you for coming with me as we join Pippi during her first year at the Windia Inn. I promise you a safe space, laughs, magical characters, many smiles, and also, some tears. In this story, we will touch upon themes of grief and loss, including the loss of children, a partner, and parents. We imagine what happens to the people we love after they pass on and how they stay connected to us. Maybe you're not ready to read about these subject matters now, or maybe it's just the right time for a story like this.

With love and respect,

Erin

For Mom, who taught me to write my first story.
I promise I won't forget.

Lorilee Ivy Borchers
1954-2024

Chapter One

It was strange to think she would experience feelings of excitement at her own aunt's funeral, but that was the exact state-of-mind Pippi Jennings found herself in on that late summer day. She took a deep breath to calm her skipping heart, refusing to look up from the small footstool she had locked her eyes on. She could *feel* the other funeral guests studying her face from behind their refreshments, looking for any hint of expression that could provide insight into the thoughts that raced through her mind. *What now?* Pippi imagined them whispering. *The girl knows nothing about the inn! Oh, this is a mess. What in the world was Hazel thinking?*

The wake for Hazel Jennings was held in the adorable house of cousin Winifred, a short drive from the cemetery they'd all gathered at not more than an hour before. Paintings of cats dressed in aprons in various kitchen scenarios decorated the heavily-wallpapered walls, along with extremely dated family photos and an overwhelming number of lighthouse sketches. But still, the house put Pippi at ease the moment she walked in, even with her head down, searching for the most out-of-the-way seat she could find.

A steaming teacup was placed upon the footstool, directly into Pippi's line of sight. She had no choice now but to look up, right into the smiling face of cousin Winifred.

"If you don't get up and come join us at the table then we'll all have to get up and come to you, and I just cut myself a giant piece of cake I'd rather like to enjoy eating from a flat surface."

Winifred tried to sound scolding but the badly-concealed smile gave away her true nature. As the closest of Hazel's distant cousins, Winifred had been the obvious choice as hostess of the wake. That, and no one else volunteered. She was dressed the part in head-to-toe black, as they all were, and her short blonde hair was pinned perfectly into neat curls. She wore a pair of dangling cat earrings and her wrists jingled with bracelets as she pointed to the table behind her.

Pippi nodded and smiled back weakly, the teacup rattling loudly in her hand as she stood from her chair. She took a moment to smooth out her black calf-length skirt and long silky blouse, which Pippi imagined showed every patch of sweat she felt on her back, chest, and armpits. Her feet were killing her in the only pair of black shoes she could find in her closet, a shiny pair of Mary Janes that Pippi now suspected she had intended to return for being too small. Pippi smoothed her wavy brown hair back behind her ears; she'd attempted to wear a thick black headband but ditched it halfway to the cemetery.

"Ah! The lady of the hour! Finally!"

The faces gathered around the table looked up at Pippi in a wave of halted conversations. They varied in age from eight to eighty and in their upturned faces Pippi saw a faint flicker of her own. All day she'd been wrestling with (amongst other things) the feeling she'd met all these people before, but in truth she had, each at a time she was too young to remember. But somewhere inside did.

What came next was a symphony of overlapping conversations as each person tried to call their question out louder than the other. Winifred silenced them with a whistle and a raise of her hand.

"Now, now! First of all, can we make room for the girl?" Winifred scolded, shooing away the youngest at the table, who seemed more invested in the cookies and cream crumble located in the center of the oversized table. Winifred gripped Pippi by the shoulders and gently (but firmly) sat her down.

"Can I tempt you with a treat?" Winifred whispered close to Pippi's face, her breath smelling heavily of mint.

"Oh, no thank you, I can't do gluten," Pippi answered, eyeing the cookies and cream crumble that was decidedly *not* gluten free.

"Phillipa Jennings," an elderly woman directly across from Pippi exclaimed, wagging her finger in the air. "Where *have* you been?"

"Oh, it's just Pippi," Pippi corrected. To her, *Phillipa* sounded like a character in a book. "And, honestly, that's a question for my mother."

Another clamoring of voices followed, some seemingly enraged and others full of pity. It wasn't a lie but Pippi felt a teensy bit guilty putting her mother in the direct line of her relative's ire, but all's fair when it comes to surviving family gatherings. Again, Winifred stepped in to quiet the room.

"Now, now, we all know about Rose and Hazel's, well, *falling out*." Winifred whispered the last part of her statement, as though she was disclosing a dirty little secret.

Pippi took a sip of her now cold tea. Rose was her mother, notably absent from her own sister's funeral. And Rose had also made sure Pippi was absent from this entire side of the family for the past twenty-five years, all stemming from this notorious *falling out* Pippi knew very little about. That is, until recently.

"Honestly, I only have a few memories of Aunt Hazel," Pippi admitted to her enraptured audience. "I was only five, maybe six years old the last time I saw her, when the *falling out* happened."

"At the inn, right?" another family member Pippi had-yet-to-reacquaint-with ventured.

"That's right."

Over the years, Pippi had played the scant flashbacks of that day over and over in her mind, in hopes of remembering the fuzzy details but also trying to decode them. She and her mother had been at Aunt Hazel's inn for a visit, as she was told they often did. The inn felt like the biggest building little Pippi had ever seen with endless hidden cubbies and stairs that made her legs ache. She remembered a kitchen that smelled like a restaurant, the salty breeze of the ocean that shone like diamonds in the distance, and the way the light refracted through the thick window glass.

Aunt Hazel herself was a tall enigma in these memories, a childless woman who wore linen overalls and gave out hugs as often as she did candy - which was a lot. She cried, she shouted, she pleaded, and all those things were what Pippi remembered last as she was carried away by her mother, sharing one last look with her aunt before the front door slammed shut between them.

"We did try to reach out to your mom, you know," Winifred sighed. "But as a mother myself, I really can't blame her for trying to protect you."

"Trust me, I've heard all about it." Pippi's voice turned colder than even she expected, recalling countless emotional conversations with her mother in the weeks between her aunt's passing and the letter arriving from the attorney. The letter that informed Pippi she'd inherited her aunt's inn in the little northern Oregon coastal town of Windia. "But this is my decision, now," Pippi told herself, everyone at the table, and her mother, who was hundreds of miles away.

"And you know *all* the details?" another yet-to-be-reacquainted-with family member asked. He leaned forward and made a spooky ghost sound.

"Roger! Really?" Winifred scoffed. "Grow up."

"Yeah, this is serious business, you fool," the finger-wagging cousin admonished.

"I do," Pippi assured the table. And she did. Her mother may have been against her accepting ownership of the inn, but there was nothing she could do about Pippi's natural-born gift to see the dead. A gift Rose did not have herself, but Aunt Hazel certainly did. In fact, Pippi saw a few spirits in the dining room at that very moment, some resting hands on a loved one's shoulder, a few exchanging knowing looks over inappropriate conversation, and others sighing as they watched a relative take a big bite of a fudgy chocolate cake that looked especially delicious.

Funerals and wakes were popular visiting events for spirits; Pippi always imagined it was for convenience sake as everyone was gathered together all at once. Other popular events that seemed to attract the dead were obvious ones like weddings or baby showers, but also seemingly insignificant ones like buying your first bra, haggling over a car purchase, or accidentally stepping on a hidden fragment of glass from a vase that broke months before. Really there seemed to be little rhyme or reason to when or why a spirit would visit for a few hours, and most smiled and nodded their head in Pippi's direction when they made eye contact, unable to hide the hint of sadness that only Pippi could see them and not the loved one they were *really* there for.

Pippi could share a hundred, maybe a thousand, other scenarios where spirits had shown up in her thirty-one years of existence. It had never been scary or strange for her (probably because she's seen them since she could remember) and the spirits certainly didn't look anything like what movies or television made them out to be. In reality, they appeared more like regular people in sometimes-dated clothing who never said anything, usually content to just sit and watch, happy to be part of their family again for an hour or two.

"There is just one thing," Pippi spoke up. "The inn itself is...special?"

Hushed snickers circled the table like a hot wind. Some relatives shot each other looks that seemed to say *poor girl* while others clearly stated *see, this is what I was talking about*. Winifred interrupted the display with a threatening throat clearing. One of the spirits nodded approvingly.

Winifred took Pippi's hand. "Don't mind them, dearest," she sighed. "You'll figure this out. Hazel wouldn't have left the inn to you if she didn't believe that."

"But she didn't really know me," Pippi voiced her hidden fear to the group. "And I don't know the first thing about running an inn, much less an inn for the dead."

A collective gasp made its way around the table.

"Oh stop, like y'all didn't know," Winifred reprimanded. She turned to Pippi and lowered her voice. "I think they're more surprised that *you* know what you're getting into," Winifred explained. "And still agreed to it."

Pippi clicked open the small black purse she'd been balancing on her lap. She pulled out a crumpled envelope, holding it up for the crowd that had expanded to include the remainder of the guests, who now gathered around the table.

"What's that?" Winifred whispered, her chair creaking as she leaned forward.

"I got this letter the day Aunt Hazel died." Pippi removed a sheet of battered stationery, shaking out the wrinkles in the paper. She looked around the table, glancing up at a few of the spirits gathered, half expecting Aunt Hazel to be there. "And it's from Aunt Hazel."

A collective gasp rippled around the room again, which was getting quite warm from the amount of body heat crammed into the small space. Even the spirits looked a bit cramped.

"Well?" demanded finger-wagging cousin. "Are you going to read it or not?"

What happened next was a commotion of shrieks, chairs overturning, toes getting stomped, tea spilling on Sunday best, Winifred's pet beagle diving for the cookies and cream crumble, and the spirits leaving to get some air in the backyard. The source of the kerfuffle was a small, reddish orange fox that had sauntered in from the adjoining kitchen, unseen until hopping up to the tabletop and sitting down complacently. The fox looked straight at Pippi, who was now standing, clutching her aunt's letter to her chest. The fox finally looked away and coughed loudly before asking, "Wouldn't you rather hear it straight from the source?"

Pippi sat in silence on Winifred's front porch where she'd been watching the transition from cherry sunset to moonlit clouds. Beside her on the wicker loveseat sat her temporarily-deceased Aunt Hazel, who now appeared to be reincarnated in the form of a talking fox.

Hazel snickered to herself in the way a fox snickers.

"What?" Pippi asked, taking a long drink of the wine that Winifred had been generously distributing.

"I'm just thinking back to that scene in the dining room," Hazel explained, shaking her head. "Everyone running away and you just standing there."

"I mean, for me, a talking fox isn't that much of a stretch," Pippi shrugged.

"Well, this is a stretch for *me*," Hazel scoffed, holding up a paw for investigation. "I certainly wasn't expecting this." She turned her deep brown eyes to her niece and Pippi saw a flicker of humanity there.

Pippi swiveled in her seat. "I hope this isn't too personal but...what was it like?"

"I presume you're talking about death," Hazel clarified dryly. "I don't have much to reveal. All I remember is closing my eyes for a few moments and when I opened them again I was myself, but inside a little fox body, sitting outside Winifred's dog door."

Pippi sat back. "I wonder why a fox?"

"That'd be me," Hazel admitted. "Always loved foxes, I doodle them on everything. Although I think I would've doodled something else if I'd known this was going to happen."

Hazel reached a paw out and laid it on Pippi's hand, her fur soft yet coarse, her claws still sharp even though retracted. "Don't worry, kid. I'm not here to take the inn back from you."

"Oh no," Pippi exclaimed far too loudly. "No, no, that's not something I was...well, if you want it back, of course, it was yours-"

"Pippi," Hazel interrupted firmly. "The inn belongs to you. But maybe I can help with the transition." She drew away her paw and sighed. "I sure would have appreciated that when I started." A thought came to Hazel's mind. "Maybe that's why I'm here."

"Yes!" Pippi agreed. "*Yes*, I will gladly take any help." The knot in her stomach loosened a bit at the prospect of receiving some sort of guidance in this new venture, even from a talking fox.

"You've got it, kiddo," Hazel yawned, stretching as she jumped to the porch floorboards. "For however long I'm here, which I have no idea about."

The screen door opened and Winifred stuck her head outside.

"Hi," she whispered in a high-pitched voice. "You ladies still catching up?"

"I think we've scratched the surface." Hazel looked to her niece. "Right?"

Pippi agreed they *had* scratched the surface of a very big lake of questions that had heavily iced over. It was as though their tete-a-tete on the porch was a casual coffee shop catch up scheduled over a short lunch hour while Pippi was on her way through town, where the conversation stuck to *How have you been?* and *Tell me about your mom's dog Pedro.*

But Pippi could barely get a word out before Winifred interrupted enthusiastically. "Great! Because we *all* have so many questions and honestly, Hazel, I'm so glad I'm going to have a chance to get your marvelous pecan pie recipe before you, well, I don't know. Anyway, come back in! I'll heat up some, um....what do you want, Hazel? Acorns? Anyway, come in!"

"Aunt Hazel, one more thing," Pippi quickly added.

Hazel nodded for Winifred to go inside and the screen door slammed shut.

"The letter," Pippi said, surprised at how her emotions were getting to her. "You meant it all?"

"Every single word," Hazel replied without a beat.

Pippi smiled and she thought Hazel smiled back. *This was going to take some getting used to.*

Hazel looked at the screen door and back at Pippi. "Do you mind?" She tilted her fox head towards the door. "This is going to take some getting used to."

Pippi jumped up and opened the screen door for Hazel, who trotted in to face the relations waiting inside for her. Pippi returned to her seat, allowing herself an extra moment of quiet. She pulled out the letter she'd received on the day that changed everything.

Dear Little Precious Phillipa,

I know you like to be called Pippi, but allow me this address as this was what I called you the first time I held you in my arms. When I say I am sorry for the time we've lost, it doesn't come close to capturing how sorry I really am. People fall out, but my love for you and Rose never waivered. That being said, I've always planned to leave you the inn, and with my passing, it's yours. You may think you don't know what to do, or how could I run an inn? Please don't worry, you and the inn will hold each other up so you both succeed. This job is bigger than you and me, you'll see.

The Handbook will tell you more. (Don't go up to the attic until you read it. <u>Trust</u> me.)

Love,

Aunt Hazel

Chapter Two

It was a mountainous shot north and a windy jaunt west from Winifred's house in Eugene to Pippi's new inn in Windia, Oregon. *That's right, I'm going straight from here to my new life,* Pippi told herself as she sat on the sidelines of the wake-turned-celebration-of-Hazel-returning-as-a-fox. She thought about how she'd feared she would back out, selling all her belongings and leaving the keys to her vacant apartment locked inside, ensuring there literally was no chance of return.

"How can you do this?" her mother had asked at their final goodbye. "After all I've done and sacrificed for you? You're going to that inn? What are you thinking?"

Pippi looked in the rearview mirror at the sleeping fox nestled atop a pile of coats and bedding. She readjusted her grip on the steering wheel and focused again on the forest-lined road in front of her, away from the realization she didn't have an answer for her mother then and she doesn't have it now. And that was absolutely, magically, deliciously, thrilling.

Hazel slept the entire three and a half hour trip, her whiskers occasionally twitching with new fox dreams. Pippi couldn't blame her for sleeping; the morning breakfast at cousin Winifred's hadn't exactly been relaxing and had followed a night of restless, heart-pounding sleep. The family had gathered on the porch to wave goodbye to the novice innkeeper and her animal companion, some of them shaking their heads while others nodded and said to each other, *I think she can actually do this.*

Whether the length of the nap had been suffice or she simply recognized the familiar twists and turns that led to her old homestead, Hazel woke as they passed the sign that announced their arrival in Windia. A town of less than a thousand, Windia was the quintessential Pacific Northwest coastal town with roots in the canning industry and where weather-beaten shanties lined the road next to shopping stores like Windia's Wonderland that sold all the essentials residents would need and everything else would have to be shipped in or require a drive back down the highway. Even through the closed car windows, Pippi could smell the ocean just a short reach away, as though Windia had washed up on shore one misty, mysterious morning when the tide was especially high. The fog was so thick that Pippi felt like she was driving through a cloud, as though descending from a marine layer was the only appropriate way for one to enter Windia.

"Keep on this way," Hazel instructed, moving to the front passenger seat. She propped her paws up on the dashboard. "Follow this through town and into the forest."

"I remember some of this," Pippi commented, waiting patiently at a crosswalk as a couple carrying enormous coffees crossed the street. They waved a *thanks* to Pippi, doing a triple take at the fox head poking up from the passenger seat.

Hazel settled back. "You loved the ice cream shop, it's still there, as a matter of fact." She sighed. "Couldn't bear to go back again after you and your mom left for good."

A heavy silence sat between them. They drove in that silence through the remainder of Windia, until the car broke back into the thick forest, the ocean obstructed from view, the fantasy ending abruptly. Hazel scratched at the window and Pippi slowed to discover a gravel road on the right side of the freeway, the entrance shrouded by a heavy canopy of oak trees. Pippi barely had time to signal before turning and if Hazel hadn't warned her, she'd surely have kept driving, never knowing anything existed there but a temporary break in the trees. It was a straight climb up the mountain from there as Pippi leaned over the steering wheel to get a good look up ahead. The thought of driving this poorly-graveled road in the winter was daunting as Pippi's car tires spun out more than once in the bare ground.

But finally the inn appeared into view, rising up right out of Pippi's memories. *Her* inn. A two story Victorian with a faded yellow paint job, the inn looked perfectly placed amidst the trees, like a lighthouse of sorts in the thick deciduous waters. A dozen memories reawakened in Pippi, of running up a staircase and the ocean view that she now glanced in her rearview mirror. A wrap-around porch both embraced the building and protected it like a halo, littered with chairs and rocking benches all facing westward towards the best view in town.

The car pulled to a stop in the driveway. Pippi opened the door and Hazel lithely brushed past her. The smell of the nearby ocean hinted to a time before, as though Pippi's senses had retained the memory of this place even though her mind urged them to move on. She followed Hazel up the river rock path that led to the wide wooden porch steps of the inn, lined by neatly-manicured miniature rose bushes and potted lavender. The heavy dark oak door, which was dominated by thick stained glass artwork, creaked open. An older woman emerged, easily in her early seventies, dressed in long black velvet overalls with big yellow rain boots, her white hair pulled up in a braided bun. She wrapped a thick black cardigan around herself and blocked the entry with her tiny body.

"We have no room for you, missy," the woman announced firmly, glowering down at Pippi. "There's a little motel about fifteen miles south, they'll take you in."

Pippi stared up at the woman, immediately threatened by her formidable presence, and chose to stay a safe distance away.

"Uh," she stammered finally, looking around for Hazel, who was nowhere to be seen. "I'm not here for a room. Well, actually, I *am* but-"

It was at this point that Hazel trotted up to the porch. The woman in the doorway took a step forward, her eyes widening as she crouched down to bended knee.

"Hazel Jennings," the woman whispered. "Is that you?"

"Yes, Pearl, it is," Hazel said with a nod.

Tears sprang to Pearl's eyes. "Why, Hazel! Praise to Mother Gaia! I see she wasn't done with you yet!"

"And I see you've been keeping good on your promise." Hazel motioned past the front door with her paw.

"Well, yes, of course." Pearl straightened and smoothed out her velvet overalls. She took on a serious tone. "Which is why I wasn't at your funeral, old friend. I wasn't about to leave the place unattended."

A realization visibly crossed Pearl's mind as she turned to Pippi with softer eyes. "So that makes you Phillipa," she said with a deep breath of relief.

"Pippi."

"Pippi, then. I'm glad to see you here."

"We had an agreement she would come watch the inn if anything ever happened to me," Hazel explained, swatting at a mosquito.

"And let me tell you, I am flying blind. Literally," Pearl complained.

"She knows about the inn? *All* about it?" Pippi asked carefully, dying to go inside and investigate every nook and cranny but manners deemed she engage in this conversation.

But Pearl had already turned her back, reaching in and rummaging around just inside the doorway. She returned with a small tote bag and an oversized broom, pushing stray strands of white hair out of her flushed face.

"Don't worry about that. No explanations needed here, dearest," Pearl said, giving Pippi a kiss on each cheek. "Welcome to Windia."

Pearl patted Hazel on the head as she skipped down the stairs. Hazel lowered her ears in response.

"I'm glad you're here too, old friend," Pearl added. "But this is the changing of the guard and I'm off to see my man. He promised me a trip to the hot springs and girls, do I need it."

"Can I give you a ride?" Pippi offered, seeing no other vehicle than her own on the hilltop property.

But Pearl had walked over to a clear spot of grass, dragging her broom behind her. She licked her finger and seemed to be determining the wind direction. Nodding, she hoisted herself atop the broom, which promptly floated to meet her. Pearl pulled a pair of goggles out of her tote bag and waved sweetly towards the girl and fox on the porch as she ascended into the sky.

"See you later, you two! Kisses!" she called out then shot off with the wind.

"Oh, she's a witch," Pippi observed. "Got it."

"Seemed the best option for an inn full of ghosts," Hazel admitted. "It was either her or the mortician."

Pippi watched Pearl disappear into a particularly puffy patch of clouds, no doubt for the concealment during the daytime, if that was a concern in Windia, Pippi considered. When she turned back, Hazel had disappeared as well, presumably into her old home and place of business. Pippi stared towards the open doorway with pause, frozen in a kind of out-of-body experience that said *If you make this choice, life will change in a completely different direction.* But the short glimpse of warmth she saw inside urged her to recognize what she knew was true. It was a place, a feeling, she trusted deep in her heart and there is no guide more fitting than that.

All her senses were overwhelmed at once when Pippi entered the inn. First, she smelled cookies, warm and buttery and she could almost taste the slightest hint of vanilla. Her feet sank into the plush emerald green carpets that stretched from wall to wall, occasionally marred with deep indentations left by heavy furniture long since moved away. Her eyes could not take in all the trinkets and dried flowers and tiny paintings and seashell charms that seemed to inhabit every nook and cranny while still remaining tasteful and uncluttered. Over the previous few weeks, Pippi had been imagining a bustling inn with guests coming and going, chatting and laughing as they went. Instead, it was completely quiet, except for the sound of a coffee pot hissing somewhere in the building and the tiny voice of Hazel down the hallway.

"In here!" she hollered.

Pippi closed the front door and left the cozy entryway, following her aunt's voice down the hall to where she also found the source of the hissing coffee pot. Hazel sat perched atop a long dining room table, easily the size of three or four average tables pushed together, gingerly lapping at a bowl of coffee. A well-stocked coffee station was tucked into the corner, filled with about every syrup imaginable.

Pippi had a sense the spirits of the inn were hiding, reduced to little flashes out of the corner of her eye, like mice darting out of sight. She knew they'd show themselves in time (they always did when they figured out who she was) so Pippi focused on the inn itself and how the light hit the corner or how the squeak of the floorboards reminded her of memories neatly tucked away.

Hazel let out a long, satisfied sigh, halting halfway through her bowl of coffee. "Oh, the fatigue," she sighed again. "This coming-back-from-the-dead business is exhausting."

"What should I do?" Pippi's heart rate started to escalate as though she was the one who drank half a bowl of coffee. "I…should I, well, read something? Unpack? Get dinner ready? Do the guests eat? What about you? Do I need to gather you grass or bugs or-"

Hazel raised a paw. "Child. Breathe. Please breathe."

Pippi breathed.

Hazed lowered her paw. "Here's what I would like you to do."

Pippi waited.

"Go for a walk."

"Where?"

"Around the inn." Hazel settled down into a curled ball, her eyes heavy. "Reacquaint yourself with the place. Introduce adult Pippi to the rooms. Do some pondering in the yard."

"I don't know my way around," Pippi protested, the ceiling suddenly looming fifty feet above her.

"Yes, you do," Hazel yawned. She snored lightly for a few beats before reiterating, "Yes, you do."

CHAPTER THREE

ENTRYWAY

Pippi backtracked to the front entryway, to the heavy front door that seemed, up close, twice the size of a normal front door. The stained glass etchings provided light and privacy, displaying scenes of a rose garden and ocean sunset and, strangely enough, a cute spider poking its head over the top of a heavily-decorated Christmas tree. Beyond the door the ocean called, but it was like white noise in a quiet room, that consistent rushing of blood that's always there, only presenting itself when a person really listens.

While the front door and its mysterious stained glass were certainly eye-catching, it was the dark cherrywood front desk that called to Pippi. It was enormous, almost as tall as she was, and a small step stool had been placed to provide a view over the desktop. The desk was mostly clean except for a rotary phone, which also looked oversized in comparison to modern phones of the day. Pippi picked up the phone and listened; no dial tone. Near the phone was a laminated sign that read *No outside calls*.

She continued to dig through the desk, finding a box of old receipts from 1993, a ring of keys, a graveyard of stretched-out rubber bands, and a leather bound book titled *Handbook for Housekeeping*. Photos of past proprietors adorned the walls and in their faces Pippi saw glimpses of her own. At last she found a picture of human Aunt Hazel, as she remembered her, standing on the front steps with Pippi as a child. Her mother had taken the photo and both woman and girl grinned ear to ear in the sunlight of that spring day.

PARLOR

A crash came from the room off to the left of the entryway, yanking Pippi from her stroll through the past. She decided to investigate but did not think much of the sudden sound, since new ghosts were notorious for accidentally knocking over objects or bumping into photo frames as they clumsily learned the art of concealment.

Much like the style of the grand desk in the entryway, the furniture in the parlor looked straight out of the 1920s, which Pippi made a mental note to ask Hazel about. A plush raspberry velvet sofa was parked in front of a large bay window, its view obscured by gauzy ivory curtains that pooled on the hardwood floors. The room was packed with comfortable seating and an oversized hutch displaying several dozen tea sets. Pippi found the source of the crash fairly quickly; a tiny figurine of a lighthouse had been knocked off an end table and belly flopped onto the floor. Pippi picked it up and returned the figurine to the table, doing so quickly as to not embarrass the spirit she assumed was hiding somewhere in the room.

LIBRARY

Deciding to give the spirit a break, Pippi crossed the entryway to the room directly across from the parlor, a library. Besides a well-worn window seat, every wall of the modest room was covered with packed bookcases of literature of every shape and size, along with a fireplace that burned low. Pippi read occasionally but as she perused the shelves, more than one title caught her eye. Intermixed with the usual classics like *Beowulf* or *The Great Gatsby* were unexpected titles like *Daughter of the Forest* and *Pride, Prejudice, and Zombies*. As Pippi turned back to the entryway, she spied a sign over the library entrance that stated *Writers and readers meet on the bridge of words.*

THE INNKEEPER'S ROOM

Off the front entryway was a tiny hallway, separate from the big hallway that led to the dining room. At the end was a single door and when Pippi opened it, she immediately recognized the scent of bar soap with the faintest hint of lavender, mixed with the inexplicable aroma of clean sheets. This had been her aunt's room, Pippi recognized it from the scant memories she did remember. And now, she supposed, this was her room.

It was modestly sized for the proprietor of an inn, containing a queen size, four-poster bed, a deep, long dresser with a mirror and a simple jewelry box. A window opened up to the east and offered a look over the backyard. A small door revealed a narrow walk-in closet from which a light bulb chain hung from the ceiling. Pippi pulled the chain and discovered her suitcases tucked into the corner. She pulled one out, startled at how light it felt. *Empty?* She scanned through the clothes hanging in the closet but nothing looked familiar. Back out in the room, the dresser was packed with clothes but none of them her own.

A plush, clay-colored cardigan had been laid out on the bed. Pippi touched it, picked it up, and smelled it. *Clean.* After looking around to see if anyone was watching (she didn't see any spirits in here, maybe it was off limits) Pippi pulled on the cardigan and sighed. *Comfort.*

UPSTAIRS

After peeking into a simple but cozy en suite bathroom, Pippi returned to the front of the inn. Even though her stomach was growling, she could hear her aunt's foxy snores from the dining room and didn't want to wake her. Besides, the grand staircase in the entryway was calling her, and she assumed all the spirits in the inn had scrambled upstairs or were hiding in the backyard.

But when Pippi reached the top of the stairs (a bit winded) she found every single door locked. There were approximately twelve to fifteen doors, all numbered something different in an order that made no sense, apparently leading to bedrooms, which was surprising considering the size of the inn from the exterior. In one corner a string fell from the ceiling with a tiny note attached to it, reading *Attic entrance - DO NOT ENTER before reading the Handbook for Housekeeping!*

Pippi wrapped her cardigan around her a bit tighter and made a mental note to ask more about *that*, in addition to where all her clothes were. She tried to open a few of the doors but they were locked. She wondered if all the spirits were behind them, listening to her in the hallway. Pippi wished she could say something that would calm their nerves, but the only thing she could think of was more of a statement than a comforting sentiment.

"Lovely up here! I'll just go down and eat some food!" she announced loudly, backing towards the stairs. "Maybe you'll all join me there later?"

Pippi screamed when she turned and came face-to-face with a ghost.

"Who are you talking to?" the woman asked. She was late-middle aged, her thick brown hair stuffed under a wide brim sun hat. She repositioned a large tote bag from one shoulder to the other, which appeared to be stuffed with magazines, a camera, water bottle, and sunscreen. Her long kaftan pooled around her perfectly-pedicured toes.

"Hi," Pippi gulped. This was the most alive-looking spirit she'd ever encountered. She could practically smell the coconut sunscreen on her tan skin.

"Hi," the woman replied slowly, her eyebrows raised at Pippi's frozen demeanor. She stuck out her hand. "Lucy."

Pippi shook Lucy's hand, which felt cool and greasy. "Nice to meet you. I'm Pippi."

Lucy's face brightened. "The new innkeeper?"

"Yes, I am. But I'm *very* new."

"Oh, anyone's better than that grumpy old witch woman," Lucy sneered. "She couldn't hear a word we said and sat around drinking coffee all day." She shrugged and walked past Pippi towards the guest rooms. She paused before opening a door. "Did you think there were guests behind the doors?"

"Well, yes," Pippi admitted.

"Why would we do that?"

"Uh, well, to hide?"

"From what?" Lucy seemed genuinely puzzled.

Pippi didn't quite know how to answer.

"There's no one here, you know. We're all down at the beach. And the inn locks these doors, not us. Did you say you were getting something to eat?"

Pippi nodded.

Lucy smiled. "Then you'll see."

DINING ROOM

Hazel was still asleep in the dining room as Pippi passed through, her tongue hanging out and sprawled across a large silver plate that had appeared beneath her snoozing head. In fact, large silver plates had appeared all along the enormous table, along with pitchers of water and iced tea, steaming carafes of coffee, and, from the smell of it, bowls of yeast rolls. From the number of place settings, there had to be at least a dozen guests expected, in addition to Hazel's plate and a setting at the head of the table that Pippi wondered if was meant for her.

Pippi's mouth literally watered as she tiptoed by the table to the adjoining room that could only be the kitchen. She planned to introduce herself to the cook and break the news on her gluten-free lifestyle.

KITCHEN

While the adjoining room *was* the kitchen, there was no cook to be found. In fact, it looked like the cook had literally just stepped out, judging from the boiling gumbo, half-chopped chopped salad on the countertop, and the stand mixer still mixing what appeared to be chocolate cake batter.

"Hello?" Pippi called out over the whir of the food processor. She walked over to turn off the food processor but the button wouldn't budge. She jumped back as a bowl of shrimp swiftly lifted itself into the air and dumped its contents into the steaming vat of aromatic gumbo.

Pippi took a few steps back out of necessity, as various other kitchen gadgets, ladles, and food items cascaded through the air in a swift symphony of movements that signaled everything was getting done at once. Pippi squinted her eyes, rubbed them, and squinted again. She didn't see a single spirit, not at the stove, not in the cavernous pantry, and not in the breakfast nook that had a glass of red wine, half empty, sitting on the table. So if there weren't any spirits...*how was everything moving?*

With no one to actually tell about her gluten sensitivity, Pippi returned to the dining room to find twelve expectant spirit faces and a fox waiting for her at the table.

Chapter Four

A second later, Pippi realized these expectant faces were not for her but for the food that went whizzing out through the kitchen door behind her. Individual bowls of steaming gumbo plopped down in front of each guest with not a drop spilled on the lacy tablecloth. Beignets, fried okra, deviled eggs, and giant bowls of rice followed next, which the guests piled onto the plates. Hazel delicately picked up a beignet with her teeth and dropped it on her plate to tear apart.

The dining room filled instantly with the hubbub of conversation, spoons clinking against bowls, and the occasional *whoops* as a cup was knocked over and an invisible force came to sop it up with a towel, then whisk the towel away back to the kitchen. The only guest that paid Pippi any attention was Lucy, who offered a little wave as she sipped on a cup of coffee. She had changed out of her beachwear kaftan into a dinnertime kaftan, but the other guests still showed signs of their time at the beach with smears of sunscreen on their nose or the telltale sign of hair mussed by the ocean wind.

Pippi walked down to the only empty seat available, the seat she had guessed belonged to her, at the head of the table. Her stomach ached as she stared at the food, resigned to the fact she'd be stuck with eating a plate of deviled eggs in this sea of gluten. But when she sat down, a packed plate of food was before her; gumbo, rolls, beignets, and, of course, deviled eggs, all topped with a little flag that touted *Gluten free!* She looked from her plate to Hazel, who'd been watching her niece's expression.

"The inn takes special requests," she winked.

"Delicious," Pippi mumbled through a mouthful of food. "So," she continued through a beignet. "You neglected to tell me that the inn is alive." *The strange sounds. The locked doors. The floating kitchen utensils.* Now, it made sense.

Hazel snickered. "It's just more fun for me to watch you find out for yourself. Except I was napping..."

"And where would the inn have placed my clothes? My suitcases are empty."

"Oh, they're long gone," Hazel explained matter-of-factly. She paused. "I can't even remember how I used to dress before taking over here." She shrugged her bony fox shoulders and began lapping at her gumbo.

"Excuse me?" Pippi was wearing her favorite pair of jeans, a long sleeve henley, and the oversized cardigan she'd found in her room. She liked this outfit but not enough to wash and rewear it every day.

"The inn will pick your clothes each day," Hazel explained. "This is a proper establishment, dear. We have a reputation to upkeep. No offense to your jeans with the holes in it. I'm sure they're very comfortable." She chewed on a piece of meat that the inn had deemed safe for a fox to eat. "On the plus side you'll never do laundry again."

"So, the inn dresses me, cooks for us, and I'm assuming also does the yardwork?"

"No, that's you."

"Okay. Dishes? Cleaning? Grocery shopping?"

"All the inn. And don't even ask me about the food, I have *no* idea how the inn takes care of that."

"And me...?" Pippi opened her hands and left the sentence unfinished.

Hazel leaned forward. "*You* are here for our guests." She crooked her head in the direction of the guests who were completely absorbed in their food and conversations. "And you will soon see why."

Before Pippi could press further, Hazel trotted into the middle of the table and cleared her throat, which came out more like a whimpering growl. Somewhere, the inn clinked loudly on a glass for attention and the table fell silent.

"Thank you," Hazel told the inn. She turned her attention to the guests, none of which looked surprised to see a talking fox.

"Hello, all. I'm Hazel, the former proprietress of this inn. Some of you know me from before (*Hello, George, I look different, don't I? Haha!*) but I see a few new faces. Thank you for being so understanding in this time of transition."

The guests nodded.

"This is my niece." Hazel motioned with her tail towards Pippi. "While there will be a few bumps in the road, I assure you that you're in capable hands and I will be here in a training capacity as long as I can."

"And the phone calls?" one woman spoke up. She was young, maybe early thirties, and she had caught Pippi's eye not only because of her youth but for the two young boys she had with her, maybe six and eight years old. One of them sat on her lap as she had spent the last twenty minutes encouraging him to try gumbo until the inn finally brought out a bowl of macaroni and cheese.

"No phone call will be missed, I give you our word," Hazel assured them.

"The phone rang a few times when that witch was here," another guest spoke up. "She didn't answer it." This guest had spiky red hair that was shellacked with gel.

"I understand. I told her not to. We have a backup voicemail system," Hazel explained. "I understand it's not ideal and my niece will check it right after dinner. But that will never happen again."

The guests looked relieved although solemn. The mood in the dining room had significantly shifted. The inn clearly picked up on the change and lowered the lights. A drum roll rattled and the kitchen door flung open as a spotlight pointed directly at Pippi's frozen face.

"With no further ado!" Hazel announced, her voice projecting as if through a loudspeaker. "I officially introduce to you our lovely new proprietress...Phillipa Hazel Jennings!"

The guests gasped and applauded as a giant cake topped with sparklers rolled out of the kitchen, sliding to a stop at Pippi's side. She stared at the monstrous cake which boasted *Welcome, Pippi!* with a smaller message below reading *Gluten free*.

Each guest got their own slice of cake and personal sparkler, which roused the spirit's spirits and had them laughing and chatting again in no time. They waved their sparklers in the air and chanted, "Speech! Speech!"

"*Oh no*," Pippi muttered under her breath as she slowly stood to her feet. "Um," she started and the table fell silent other than the hissing sparklers. For the first time she made eye contact with each and every guest there. Some young, some old, some sadder than others. She'd never made *real* eye contact with a spirit before; they always seemed preoccupied or uninterested in Pippi's attempts at conversation. Now, she realized, as these guests stared at her with complete trust, those spirits simply felt alone. Here, they felt found.

Pippi cleared her throat. "First of all, you can call me Pippi, not Phillipa. And I see all of you. I *really* see all of you. I've always been able to see others like you. I don't know a lot yet about this business here, but I figure that's a start? Thank you."

The guests offered a few nods and a polite clap then immediately returned to their conversations and cake. Pippi had only taken one bite of her own slice before Hazel motioned for her to follow. Reluctantly leaving the cake behind, Pippi followed her aunt into the entryway.

Hazel hopped up to the registration desk. "We need to check the voicemail before they go to bed," she explained, pawing at the rotary phone. "Hopefully this is the only time we will have to check it. It's very important we do *not* miss calls."

"Who are these calls for?" Pippi asked, sitting down on a nearby stool that was topped with a fluffy, plush cushion. By the way the cushion sunk it was obvious this seat had been utilized quite a bit.

"The guests."

"What?"

"*The guests*. I hate repeating myself Pippi, really," Hazel huffed. She pawed a pen and notepad in Pippi's direction. "I'll do the first message so you can see what notes to take. You do the second." She paused for a beat. "You'll understand after that."

Hazel walked Pippi through the voicemail retrieval process, which involved simply dialing zero and entering Pippi's birthday as the passcode. Pippi held the receiver up to Hazel's ear and waited for note dictation orders.

"It's for George. Two days ago," Hazel began, then stopped to listen. "His wife." There was a long pause. "Sam passed his exam." Hazel closed her eyes then and blinked a few times.

Pippi's throat tightened.

"I don't think George needs more than that," Hazel said. "Your turn. Press seven to erase and it will play the next message."

"Okay." Pippi slowly put the receiver to her ear. She pressed seven.

"Message erased," a soothing voice confirmed over the line. "Next message for...Lidia. From Claire. One day ago."

Pippi took a fresh sheet of paper and scribbled down the name and date. She glanced up at Hazel, who watched her every move.

When the recording first started, all Pippi could hear was what sounded like white noise. Long, stretching white noise. Then she heard quiet sniffling.

"Someone's crying?" Pippi whispered to her aunt, who nodded. This didn't seem to be startling.

"I miss you." It was a female voice, barely a whisper. Pippi had to strain even to make out those words. "I just really miss you."

The hairs on Pippi's arm stood on end. She could feel the overwhelming emotion in this woman's small, whispered words.

"Message complete." The calm voice returned followed by a chime. "To repeat, press one. To erase, press seven. To save, press nine."

Pippi pressed seven.

"Thank you," the recorded voice responded. "There are no further messages. Goodbye."

Hooking the receiver back onto the phone with a satisfying *click*, Pippi paused before looking at her aunt.

"What did they say?" Hazel asked.

"Her name was Claire. She just said that she missed her." Pippi felt sick to her stomach, like she'd been tossed around on an amusement ride and her body was just now catching up. Or like she'd just eavesdropped on a conversation that was not meant for her.

"Write it down," Hazel instructed. She glanced down towards the dining room. "They're wrapping up dessert."

Pippi did as she was told, writing simply *Claire really misses you*.

As she finished the note, the guests exited the dining room and strolled down the hallway. The inn was already clearing the table in a whirl of dishes that whisked off in the direction of the kitchen.

"Lidia? George?" Hazel called out from her perch atop the reception desk. She turned to make sure Pippi was watching and learning. "Can I have a moment?"

The guests all exchanged looks, some relieved, some with pity for Lidia and George. George had been one of the friendliest faces Pippi had identified at the table, with a gentle countenance shining from behind his wrinkles and perfectly slicked back white hair. Lidia was the woman with spiky red hair that had reported the missed phone calls. Maybe somehow she knew one was for her.

Lidia and George approached the reception desk, like two children reporting to the teacher's office. Pippi took this as her cue to hand over the messages, which they accepted and immediately read. George nodded *goodnight* to Pippi and Hazel and turned to lumber up the stairs. Lidia lingered longer, staring at the simple message. She turned her eyes on Pippi.

"Was she very upset?" she asked.

Pippi glanced at Hazel out of the corner of her eye and wished she could read her aunt's fox expression for a clue on how to proceed.

Follow your gut. "No. I think she just wanted you to know," she said (convincingly, she hoped.)

Lidia took a deep breath and nodded, following the rest of the guests upstairs. Pippi waited until she heard the last door shut before making eye contact with Hazel again.

"I lied," she burst out. "The woman on the message was sobbing. Did I do wrong? Am I fired?"

Hazel chuckled. "Well read! And, of course you're not fired. It would take much more than that."

"These calls are...?" Pippi raised her eyebrows for her aunt to finish.

Hazel leaned in for Pippi to finish her own sentence.

"...family members of the spirits?"

"Guests."

"Family members of the *guests?*"

"Family, friends, lovers. Sometimes even enemies to repent their sins."

"How?"

"Really? You're standing in a building that's currently washing the dishes by itself with a dozen dead spirits upstairs and you're asking *how?*"

"*Guests.*"

"Now you're catching on." Hazel plopped down to the ground. "Honey, honestly, I don't know how the phone works, it just does. I've tried unplugging it and it still rings."

"What do I do if it rings? You said don't let it go to voicemail. What if I can't make it here in time?" Pippi felt on edge. She'd never been good on the phone.

"You'll have a cell phone to keep with you at all times. The cell phone and the inn phone are connected and ring at the same time. Got it? And you don't have to say anything special," Hazel assured. "Just answer the phone, listen for the name, say *one moment, please* and go get the guest. They'll come take the call. If they're not here, by chance, take a message."

"So the spirits - guests - talk back to the caller?" Pippi had to know every in and out of this if she was going to sleep tonight. And she felt very, very ready for sleep.

"No, unfortunately they can't talk back. But they never try. Still, it helps, somehow. It helps the guest to be there for the caller and it helps the caller to feel a closeness, I presume. Have you ever experienced that? When you feel like someone you lost is very close?"

"Yes," Pippi smirked. "I've been feeling that quite a bit lately."

"Ha. Ha." Hazel wandered up to the front door, which opened on its own.

"And where are you going?" Pippi asked.

"I don't know, I feel like roaming," Hazel explained. "Must be a fox thing. I mean, I did nap most of the day." As the door closed behind her, Hazel called out, "Goodnight!"

Pippi needed no further prompting. After double-checking the phone receiver was securely on the hook, she walked to the warm light coming from her bedroom and shut the door behind her. A set of pink silk pajamas had been laid on the bed, which was turned down. A candle on the nightstand released a cozy vanilla scent. Pippi slipped into the pajamas and pulled the covers up, revealing a book that'd been nestled in the layers of cotton sheets. It was the book she'd seen before at the reception desk, titled *Handbook for House-keeping*. Enough had happened on Day One that Pippi stopped questioning how the book got there. Although she felt ready to fall asleep on the spot, Pippi picked up the book and started reading.

When Your Aunt Leaves You an Inn and You Have No Idea What To Do

Welcome to your new inn! Before you curse your aunt for leaving you this responsibility - that you did not ask for - stop! The inn is listening and does not care for crotchetiness. Do not let that frighten you, however; no harm will come to you within these walls. (At the very worst, you may run out of toilet paper and the inn will hide all the extra rolls, if you deserve it.)

This is your inn. It has always belonged to a Jennings aunt and has always been passed to a Jennings niece. Which is you.

The inn is not for living humans and is to be kept from them. It is a private affair for spirits only. Specifically, those that are between death and the afterlife.

Did we just say spirits? Yes, we did. After death, spirits are allowed a period of travel on earth before continuing to the afterlife. Most spirits use this time to see those places they always wanted to go. (The Pacific Northwest is a popular travel spot!) See the chapter "The Guests" for more information. But this time also allows the spirits (our guests) an opportunity to be nearby for grieving family and friends. See the chapter "Phone Messages for Guests" for more information.

The inn handles most of the daily tasks for you such as meal prep, dishes, etc. (all detailed here in this handbook.) But you will need to tend to guests, take messages, and any other duties a sentient inn simply cannot deal with. Treat the inn respectfully and it will do the same to you. Rather simple, right?

Is this peculiar? Yes. But take a breath. Somewhere inside you already knows what to do.

Pippi flicked next to the chapter.

The Guests

After death, spirits are allowed a period of time to visit the places they always wanted to see before continuing on to the afterlife. The guests decide when it is time to move on, often after their human form is put to rest.

Many are drawn to Windia due to its "supernatural" history and ocean views. While the guests know they are dead, their method of death is unknown. They will appear in their last living form, although they will not show themselves to living humans. That is frowned upon, unless the living human is residing inside the inn. (Which would ONLY be you, right?)

Guests can receive messages from family and friends. They may listen and feel present for those left behind. Under no circumstances can a guest reply to a message.

"One more," Pippi told herself.

The Attic Spiders

Pippi sat up straight in bed.

*The inn's spider companions live in the attic. They are LARGE, semi-retired battle spiders who protect the inn from The Bats (see chapter "What to do When the Migrating Warrior Bats Come to Visit Every 101 Years.") They also assist the inn *as needed* and manage the attic space for you. They will bring down holiday decorations in exchange for gift baskets. DO NOT come empty handed or they will help themselves to something else. (Probably you.)*

"Okay, then." Pippi fanned her hot face, looking up at the ceiling. She needed a happier chapter to read before bed, turning to *How to Make Breakfast.* Drifting off at some point, Pippi dreamed of cities made of pancakes and lakes of syrup, where ghost people kayaked on waffles with oars of cinnamon sticks on which were inscribed, with bright red letters, the words *Gluten free!*

Chapter Five

Pippi thought she was still dreaming when she woke up to the un-mistakable aroma of melted butter and warm syrup. She wiped her face to find she'd been heavily drooling through the night. Beside her laid the open *Handbook for Housekeeping*. Her mind and body had to adjust to the newness of her bedroom, which felt alien compared to her old cramped apartment in the city. It was so quiet, there were no cars whizzing by outside or crosswalks beeping, just absolute silence, and even the light looked different in the way it poured in through the window and pooled on her bed.

She kicked off her blankets and turned on the shower in the tiny adjoining bathroom. Although her packed clothes had been whisked away to an unknown location, the inn had been accommo-dating enough to let Pippi keep all her toiletries and an inspection under the counter revealed back-up refills for all her toiletries, as well. The water in the shower was not *quite* as scalding as she pre-ferred, so Pippi ventured, "A little hotter, please?" After a few clinks and clanks behind the wall, the water temperature went up several degrees.

When she got out of the shower, a perfectly-pressed outfit laid ready for Pippi at the end of the bed. She had never been one to care *too* much for fashion but she was particular about fabrics. Nothing itchy, nothing constricting, and *nothing* that couldn't go in the dryer. But the outfit was perfect; a soft, white long sleeve undershirt paired with sage-colored linen overalls with wide legs that ended just perfectly at her ankles. And there were pockets. So many pockets. On the floor were a pair of shiny black sneakers and plush, cotton socks. Pippi combed her wet hair and looked at herself in the mirror. It was not an outfit she would have ever picked, but somehow, it was her.

Before leaving her room, Pippi vaguely remembered something she'd read before falling asleep. *Or had she?* She flipped through the handbook until she found the page about breakfast.

How to Make Breakfast

Breakfast will be served promptly at 7:37 am each morning, based on the proprietor's dream from the night before. On the chance there is no dream or the proprietor does not sleep, then breakfast will default to dry cereal (no milk) and lukewarm, weak coffee. (Allergies will still be accommodated.)

Even before entering the dining room, Pippi's hopes were confirmed simply by the aroma that wafted down the hall. The guests were already indulging in their own personal towers of pancakes and waffles, each structure dripping with a buttery brown waterfall of steaming syrup. There was a bowl of cinnamon sticks, although these were not inscribed with *gluten free* as in her dream but the detail really wasn't necessary. There were several appreciative nods from the guests as Pippi sat down in her seat, but no one seemed more excited about breakfast than Hazel, who had decimated her tower into a pile of wet crumbs.

"That was so good," Hazel murmured, sitting back in her seat. "Great, great choice."

"Is it true what happens if I don't dream of anything?" Pippi delicately removed the *gluten free* flag from the top of her tower. She grabbed a waffle and took a bite. *Heaven.*

"Don't worry about it. Now that the idea is planted in your head you'll dream every night, at least I did." Hazel lapped at her bowl of coffee. "Love the outfit."

"And the giant spiders?" Pippi said through a mouthful of food. "Can you elaborate on that situation?"

"What about it?"

"*What about* an attic of spiders that are large enough to move a box of holiday decorations?"

Hazel blinked slowly. "Dearest," she began. "They are the sweetest babies, a little shy, that's why we do the exchange at night. When everyone's sleeping they bring down what you ask for and pick up the little thank you gift you leave them. I shower those sweeties with goodies whenever I can. In fact, last time I was a human in town I saw this crochet pattern for sweaters, I think if we played with the measurements we could upsize them to fit. They'd love that."

Pippi stared. "Upsize them?"

"I'd say they're an adult extra, extra large? They like a snug fit. Of course, we need to add more sleeves. Rich, deep jewel tones are their favorite."

"But-"

"And do you think anyone is going to mess with this inn with giant spiders in our attic?" Hazel lowered her voice. "They're *very* protective of the ones they love."

Pippi straightened in her seat. "Keep the spiders happy. Got it."

"Now," Hazel yawned. "I think it's time for a morning nap."

Pippi took a swig of tea. "I was hoping you'd walk through the day with me." She cocked her head towards the guests. "And help me with *them*."

"Girl, I was wandering the beach all night," Hazel yawned again. "No idea what I was looking for. I'm still adjusting to this whole animal instinct situation, you know. I'm myself but..." She shrugged and pushed forward a sheet of paper with her snout. "Besides, I wrote up an itinerary for you. Well, the inn helped me write it."

Pippi looked over the paper, which was written with the most neat, ornate penmanship she'd ever seen.

The inn will take care of breakfast, lunch, dinner, and midnight tea. You start with the morning yardwork, sweep the deck, join the guests for lunch, have an afternoon nap, then dinner, then stay up for midnight tea. Be available for guests at all times and ALWAYS have your phone with you!

"You missed midnight tea last night but it's fine." Hazel jumped down from her chair and stretched.

"I'm not really a napper." Pippi scratched her head. "And what-" She reached into her front overalls pocket, where she suddenly became aware of a bulge. "A cell phone?" The cell phone was oversized and dated. She flipped it open to a dreamy bright screen that read *No missed calls.*

"Well, you're a napper, now," Hazel said, slinking away. "And speaking of naps, I'll see you at lunch."

Pippi became extremely aware of the sudden silence in the dining room. She looked down at her food and peeked up to see the guests all watching her. She took a sip of tea for courage.

"Morning, all!" she greeted loudly.

The guests nodded pleasantly, some echoing back the same sentiment.

"Sorry about midnight tea last night," Pippi managed. "I just heard about it this morning."

"That's fine, we know," Lucy spoke up. "We're just glad you're here."

Pippi blushed. She looked around at the other faces at the table. They actually *did* look glad she was there. She stood up, holding the itinerary in her hand.

"I'll just be outside." She glanced out one of the large bay windows at the gentle precipitation dripping down the glass. "Doing yardwork."

Tucking the cell phone back safely in her front pocket, Pippi exited the dining room and made her way towards the front door. If there was another entrance for the inn she hadn't found it yet. She paused at the reception desk first, which was clean and looked the same as last night. She glanced around to see if anyone was watching and picked up the phone receiver and listened. *Complete silence.*

The inn had hung a long, waterproof rain slicker on the coat rack along with a similarly waterproof bucket hat and a pair of rain boots. Upon further inspection of the rainwear, which all matched with the same shade of dark hunter green, Pippi discovered it was also covered with a tiny little fox face pattern.

"Nice touch," Pippi said to the inn, who swung the door open for her, revealing a blustery coastal morning. In the distance, the ocean roared and tossed, disguised by the heavy marine layer.

She slipped into her rainwear, which, as expected, fit perfectly, and exited the inn. All necessary sweeping and yard tools were propped up on the front porch for her. Pippi started with the sweeping in case any guests came out for storm watching, methodically making her way across the wraparound porch. There wasn't much to sweep up which Pippi suspected was due to the daily attention. When the floor looked clean (enough) Pippi shook out the cushions on the porch furniture, which were completely spider-free.

"Oh, of course," Pippi gulped, looking up towards the attic.

She waited a few moments to see if the rain would stop but it seemed determined to continue on in a constant drizzle that wasn't going anywhere. The air was so thick with moisture that Pippi could feel it on her face even before she stepped out into the rain, like she'd been misted with an odorless perfume when she wasn't looking.

Dragging the yard tools down the stairs with her, Pippi looked back behind the inn. Heavily forested with a mix of evergreen and deciduous trees, a mountain rose impressively like a protective older sister having its little sister's back, shielding the inn from what-ever stretched behind her, which Pippi suspected was just more heavily-forested mountains. The air certainly smelled like trees were nearby but occasionally the wind would shift and deliver a whiff of that unmistakable ocean aroma of salt and marine life.

Leaving the tools behind, Pippi inspected the yard to see what actually needed done. Since summer was winding down the yard was too; the rhododendron bushes were long past their bloom and the rose bushes were heavy with uncut buds that now wilted over with shriveled petals. The lawn was short and mostly on the dry side. Pippi followed it around to the back of the inn where she found a courtyard and a tiny shed, painted the same pale yellow of the inn. She peeked through the window and discovered a lawn mower and various other yard tools.

A loud rumble erupted in her chest and Pippi practically jumped out of her skin. Breathlessly, she yanked off her gloves and reached down into her overall's pocket, pulling out the ringing cell phone. *How many rings until it goes to voicemail?* She had to be on ring three or four by now. *Fifth ring.* Pippi steadied her breath. *Answer it now.* She flipped open the phone, the screen blasting *incoming call!* She pressed the green phone icon and held the phone up to her ear, tucking it safely under the protection of her bucket hat.

"Hello?" she whispered.

There was a click and the same calm voice from the voicemail said, "Incoming call for Stephanie from Paul. Ready to connect?"

"Uh, wait!" Pippi blubbered, stumbling over her boots as she raced towards the front of the inn. "Can you wait?"

There was no answer.

"Hello? Please wait!" she panted, bounding up the front porch steps.

"Ready to connect?" the calm voice asked again.

At least Pippi and the calm voice on the other line seemed to be in a holding pattern. Once inside, Pippi stomped down the hallway, still in her rainwear, to the dining room. *Empty.*

"Ready to connect?"

"No, no, not yet!" Pippi panicked. She ran back to the reception desk and rummaged through the drawers. Who was Stephanie? She hadn't met a Stephanie yet. Was there a guest log somewhere? A room map? An emergency alarm button she could press that would send a firework signal in the air for her aunt?

"Ready to connect?"

"A little help here?" Pippi yelled at the inn.

A bell *dinged* somewhere upstairs. Pippi raced to the foot of the stairs as one of the bedroom doors opened. The younger woman she'd seen before with the two children appeared at the top of the stairs and looked down at Pippi.

"Did you hear that?" the woman asked.

"*Ready to connect?*"

"Are you Stephanie?" Pippi called up.

The woman went white as a ghost.

"Yes." She already looked emotional as she descended the stairs, still in her pajamas with her reddish brown hair wrapped in a top knot. "Is it for me?"

Pippi breathed again. "Yes, yes it is."

Stephanie went directly to the stool behind the rotary phone, her face solemn.

"Ready to connect?" the voice on the phone queried.

"Are you ready?" Pippi asked.

Stephanie placed a hand on the phone receiver and paused. "Will you go up with my boys? I don't want..."

"Sure," Pippi assured. "Anything."

"Okay." Stephanie took a deep breath. "This is my first time."

"Mine too."

"Ready to connect?"

"I'm ready." Stephanie picked up the receiver and pressed it to her ear. She closed her eyes.

"Yes, we're ready," Pippi said into her cell phone and she knew by the look on Stephanie's face when it was time for her to hang up.

Chapter Six

Pippi found Stephanie's sons upstairs in the room with the only open door. They were sprawled out on the floor, looking over a large map of the world, and appeared the least bit surprised to see Pippi in their doorway.

This was her first time inside of a guest's room, which was much bigger than she imagined. The ceiling reached at least fifteen feet into the air, with floor-length windows that lined the wall and looked out to the forest behind them. It was a full living room with an oversized sectional, a desk for writing, and a sixty inch television mounted over the fireplace, a fireplace for which Pippi had not seen a chimney. There were multiple other doors which she assumed led to bedrooms and bathrooms. If spirits needed that.

"Hi!" Pippi tried hard to calm her breath, which was still shaking from the run up the stairs. "Your mom is busy so I'll be hanging out with you. What are your names?"

"Anthony," said the older boy.

"I'm Caleb," said the younger boy, grinning to display his missing two front teeth.

"What are you up to?" Pippi asked as she entered the room.

"Looking at our next vacation spot," Caleb said, holding up the map. "I want to go to Disneyland!"

"Caleb," Anthony snapped. "Mom said she hadn't decided yet."

Pippi had no idea what they were talking about. If the spirits wandered all the way down to Disneyland, how would she get a hold of them if a call came through?

When Stephanie returned to the room she found Pippi at the desk with the boys, compiling a list of her recommended rides at Disneyland and which order to try them in. Anthony took the list from Pippi and looked it over.

"You left off the Haunted Mansion," he noted, eyes twinkling.

It was Pippi's turn to go pale. "Uh, um…"

Both boys burst out laughing.

"Okay, okay," Stephanie chided, although she couldn't help looking amused at Pippi's embarrassment. She met Pippi's gaze and mouthed *thank you.*

"How'd it go?" Pippi wasn't sure if she should ask but she also couldn't help herself.

Stephanie didn't answer at first. "Hard," she said at last. "But good. He couldn't find something in the house. It made him sad to remember how I always knew where everything was." She chuckled to herself and shook her head. "But at the end of our call…I heard some relief." Stephanie looked at Pippi intensely. "Did he really know I was there and listening?"

"That's what I'm told."

Stephanie sighed deeply. She looked over at her sons. "They tell you about Disneyland?"

"Yes, they did," Pippi admitted. "I'm excited for you all but how will I reach you if…?" She made a hand gesture as though holding a phone to her ear.

"Well, it would be the other innkeeper who would get me." Stephanie seemed genuinely confused at Pippi's confusion. "Or am I wrong about that? The brochure said we could go to any of the inns?" She shrugged. "I just thought the coast sounded relaxing for the start."

"Brochure?" *Yet another thing her snoozing fox aunt had forgotten to tell her.*

"Yeah. I have it here somewhere." Stephanie proceeded to dig through her bottomless beach bag until she pulled out a glossy brochure and handed it to Pippi. "Take a look."

Pippi perused the brochure, titled *Travel like you always dreamed!* with a smiling couple pointing at the Great Sphinx of Giza. The brochure gave very little information other than a brief list of *popular locations* that included Disneyland, the Nile River, Las Vegas, Paris, London, Sydney, and *many, many more*. There were more pictures of happy couples, toasting with champagne glasses and strolling hand in hand. *Enjoy this time while still being present for your loved ones,* read another caption below a photo of a woman sitting on a couch with a book and a phone. *See your innkeeper for transfer details!*

A chime rang out.

"Lunch!" Anthony and Caleb shouted, fighting each other to see who could fit through the door first.

"Thank you." Pippi handed back the brochure. "I guess come see me when you want to be transferred to Disneyland. I'll have it figured out by then." She wanted to ask how Stephanie had obtained the brochure in the first place, but didn't.

"I will," Stephanie said. She paused and added, "But I think I'll stick around for now."

Pippi deposited her rainwear back on the coat rack before entering the busy dining room for lunch. It appeared to be a make-your-own-sandwich buffet as the guests lined up along the wall and waited their turn at the lunchmeat and condiment station, where they gave their order to the inn, who assembled their sandwich in front of them. Pippi took her spot in line and perused the menu, which consisted of meats and mustards she'd never even heard of but certainly sounded fancy. At the bottom of the menu was printed in bold *Innkeeper's sandwich at her seat.*

"Oh, okay." Pippi walked dutifully to her seat, eyeing the other guests' towering sandwiches. Mostly she coveted the bread, a staple she'd missed the most since learning of her gluten intolerance. She'd tried many gluten-free bread alternatives but was always left with a distinct aftertaste that didn't make it worth the inflated price she'd spent to chance it.

But sitting in front of her, topped with the usual *gluten free* flag, was the most gluten-stuffed-looking-gluten-free sandwich she'd ever seen. The crispy, toasted texture, the smell; Pippi ripped off the flag and took a bite without even checking to see what else the inn had included. But it was perfect. Absolutely, perfect. She closed her eyes as she savored each bite, transporting back to her favorite restaurant with the yeast rolls and honey butter she'd go to every birthday. She sat back in her seat and wiped away relieved tears. She was getting emotional about bread and she didn't care who saw it.

Hazel tried to act like she didn't see her niece wipe her tears. She had her own customized plate, a fox-appropriate charcuterie platter of berries, toast cut into cubes, and some sort of roasted meat.

"How'd the yardwork go?" she finally asked.

"Fine," Pippi said through a mouthful of sandwich. "Other than I got my first call."

"And?"

"And it was terrifying."

"But you made it through?" A corner of Hazel's jowl pulled into a knowing smile.

"With the inn's help." Pippi had a list of things she felt she should thank the inn for, most of all, the bread.

"Well, of course," Hazel nodded.

"Speaking of the inn." Pippi motioned around with her remaining half of sandwich. "There are more inns?"

"Loads of them." Hazel outstretched her claws and skewered a blueberry before popping it in her mouth. "I like to think we're one of the best, though."

Pippi reluctantly laid down her sandwich but felt she needed both hands to make a point. "I really need you to tell me these things."

"You're doing fine," Hazel patted Pippi's hand. "I'm not just napping, you know. I need to be out of the way so you and the inn can work out your *own* system, you get me? I'm not sure yet why I'm back here, but I do know it's not to interfere with a relationship as old as time."

"Can you at least show me how to fill out a transfer?" Pippi sighed. "Stephanie and the boys are planning a trip to Disneyland."

"That I can do. And I promise to spend the rest of the afternoon with you." Hazel smacked her lips contentedly and pushed away her plate.

"Which happens to include an afternoon nap."

"Yes, it does happen to include that."

Pippi looked around the table at the guests. They all seemed to be equally enthralled with their customized sandwich.

"How long are they here? Not our inn specifically, but *here*?" Pippi asked quietly.

"It's different for every single one," Hazel shrugged. "I've seen some guests for a day and others for years."

"But, why? And do they know why? Or do they just one day..." Pippi snapped her fingers.

"I have my suspicions." Hazel tried to cross her fox arms. "I think it has to do with the people left behind. On average, I see a guest for a week or two before they move on."

"So the time of passing to...the funeral?"

Hazel nodded. "Funerals or celebrations of life create closure for the living. I believe the guests hang around until they feel that shift."

"And the guests who stay longer?"

"We all grieve differently, kid," Hazel sighed. "I guess that goes for the living as well as the spirits. They've lost someone, too."

Lunch wrapped up and the dirty dishes started their journey back to the kitchen sink. Hazel did stay with Pippi, explaining the different log books at the reception desk and walking her through a practice guest transfer, which Pippi was surprised to hear consisted of completing a simple form online, a recent upgrade from pigeon deliveries, Hazel advised. Pippi also learned there was a comment box where she could drop notes to the inn and there is a master key to the inn's front door that stays hidden until the inn *fully* trusts her.

It was amazing what a few hours of training and answered questions did for Pippi's confidence. That, along with an hour of yard-work and a satisfying (but heavy) lunch of lots of bread, did make an afternoon nap sound appealing. She and Hazel curled together in the warm sunlight that had crept up to the pillows on Pippi's bed, and the last thing she remembered before falling asleep was her aunt's soft fur and rhythmic snoring.

Pippi had never, *ever*, napped like that. Not when she had pneumonia, not when she'd accidentally fallen asleep in the airport after staying up all hours the night before, not even in any childhood memories of waking up from a much-needed nap after a day of swimming. Her limbs were heavy and slow to wake as Pippi dragged herself into a sitting position. Outside the window, day was fading as the afternoon light retreated into the mountains, preparing for the approaching transition to night. She fumbled with the cell phone in her chest pocket and flipped it open. *No missed calls.*

Hazel was gone and the door to Pippi's room was cracked open just enough for a fox to fit through. Pippi looked in the bathroom mirror and washed the sleep from her eyes. While she felt deeply rested she wasn't sure how she liked this huge time drain from her day. Her stomach audibly growled.

"Seriously?" Pippi asked herself.

A jaunty tune played in the air followed by thundering footsteps upstairs, signaling another meal was ready for the guests. Pippi checked on the reception desk (it looked all clear) on her way to the dining room, which had transitioned to warm, muted lighting to fit the mood of the meal, which appeared to be prime rib, cooked to each guest's preference, of course. The air filled with the sounds of utensils clinking against plates and laughter as Pippi looked for her aunt, whose seat was empty although a plate of perfectly-cubed prime rib had been readied for her.

So the inn had expected Hazel. Pippi looked around the dining room again before starting her meal. It was perfection, each bite better than the next. After the dinner dishes were cleared, an assortment of cheesecakes were delivered and Pippi received a slice of mango lime coconut cheesecake, topped with her *gluten free* flag.

The guests seemed more willing to linger and visit with Pippi this evening; maybe it was the prime rib or maybe they were warming up to her. The guests loitered on the front porch, watching as the last hint of daylight sunk into the horizon, absorbed into the depths of the sea. The outdoor lights flickered to life, allowing for conversations to continue. Pippi finally met each guest and had a name for every face. The air began to take on a chill (whether the guests felt it or not, she wasn't sure) so the inn opened the front door to encourage a transition inside. Pippi followed the guests, looking once more into the dark for a glimpse of Hazel trotting up to them. She left the door open just wide enough for a fox, just in case.

Books, movies, songs, foods, family, scents, jokes, animals, fears, loves, hates; the conversations flowed between Pippi and the guests like the tide rising and receding, steady and natural. The clock chimed the passing of one hour to the next. Pippi moved from the parlor to the library, carefully weighing time spent with each guest so everyone felt included and had an opportunity to share.

Then the phone rang.

Jovial conversations snapped to a stop. First, Pippi's cell phone rang, then a beat later, the reception phone. All eyes followed Pippi as she walked to the desk and answered the phone.

She cleared her throat. "Hello?"

"Incoming call for George," said the voice on the other line. "From Wendy. Ready to connect?"

George, the striking and quiet older gentleman with perfectly-combed white hair, approached the desk without Pippi even looking at him. He offered a small but warm smile and outstretched his hand.

"It's Wendy," Pippi informed him. "Are you ready?"

George nodded politely. "Yes."

"Yes, we're ready," Pippi confirmed, then handed the phone to George.

George maneuvered around the reception desk and sat stiffly on the stool. He rolled his shoulders and pressed the receiver to his ear. The lights over the reception desk dimmed for privacy.

Pippi joined the other guests in the library. The mood had turned somber as the guests sat in thought or looked out the window to the darkness.

"I think he knew who was calling," Pippi said to Lucy, who was dressed in a formal, evening-wear kaftan.

Lucy nodded. "It's his wife. It's always her. She calls most nights. He stays up to make sure then goes to bed."

Pippi's heart dropped. "Oh."

Lucy seemed to anticipate Pippi's next question. "George has been here the longest of all of us." She shook her head. "And I don't think he's going anywhere."

This dilemma hung so heavy in the room that Pippi could almost see it. An unsaid concern that all the guests shared. What if their loved ones never stopped needing them? *Really* needing them? Tears threatened Pippi's eyes but she didn't want the guests to see. This wasn't all vacation and fancy meals. This was the dead comforting the living left behind.

They tried not to listen, not that there was anything they'd be able to hear as George could not talk back. But still, the other guests and Pippi jumped when they heard the *click* of the receiver being replaced on the phone hook. Pippi recognized the scoot of the stool, the creak of the first step on the staircase.

"Wait!" Pippi exclaimed, quickly rounding the corner.

George's back was to her as he paused on the first step. "I'm off to bed, thank you."

"It's time for midnight tea," Pippi said gently but firmly. She heard the other guests shuffle in and stand behind her. "You don't want to miss that."

George stood on the step, frozen. Pippi approached him and offered her arm. She could smell him; he was newspaper ink and banana and bran and a cologne that faded with potency as the day wore on. George turned and looked at her, heavily. He didn't take her arm but nodded, descending back into the entryway.

On cue, the inn rolled out several carts topped with steaming teapots, very fragile teacups, and an assortment of baked goods and crackers light enough to eat before bed. They shared tea in the parlor and Pippi watched George visibly unwind, allowing himself to be coaxed into an extra cube (or three) of sugar. She caught a few approving glances from guests thrown her way, as well.

"What's up?" Pippi whispered to Lucy.

She smiled. "This is the first midnight tea George has attended." Lucy looked like she was holding back tears, as well. "Good job."

Pippi flushed deeply, down beneath her skin, up to her hairline. She sipped on her tea so no one would notice, glancing back at the front door which was still left open for any foxes out past bedtime.

CHAPTER SEVEN

Before going to bed that night, Pippi tried to will herself to dream of lobster omelets, steak and eggs, even corned beef hash sounded amazing. There was a small notepad on her nightstand (printed with her monogram) on which she jotted down a few notes before drifting off to sleep:

-Dream of lobster

Tell the inn we need:

-A fox door

-New (more comfy) chair at desk

-A hairdryer

Pippi woke the next morning to rain pitter-pattering on her bedroom window like little wet feet racing down the glass. She sat up straight in bed, panic rising in her throat. *What did she dream about last night?* Anything? Nothing that she could remember. She swung out of bed and glanced at the note from last night. It was the same list, but now with checkmarks.

After a quick shower, Pippi braided her wet hair and found what outfit the inn had picked for the day. It was another pair of linen overalls, this time light tan with a black tank top and an oversized blush pink pullover sweater that Pippi assumed would be itchy but actually felt like warm cashmere. On top of her clothes was a hairdryer, still in its plastic packaging.

"Oh, thank you, I appreciate that," Pippi said out loud. She'd already braided her hair so she deposited the hairdryer in the bathroom and slipped on her shoes for the day, a pair of athletic sneakers with a flourish that matched her pink sweater perfectly. She placed the cell phone safely in the front pocket of her overalls and left the room.

Passing by the reception desk, Pippi halted at the addition of a new chair behind the desk. It was a major upgrade from the crotchety stool, with a high wingback, oversized arm rests, and a deep cushion. She looked closer at the embroidered fabric, which showed little miniature scenes from around the inn; there were the spiders peeking over the roof, there was Pippi sweeping the porch, the beach at sunrise, the pattern from the teacup china.

"Wow, you are good," Pippi marveled. Remembering her last remaining request, Pippi turned to find a swinging panel installed into the front door, just big enough for a fox to fit through when she pleased.

After writing up a small thank-you note and dropping it in the comment box, Pippi cheerfully trotted into the dining room, only to find the complete opposite energy there. The guests sat before a bleak breakfast of dry cereal (some sort of mix of puffed corn cereal and chocolate crisps,) weak, almost pale-beige tepid coffee, and not a hint of juice or milk in sight. The guests turned and looked at Pippi as she entered the room, betrayal in their eyes.

"Morning," Pippi mumbled as she took her seat. Hazel's seat was still empty. Before Pippi was a similarly dismal-looking breakfast of dry cereal with her customary *gluten free* flag, although this flag looked tattered and weather-beaten. She gingerly took a bite. If she'd been the source of everyone's suffering, she felt obliged to join them. The cereal was damp yet dry, terribly stale, as though the bag of cereal had been left open for several days before that morning.

Pippi pushed the bowl away and cleared her throat. "Sorry about that. I'll see if we can make a change to this."

The guests tried to look encouraging as they stood from the table but Pippi could feel their hangry-ness emanating towards her like a solar flare. She returned to her room and grabbed the notepad, writing:

Please change the non-dreaming breakfast meals to lox and a bagel assortment, cream cheese, a fruit tray, HOT coffee, and apple juice. It's not fair to punish the guests because I didn't dream. I am open to discussion of this matter.

She slammed down the notepad. Hopefully that would get her point across to the inn. She paused and added:

Where is Hazel? I still need help!

The fact that she could hear the rain pummeling on the roof only added to Pippi's dread of doing yardwork. The fox faces on her rain gear had been replaced with a neon green question mark pattern. Pippi transitioned from annoyed to concerned for her aunt. What if another animal had found her? What if she was injured? Lost? She was new to being a fox. Hazel said herself she felt her animal instincts on the edge of her mind. *What if it had taken over for good?*

As if reading her mind, or anticipating her behavior, or even hoping Pippi would get the hint, the inn had included with her raingear a small backpack containing a rolled-up map, thermos of blessedly-hot coffee, a blanket, first aid kit, and other hiking essentials. The broom and other yard equipment previously on the porch had been replaced with a walking stick. Apparently, the inn was letting her out of yardwork for the day and sending her on a quest to find Hazel, instead.

Pippi slipped into her boots and her raingear, gasping at the discovery of something warm in her pocket. She pulled out a buttery English muffin with a sausage patty and thick cheddar cheese slice sandwiched in-between. Pippi snuck outside and ate her secret breakfast sandwich as she unfurled the map, finding that the inn had circled a few spots of interest. Wiping her mouth clean with her sleeve, Pippi pulled her bucket hat down hard and stepped out into the rain.

The storm, while beautiful, was causing a great deal of mud and slippery situations for Pippi as she struggled down the side of the hill to the first location suggested by the inn. She was able to stomp her way through the small blackberry vines low to the ground, but the larger ones took untangling with the walking stick. Pippi was soaked with sweat, not rain, when she finally reached the largest untamed blackberry bush she'd ever seen in her life. It must have stood at least twenty feet tall, with ancient thorns that had grown confident with age.

Pippi checked the map again and confirmed she was in the right spot. She supposed if she was a tiny wild creature then a labyrinth of blackberry bushes would be an ideal place to hide.

"Aunt Hazel?" Pippi shouted, but the only response was the flight of a startled crow that had been rooting at the soil.

There was absolutely no way Pippi could reach the center of that blackberry bush without the help of heavy machinery. She crouched under the protection of a nearby fir tree and opened her backpack, pulling out a flashlight.

"Aunt Hazel? Are you in there?" she shouted, approaching as close to the bush as she dared, yanking her coat free of thorns that caught her. She pointed the flashlight beam deep into the farthest darkness of the brambles and froze when three pairs of eyes looked back at her.

Pippi exclaimed and dropped the flashlight, retreating to the safety of the fir tree. She pressed her back against the tree trunk and waited, watching for an animal to reveal itself. *Nothing appeared. Nothing moved.* She held her breath. The only sound she heard was the steady sprinkle of rain and the roar of the ocean in the distance.

She finally convinced herself if it had been a predator it would have lunged out at her by now. Creeping back towards her discarded flashlight, Pippi tried again. She was prepared for the three sets of eyes now.

"Aunt Hazel?" she whispered.

The eyes blinked. Pippi's own eyes started to adjust, revealing to her a doe and two fawns, nestled in the farthest reaches of their blackberry fortress. They watched her with the hesitant familiarity of a creature who had spent their entire life around humans who've let them be.

Clicking off her flashlight and finally breathing again, Pippi returned to her backpack and consulted the map for the next potential fox spot. Based off the thick brown line that Pippi took for the driveway, the map appeared to be leading her to the bottom of the drive where it met the main highway. A small mailbox popped up in the middle of the next circle.

Grateful for the easier trek to the next circle, Pippi surveyed the property on her way down the hill. Most of it was overgrown with blackberry bushes, concealing the earth beneath with its intricate stitching of thorns. The occasional oak or fir tree would rise from the entanglement, stretching triumphantly from the chokehold of the constricting vines below, even as they wrapped around the trunk, threatening to climb and conquer. Pippi walked on in silence, the gravel crunching beneath her question mark boots, the forest surveying this new owner of the inn.

A solid twenty minute walk later, Pippi traversed the final steep slide down to the intersection of the gravel drive with the paved main highway. It felt like a million years, another lifetime, had passed since she'd been there last. A yellow mailbox was at the bottom of the drive, tucked into a blackberry bush, just as the map had indicated.

Hazel obviously wasn't inside the mailbox but the beating circle on the map didn't falter. Pippi opened it just in case. *Empty.* She used her walking stick to dig through the blackberry bushes around the mailbox.

"Oy! Watch it!" a deep, gruff voice shouted.

Pippi jumped back into the deserted highway.

"Aunt Hazel?" Pippi ventured. *Maybe she was sick?*

The blackberry bushes rustled. Pippi stood at the ready, her walking stick raised to strike.

"Who goes there?" the voice demanded.

Her hands clenched tighter around the stick. "Pippi!"

The bushes stopped shaking. Out crawled a gnome, small enough to scoot beneath and between the thorns that obviously guarded the entrance to something. The gnome was dressed as a gnome would be expected to dress, as though it was a lawn ornament come to life. And around here, it very well could have.

The gnome dusted himself off and straightened his red cap. He pulled out a twig from his long white beard.

"Was wondering when you'd get down here and make introductions," the gnome huffed in the same deep voice. "Rude it took this long, really."

"Sorry. I didn't...well, yes, I'm Pippi. And you?"

"Mauricio. But you can call me Mo." He sized her up from the ground. "Hazel really didn't tell you about me? Well, 'suppose there's a lot to tell about this place. What's with the getup? You got a question?"

"Actually, speaking of Hazel-"

Mo puffed out his chest. "I'm security around here. You ladies and guests are safe and sound up there with me, ma'am."

Pippi blinked. "You?"

Mo didn't catch on. "The inn and I have a system worked out, you see. No one gets by me that I don't want up at the inn, you get me?"

"Have you happened to see Hazel around?"

"She's a fox now, ain't she?" Mo thoughtfully pulled at his beard. He shook his head. "No ma'am, haven't seen her."

Pippi deflated.

"But you might try down at the beach." Mo pointed across the highway. "There's a path there, you'll see it. Walked enough times to keep the blackberries at bay."

Pippi consulted her map. The circle on the mailbox popped away, with the remaining circle floating over the coastline, presumably where Mo had suggested.

"Thanks, I'll check there." Pippi rolled up the map. "If you see her, please let her know I'm looking for her."

Mo saluted.

"And nice to meet you," Pippi called out as she crossed the high-way. "Glad to know you're looking out!"

Mo watched as Pippi found the path and descended down towards the beach. He shook his head, muttering, "Funny world we live in."

The sea appeared to Pippi as if in a dream, a misty dream, a dream where she was someone else, walking down the path and catching glimpses through the tree breaks. It whispered her name with every crash against the sand, a familiar call that stirred her somewhere deep within, where heart speaks to heart and words can go unsaid. Pippi had to remind herself to watch her footing on the gradual decline, which had become slippery from the consistent rain. But she couldn't look away from the picture-perfect-postcard view of the Pacific, painted just for her.

The path bottomed out at the beach, and after climbing over rocks and driftwood, Pippi was finally on the open sand. The wind grabbed for her, both bringing her oxygen and taking her breath away at the same time. She was the only one on the beach as far as she could see, which was not far, as much of the coastline was shrouded in fog. Pippi removed the map from the protection of her jacket and walked in the direction of the circle. The map led her to where a makeshift windbreak was erected against a deep dune, constructed of driftwood that had been layered into the crude shape of a sort of chair.

The sea throne. The hairs on Pippi's arm stood on end. She'd been here before, she'd been here when this was built, she'd sat on it for the first time. She'd *named* this. And from the looks of it, the little driftwood throne had been frequented many times. The wood was smooth with wear, nailed together for good measure. Pippi had been here with Hazel. The walk to this beach hadn't lied. She had been another person. It had been a different life.

Carefully, Pippi lowered herself into the throne. Tears filled her eyes as she sat back and breathed. Breathed deep. She wiped away the tears hard with her hand. *What was she crying for? Who was she crying for?* There was no sign of Hazel, not even a hint of red fur or a fox paw print in the damp sand. But her aunt had been here many times, preserving a memory, tending to it so that when Pippi returned it was here for her.

Pippi didn't try to stop herself from crying this time. The falling rain encouraged it, mixing with the tears on her cheeks. The wind met her big sobbing breaths, stealing them to dispose discreetly. Something about the endless expanse before her allowed Pippi to cry without reason, to just accept the overwhelmingness of life, and now, death. And that releasing those feelings would affect nothing negatively, much less the sea, who carried the tears and dreams of many.

With her last tear shed, Pippi sat in silent thought. The fog masked the passing of time but Pippi wasn't in a rush. She'd already messed up breakfast, the inn would take care of lunch and dinner. Really, the guests were fine without her, if she thought about it. Her phone had not rung once and Pippi had been sure to check she had service throughout the day. She unrolled the map once more. The last circle was long gone. Maybe Hazel was long gone, too. She closed her eyes and sighed.

What had she gotten herself into?

"Pippi?"

Pippi turned sharply. But it wasn't Hazel who stood there. It was Lucy, and George, and all the other guests, all dressed in their rainwear. They were all there, concern clear on their faces.

"Hi." Pippi stood stiffly. She rubbed her swollen eyes. "What's going on?"

"We've been looking for you," Stephanie piped up, carrying Caleb on her hip.

"Do you all need something? I have the phone-"

"We were worried about you," George said. He looked back at the group, who collectively nodded.

Pippi's throat thickened. "Really?"

"We don't care about the breakfast," Anthony shrugged. "I mean, it was terrible, but..."

"Did we hurt your feelings?" Lucy fretted. "Oh, I'd hate to think that."

"No, no," Pippi insisted. "I mean, I did feel awful about breakfast. But I left to look for Hazel."

"Who's Hazel?" Caleb whispered loudly.

"The old innkeeper. The fox," his mother clarified.

"Oh, her. She said she'd bring me candy when she comes back," Caleb yawned.

All eyes turned to the little boy.

"Caleb," Stephanie said firmly, nudging him from sleep. "When did you last see the fox lady?"

"Hmm, yesterday." He thought for a moment, then nodded. "Yes, that's right. Because I snuck a sucker and she said, *oh, you like candy?* I said, yes. So she said, *I'm going off for a surprise and I'll bring you back candy.*" Caleb slapped his head. "I was supposed to tell the new inn lady."

"Pippi," Stephanie sighed. "You were supposed to tell Pippi."

Caleb tried to snap. "That's it. 'Cause foxes can't write notes, you know."

A collective exhale went through the group and Pippi couldn't help but laugh, which significantly lightened the mood.

"Thanks for the message, Caleb." She picked up the discarded map and clicked on the flashlight. "Let's go home."

CHAPTER EIGHT

That night, the inn snuck a little brandy into their midnight tea to scorch away the last of the ocean chill. Pippi slept hard, her eyes still swollen from crying, but her heart at peace knowing her aunt was fine. The fireplace burned a little warmer that night as the inn took extra comfort not in the return of Hazel, but in how Pippi had handled the whole situation.

The morning consisted of a relaxed breakfast of more donut varieties than Pippi knew existed (but did dream of) and coffee served from ornate percolators, which was a special thrill to the guests who *still* had a taste in their mouth from yesterday's cold coffee.

Pippi had just finished sweeping the front porch when Hazel showed up. She carried a small plastic bag in her mouth, which she deposited on the clean porch, smacking her lips afterwards.

Pippi crossed her arms. "Candy, I presume."

"Salt water taffy to be precise," Hazel replied. "A fox door! I'm flattered."

"Would've been great if you told me where you were going," Pippi said as she settled into the same porch chair used by proprietors of the past.

Hazel smiled to see it. "Seemed rude to wake you, plus, I was planning a surprise." She visibly eyed Pippi's outerwear for the day, which the inn had splattered with photos of Pippi outlined by a giant red heart, as though marked up by an adoring fan. "What's this about?"

Pippi admired her boots. "The inn is feeling especially loving towards me after yesterday."

Hazel raised an eyebrow. "What was yesterday?"

The phone rang. But Pippi had already felt the stir in her chest, like the breath before a heartbeat, and knew it was coming before anyone else did. She was on her feet in an instant.

"Just a second," she excused herself, casting away her yard gloves, which also sported the heart pattern.

"Of course," Hazel nodded deeply.

The guests were all in the backyard, playing a rousing game of cricket, unaware of the phone ringing. It didn't call to their hearts like a usual call would, as this was business for the proprietor only. Hazel watched as Pippi answered the phone, exchanged a few words and hung up, depositing her outerwear at the door before rejoining her aunt.

"It was just confirming the transfer for Lidia tonight," Pippi explained, sitting on the step next to Hazel. "So it happens when she goes to sleep?"

"That's right," Hazel confirmed. "She goes to sleep with bags packed and wakes up in...?"

"London."

"London. Easy at that." Hazel started to bat at a fly, then stopped. "But poor Lidia, she'll miss out on the field trip."

"Oh, what's this?" Pippi sighed.

"Well, I like to take the guests on a little outing now and then, you know, show them the sights. You've been asking for help, so I figured I'd plan your first one."

Pippi thought back to her picturesque yet incredibly short drive through Windia. Other than their private little beach across the highway, she couldn't think of another tourist spot that would be safe enough to bring a group of ghosts.

Hazel interrupted Pippi's thoughts. She waved her paw through the air as though pulling back the curtain on a big reveal lit up on a marquee.

"We're going to see *Lonesome Lily*."

The shutters on the porch clapped with excited applause.

"Thank you, thank you," Hazel said to the inn. "It wasn't easy to arrange, let me tell you."

Pippi began to sweat. This was an understandable reaction for a living person, considering Lonesome Lily was one of the most difficult islands to reach on the Pacific Northwest coastline. If it could even be called an *island*. Lonesome Lily was more of a giant rock that some mad person decided was as good a spot as any to erect a lighthouse. And while Lonesome Lily had doubtless saved a great many ships and an even greater number of lives from crashing into the jetty's hazardous rock outcroppings, the harsh conditions of the island were enough to drive a person mad. And maybe it even had.

"I have a brochure in here." Hazel nudged the bag of salt water taffy towards her niece. "It's not a functioning lighthouse anymore. They converted it years ago. It's a columbarium now."

"A what?"

"You know, for urns."

"That's so insensitive! Why would we take the guests to that?"

"Because it's the hippest club for the undead for *thousands* of miles around. It's practically impossible to get a reservation, the waitlist is eons long. I only got one because the manager had never seen a talking fox before!"

Pippi paled. "It's a ghost nightclub?"

"Well, what else would you expect from an abandoned lighthouse full of urns?" Hazel folded her paws matter-of-factly.

Pippi grabbed the bag of salt water taffy. "Let me see this brochure."

Experience a dazzling after-dark experience like none other! the brochure touted alongside a photo of a dancing couple with the outline of Lonesome Lily in the background. *Our exclusive, private club has been designed with your special needs in mind, featuring a delectable food and drink selection with a Pacific Northwest flair. Evening attire required. Join us from dusk to twilight. Magic happens at midnight.*

"This sounds amazing for you all," Pippi admitted. She replaced the brochure in the bag and patted it closed. "Have a wonderful time. I'll stay here and hold down the fort." Pippi was already imagining a relaxing evening by the fire, curled up with a book and a giant hot cocoa.

"Oh no, no. You're coming," Hazel insisted.

"No, thank you."

"The guests can't go if you don't go." Hazel motioned to the tiny cell phone tucked safely in Pippi's overalls pockets.

"Who would watch the inn if I go?"

"Seriously? You think the inn can't take care of itself?"

Pippi hung her head in defeat. While normally a lighthouse full of urns wouldn't be a problem for her, it was the necessary mode of transportation that was the issue. The only way to the lighthouse would be by water or air and Pippi got terribly seasick and had a massive fear of heights.

Before she could become anywhere near adjusted to the idea, the inn spilled the beans on the upcoming visit to the mystical Lonesome Lily by distributing flyers under the bedroom doors. The guests were abuzz with the news and Lidia immediately asked to cancel her transfer to London. Pippi slept restlessly that night in anticipation of the trip, dreaming of underwater sea life, which the inn interpreted in the form of a seafood buffet for breakfast with mimosas, extra heavy on the champagne for Pippi's sake.

The inn had prepared a special outfit for Pippi in honor of the trip; a knee-length overall dress featuring a nautical print of tiny lighthouses with the silhouettes of happy ghosts drinking martinis in the windows. On the front of the deep blue overalls, right over the heart, was a small pocket lined with waterproof material to protect the cell phone from any moisture. She was also provided a light blue cardigan with a frilly collar and dainty white satin gloves. For what, she had no idea, but tucked them in her pocket anyway.

Everyone waited for Pippi in the entryway, each guest dressed in their own interpretation of evening wear. They talked over each other with breathless excitement, falling silent when Pippi entered. Hazel jumped atop the reception desk and looked Pippi up and down heavily.

"Are those ghosts drinking martinis?" she asked, stifling a laugh.

Pippi pulled her cardigan closed tighter.

"Well, I love it," Stephanie piped up. She pushed Anthony and Caleb forward, who both pulled at their collared shirts. "Hazel said it was okay for the boys to come?"

Pippi forced a smile and nodded. More like they *had* to come. She looked from one elated face to another. Apparently she was the only one dreading this. But Pippi supposed they had nothing to fear, since, not to be crass, but they *were* already dead. What could a fiery crash from a malfunctioning helicopter do to them? Actually, what *would* happen to them if Pippi died? Would they blink and be back at the inn, or would they be forced to move on before they wished? And what would happen to her?

Her thoughts of imminent death were interrupted by the approaching sound of helicopter blades slicing through the air. Pippi's stomach leapt into her throat while the guests clamored over each other for the best view out the window.

"You'll have to carry me in this, please." Hazel nosed forward an inconspicuous black backpack laying atop the reception desk. She crawled inside, tucking it closed with just enough room for her snout to get air. "See? Perfect," her muffled voice assured.

Pippi strapped on the awkward backpack and stepped outside, securing the door behind her just as the helicopter came into view. She'd already been briefed on the plan for the next twenty-four hours, such as the helicopter pilot was expecting Pippi and no one else (not that he needed to know about a weightless gaggle of ghosts and an old fox.) The day was quiet and still, perfect for a flight out to Lonesome Lily, which was notoriously difficult to reach at its perch amidst the stormy Pacific swells. The pilot (a local who was ironically, or not so ironically, known as *Chopper*) was the expert in the area on Lonesome Lily and all her dangerous quirks and charms. The plan was to leave Pippi (disguised as Hazel, disguised as a young scientist collecting data on the island) overnight and pick her up the following morning. That is, weather permitting.

"And what if the weather is not permitting?" Pippi had asked her aunt. "Am I stuck there?"

"Oh, pish posh," Hazel had tutted. "No one is going to leave a young lady out there."

"Let's talk about how the lighthouse got its name, shall we?"

"No, thank you," Hazel had replied, then run off.

The helicopter landed on the lawn with galeforce winds that shook the last dry leaves of summer out of the nearby oak trees. Pippi descended the steps and looked behind her. The guests were gone yet...not.

Chopper met her on the steps, a strapping senior that stood over six feet tall. Dressed in cargo pants, a white shirt, and a leather vest, he buried his aviator glasses in his thick white hair.

"You Hazel?" he spat, literally spitting a wad of gum on the lawn that Pippi made a mental note to clean up later.

"Yes...yes," Pippi stammered, shaking Chopper's large, coarse hand with her own sweaty one. "Nice to meet you."

Chopper looked Pippi up and down and spit out yet another piece of gum. "You the same one I talked to on the phone?"

Pippi had been instructed to say *yes*. "Yes."

"Changed your mind? The old lady isn't for the faint of heart."

Pippi didn't care for a craggy, washed-up lighthouse being referred to as an *old lady* and she didn't care for being called faint of heart either, but nodded anyway. "Understood."

"Got a bag?"

"There, on the steps." Pippi motioned to the duffel bag the inn had packed for her. She adjusted the Hazel backpack. "I'll hang onto this one."

Chopper slapped his thigh with his thick leather gloves. "Alright then, let's get going before I change my mind." He paused. "You know, it's only because you did a solid for Old Herman that I'm doing this. I have a waiting list as long as my arm for a trip to old Lily."

Pippi nodded with clenched teeth. *She had no idea what he was talking about.*

Against all her better judgment and sense of self-preservation, Pippi climbed into a helicopter for the first time. She couldn't recall much of the trip with her eyes tightly closed, other than Chopper calling out commands to his concerningly creaky craft, the dry plastic of the handhold she grasped for dear life, and the warm Hazel backpack strapped into the seat beside her.

"There she is, the old crone!" Chopper hollered, turning in his seat to look at Pippi. "Oh, for Neptune's sake, take a look! You'll miss her!"

Chopper's bellowing voice startled Pippi enough to open her eyes. In the churning seas below was unmistakably Lonesome Lily, a white cathedral-like lighthouse who indeed looked on her lonesome far from the safety of the coastline. She was built atop an outcropping of the tiny rock island with hordes of roaring sea lions scattered around like sentries. They belly flopped into the water when the helicopter got too close for sea lion comfort, barking loudly to show their annoyed displeasure but watching from the waves nonetheless.

Now that her eyes were open, Pippi couldn't look away as Chopper expertly landed the craft on the narrow beach. She could understand why this trip would be impossible without perfect conditions; with no mountains or trees to slow the wind's progress, the element was viciously free to push, pull, and have its way with no thought for life or death.

The helicopter's motor whirred to a stop and Chopper jumped out to open the door for Pippi. Grabbing the Hazel backpack, Pippi's legs wobbled when her feet touched the solid rock. Even though she knew there was a substantial amount of earth beneath her, solid literally as a rock, Pippi still felt like the whole island was swaying. It smelled overwhelmingly of sea lion waste (both leftover food and the *other)* and the slick moss that covered the rocks made it difficult to traverse up the awkward pathway to the lighthouse. Duffel bag lugged over his shoulder, Chopper followed behind Pippi to make sure the crazy girl didn't slip and break her neck on his watch.

Collapsing against the harsh stone exterior of the lighthouse, Pippi tried to catch her breath after the treacherous climb. From this view, the Pacific looked both breathtaking and terrifying; endless depths that stretched for endless lengths into an unreachable horizon. Even with the still air, waves crashed violently against the rocky cliffs, wearing the exterior down a little bit each time. After a short battle with an oversized key, Chopper shouldered his weight against the door and they rushed inside.

The interior of Lonesome Lily looked much like what would be expected of an abandoned lighthouse. It was one huge room with a spiral staircase that led up to the giant orb in the sky, to the now-extinguished lamp that once guided sailors through the mist and darkness.

"There's a bathroom around there," Chopper advised, jerking his thumb towards a narrow hallway off the main room.

"There's running water here?" Pippi asked hopefully.

Chopper blinked. "It's a hole in the ground." He dropped Pippi's bag and checked his watch. "Right. I'm off. I'll be back at noon tomorrow." He frowned. "You good here?"

Pippi nodded, a cold pit spinning into a tangled mess inside her stomach. She wanted to say *nope, forget this* but felt a dozen pairs of invisible eyes intensely giving her knowing looks to stay put.

"Yep. Thank you," Pippi managed through chattering teeth.

Chopper shook his head and walked away, then stopped. After a short, grumbling conversation with himself, Chopper reached into his jacket and pulled out a radio. He shoved it in Pippi's direction.

"Here."

Pippi accepted the device. "What's this?"

"I don't give out my equipment for nothing, you know! I'm expecting that back in perfect condition." He sighed and muttered, "Just for you, Old Herman."

"Do I use this to call you tomorrow?" Pippi ventured.

"Dag nammit!" Chopper bellowed. "It's if you need me, you hear? *Only in emergencies*, got it?" He shook his head and left the lighthouse, slamming the door behind him. Pippi watched him leave through the open window frame, grumbling the entire way back to the helicopter. A minute later he was in the air and making the trip back to town.

Pippi lowered the Hazel backpack and let her aunt free.

"I've got to know about Old Herman," Pippi said.

"No, you really don't," Hazel replied, shaking her matted fur back into place. "Where are the guests?"

"Right here!" George exclaimed, poking his head around the corner of the hallway. "We were checking out the bathroom situation."

"And?" Pippi asked.

Lucy wrinkled her nose.

"Great," Pippi sighed. "And where's the party?"

"The nightclub doesn't open until the sun sinks into the sea," Hazel said, leaping from dusty chair, to crumbling bookcase, to crooked table, which collapsed a little more under Hazel's weight. "So we'll just have to keep ourselves entertained for the time being."

Pippi, Hazel, and the guests spent the next few hours exploring the island and the lighthouse itself, a feat that was significantly easier for everyone other than Pippi, who had the limbs and stamina of a living person. Mostly they found sea lion waste, fish bones, armfuls of seashells, stunning green kelp, ancient driftwood, and a miscellaneous collection of garbage.

Some guests hoped to find treasure, but the real jewel on Lonesome Lily was the spectacular lighthouse herself that had withstood more tempests than time could tell. Pippi climbed step after step of the grand winding staircase with her back against the sturdy wall; if she fell to her death here they'd all be stuck on Lonesome Lily interminably. The excited guests rushed past her and when Pippi joined them at the top they shared an awe-filled silence, humbled by the grandness of the view. The lighthouse lamp gazed at them like a giant eye, forever watching, forever guiding, heavy with the burden of protecting those that traveled her waters.

The inn had packed Pippi a dinner-to-go of sandwiches, fruit, and seltzer water, which she shared with the guests on the top landing of the lighthouse. A call came in for George, which alarmed all the guests, who were unaccustomed to him receiving a call anytime other than late at night. Pippi passed her cell phone to him; she'd set the inn's phone to call forwarding before they left, just in case. After the call, George sat quietly to himself, thoughtful as he observed the ocean and seemed to look for a message in those ancient waves.

They were almost through the meal when Pippi heard the sound of a helicopter, and soon enough, Chopper's aircraft appeared as a quickly-approaching dot in the distance, circling Lonesome Lily as it prepared for landing.

"What's this about?" Pippi asked, peering out the window as the helicopter touched rocky ground.

Hazel shrugged her tiny shoulders. "Beats me. I didn't ask for anything else from him. Other than tomorrow's ride."

As Pippi was the only one who could investigate, she descended back down the lighthouse steps one crumbling step at a time. She finally reached the ground when the door burst open with a gust of Pacific wind, ushering in Chopper and another man.

"What's going on?" Pippi bristled.

"This here is Cecil." Chopper jerked his finger to the thirty-something man beside him. "He's staying for the night as well."

The man offered a small wave to Pippi. Bundled in a hooded coat that looked more appropriate for the Arctic than the Oregon coast, his bleached white hair hung over his dark plastic glasses and into his light blue eyes. He looked ridiculously lanky compared to Chopper's stout frame and also a little taller, if that was possible.

"What?" Pippi snapped. "Absolutely not!"

"Now, look here. I told you I've got a right long list of people that want out to Lily and I had to take advantage of the wind," Chopper explained. He adjusted his coat and shuffled his feet. "Plus, it ain't right for a young lady to be out here by herself. Just ain't."

"I'm not by myself!" Pippi blurted out before slapping a hand over her mouth.

The men looked around the abandoned lighthouse.

"I have the radio," Pippi offered.

Cecil turned to Chopper. "You'll take good care of my bag, right? There's expensive equipment in there and I can't exactly get insurance in my line of work."

Chopper dismissed the younger man. "Your business out here is none of my business. I'll lock the door on my truck tonight, that's about all I can promise."

"Great," Cecil mumbled. He looked Pippi up and down. "So she's why I couldn't bring my bag, huh?" He stepped forward and offered his hand. "Cecil."

"Pippi," she replied, quickly adding, "Hazel." She shook his hand and glanced over her shoulder at Hazel who was watching from a darkened stair.

Chopper nodded. "That's right, there's a small window with the wind, you see. I've got to get you both out tomorrow in one ride and the girl packed her every possession in that bag."

"That's because I was supposed to be the only out here tonight," Pippi grumbled. "What would Old Herman think of this?"

Chopper was clearly wounded. He swung open the front door. "That's below the belt, young lady! Good day!"

"Wait!" Pippi called out, but Chopper slammed the door behind him. She sat down on the step, peeking over her shoulder at dozens of disappointed eyes that only she could see.

"Looks like you're stuck with me." Cecil shoved his hands in his coat pockets. "Also, it looks like you'll be feeding me. Because other than my camera, this is literally all I have on me." He revealed a spiral notebook and a pen.

Pippi ignored him, trying to communicate with the guests through her eyes. Cecil watched, trying to see what she was looking at.

"Is it Pippi or Hazel?" he asked.

"What?"

"Your name."

"It's Pippi. But to Chopper, it's Hazel. It's complicated."

"I'm gathering that. And Old Herman?"

"That I don't know."

"How about what are you doing out here?"

Pippi stood up. "How about, what are *you* doing out here?"

Cecil raised his hands in surrender. "Look, I get you're annoyed I'm out here. I'm sorry about that. But I've been trying to get to Lonesome Lily for over six months, and as far as I knew, I was next on the list." He pushed up his glasses. "Then all of the sudden you cut in line. I'm just curious what was so important to allow that."

We wanted to attend a high-end ghost nightclub. "Research," Pippi lied.

Cecil crossed his arms. "Me too. What are you working on?"

A loud and perfectly-timed clattering distraction interrupted their conversation.

"Hold that thought." Cecil turned a page in his notebook and wrote something. He poked his head around the corner and disappeared down the hallway towards the bathroom.

The second Cecil was gone, Pippi swiveled around to the guests, who had been watching the exchange with either their eyes, ears, or mouth covered. Hazel flicked her tail from the shadows.

"What do I do?" she whispered sharply, wringing her sweaty hands.

"Get rid of him!" Hazel hissed.

"How am I going to do that? Make him swim back to Windia?" Pippi hissed back.

Cecil rounded the corner quickly. "What's that?"

Pippi swung back around. "I said, what are you doing?"

Cecil tucked his notebook into his coat. "Sorry, habit. My ear is tuned to weird sounds like that. I research the paranormal, it's a personal passion of mine and I'm trying to turn it into my career." He reached into his jeans and pulled out his wallet, removing a business card that he handed to Pippi. "That's me. Right now I'm focusing on paranormal activity in Oregon, since that's what I know best. I'm starting a podcast, too."

Pippi's breathing went shallow. Every alarm went off in her mind as she accepted Cecil's business card, which included his contact information and *Cecil's Ghost Explorer Agency* written in scrawling letters beneath it.

"You're a ghost hunter?" Pippi asked, the words dry and strange in her mouth.

"No, I'm a ghost *explorer,* actually," Cecil corrected immediately. "There's a big difference. You see, a ghost hunter is more interested in-"

"Why is this happening?" Pippi panted as the room swayed. Still holding Cecil's business card in her hand, she started a slow collapse down to the bottom staircase step.

Cecil reached out and caught Pippi by the arms, gingerly lowering her down to the step. "Whoa, are you okay?"

Pippi both nodded and shook her head at the same time. She fanned her face with Cecil's card.

"I'll find some water," Cecil decided, looking upstairs, where, unbeknownst to him, a small army of invisible ghosts and a cranky fox were ready to block his way. "Is your bag up there?" He started a quick but careful ascension up the staircase.

"Wait!" Pippi called out.

She jumped up and grabbed his arm, immediately losing her balance and falling into Cecil, sending him crashing back against the wall, his huge puffy coat protecting him from any injury. Pippi's heart leapt and a beat later, the cell phone rang from its waterproof nest in her overalls. They both looked down towards the ringing phone.

"You get cell service out here?" he marveled.

"You've got to leave," she ordered, continuing her hold on Cecil's arm as she attempted to drag him down the steps.

He laughed and allowed Pippi to manhandle him. "But I just got here!"

Pippi planted her feet and tried to open the rusty front door to no avail. The phone rang harder and harder against her chest, burning warmer and warmer with each missed ring. Cecil reached around Pippi and heaved open the door.

"Thank you," she breathed. "I need to pee. Just wait outside. Just for a little." Pippi shoved Cecil outside. "I'll tell you when you can come back, okay? Just wait here."

"Okay..." Cecil agreed as Pippi heaved her weight against the door, shutting it in his face.

She answered mid-ring. "Hello? I'm here."

"Incoming call for George from Wendy. Ready to connect?" the calm voice on the line asked.

The guests were at Pippi's side in a heartbeat. Hazel descended the stairs from where she'd been perched and ready to strike Cecil if needed. George already had his hand out, his face grim. He placed the phone to his ear, but this time he didn't walk away for privacy. The other guests huddled closer, forming a protective circle around George, whose erratic breathing was seriously concerning Pippi. He closed his eyes and silently wept. He handed the phone back to Pippi.

The phone rang again immediately.

"Hello?" Pippi sniffled, overwhelmed by the clear anguish on George's face.

"Hi, Pippi, how are you this afternoon?" a voice greeted on the other line.

"Fine." She wasn't used to talking to a live person on this phone, much less in such a casual way.

"Good to hear." Pippi heard typing in the background. "We have a new guest we'd like to send your way today. She'll be ready in a few hours. She's resting at the moment."

Could it be? "Of course. Yes, absolutely. I'm new to this, I'm sorry. What's the guest's name?"

"No problem, you're doing great. Wendy is the name. She's the spouse of a longtime guest."

"Yes. Yes, I know."

"You'll see this a lot."

"See what?"

"A partner waiting for the other."

Pippi looked at George, who met her gaze back.

"So they can move on together," the voice explained further.

"What do I need to do? I'm not at the inn right now," Pippi asked, turning away as the guests embraced George.

"No worries, I'll email you the forms to complete at your earliest convenience. Have a wonderful day."

"Wait!" Pippi called out before the line clicked and the other caller was gone.

Cecil knocked on the door.

"Not yet!" Pippi shouted.

"This is terrible," Lidia lamented. "He's going to ruin everything. We can't be ourselves with him around! It won't be the same."

"He can't see us, right?" Stephanie whispered. "I'm pretty sure he can't but there's something about him..."

Hazel glared at the door. "No, he can't see us, but he's obviously trained to look for tell-tale signs," she harrumphed. "Ghost explorer, my-"

"Wendy." George approached Pippi and held her hands in his. They were cold, like the first touch of frost in the morning. "She's coming here? Tonight?"

Pippi squeezed George's hands. "I think so. And you all are having this party, I'll see to it. If I keep him outside tonight, the ocean should be too loud for him to catch onto anything."

"Pippi, it'll be freezing!" Stephanie protested.

"I've got my sweater," Pippi replied, motioning to her thin cardigan.

"And what if you get a call?" Lucy added.

"Then I'll come inside to...pee," Pippi countered.

George looked on the verge of panic. "Will that be enough?"

"You guys, I've got this," Pippi announced firmly. "I promise."

This last statement seemed to convince the group, who took a collective sigh of relief. The guests walked together back up the stairs to finish the last of their dinner, taking extra care to keep George steady.

Hazel stayed behind and sized up her niece. "Look at you."

"Yes, look at me." Pippi's hands shook as she replaced the cell phone back in her waterproof pocket and fumbled with the zipper.

Cecil knocked on the door again.

"Almost done!" Pippi called out, rubbing her palm across her forehead. She turned to her aunt then started up the stairs. "I better grab the bag if I'm going to get through the night."

Hazel flicked her tail. "You know, if things get dicey out there, you can always call the Guardian."

Pippi stopped. "What?"

Hazel's eyes twinkled. "Lonesome Lily's guardian. The old girl is still at it, even after she passed."

"Are you being serious?"

"I don't know. Am I?"

Pippi paused. She couldn't read her aunt's expression and was still adjusting to Hazel's sense of humor, including her lack thereof.

"I know, you've got this covered," Hazel said as she slinked by her niece and bounded upstairs. "I'm sure it'll all work out swell."

Chapter Nine

With the help of the guests (who promptly disappeared out of sight) Pippi opened the front door of the lighthouse. She was met with a burst of cold air and discovered Cecil sitting on a nearby rock, hands in his pockets, jacket hood pulled up over his head, which the wind kept yanking back. He looked up at the sound of the door creaking open.

"Am I going to have to do this every time you need to pee?" he asked.

"How's the temperature out here?" Pippi asked, trying her best to sound chipper.

"Cold." Cecil said, standing up stiffly. "Can we go back in? Hold on, what's that?"

He watched as Pippi dragged behind her the heavy duffel bag packed by the inn. With one last tug, the bag passed the threshold of the doorway and Pippi reached out to swing the lighthouse door shut with a ringing thud.

"Because you and I are spending tonight outside," she announced.

Cecil scratched his head. "We are?"

"It'll be great for your research," Pippi continued, attempting to swing the duffel bag over her shoulder.

"Let me," Cecil offered. He picked up the duffel bag and heaved it onto his back, which wilted significantly under its weight. "What's in here?" he panted.

"Just a few things." In fact, Pippi wasn't entirely sure what the inn had packed, but she knew there were at least some snacks. She buttoned closed her cardigan and tucked the sleeves around the ends of her hands. She remembered her satin gloves and pulled them on over her frozen fingers. Cecil was right, it was *cold*.

Cecil watched her. "Are you sure about this?" He looked up at the lighthouse. "Because an abandoned lighthouse seems ideal for paranormal activity, if you ask me. And a heck of a lot warmer, too." He looked out to the west, where the farthest waves were slowly taking on an amber hue, preparing for the arrival for sunset.

Pippi was also aware of the impending sunset. She had to get Cecil away from earshot of the lighthouse before nightfall and the nightclub festivities began.

"Well, it's up to you," she shrugged. "I just thought you'd want to look for the Guardian."

Cecil's bright blue eyes brightened even more. "Who's the Guardian?"

"Lonesome Lily's guardian," Pippi said, pretending to shield her gaze from the sun. "You never heard of her? She's said to come out at night and look for intruders on her island." She looked at Cecil out of the corner of her eye to see if he was buying it.

Cecil rubbed his hands together. "Let's do it! We should probably set up camp close to the water, we might be able to find some cover and break from the wind down in the rocks." He slapped his thigh, a boyish grin on his face. "Wow, what an opportunity! Now, *this* will be great for my podcast!"

"Yeah!" Pippi felt a twang of guilt after seeing his enthusiasm over the prospect of finding a most-likely-fictional island guardian, when a literal ghost party would be unfolding right under his nose. He actually seemed like a perfectly amiable and decent guy. It wasn't his fault he crashed her field trip.

"He's sweet," Stephanie whispered in Pippi's ear.

Pippi jumped, hand on her heart. Stephanie stood in the doorway behind Cecil, who was preoccupied with talking himself through camp options for the night and his plans for a campfire. Stephanie had prettied herself up even more for the night ahead, her soft hair curled and decorated with twinkle lights. She snuck right up to Cecil's back and gave a thumbs up.

Pippi was still shooing her friend back inside when Cecil turned around. She stopped.

"Ready?" he asked, extending his arm.

Pippi hesitated. She knew Hazel and all the guests were watching, whether through the windows or hanging from the lighthouse rooftop. She even felt like the sun was staring, delaying its retreat into the horizon to see how this played out. Her face burned hot, camouflaged by the pink sunset.

Cecil looked down at his arm and back at Pippi. "It's slippery," he explained, arm still outstretched.

"Thanks," Pippi said, hanging onto Cecil's arm to traverse down a path she'd climbed just fine.

They continued on like this, both acutely aware of each other's closeness, down the strange rock hallways of Lonesome Lily. Once the sun completely set, the island transformed into a dark moonscape, devoid of all plants and living creatures besides the snoring sea lions that lolled on the beach. Cecil crouched down so Pippi could look for a flashlight in the bag, which she found immediately in her magical Mary Poppins-esque bag of supplies. Between the pitch black beyond the illumination of the flashlight beam and the creepy moaning of sleeping sea lions, Pippi found herself gripping Cecil's arm harder and harder. She started to seriously consider Hazel had been telling the truth about a lurking Lonesome Lily guardian.

When they reached the base of the rocky cliffs that bottomed out near the sea, Pippi and Cecil found a camping spot that was (mostly) free of sea lion waste with an outcropping that provided a slight break from the wind. Cecil dropped Pippi's bag to the ground with a loud thud and stretched his shoulders. He started pacing their new campsite.

"Let's see if we can gather some driftwood," he said, arms propped on his waist as he looked out across the inky sea. "Did you pack any matches?"

Pippi was already digging through her bag, hoping to find a thicker coat now that she didn't have Cecil's body heat to warm her up. She pulled out a canister of waterproof matches, a bottle of lighter fluid, a small pack of kindling, several well-seasoned logs, and a miniature fire pit. She tossed them to the ground as she continued to rummage through the bag.

Cecil watched, mouth hanging open. "That's...exactly what we need."

"What?" Pippi said absently, her teeth chattering. "Oh, fire stuff. That is exactly what we need, isn't it?"

"Here, take this," Cecil offered, unzipping his coat.

"No, no," Pippi protested, jumping up and down to stay warm. "I must've left my coat at the lighthouse. I'll just run up and grab it." *And see what's happening at the party she'd been hearing since nightfall.*

"You stay, I'll go get it," Cecil insisted, handing over his coat.

"No, you'll never find my coat." *In fact, she wouldn't find one, either.*

"Then I'll go with you."

"Look, I have to pee, okay?" Pippi said, falling back on her trusty excuse.

Cecil thought on that. "Okay, I'll start the fire."

"Great." Pippi grabbed a flashlight and raced back up the hill, trying to ignore the dark walls that seemed to close in on her. She preoccupied herself with moving fast to keep warm and promising herself a brief visit inside the lighthouse to thaw out.

But when did she arrive at the lighthouse, there was no way Pippi was going inside. Even if she had tried, *it wasn't for her*, the light-house seemed to say as rainbow colored lights outlined the doorway. Instead, Pippi peeked through the windows, finding the formerly mud-streaked walls of the lighthouse now draped in deep green velvet that she longed to reach out and run her hand across. The lighthouse lamp had dropped down from its perch and transformed into a sparkling disco ball that cast radiant prisms around the room, illuminating the faces of the packed crowd of revelers. The music in the nightclub was a mix of instrumental covers of popular songs and some classic waltzes that some ghosts were more excited about than others. They were all dressed to the nines, dripping in jewels, hair whipped up high or tumbling down to the floor, in pointy shoes with ankle-breaking heels that no living person would want to wear. The spiral steps to the top of the lighthouse had been replaced by a grand staircase carpeted with that same deep green velvet. Revelers seemed to enter the party this way, passing by the loiterers who watched the crowd below.

Pippi shivered intensely as she searched the crowd. She found Lucy and Lidia, dripping in furs and drinking from giant martinis as they laughed so loudly their earrings fell off. Stephanie and the boys were easy to spot as the beleaguered mother urged the boys to stop sliding down the ornate banister. Even Hazel seemed into it, sitting on the bar with a black tie around her neck, lapping from a fox-safe concoction served in a wine glass.

But there was one face she was really looking for. George was the definition of old school glamor in a black and white tuxedo with tails, his white hair slicked back, which he checked frequently with his white gloves. He was definitely waiting for someone, his eyes locked on the top of the stairs, pacing a hole in the carpet.

"Hey!" the faraway voice of Cecil shouted into the wind. "You lost?"

Drat. This was just starting to get good. Pippi turned and gathered her breath, shouting through numb lips, "Nope! I'm here!"

Hopefully he heard her. Pippi's heart skipped a beat as she covered her mouth with her trembling hand.

There was Wendy. Dressed in a white floor length gown, her head was crowned with the same shade of silky white hair, her frail neck adorned with sparkling diamonds in the shape of a tree. Pippi knew it was her before she even saw George move. He climbed one step at a time, with agility Pippi hadn't seen from the old man before, until he finally reached her hand. Pippi wiped furiously at the tears in her eyes that obstructed her view of George and Wendy's reunion. Their embrace challenged everything she'd thought most beautiful before; this was two souls recognizing and reconnecting, like a star that waited for the dawn.

Pippi took a deep breath of cold air. George and Wendy together again. The party began to fade dark. Was it supposed to? Was it supposed to be getting darker, and darker, and darker, until...nothing?

Like a quiet ember, Pippi felt warmth slowly pulsing through her body, branching out from the glowing center and spreading until she was completely ignited. That's when she opened her eyes and saw the real fire within arm's reach, crackling and smoking under the crisp, cloudless night that showcased innumerable stars. Pippi tried to sit up but she was stiff and also bundled under multiple layers of blankets. But she could move her head, and that's how she spotted Cecil on the other side of the fire, staring into the flames.

He stood up at Pippi's stirrings and came to crouch at her side. "Well, hello there. Glad you didn't die on me."

"What happened?" Pippi croaked, forcing past the weight of the blankets to sit up.

The cell phone. She fumbled with her waterproof pocket and pulled out the cell phone. *No missed calls.* Pippi replaced the phone in her pocket as Cecil sat down next to her.

"I guess no more bathroom trips without a coat, huh?" he suggested, a smile at the corner of his lips.

"I didn't realize how cold I was." Pippi rubbed her head. "At least I found my way back."

Cecil chuckled. "More like I found you face down on the ground like a popsicle. Chopper refused to come out in the dark so I did what I could."

"You carried me back here to camp?" Pippi squeaked, her face burning. "Thank you."

"It's not as heroic as it sounds," Cecil shrugged. "You and I slid down the slippery points, I'll admit it. But you're still easier to carry than this bag of yours."

He reached over for Pippi's giant bag and pulled out a thermos. Cecil poured her a mug of tea, which was steaming hot when it absolutely should not have been.

"I have to commend your packing skills," he said, pouring himself a mug of tea, as well. "I found about everything but the kitchen sink in there."

"If you kept looking, you probably would have," Pippi said to herself, taking a sip.

"For example." He held up one of the partially-crocheted spider sweaters that Hazel had been working on. Apparently the inn had packed it with the intention of keeping Pippi busy. "What's this?"

A sweater for a giant attic spider. "Just a sweater for my brother that I'm working on," Pippi lied, quickly taking another drink and burning her tongue.

Cecil held up one, two, three, four different sleeves before Pippi snatched it away.

"It's not polite to go through a lady's bag, you know," she bristled.

"You're right, I'm sorry. Honestly, I was just looking for something to get you warm."

Cecil crossed to the other side of the fire and tossed another log on the fire pit, sending a spray of sparks into the air. Pippi watched from behind her mug as he puttered around their small camp, halting whenever he heard a sound of interest.

"Are you from Windia?" she finally asked.

Cecil sat down, the fire reflecting off the lenses of his glasses. "No, Portland. But I've been camping in my van down by the beach for the last few days, just in case Chopper called." He paused for an extra loud sea lion bellow. "You?"

"I live here, but I'm not *from* here," Pippi divulged. "And your ghost hunting. Does it pay the bills?"

"I'm a ghost *explorer*," Cecil corrected wearily. "And I'm still trying to get off the ground. So, no, it does not pay the bills. But one day it will." He tossed a rock into the darkness. "It has to."

"It has to?" Pippi repeated.

"I quit my job."

"Oh."

Cecil ran his hands through his thick bleached hair, which stuck straight up thanks to the salty deposits from the ocean wind. "I had this epiphany, right? I don't know what it was. Well, I do, actually. You see, I had my fair share of paranormal experiences as a child, plus, my dad was really into it. It was my dream to study the paranormal and make it my *job*, whatever that means to a kid."

"I see." Pippi wondered how Cecil's paranormal experiences compared to her own, starting with the ghost nanny who kept her company all night after transitioning to her toddler bed. Or, perhaps, running an inn for spirits on vacation.

"A few months back it was the anniversary of my dad's death. And it made me remember some of the things he'd said." Cecil paused, looking away. He removed his glasses and turned back to Pippi, his eyes transforming into twin blue flames. "So I had to make a change.

Go back to that thing I've been missing. Have you ever had one of those moments?"

Pippi had to remind herself to breathe. A chill ran up her spine and it wasn't from the cold. "Yes," she found herself saying.

"Yeah? Turns your world upside down, doesn't it?"

Cecil waited for Pippi to share. She sat in that moment, staring at him. *She couldn't have said it better herself.*

"What kind of research are you doing out here?" he finally asked.

"Actually, I'm not a researcher." Pippi said, then stopped, pressing her lips together. *What was she doing?*

Cecil replaced his glasses and nodded. "Okay. Then what do you do?"

Suddenly, a giant splash thundered over the snores of the sea lions, waking them unceremoniously while also silencing them immediately. A low rumble vibrated through the island, causing the ground to tremble and huge waves to crash upon the rocky shores. Cecil jumped to his feet as Pippi dropped her mug and fumbled through the blankets for her flashlight. The tiny earthquake stopped as suddenly as it started as the very-much-awake sea lions howled and fled into the sea.

"What was *that?*" Pippi shouted, slashing through the darkness left and right with her flashlight beam. She placed a hand over her racing heart.

Cecil's wide eyes turned to Pippi. "The Guardian!" he whispered. He pulled Pippi up from the ground and took off his coat, tossing it to her as he dove for his notebook. "There's a camera in the front pocket. Be ready!"

Pippi yanked on Cecil's oversized coat and was running after him before she even knew what she was doing, their steps illuminated by their shaky flashlight beams. Another splash, this time accompanied by a sound that could only be described as if the entire horde of Lonesome Lily sea lions roared in unison. Cecil turned sharply, following the sound near-blindly, skidding over wet rocks. Pippi tried to keep up, her eyes on the ground, until she ran right into Cecil, who had stopped abruptly at the water's edge. Beyond them, the dark sea was ominously still.

Cecil's heavy breathing sounded especially tight in the strangely-still air. "Do you see anything?" he panted.

"Nothing! I can't see a thing!" *Was this what everyone else in the world felt like about ghosts?*

A menacing grumble issued a clear warning. The sea lions barked at the stupid humans to run away as they swam further out to sea.

"It has to be the Guardian," Cecil whispered, rubbing his hands together like it was Christmas morning. "I can feel it."

But she can't. "Maybe it is?" Pippi asked herself, peeking over Cecil's shoulder.

"Get the camera ready."

She reached into the front pocket of Cecil's coat and pulled out an old SLR film camera. At the bottom of the deep pocket was an external flash that she attached as well for good measure.

The waters parted soundlessly as a barnacled tentacle writhed in the air, followed by another. And another. And another. And *another.* Soon, a beastly head rose from the water, a monstrous silhouette against the starry sky. The guardian of Lonesome Lily was a colossal kraken, now in ghost (but still very capable) form. She focused her red eyes right on Cecil, flashing with rage.

Pippi swallowed a scream and grasped Cecil's shoulder. She pointed a quivering finger at the monster rising higher and higher into the air.

"What? Do you see it? Where?" Cecil swiveled back and forth, pencil at the ready, as if he was going to attempt a quick sketch of the creature.

"There! There!" Pippi cried out.

"Where? Where?" Cecil swirled around.

The ghost kraken summoned all her tentacles into the air, causing a crash of heavy ocean water that drenched the two humans. She opened her mouth in preparation for the treat she was sending her tentacles to retrieve.

"Oh no," Pippi gasped. "She's coming!"

Pippi didn't fear for herself in this situation; ghosts naturally had a soft spot for her, even a ghost kraken. Time slowed as she watched the muscular tentacles curl towards Cecil's innocently smiling face. Now, she got it. Hazel knew no ghost would hurt Pippi, but a ghost hunter? She shook her head. *I'm sure it'll all work out swell* came to mind.

"Oh, geez. What do I do? What do I do?" Pippi fumbled inside Cecil's pocket for some sort of weapon, rock, piece of cake, *anything* she could hurl at the ghost tentacle stealthily approaching Cecil's neck.

"If you see it, get a picture!" Cecil seemed to have some sort of awareness to stay still, perhaps in fear of scaring away the invisible creature. He crinkled his nose at the sudden and very overwhelming smell of rotten fish.

"Okay, oh my gosh, hang on, hang on, hang on," Pippi panicked. "Just keep breathing."

"Me or you?" Cecil asked, starting to sound concerned.

With a snap and a flash, Pippi discharged the camera and took a picture of the kraken. The ghost recoiled at the bright flash, shooting Pippi a grumpy look before slinking away back into the dark Pacific without causing even a single ripple.

"Yes! Woo hoo!" Pippi cheered, jumping up and down around the rocky beach. "I did it! I did it!"

"You got a picture?" he called out. "I can't believe I didn't see it! What the heck?"

Pippi breathlessly wrapped her arms around Cecil's neck and hugged him. She was exhilarated; she'd never *saved* someone before. She'd also never interacted with someone else that was living (and was not a fox or her mom) about *ghosts* before. Her racing heart pressed against his as she breathed in his cologne and sweaty, salty pheromones. Cecil slid his arms around Pippi's waist, beneath his coat, squeezing her tight. Her cheek brushed against his as she pulled back and looked up into his face. Cecil lifted his steamy glasses and they stared at each other, breathing hard.

Finally, Pippi stepped back and patted the camera on Cecil's chest. "We're even," she panted.

They stayed up all night as Pippi recounted every detail about the ghost kraken, telling the story by firelight over and over to Cecil, who filled half his notebook with her information and his attempts at sketches, cursing himself for somehow missing the giant creature with his own eyes. The words spilled, the laughter echoed in their little campsite, and their excitement kept them warm until sunrise, when Pippi caught one last parting tentacle wave from the Guardian as her watch came to an end until the next sunset.

Since Pippi didn't sleep, she didn't dream, but she still managed to avoid making breakfast. Cecil fried up eggs and bacon, kept at a safe temperature until ready for consumption inside Pippi's magical bag, which also produced a perfectly-seasoned cast iron skillet.

"So what's the rest of your day look like?" Cecil asked as he stuffed their camping gear back into Pippi's bag, taking periodic looks inside and scratching his head.

Pippi folded the blankets and handed them to Cecil. "Just my usual stuff around the inn." She turned away and shook her head.

Cecil wiped the ashes from the fire pit. "What inn?"

Too late now. "The inn I work at. Well, the inn I run."

Cecil straightened. "You *run* an inn? How did this not come up?"

Pippi shrugged sheepishly. The fact it *hadn't* come up was pretty amazing, considering they touched on so many subjects during their many hours together, including favorite movies, where they went to school (but didn't finish,) their thoughts on Pho, and many, many more seemingly insignificant things that kept the conversation ceaselessly rolling until sunrise.

"So what was an innkeeper doing out here alone on Lonesome Lily?" Cecil pressed.

Pippi handed Cecil back his coat and sniffed indignantly. "I can't really say."

The sound of Chopper's approach cut through the still air. Cecil looked up into the clear blue sky and crammed the fire pit into the bag, zipping it shut.

"I guess the adventure is over," he said.

Pippi rocked back and forth. "I guess so."

Cecil patted the pocket of his coat. "Thanks for the picture."

Pippi nodded, disappointed for Cecil, knowing he wouldn't find anything in that photograph. "Glad I could help."

They stared at each other in an unfamiliar conversation lull as Chopper whipped past overhead. Pippi and Cecil (laden with Pippi's bag) trekked back to the lighthouse in virtual silence, with the occasional *slippery bit here* or *gonna be a beautiful day* tossed in. Pippi stole glances at Cecil, who appeared deep in thought about something. Maybe he was thinking about the way she shirked away from any questions about herself. Or maybe he was thinking the same thing she was. *She didn't want their time together to end.*

When they reached the lighthouse, Chopper was pacing around his helicopter. "So Old Lily left you alone last night! Lucky two!" he hollered at them.

Pippi excused herself and slipped inside the lighthouse ("to go pee before they left") and reconnected with the guests, who were strung, bleary-eyed and partied-out, across the floor. Except for George and Wendy, who sat on the stairs together, hands intertwined, deep in conversation. All signs of the nightclub had been completely cleared away, returning the lighthouse to its usual dilapidated state.

"Oh, my," Pippi sighed, surveying the lot. "Looks like it's time to go home."

Hazel stretched and yawned, her bow tie unraveled and dragging on the ground. "And how was your night?" she asked, digging around for the travel backpack she'd ride back to Windia in. "Any run-ins with the Guardian?" she added with a conniving sneer.

"I'll talk to you about *that* later," Pippi said firmly.

Hazel closed her eyes and sighed. "Looking forward to it."

As the guests rallied themselves for the ride back to the inn, Pippi approached George and Wendy. They looked up from their discussion.

She held out her hand. "Hi Wendy, I'm Pippi."

Wendy offered her delicate hand. "Pippi. Thank you for a beautiful night."

"Beautiful night," George echoed.

Pippi beamed. "That's all I wanted."

Chopper banged on the door. "The wind's picking up! C'mon now, can't you hold it?"

Pippi could hear Cecil arguing with Chopper to *let her pee in peace*, so she strapped Hazel to her back (and the guests strapped into her?) and remerged outside. The men stopped arguing when she exited and passed by.

"What are you waiting for? Let's get out of here!" she admonished, climbing up into the helicopter and over her giant bag. She secured her seatbelt, carefully stretching Hazel across her lap with her aunt's snout pointed away towards the window.

Cecil jumped into the seat next to Pippi. He attempted to talk to her over the ride home, but between Pippi's motion sickness and the roar of the engine, it was a failure. As the inn was closer to Lonesome Lily than Windia, Chopper stopped to drop Pippi off first.

The helicopter plopped to the grassy lawn of the inn, the engine whirring as Chopper climbed out. Pippi gathered her aunt and slid past Cecil.

"Wait!" Cecil called over the noise. "Can I get your number?"

Pippi immediately nodded, then stopped. "Here's the thing!" she called back. "I don't have a phone number, actually!"

Right on cue, Pippi's heart leapt and the phone in her chest rang louder than it ever had before. Cecil's eyebrows scrunched together.

"It's hard to explain!" Pippi fumbled with the phone. "I gotta go!"

Pippi leapt from the helicopter. She looked at Cecil, wanting to say something else, but what could she say? He couldn't call her, he couldn't come to the inn. As her cell phone rang louder and louder, the escapades of her night spent with Cecil became more and more like fiction. A ghost hunter and the proprietress of an inn for ghosts. That was the stuff of fantasy.

"Bye, Cecil," she said, turning away. She thanked Chopper and ran to the front door, which the inn had already opened for her. Chopper placed Pippi's heavy bag on the grass and shook his head as the front door slammed shut on its own.

"Only for you, Old Herman," he grumbled. "Only for you."

Chapter Ten

It turned out the Lonesome Lily guardian was actually a ghost kraken named Susie and she was very protective of her lighthouse and all her sea lion companions. Hazel explained Susie used to host a very popular morning yoga class years ago but attendance dropped when Susie moved the classes from the beach near Windia out to Lonesome Lily. But she couldn't help herself, Hazel explained. Home is home, even for a ghost kraken.

"She looked rather menacing, I have to admit," Pippi recounted. "For a practicing yogi, especially."

"She could probably smell that ghost hunter a mile away." Hazel added a sniff for good measure.

"Ghost *explorer*," Pippi corrected. "And his name is Cecil."

"Yes, so you've mentioned." Hazel studied her niece. They were sitting on the front porch, soaking up the mid-September afternoon sun which was soon to be replaced by months of solid rain. They were putting the finishing touches on the gift basket for the attic spiders; five appropriately-sized sweaters for giant arachnids (featuring fall motifs of spiced pumpkin lattes and autumn leaves,) a handful of fidget spinners, a selection of large print movie trivia crossword puzzles, and some baked goods provided by the inn that Hazel strictly advised Pippi *not* to sample. Pippi wrapped the offering/gift in brown parchment paper and finished it with a bow.

"Read me the letter again," Hazel sighed, closing her eyes in concentration.

"Hello darlings," Pippi began. "We hope you enjoyed your summer. Thank you for keeping the mosquito situation under control. You've probably noticed, but Hazel is now a fox and Phillipa (preferred name is Pippi) is now the inn's proprietress. All is well and under control. Please enjoy these gifts and we have a few requests at your earliest convenience."

Pippi paused and Hazel nodded for her to continue.

"We need the fall decorations out of the large blue bin," Pippi continued. "The dark green table cloths are either in the small blue bin or wrapped in a paper bag. Please no Halloween decorations yet, we will come back next month for those. Let us know what you need and we will deliver them then. Hugs and kisses. Love, Hazel and Pippi. P.S. Can you also do something about the wasp nest in the eaves of the northwest corner? We can't reach it. Thanks so much!"

"Excellent," Hazel approved. "You can take it upstairs tonight."

"Can you?" Pippi gulped.

Hazel looked at her pointedly.

"I'll do it," Pippi mumbled.

A breeze blustered by and scattered the scraps of parchment paper across the deck. Fall was truly approaching, ushering summer out gently with earlier nights and surprise storms, the air tinged with hints of wood-burning smoke and damp undergrowth, teasing an aroma that promised to be within reach soon. The ocean was restless with the approaching transition; gentle during the day and roaring at night, calling out farewells to the leaves that fell with the wind's midnight sigh, promising to return in another way, another day.

Pippi was still picking up scattered paper when George and Wendy stepped outside, arm in arm, completely unaware of anyone else's presence. Since Wendy had joined George, it was like no one else existed. They spent their dinners with heads together, sharing food and hushed conversations. They walked for hours, coming home late at night, their forms flashing spirit-like under the breaking moonlight. Sometimes it seemed to Pippi like they were slowly fading away a little more each day but then they'd share a rousing game of Rummy and seem more alive than ever.

"It won't be long, now," Hazel noted, nodding to the ghost couple from her perch atop the porch railing.

"I know." And somewhere inside, she *did* know, like a scratchy throat that signaled a full-blown cold was coming soon. This would be Pippi's first official passing; moving on, ascending, descending, whatever it should be called. A lump formed in her scratchy throat and it wasn't about the paperwork that would follow the big event. Was this a loss or a blessing? Wasn't this what she was here for, partly? And this would happen again and again, for years and years, over and over, an endless rotation of occupied rooms that vacated only to be filled again. How attached should she - could she - get?

Pippi was dreaming of piling her plate high with treats from a quaint Paris patisserie when she heard the twang of a loud bell ring.

She looked up at the heavily-mustachioed dream baker behind the counter, who shrugged and pointed at her before saying, "C'est toi!"

She sat bolt upright as the sound of the bell pierced through the air again and immediately searched for her flannel bathrobe buried in her bedsheets. It was not quite night but not quite morning, it was that time of transition in between, when dawn outlines the curtain edges and darkness begins its retreat.

Pippi wrapped her robe around herself and checked her cell phone, on which a notification had appeared.

Guests at the front desk.

Pippi tiptoed down the hallway. The inn still seemed to be asleep and the front desk was on after-hours service with the lights turned down low. She peeked around the corner, jumping at the sight of George and Wendy waiting at the front desk, their arms entwined, coats on, bags packed. Pippi dragged herself to the front desk, averting eye contact.

"Can I help you?" Pippi managed, her voice barely above a whisper. When she was finally brave enough to look into George and Wendy's faces, she saw the tell-tale sign of impending death, that unmistakable drooping of the skin and hollow eyes. They were slipping away.

"Yes," George said flatly. He repositioned his Fedora. "Checking out."

Pippi had to crack her knuckles to steady her shaking hands as she moved the computer mouse to awaken the front desk computer. Hazel had walked her through this part but experiencing the check out of a customer in reality was a whole different experience.

"Thank you for taking care of my George." Wendy's voice was tight and weak, a woman of few words as Pippi had learned in her short stay there. Her eyes trailed in stiff, slow motion to George. "While he waited for me."

"You sure you don't want to see somewhere else?" Pippi choked. "I hear Cairo is nice this time of year?"

They didn't need to answer; Pippi knew it was time. There hadn't been a single call for Wendy since she joined George at the inn. Which either meant there was no one left to mourn her, or maybe they were at peace with her passing.

Pippi took a long breath as she pulled up George and Wendy's reservation. A large red button pulsed with the message *check out* in bold letters. One afternoon she'd taken a peek at their reservation only to find this button deselected with a large lock icon over it.

She clicked the button, which prompted a pop-up box asking *Checking out George and Wendy. Are you sure? Yes or no?*

Pippi forced herself to look from George to Wendy, who were quite literally fading before her eyes. And then, with the most professional innkeeper voice she could muster, she said, "It's been a pleasure having you stay with us. Goodbye."

She confirmed *yes* and the front door to the inn opened on its own, revealing the blinding sun of dawn. George and Wendy turned to walk through, the door shutting behind them.

Immediately running around the desk to the window, Pippi peeked through the curtains to the empty front porch. She then turned to the staircase and bounded up the steps two by two, creeping quietly through the dark upstairs hallway until she found the door to George and Wendy's room cracked open, revealing a room empty of all personal belongings, barren even of standard cozy inn furnishings.

An envelope sat propped on the windowsill.

Pippi,

Time is fleeting for a reason. If you embrace it with someone you love, you'll find out why. Even the most beautiful things can't stay forever.

Thank you for that midnight tea.

George & Wendy

Pippi tucked the note into her robe. As she would learn later, every guest that passed on would leave her a goodbye card as a way of closure for both parties involved.

Wiping away her stinging tears, Pippi turned to leave the room. The inn was probably already preparing for the next guest, which would consist of a deep cleaning and whole new room design. Gently closing the door behind her, Pippi tiptoed across the dark hallway and instinctively froze, immediately drenched in a cold sweat.

The hatch to the attic was open.

In the faint light of the dimmed hallway sconces, Pippi could make out the outlines of nothing else but giant eight-legged creatures, so tall they crouched and still brushed the nine foot ceilings. They appeared to be investigating the basket of goodies, admiring each sweater and holding them up with approving ticks. One of the spiders seemed to be *reading* the letter aloud with a series of grunts and clicks.

Pippi couldn't hold her breath any longer, letting out a burst of shaky air that prompted the shadowy shapes to snap in unison in her direction. Pippi caught one glimpse of the dozens of friendly glinting brown eyes before forcing shut her own, her breathing bordering on hyperventilation.

A commotion followed that was as silent as a gentle breeze and when Pippi finally dared to steal a peek, the hallway was empty again. Two sweater-clad legs lowered a blue bin gently to the hallway floor, followed by a plop of folded dark green table cloths. The two legs adjusted its sweater (which Pippi would have to tell Hazel later were a touch too short) and then offered a little wave before silently pulling the attic steps back up behind them.

Pippi walked slowly and calmly to the staircase, descending a few steps before daring to look behind her, but the giant spiders were definitely gone. She collapsed to the stair, leaning her sweaty face against the cool banister. The inn was slowly waking, she could feel it more than she could hear it or even smell it as the aroma of those French pastries she'd dreamed of filtered through the air.

Outside on the front porch, the still morning air ferried in the sound of high morning tide to Pippi, where she sat for a long while in the rocking chair, thinking, processing, and remembering George and Wendy in a way she felt she should.

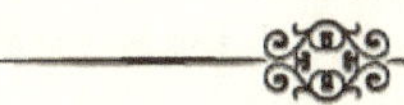

That night, well past a rather somber midnight tea, Pippi couldn't sleep. While sleep had never been an issue for her in the past, it was the knowledge she *had* to sleep in order for anyone to have a decent breakfast that occasionally kept her up at night. She remembered her grandmother would often play Solitaire on her old buzzing computer when she couldn't sleep, so that had become Pippi's new bedtime routine to unwind before hitting the sheets. Lights down low, it was just her, the blazing computer screen, and a deck of virtual cards that matched whatever design was currently displayed on the front door's stained glass, which at that moment, was a giant white moon floating over a dark sea. Behind her, Pippi could hear the inn deep cleaning the kitchen, which seemed to be scheduled for every Tuesday night.

No moves left. Pippi waited for the deck to reshuffle, glancing around her mostly-organized desk. Her eyes trailed (for the fifteenth time) to Cecil's business card, which she'd *somehow* forgotten to throw away. Looking around the empty entryway, Pippi slid the card next to the keyboard.

It was a simple card, plain white and nothing fancy, as though Cecil had just picked the first design he'd seen and went with that. Pippi ran her fingers over the raised lettering, tapping Cecil's email address. Another thing her grandmother did when she couldn't sleep was write a letter to someone that she'd never send. These letters were usually pretty juicy, filled mostly with delayed comebacks or scathing commentary like *that outfit from Sunday was pure trash, by the way!* Some of the letters Pippi wasn't allowed to read, tucked away instead of thrown away, containing the most personal unsaid confessions of all.

With one more look around the still-empty entryway, Pippi logged into her innkeeper email and opened up a new, blank message. *Dear Cecil,* she started, then quickly erased it.

"Can't sleep?"

Pippi exclaimed and jumped back in her seat, grasping her breathless chest. Stephanie stood next to her, dressed in a long white gown that looked appropriate for her current state, her hair tied up in pink sponge curlers.

"Stephanie," Pippi breathed. "What's going on?"

"I just came down for some warm milk for the boys," Stephanie replied, eyeing Pippi's computer screen. "Still up working this late?"

Pippi quickly clicked back to Solitaire. "I was just playing a card game to unwind."

"I see." Stephanie looked at Pippi closely. "Anything you want to talk about? I mean, about George and Wendy..."

Pippi reached out and held her friend's hand. "That is so kind. But I am fine. And you?"

"Fine," Stephanie admitted with a shrug. "Ish." She looked over at the computer. "Can I give it a try? I could use a distraction, too."

"Sure, of course," Pippi said, offering her seat to Stephanie. "How about you try a round and I'll go get the boy's milk. Extra hot, right?"

"You got it." Stephanie turned to the computer screen. "Oh look, an ace!"

Pippi took one last look at Cecil's business card, half concealed by the keyboard. Stephanie seemed engrossed enough with the card game to miss its presence, which was Pippi's first mistake. Her second mistake was taking too long in the kitchen, negotiating with the cranky inn that did not want to interrupt its deep-cleaning-Tuesday for two milk steamers. Her last mistake was not questioning why Stephanie had shut off her computer, admonishing Pippi to *just go to bed and let the night be* as she appeared to float upstairs, her long white nightgown trailing behind her, two milks in hand.

Chapter Eleven

"If you die, what then? I don't have time to train someone new."

Pippi held her breath and stretched as far as her right arm would allow, while her left arm hooked around the porch post. Her nose itched in concentration as she repeated to herself over and over *don't look down, don't look down*. The ladder trembled as she stood on her tiptoes to loop the string of orange and purple twinkle lights on the last, faraway nail.

Successfully looped, Pippi clung to the porch post as she caught her breath. She looked down at Hazel, who was watching the Halloween decorating spectacle from the safety of the lawn.

"Well, I don't think you have opposable thumbs right now, so who else is going to do it?" she panted.

Hazel licked her paw. "We're an inn for spirits," she said dryly. "Spirits that can float. This is an inn that takes care of itself. Giant spiders?"

"You're right," Pippi admitted, her head spinning. "I'm coming down."

It was early October and the clear, crisp autumn days were quickly becoming outnumbered by the rainy alternative. Which no one complained about, from the summer-parched plants, to the guests who came to the inn for the stormy coastal experience, to Pippi herself, who had so many memories rooted in the inn on cloudy days that she wanted to revisit.

In exchange for a giant basket of socks, the attic spiders had obligingly delivered all the Halloween decorations, depositing them in front of Pippi's bedroom door, which she desperately didn't want to think about although Hazel assured her that the spiders must *really* like her to go the extra mile like that. And while no trick-or-treaters or Windia townsfolk ever ventured up the long road to the inn, Pippi and Hazel decorated for the guests, who had all been excitedly discussing how they were going to be actual *ghosts* at a *haunted inn* on *Halloween* and how just being *themselves* was the most hilariously appropriate costume ever.

Pippi was halfway down the ladder when an unfamiliar noise caught her attention. She squinted into the distance.

"Is that a car?" she called, observing the tell-tale sign of dust kicked up by the dry gravel road. She couldn't be sure because no one came up there, ever.

"Impossible," Hazel huffed, jumping up on the porch railing for a better look.

From her viewpoint, Pippi watched as Mo the guardian gnome jogged up the drive, laboriously huffing for breath as he dodged branches and slipped on larger rocks, finally collapsing on the front lawn.

"Intruder!" he gasped, raising his little hand to point behind him. "*This is not a drill!*"

Sure enough, the tell-tale sign of dust was followed by the tell-tale crunch of car tires over gravel. The crunching tires belonged to a large red Aerostar van with some sort of faded logo painted on the side, which became clearer as the van gradually crept closer.

"Cecil's Ghost Explorer Agency," Pippi read aloud from the top of the ladder. "Oh, boy."

"That ghost hunter boy!" Hazel hissed, teeth barred and fur standing on end.

"I'll tell the spiders to armor up and get to battlestations!" Mo announced, forcing himself to stand.

"I've got this, it's just Cecil," Pippi assured as she dropped rung by rung back to the firm earth. "Hazel, you go and tell the guests to hide. Mo, back to your post, please."

"Well, if you say so, ma'am." Mo disappeared into the bushes, grumbling, "There's a thanks for you. Pretty sure I pulled something on the way."

Hazel shot her niece a look before she raced inside. Pippi quickly dusted off her matching-to-the-twinkle-lights orange overalls and purple shirt as the Aerostar whined to a stop in the drive. Cecil manually rolled down his window and poked his head outside.

"Hey, Pippi," he greeted, switching out his sunglasses for his usual round spectacles. He reached to open his door from the outside and rolled the window back up before shutting the door. "The door handle inside stopped working about a year ago," he explained, shrugging. "How've you been?"

Cecil wore a black beanie over his bleached hair. He wore dark pants with a silver chain, presumably attached to his wallet or Aerostar keys, a very crisp white shirt, and black boots that were well worn and looked excellent for ghost hunting. His icy blue eyes stood out, almost out of place behind his thick black eyeglasses. His eyes looked like they'd be better suited for a fancy real estate agent that takes his lattes extra hot and seals each deal with his winning smile. But instead, they belonged to a gangly ghost explorer.

Pippi meant to say, "Doing well, and you?" Instead, she blurted out, "What are you doing here?"

"I got your email," he said, stuffing his hands into his pockets.

"My email?" *Had she actually sent an email that night?* She looked over her shoulder, where she found Stephanie's face pressed up to the parlor window, watching. She ducked away quickly. Pippi closed her eyes. *Of course.*

"Sorry, it went to my spam, so I just found it yesterday," Cecil admitted. "I've been crashing at my friend's place in Portland, so...anyway, that's why I'm here today."

"Well, thanks for coming," Pippi said through gritted teeth.

He smiled shyly. "How could I say no? I was really glad to hear from you. I wasn't sure...well, it was good to hear from you."

Pippi started sweating. *What did Stephanie write in that email?*

Cecil looked over his shoulder at the glistening sea. "I bet that never gets old. Stunning. Looking forward to my stay." He yanked open the sliding door to his van, revealing a myriad of monitors, camera equipment, a sleeping bag, and crates full of wires and other electronics.

"Your what?" Pippi faltered.

Cecil grabbed a black duffle bag and slid the van door shut again. "My stay?" He paused. "Did you get my email back?"

"Could you give me a second?" Pippi wheezed, backing up towards the front door. "Just *one* second."

"You need to go pee?" Cecil teased, dropping his bag to the ground.

"Right," Pippi laughed tightly. "One second."

She raced up the porch stairs and rushed inside, slamming the door shut and bracing her body against the hard glass.

"Stephanie!" she bellowed, skidding over to her computer and pounding the keyboard to wake it from sleep.

"I only meant to help," Stephanie's tiny voice called out from the parlor, where she was hiding behind a curtain.

Pippi navigated to her email, scanning through her *sent* messages until zeroing in on a message sent at 2:03 am to Cecil on the day George and Wendy passed on. She clicked it open and hung her head at the lengthy paragraph.

Dear Cecil,

Hi! How are you? Just thought I'd drop you a note to say I really enjoyed our time together out on Lonesome Lily. What a night, huh? Although it wasn't my original plan, I'm glad you were there. I was just thinking, I could use your help here at the inn, if you have the time. It can be pretty quiet around here. Maybe it would give us a chance to get to know each other better, too? Stop by whenever works best for you, I'll find you a room.

Yours truly,

Pippi

"Yours truly?" Pippi repeated, covering her face. Heart pounding, she clicked over to her inbox, where she found Cecil's reply, nestled amidst a slew of ads.

Dear Pippi,

I'm so sorry I didn't see your email until just now. I wish I had seen it sooner, it's been the best part of my day. I'm staying at a buddy's house in Portland right now, he's letting me use his internet and crash on the couch for the time being. He's also going to be my partner for the podcast, we're still coming up with names. I have a bunch to tell you.

I think about Lonesome Lily all the time. Yes, I would love to come see you and help at the inn. I'll be there sometime tomorrow afternoon.

Best,

Cecil

"Stephanie, why?" Pippi moaned, peeking one last time to see if Cecil had closed his email with *yours truly* as well.

Stephanie poked her head out. "I'm sorry!" she sniffled. "But he just seems *so sweet* and you keep looking at his business card, I just thought...I just thought...a *teensy* push..."

"Oh, it's okay, it's fine," Pippi consoled, rounding the desk to give Stephanie a hug. She embraced her friend and took a peek out the window at Cecil, who was leaning against his van and kicking at loose gravel. "It'll be fine."

"Will it?" Hazel piped up, sticking her snout out from under the couch. "Because we've got a ghost hunter with an overnight bag out in our parking lot, if you haven't noticed."

Pippi rolled back her shoulders. "I will take care of this right now," she told the other hidden guests (and herself.)

Opening the front door with a flourish, Pippi stomped down the front porch steps. She stopped on the bottom step to remain at eye level with Cecil, who straightened up at Pippi's approach.

"I'm sorry, I can't let you stay here," she announced like a general commanding her troops.

"Oh." Cecil's face fell. "What happened?"

"I just can't." Pippi's heart broke a little. But she can't let him stay. She won't let him stay. *She shouldn't let him stay.*

Cecil opened the van door. "It's okay. I get it, you sent me that email weeks ago. You're booked solid, I'm sure, considering Halloween is coming up."

"Thank you for understanding," Pippi said, then pivoted. "What's that about Halloween?"

Cecil looked up at the inn. "Well, the whole haunted thing."

Pippi suddenly felt the presence of a dozen faces crowded around the window behind her, watching and listening. She audibly gulped.

Cecil dropped his duffel bag and rummaged around inside, finally pulling out a thick pamphlet made of newsprint paper. He held it in the air. "I knew something about this place seemed familiar when Chopper dropped you off. So I dug around through my dad's stuff and found his stack of old *Haunted Oregon* magazines. They haven't printed these for ages but leave it to my dad to keep every issue."

The hairs rose on the back of Pippi's neck. "Sorry, my inn is *in* that magazine? Can I see it?"

Pippi's mind raced as she flipped by other Oregon (not inn-related) haunts like Bohemia Mountain and the Shelton McMurphy Johnson House. The magazine definitely looked dated, with an ad for the soon-to-be-released 1984 *Ghostbusters* film and some soda she'd never heard of before. Finally, at the end of the magazine, she found the Windia Inn, featuring a black and white photo of the inn with the heading *A true hidden gem on the Oregon coast.* In addition to the inn's address with detailed directions (*Look for a yellow mailbox tucked into the blackberries!*) there was also a short blurb on nearby Windia (including an even shorter blurb on Lonesome Lily) and a recap of the weather for the year. A short description of the inn stated, *Be one of the first to experience the hospitality of Oregon's most secret haunted establishment. While the history of the Windia Inn is closely guarded, the astute visitor will see (and hear) clues to the undead throughout the property. The food is unbeatable and the views are spectacular. Cost: contact innkeeper for reservation details.*

Cecil continued on as Pippi limply handed back the magazine. "When I got your email, it really got me thinking. I figured I could help you out, get some readings, gather some evidence…you know, do a little spotlight on the place? Maybe it would send some more customers your way? The whole haunted angle is part of the charm, right? But it's all good, maybe another time." Cecil zipped his duffel bag closed again. "I'll still give you a shout-out on my podcast."

"That is definitely *not* necessary."

"I'd love to, seriously. I already told my friend about your place, and he agreed-"

"Actually, you should stay," Pippi blurted out.

She had to protect the inn. And part of staying safe was their anonymity. She couldn't have Cecil spreading the word more than she couldn't have Cecil staying there. She could control one living person, but two becomes five, and five becomes twenty, and twenty becomes an angry horde with pitchforks, singing in unison as they stomp up the hill, waving their torches.

"Really?" Cecil nudged.

"Yes!" *She'll invite him to stay, keep the guests hidden, he'll find out there's nothing here, and nothing to share on his podcast, and everything will go back to normal.* "I'm sure we can make it work."

"Great!" Cecil shouldered his duffel bag. "Lead the way!"

As they approached the front door, Hazel ran out in a flash of reddish orange, tripping Cecil and sending him tumbling down the front steps. He looked up through a cloud of dust.

"What was that?" he panted, jumping up and brushing himself off.

"I don't know?" Pippi shrugged, turning before he saw her lie. "Giant rat, maybe?"

"Okay, hold on." Cecil returned to his van and slid open the side door again. He pulled out the same camera from the night on Lonesome Lily and hung it around his neck.

Cecil rejoined Pippi at the front door. She took a deep breath, preparing herself for the next lie/excuse she'd have to sell Cecil. *There's no way the inn would let him inside.* But to her visible surprise, the door opened without even a creak.

Inside, Pippi led Cecil to the front desk. As he looked around, taking in all the details of the inn, the guests watched him, out of sight around the corner. Pippi tried to wave them away but stopped as Cecil plopped his duffel bag up on the front desk and waited.

"I'll just see what I have available." Pippi tapped the computer keyboard, intending to click at nothing until she figured out what to do next. As soon as the screen lit up, a flashing green notification appeared at the bottom of the screen.

NEW reservation details

*For: Ghost "Explorer" Cecil *ALIVE**

Room: Backyard cottage

Check in: October 23rd

Check out: November 23rd

"An entire month!" Pippi practically shouted.

"An entire month?" Cecil repeated. He rubbed his chin. "Well, that would get me a really solid collection of data. I can do that!"

"An entire month it is," Pippi confirmed in her best innkeeper voice. Her stomach was a mix of excitement over a real guest (and that real guest was *Cecil*) being there and utter despair over how this might affect the other guests' experience at the inn. And how would she excuse the phone calls? And the breakfast? *And her talking fox aunt?*

One thing at a time. "Looks like we have an opening in our back-yard cottage," Pippi announced, digging through drawers until she found a shiny new key labeled *backyard cottage.*

Cecil frowned. "I won't be in the main house?"

"Well, see, the other rooms are full." *Not a lie.* "And we reserve the backyard cottage for longer stays." *She had no idea but it sounded about right.* "And I hear it's the most haunted part of the property!" *She would pull a few strings and make sure it wasn't.*

Pippi took Cecil on a quick, top-level tour of the inn, including the dining room, *("We use this for more formal occasions. I'll probably just bring your food out to you!")* a quick peek into the kitchen, *("Sorry, kitchen is off limits. You know how chefs are!")* and a simple finger point upstairs. *("You must never go up there. Just...don't.")*

"Is that your west wing?" Cecil asked with a wry smirk.

"Uh." *If she says yes, he'd definitely go up there.* "There's toxic mold up there. Very dangerous."

The lies were starting to pile so high Pippi was about to topple over. With each little fib (well, there *could* be toxic mold upstairs) she felt a big pang of guilt. He was just trying to help her out, using the tools of his personal passion, no less. He did save her from hypothermia. He also showed up after receiving her cringe-worthy email. And was also very fun to talk to. And, she noted as he walked closely behind her, still smelled like cologne and salty pheromones.

But what about the guests.

The backyard cottage was a brilliant addition on the part of the inn. (She'd have to leave a glowing note in the suggestion box about the last-minute pivot.) Tucked away behind the inn beneath a dark archway of blackberry bushes, a brick chimney rose towards the late afternoon sky, as though it'd been there a hundred years, slowly settling, slowly burrowing, slowly becoming a part of the forest itself. The hunter green exterior paint and nutty brown roof made it appear like an alien tree hatched from a dream and grew into a special, tangible, real thing. Pippi unlocked the door and stood back for Cecil to enter, startled briefly by Hazel's glowing eyes watching from within the blackberry bushes.

To Pippi, the interior of the backyard cottage felt like a mini-inn, with similar plush furnishings, a tiny fireplace, worn but delicate rugs covering ancient floorboards, even the smell seemed the same. The one room space had a fluffy queen bed tucked in the corner, a very old television set with VHS tapes, and a door that led to a small but adequate bathroom.

"This is perfect," Cecil marveled, tossing his duffel bag on the bed. Pippi noticed he didn't take off his camera. "Thank you."

Pippi nodded. *It actually was very nice.*

"By the way, is it okay where I parked my van?" he asked.

"Oh, sure. Totally fine."

"Where are the other guests' cars?"

Oops. "Most of them...flew in. And we picked them up."

Hazel scratched at the door.

"Well, I'll let you settle in," Pippi floundered, backing towards the door. "I'll let you know about food."

"Sounds good." Cecil was agreeable and laid back almost to a fault, if that was possible. "I think I'll take a walk, check out the grounds. Is that cool?"

"Sure," Pippi replied, drawing out every letter, hoping he didn't wander *too* deep into the woods, where she was told sometimes the spiders liked to stretch their legs.

Pippi cracked the door open and slipped out. Hazel was nowhere to be seen. Cecil followed her outside, lumbering off into the woods with his camera. Once out of sight, Pippi broke into a run and didn't stop until she was inside the inn, shutting the door and coming face-to-face with a gathered group of guests crowded into the entry, with Hazel leading the pack.

Pippi held up her hands before anyone could say anything. "Let me explain!"

A chorus of concerns followed:

"But he's alive!"

"Hazel said he was a ghost hunter? Can he kill us? Wait..."

"What's for dinner?"

"I overheard he's here for a month. Is that wise?"

"How am I going to go on my hauntingly thoughtful twilight strolls now?"

"There was a lot of movement up in the attic. Do we have bats?"

"I don't know if this is a good idea."

"And you like him," Hazel said loudly, silencing the others. Her voice was firm and twinged with disappointment. "You let it cloud your judgment."

"I didn't know what else to do! I don't want him talking about the inn to the public. Who knows how many people would show up here after that!" Pippi hung her head. "And I never thought the inn would let him in."

Hazel took a step forward. "The inn will follow your heart," she said. "It was on you to tell him to leave. He needs to leave, Pippi."

"Just let him stay," Stephanie piped up, simultaneously handing snacks to both her boys.

"Yeah, what's the harm, I guess."

"I'll just go invisible on my hauntingly thoughtful twilight strolls."

"Or float over him?"

"Oh yes, there's that. Still new to this."

"Dessert is served first tonight!" Pippi announced loudly, counting on the inn to hear her, which was confirmed by loud clattering in the kitchen.

Conversation immediately pivoted from the living stranger to bets on the evening's dessert. The guests crowded into the dining room, leaving Hazel and Pippi alone.

"You shouldn't have said that in front of the guests," Pippi said.

"But you *do* like him," Hazel bristled.

"I mean, he is trying to help us, in a completely unknowingly unhelpful way. He seems like a really good guy. Am I curious about him? Sure, I guess," Pippi thought out loud.

"Phillipa!" Hazel shouted, clearly aghast. "If *they* find out we have a living human here, we can get shut down! If a guest doesn't report us first!"

"*They* who?"

"Tell him to leave and to never mention the inn again."

Pippi hesitated. She felt like the walls were watching, listening. Supporting her.

"No," Pippi said firmly, although a plume of excited panic rose in her stomach over what was to be said next. "It's my inn and I'll make the call here. He stays and I'll prove to him nothing is going on. And that's that."

Hazel stared at her niece with her large, brown eyes for a few beats, then looked at the floor, shaking her head.

"This is the way of the world, I suppose," she sighed. "To watch with wiser eyes as your own mistakes play out in front of you. And know there is nothing you can do about it." Hazel jumped down and disappeared out the front door.

Pippi followed. "Where are you going?"

"To think about why I was brought back only to watch the inn be destroyed!" Hazel called out. She stopped and took one last look back at her niece. "You've got to figure this out on your own."

And then Hazel was gone, slinking off into the blackberry bushes without the movement of a single leaf. Pippi wanted to call out *stop, come back, she'd tell him to leave, don't leave her alone with this big sentient inn of ghosts and spiders.* But she didn't call out, a voice inside told her to trust her gut, a voice she was new to listening to.

The smell of dinner wafted through the air, tinged with the distinct aroma of macaroni and cheese. Pippi wondered if Cecil could smell it, too. She'd have to figure out a way to get him food without letting him into the dining room so the guests could eat in peace. She took a deep breath and turned back, freezing as she realized the fox door had been removed from the door. She investigated the stained glass and found the only acknowledgement of Hazel was her tail disappearing into a bush.

Pippi brushed her fingers over a new addition to the stained glass; a tiny backyard cottage with a warm glow emanating from the tiny windows. Then she found a rendering of towering fir trees with a small figure walking amongst them, unaware of the giant spider shadows watching from the treetops.

First, write a letter to the spiders.

Pippi made it through dinner, delivering a plate to the backyard cottage, explaining to Cecil it was part of the inn experience and he should expect all meals like this. Cecil accepted it graciously, commenting on how quiet the woods were, likely due to all the wildlife and insects clamming up to escape notice of the giant spiders.

She had an hour before hosting midnight tea, so Pippi retired to her room in an attempt to comfort herself with everything at her disposal, including fuzzy blankets and a pile of chocolate. She wrapped herself in her robe, allowing herself a peek out the bedroom window. Where there was once thick darkness now stood a little pocket of light in the shape of the backyard cottage. She'd lost Hazel for it, but in return gained a warm sense of relief knowing there was someone else alive nearby, someone who had some semblance of understanding what life with ghosts was like.

Chapter Twelve

It was a rainy October morning that Pippi woke up to, which she convinced herself did *not* have an ominous undertone and had absolutely nothing to do with the fact that Hazel was no longer on the premises and the inn was all on her shoulders. Pippi had slept restlessly with this new development. While the inn had felt like hers for the past month or so, it was always with the understanding there was a wiser supervisor on duty that she could (and, oftentimes, did) call on when Pippi had a question. She couldn't exactly look her questions up on the internet.

But she did have something else. The inn must've been thinking the same thing, because when Pippi came out of the shower, the inn's *Handbook for Housekeeping* was sitting heavily on the end of her perfectly-made bed. She'd referenced it a few times over the last few weeks, mostly to look up the overly-complicated password for the front desk computer or to remind herself of the spider's known allergies while boxing up the next offering. She liked to think the handbook was an antiquated thing she wouldn't need with her youthful enthusiasm and innovativeness, but now she eyed it with a big sigh of relief.

Due to her restless sleep (during which, with concern, she couldn't remember what she'd dreamed of) Pippi was up far before breakfast. She took a quick peek out at the backyard cottage, where the lights were still turned down to a sleepytime low. After quickly pulling on a pair of pumpkin-patterned overalls and a long sleeved black shirt, Pippi flipped through the handbook, stopping on the chapter titled *How to Get Rid of a Ghost Hunter* which stated the obvious warnings and admonishments if the innkeeper had let the ghost hunter in, ending the chapter with the bold warning to *Keep an eye on them at all times!*

Keep an eye on them at all times! Pippi jumped off the bed and peeked out the window; the curtains were open in the backyard cottage windows and the lights were off. The door opened and Cecil exited the cottage, dressed in similar attire to the day before with the same leather jacket and a black beanie. He adjusted his glasses and wiped his camera lens.

"Oh no." Pippi had lost her early morning advantage. She yanked on some boots and took the cell phone off the charger, placing it safely in the front pocket of her overalls.

The phone immediately rang.

Pippi looked out the window for Cecil, but he was nowhere to be seen.

The phone rang again, harder. "Incoming call for Anthony and Caleb. Ready to connect?"

For both the boys, again. They'd been receiving a lot of calls lately, which caused them more excitement than grief and usually resulted in an argument over who could hold the phone first. All bickering stopped when the call started, however, as Pippi watched their faces turn more solemn than anyone their age should experience.

Stephanie already had the boys corralled behind the front desk, mid-argument about the phone. Her face was drawn, lines telling stories heavy with thoughts and dreams washed away, gone forever.

"I know," Stephanie told Pippi quietly. "I've got them ready."

Pippi said nothing and took her place behind the desk. She'd learned, through awkward trial and error, she could best serve the guests by getting down to business. No one truly wanted these phone calls; it was the sinful, unsaid thought between them all, the one time they didn't want to feel needed.

With the boys settled in for their phone call and an extra chair brought in for Stephanie's vigil, Pippi excused herself to the dining room, where she immediately rammed into a cart of breakfast-to-go obviously packed up by the inn for Stephanie and the boys. Her face reddened when she realized she must have dreamt about sushi and tea for breakfast, some of which the inn had prepared in the shape of narwhals, sea urchins, and other random aquatic life. Pippi delivered the food to the grateful mom and ravenous boys before peeking her head back into the dining room, half expecting to find Cecil mid-dip in wasabi.

But the room was buzzing with the usual array of guests who seemed to be thoroughly enjoying the unique breakfast, encouraging the hesitant ones who'd never tried sushi before, either while living or dead. Pippi scanned the room one more time and sat down in her place at the head of the table, where she had her own plate of sushi and a small bowl of tamari, on which floated a plastic steamboat hailing a *gluten free* flag.

Pippi tried to join the others in the fun but was too distracted by Hazel's empty space beside her, from which the inn had tactfully removed the chair, but somehow the blank spot made even more of an impact. The other guests didn't mention Hazel's absence or maybe they didn't notice. Or maybe they felt content enough with Pippi herself, an option Pippi didn't have the confidence to think of, yet.

In an instant, the energy in the room disappeared and to the untrained eye, Pippi was on her own in a room full of sushi. But Pippi could see the ghosts had gone incognito, wide eyed and staring at her silently. They simultaneously pointed towards the big windows, where Cecil's face was peeking through the glass. His glasses were speckled with rain, which he removed to wipe clean. He replaced them and waved at Pippi, motioning he'd come join her. Pippi jumped up and vigorously shook her head, trying to say something through her mouthful of sushi. But he insisted, making the motion *it's no problem* and in an instant, Cecil's head bobbed past the windows.

Pippi washed down her sushi with green tea and ordered, "Everyone upstairs!"

The guests ascended up to the ceiling, some trying to take their sushi and tea with them, forgetting they were transparent and the food/drink was not, resulting in a shower of sashimi and green tea raining down upon the table.

Pippi rushed up to the front desk, where the boys were still on the phone and Stephanie stood nearby, wringing her hands.

"What do we do?" she whispered.

"Stay here," Pippi ordered, bracing herself against the front door. Interrupting a phone call was definitely where she'd draw the line.

"Hello?" Cecil's voice called out from the dining room.

"It's him!" Stephanie mouthed.

Racing back down the hall to the dining room, Pippi reached the doorway and found Cecil surveying the disaster on the table.

"Good morning!" Pippi announced casually, trying to keep her cool. "Snuck by me!"

"Morning. Yeah, I came in through the kitchen," Cecil replied, picking up an egg roll that had fallen to the floor. "Everything okay in here?"

The inn created an exterior door in the kitchen. Well played.

"Yup, just finishing up breakfast," Pippi said, popping a California roll in her mouth for good measure. "The other guests just left."

"Can I join?" Cecil asked, removing his coat and shaking off the rain.

"Of course." Pippi sat down at the head of the table. She was startled to see the inn had placed a chair in Hazel's old spot and put a fresh plate of sushi in the shape of a camera and a steaming pot of tea in front of it. "Right here."

"Thanks." Cecil pulled out his chair and cleared a spot on the table for his camera. He sat down and surveyed his food. "Haven't had sushi for breakfast in awhile."

Pippi watched as Cecil started eating, apparently finding nothing strange about the situation. She sipped her tea in silence until Cecil spoke up.

"Is it an allergy or celiac? My sister has celiac," he said.

"Sorry?" Pippi paled.

Cecil motioned to the little *gluten free* flag.

"Oh, yes. That's too bad."

Cecil wiped his mouth and folded his hands on the table. "What's going on here?"

"What do you mean?"

"You can tell me. Really."

Here it comes. Pippi moved to the edge of her seat, ready to either spring into action or run for the door. Or summon the spiders she heard rustling in the attic, listening for their innkeeper's call for help.

Cecil noticed the shift but waited for Pippi to answer.

"Just having a sushi breakfast," was all Pippi could manage. But what was also on the tip of her tongue was that she was terrified on this first day on her own as the proprietress of an inn for spirits, her aunt is a fox, there's some very protective spiders upstairs, and that deep in her heart she felt intrigued by the very last man she *should* be intrigued by.

"It's very quiet here," Cecil noted.

"Most people think that's a good thing."

"Too quiet, I think. We'll change that with my podcast, though. Right?"

Change the subject. "How was your night?"

"That little cottage is great. But I would still like to try a few nights here in the main house when a room opens up."

"Well, uh, I don't-"

"The woods back there are impressive."

"Yeah, about that, maybe don't go there again. Stick to the beach."

"Got some great photos around the property. That's okay, isn't it?"

"Pictures?"

"It's all part of the process. I'll start with photo documentation and then move onto the bigger equipment. Heat sensors, EMF's, EVP's, etc."

"I see."

"I can show you, if you like, when it's time."

"Great." Pippi's responses became more and more monotone as she sunk deeper and deeper into an overwhelming chasm of panic.

Cecil lowered his mug of tea. "It seemed like you were interested in all of this back on Lonesome Lily."

"I am, it's just-" *What could she say?* "Is there a charge for any of this?"

Cecil looked borderline offended. "Absolutely not. You're helping me out, every new haunt I report on adds to my credibility. And I hope I'm helping you, too." He leaned in and lowered his voice. "Do you need help?"

Play it off. "If you know a good groundskeeper, I could use some help outside," she smiled.

Cecil sat back, observing Pippi closely. He looked at his camera. "I need to get this developed."

"Sure. Windia's Wonderland in town can send it off for you."

"Actually, I like to develop my own film," he said, gathering up his dishes. "Any dark, creepy basements available? Or an attic?"

Pippi laughed too loudly. "Sorry, no."

"It's okay, I'll figure it out," he said, standing and motioning to his dishes. "To the kitchen?"

A loud clatter in the kitchen signaled to Pippi this was not the time.

"Just leave it here, it's fine," she assured, also standing. "Thanks for having breakfast with me."

Cecil beamed, obviously bolstered by a normal comment finally coming from Pippi. "I enjoyed it, too," he agreed. "See you at lunch."

"What?" Pippi squeaked.

Cecil pulled on his jacket and hung his camera back around his neck. "No point in you bringing my food out there, especially when you've got this awesome dining hall." He pulled on his beanie and adjusted his glasses. "Plus, I want to meet the other guests."

Whether somehow Cecil knew he wasn't supposed to go in the kitchen or he just wanted to investigate, Cecil excused himself and exited through the front door, but not before snapping a few pictures and thoroughly inspecting the stained glass depictions on the front door.

Once he left, Pippi collapsed, her face pressed against the table, finally able to breathe again. She couldn't keep this up. Her stomach sank with disappointment and too much sushi. Maybe Hazel had been right. *What WAS she thinking, anyway?*

It was then that she remembered Stephanie and the boys. There was no doubt they had still been on the phone, if she could base it off the calls of the last few days. Pippi found them in the entry, the boys playing jacks on the floor and Stephanie taking her turn on the phone, as she had for all the past calls. Pippi felt like the lowest of the low as she approached them, seeing the clear disappointment in their eyes.

She'd let them down. She'd allowed an intrusion during the most sacred moment of their stay. During the very *reason* they were staying in the first place.

The other guests descended from the second floor, congregating on the stairs to watch Pippi's walk of shame now that the coast was clear. Stephanie raised a finger, waited a moment, and replaced the phone receiver back on the hook as the call ended. She took a deep breath and exhaled.

"I'm so sorry," Pippi whispered.

"It's okay," Stephanie reassured. "I told the boys to hide and I put the phone down for a moment. He couldn't have seen anything."

"But you missed some...oh gosh, I've messed this up."

"Pippi, it's fine-"

"I'll fix this," Pippi said to herself, then louder again to the others. "I'll fix this. I'll get rid of him today."

"We don't mind him that much," Lidia spoke up, her hair still in her morning curlers. "Plus, he's easy on the eyes."

"It's not the full experience," Pippi insisted. "If anyone needs to transfer while I clear this up, I understand."

"We're not leaving you, Pippi," Lucy spoke up this time. "Well, not until, *you know.*"

"It's almost Halloween," Anthony spoke up. "Let's SCARE him away!"

"He's a ghost explorer, he's going to eat that right up," Pippi sighed.

"It's worth a try," Stephanie shrugged. She looked from the boys to Pippi pointedly. "It would be a good distraction."

"And we scare him SO BAD he tells everyone to never, ever come here AGAIN!" Caleb added. "OR ELSE!"

Before Pippi could put a stop to it, the guests were packed into the front entry and the air was buzzing as they hatched plans for their first Halloween as proper ghosts doing proper ghost tricks, promising Pippi they wouldn't hurt her soon-to-be-beau (or they'd *try* not to) but they'd certainly run him off so they could go back to playing croquet in the backyard without having to go invisible.

Halloween was just days away, which the guests decided was plenty of time to plan a coordinated attack on the unsuspecting ghost hunter. In the meantime, the guests would take all their meals upstairs, spinning it into a campout situation like the second floor was a floating island and the downstairs was lava. The guests retreated upstairs, overjoyed with their new task that also incorporated their current, although temporary, identities.

Watching them leave to scheme, Pippi's heart swelled and broke at the same time. She couldn't allow this, she should march to the backyard cottage and pack Cecil's bags, lock the door, and tell him the inn is closed to the living public forever and ever and ever and to forget they even existed. But selfishly she wanted him around, she wanted more of that warm feeling knowing he was nearby, even though she knew what risk it entailed.

Behind her, the inn was already cleaning out the dining room as dishes whizzed through the air to the kitchen. This was her typical yardwork time slot of the day. Pippi pulled on her boots and matching rain jacket, this time with a pattern so tiny it would take a microscope to see, featuring miniscule icons of Pippi's face, a heart, Cecil's face, and a question mark.

Outside, the rain fell with a steady whisper that laid a misty blanket of silence on the inn's grounds and the woods, which was a kaleidoscope of erupting fall colors intermixed with the steady yearlong evergreen pine and fir. In the distance, the ocean roared with stormy winds, tossing and toiling in the vast expanse of the Pacific. A faraway foghorn broke the gentle silence, long and forlorn. Pippi closed her eyes and breathed deep, and when she exhaled and opened them again, she could have sworn she saw Hazel's eyes watching from within the blackberry bushes. But she'd been fooled by those docile dark eyes before and this time was no different; in her heart she knew Hazel had left the inn, maybe temporarily, maybe to return to the wild. Or maybe she'd wake up tomorrow with a guest checkout notification.

Down the hill, Cecil investigated a tiny shovel that Pippi knew Mo had left behind after shoveling more gravel on to the drive. *Just until Halloween.* That would give her time to convince Cecil there was nothing going on at the inn. The guests would be happy and distracted. Pippi watched him out of the corner of her eye as she raked at nothing. Cecil looked up and waved at her, motioning to the shovel. She shrugged and smiled.

Just until Halloween. Until then, how much harm could it really cause to have him around?

Pippi fumbled through the remainder of the day, made significantly easier by the guests staying upstairs and only one phone call for just Stephanie this time, a short one that rang through at 3:00 am when Cecil was safely tucked away in his cottage. Calls at that time were a rarity, which Pippi assumed was due to the living being asleep. She stayed with Stephanie for this phone call, curled in a ball on an overstuffed chair in the library.

Pippi stood up when she heard the receiver click back into place. Stephanie peeked her head around to see if Pippi had fallen asleep.

"I'm done," she whispered. In the dim light her once soft skin looked gray and dry and Pippi knew what was coming.

"How much longer?" she asked gently.

Stephanie looked over her shoulder as though afraid her sons could be listening in, which was a realistic concern with those two.

"I think soon," she admitted. "I don't know for sure. I feel…different."

"The calls?" Pippi never asked these questions, but in that moment, it felt right.

"It's always my husband." Stephanie closed her eyes and wrapped her arms around her thin frame. "At first the calls were silly. Where did I put the fabric softener? Is the mortgage paid with the first or second paycheck? But now, I think…" she paused, as though she couldn't believe she was saying these words. "I think they had our funeral recently. He's hurting, trying to find a new normal without us. But also not wanting to lose us."

Pippi listened.

Stephanie wiped her face and took a deep breath. "He'll figure it out. I know he will. He's good at figuring things out."

Pippi smiled. "And then you can get some rest."

Stephanie laughed out loud. "Right? Yes, you're right, I have help waiting on me." She nodded, as though she'd forgotten. "You're right."

The two women embraced. Pippi had an idea.

"Should we do a transfer in the morning? I can pull up a list of inns near the biggest rollercoasters."

"And miss Halloween here? Never," Stephanie said with a small smile. "Plus, I want to see how things unfold with you and your ghost hunter."

"He's not mine," Pippi flustered.

Stephanie placed her hand on Pippi's arm. "I remember one time, my husband, well, boyfriend at the time, we went to one of those survey places when we were dating, you know what I mean? They pop up in the mall and ask you to try a product and they'll pay you for your time. Anyway, the girl helping us asked how long we'd been married. Of course, I corrected her and said we're only dating. And then she said, one day you'll be married. I can see from the way he looks at you." Stephanie's eyes glazed over, remembering. "I thought that was so strange. But now I get it. The things you see differently looking in from the outside."

Pippi said nothing. She didn't want to ruin Stephanie's sweet memory with her protests.

"Anyway, I'm not saying you'll be married," Stephanie chuckled. "But if you do, remember I sent that email." She winked and turned to leave. "Goodnight, Pippi."

"Goodnight." Pippi waited until Stephanie was all the way upstairs before reaching to turn down the front desk lamp. Then she stopped. Tonight, she would leave the light on.

Chapter Thirteen

In the space between falling asleep and waking, Pippi thought she was dreaming of smoked meats, even though she could have sworn she dreamed of a pizza parlor that served giant quiches instead of pizza. She sat bolt upright, realizing the smell was actual smoke and not a dream. She'd left her window open last night, craving the calm and gentle sounds of midnight rain, and now it served as an open portal between her room and the fire outside. She could tell by the crackling that the fire was indeed outside and the smell was not from a wood burning stove. It was earthy, damp, sweet, and thick, like somehow someone had managed to catch sopping-wet moss on fire and the resulting secret scent was now revealing itself in a rare concoction of aromas that would forever be tied and known only as the smell of a burn pile.

Burn piles were very common in the area, consisting of a con-glomeration of limbs, leaves, weeds, grass clippings, old rose bush branches, and other such yard scraps collected throughout the year, covered protectively with a tarp until a perfect October day that was cloudy but rain-free, damp enough to discourage the fire from jumping and running free but not so damp as to hinder progress. Most burn pile fires happened on weekends, because monitoring the pile was typically a full day affair, feeding and tending a raging beast that chewed through the brush with a never-ending appetite. Most people found the process cathartic, primal, even. A time for silence and introspection at the turn of the season, discarding old brush onto the funeral pyre until only a flattened pile of smoldering embers were left behind, like stars fallen from the sky, as sunset ushered in the night.

Pippi used the bathroom, skipping an unnecessary shower if she was going to be hanging around a burn pile. The inn seemed to agree and placed a pair of stained overalls out for her, a familiar undershirt, and an oversized plaid jacket which was attire that seemed to go hand-in-hand with tending a burn pile. She pulled her hair up high and out of her face, securing it tightly with a handkerchief. As she pulled on her boots, she pondered how the inn had managed to start the burn pile on its own. She followed the smell of smoke to the front yard, where Pippi had been meticulously gathering brush since she arrived, covering it with a tarp, in line with burn pile lore.

Cecil was at least a good two hours into the burn pile judging by the accumulation of hot ashes. It was a good, roaring fire, big enough to be impressive but not big enough to lose control. Dressed in a sleeveless shirt and jeans, Cecil's leather jacket was tossed over a patio chair he had dragged near the fire. Next to it sat the innkeeper's rocking chair that was usually stationed by the front door.

It took Pippi a beat to absorb the whole scene, completely expecting this was just another innkeeper job she'd stumbled onto, again. It also took her a moment to catch her breath at the sight of Cecil's sweat-drenched frame, his bright hair slicked back, condensation fogging his frames. He heaved another branch onto the burn pile with an explosion of sparks and Pippi saw hearts.

Cecil wiped his glasses and turned to Pippi, surveying her burn pile outfit. "Morning."

"Morning," Pippi managed.

Cecil nodded towards the porch. "Awesome, thanks. I can use it."

Pippi looked over her shoulder, to where two hot teas sat on the porch, courtesy of the inn, along with miniature pie tins of quiche. Pippi gathered the food and Cecil motioned to the rocking chair.

"I took a guess this was your seat," he said. "It sure looks well-loved."

"It is, thanks," Pippi replied. She sat down in the rocking chair. "What are you doing?"

Cecil sniffed at the quiche. "Tending a burn pile."

"I can see that. Why?"

"You said you needed help," he shrugged. "And I love this stuff. It's been calling my name since I got here. Haven't had a good burn pile since I lived with my dad. One of the downsides to city living, I guess."

"Maybe I was saving this for myself?" Pippi suggested, only barely joking.

Cecil froze, his tea halfway to his mouth. He paled. "Oh no, I'm sorry-"

"No, it's fine," Pippi laughed. "Just let me toss in a few sticks and I'll get my fill."

Cecil laughed as Pippi demonstrated, dusting off her hands and returning to her tea.

"See?" she said. "You can have the rest. Let's be honest, I probably would have burned down the inn."

"The inn," Cecil said, using a shovel to reposition a log in the fire. "How did you come to be the owner here, anyway?"

Pippi pretended to be mid-chew with a mouthful of quiche as she formulated an answer. She decided to just go with as few details as possible.

"I inherited it," she finally said.

"Wow. Quite a responsibility."

"You have no idea."

"I still haven't seen the other guests?"

Pippi chewed slowly on another large bite. "Oh, they're around."

"I'm beginning to think you're the only one here." Cecil tossed another branch into the hungry inferno.

Pippi pshawed. "Who do you think made this quiche this morning? Certainly not me."

"Yes..." Cecil agreed. "By a chef I've yet to see, as well."

Pippi did not like where this conversation was going.

"Well, looks like you've got this covered. I think I'll head inside," she said, gathering the trash.

Cecil brushed his hair out of his face in a way that made Pippi trip over her feet. "Are you free this afternoon?" he asked.

"Yes," Pippi said before she could stop herself.

"Great, I'll need your help finding the best spots to set up my equipment before the big event," he explained.

"Wait, what?"

"It's almost Halloween," he pointed out. "The hottest night for paranormal activity. It's like the ghosts *know* it's their time to shine."

Pippi's laugh sounded tight.

"You'll help?"

Cecil looked ridiculously adorable, even with a towering inferno behind him and the prospect of this man uncovering every secret about her precious inn. So, of course, Pippi said yes.

Pippi was too distracted by the feelings stirred up from watching Cecil handle his ghost exploring equipment to worry about what that equipment could possibly expose. He stayed sleeveless in his white shirt, thin cotton that stuck to his body from sweat and the slight drizzle that started almost on cue when the burn pile was done. Cecil showed her the inside of the Aerostar van, which was decorated with twinkle lights and thin pile carpet that covered every inch of the interior of the vehicle, which Cecil explained he'd done to cover the cracking and peeling plastic underneath. Boom mics, nets, flashlights, and rechargeable batteries were strapped to the blacked-out windows while old wooden crates and plastic laundry baskets held messy nests of wires, timecode sheets, and a mix of video and audio tapes labeled with locations like Salt Creek Falls and Hogback Mountain.

Cecil explained each piece of equipment to Pippi with terms like EMF meter, radio frequency sweeper, and something called a phantom cam that she'd laughed at because no one would seriously call a piece of equipment *that*.

"This is serious," he frowned.

Pippi immediately sobered. "You're right. I'm sorry."

He nodded and handed her a coil of cables. He heaved a tripod on his shoulder and picked up a plastic case in each hand. "Ready to go."

Cecil had insisted he get coverage of the whole inn and the forbidden upstairs was at the top of his list. With the excuse of having to use the bathroom (she *really* needed a new excuse) Pippi raced up to the second floor two steps at a time, explaining to the guests the linen closet was off limits. She checked to make sure the attic door was closed tight (it was) and felt reasonably comfortable that the spiders understood the situation, as her letter had been replaced by a sticky, white checkmark made out of, she was horrified to discover, *lots* of web.

Pippi rejoined Cecil downstairs, where he'd been studying the stained glass window in the front door.

"Did the design on this change?" he asked.

Pippi looked closer. The inn had immortalized their burn pile tete-a-tete in the stained glass, down to the little tins of quiche.

"Let's go upstairs!" she said, grabbing his arm. "We're coming upstairs now!" she shouted.

Finally on the second floor, Cecil dropped the heavy cases and took in the enormity of the upstairs hallway and numerous doorways. He looked downstairs and back again.

"Wow," he marveled. "You'd never think there was this much room up here."

"Let me show you the spot." Pippi had heavily talked up this abandoned linen closet to Cecil as the most haunted room in the inn, a room which was 100% not haunted. When he'd asked for the backstory, Pippi couldn't think of a better answer other than it was rumored to be a portal between the living and the dead.

Convincing Cecil he definitely did *not* need camera coverage in the hallway, Pippi ushered him to the unimpressive walk-in linen closet, filled with musty sheets and a bare, buzzing lightbulb.

"Here it is," Pippi said eerily.

Cecil crossed his arms. "Here?"

"Yes, here," Pippi assured, her eyes trailing behind him to the giant hairy spider leg silently stretching down from the ceiling in Cecil's direction.

"Get in here!" she screamed, pulling Cecil into the closet and slamming the door shut. She braced herself against the door, panting.

"What is it?" Cecil exclaimed. "Let me look."

"No, no, it's-"

Pippi was interrupted by the sound of loud scuttling in the attic. Cecil looked up. "Rats?" *Thud.* "Big rats?"

The attic door loudly closed shut. Pippi breathed again. "Yes, big, big rats. Another reason you shouldn't come up here."

"You've got attic access out there?" he asked, gently trying to move Pippi out of the way. "I can set some rat traps up there and a few cameras too, attic spaces are great hot spots for activity."

"I feel really strongly we should stay in here," Pippi said firmly.

Cecil placed his hand on the door frame and leaned over her. "Do you?"

Pippi's toes curled. He smelled like the layered complexities of burn pile smoke. At first, Pippi thought her heart was literally jumping out of her chest, but it was just the anticipatory leap before the cell phone rang loudly from her pocket.

"Work call," she gulped.

Cecil stood back. "Sure, go ahead."

"I'll take it downstairs while you setup." Pippi cracked open the door and peeked out into the hallway.

"You want me to check it out first?" Cecil offered.

"Nope, all good," Pippi said, disappearing into the hall and shutting the door in his face. She wasn't worried about herself, but this was a minefield for Cecil up here.

"Please don't do that again! Not funny!" Pippi whispered loudly to the cracked attic door. It snapped shut quickly after her harsh correction.

The call was for Arthur, a relatively quiet guest that had checked in a few days before. He stayed mostly on the outside of the inn's drama and ate his meals in silence, offering friendly nods in acknowledgment of the table's conversation but never adding to it. Pippi gently opened the door to Stephanie's room, where the guests were camped out, waiting for the all clear. Pippi escorted Arthur down to the lobby phone and returned to the top of the stairs, perching within eyesight of the linen closet's closed door while still staying present for Arthur. She stared at the linen closet door, willing it to stay closed. She couldn't rush Arthur (even Arthur couldn't rush it, this was about the living person on the other end of the phone line) but Cecil wouldn't stay in there forever.

"Hello?" Cecil called out. The linen closet door handle jostled. "Pippi?"

Pippi smiled and shook her head. The inn had temporarily locked him in. "Nice save," she said.

Arthur was only on the phone for twenty minutes, replacing the phone receiver back on the hook gently. He ascended the steps soundlessly, nodding at Pippi pleasantly.

Pippi stood up. "You okay?"

"Oh yes, thank you," Arthur murmured. "And, if it's no trouble, I'll be transferring to England, please. The Deverills, specifically."

"Of course, no problem. I'll work on it tonight. You'll be there in the morning."

"He asked me to go, you see," Arthur offered. "In a roundabout way. He always wanted me to see where he was from."

Pippi placed her hand gently on Arthur's arm. "And now you will."

"And now I will." Arthur patted her hand. "Well, back to the gang. We're discussing appropriate sounds for Halloween night. I will hate to miss that."

Pippi walked him to the door. "Oh, but the English moors on Halloween? How much more perfect could it get?"

"Yes. Yes, you're right. Quite poetic, won't it be?" Arthur smiled. "Thank you."

Pippi shut the door behind Arthur and took one more peek at the attic before pretending to have trouble with the linen closet door handle. She opened it to find Cecil sitting on the ground, wearing oversized headphones and turning the dials on the glowing EVP machine.

He looked up at Pippi. "You're right," he said, removing his headphones.

"How's that?" Pippi sweated.

Cecil handed Pippi the headphones. "Check it out."

Pippi placed the warm headphones over her ears, reminding herself to control her expression as Cecil hovered nearby, waiting for her reaction. Through the electronic static crackling, Pippi could make out the unmistakable, undeniable, but still indiscernible chatter of her guests down the hallway, dreaming up detailed Halloween schemes. Pippi listened for a while, smothering a smile when the happy guests clearly laughed in unison or started singing together.

"Well, there's something there," Pippi said as she lowered the headphones, unable to excuse this one. "Those are some strange sounding rats!" she tried.

He took the headphones back, over the moon. "I could swear it sounds like singing!"

Probably the scary sea shanty they demonstrated for her at last night's midnight tea.

"I just don't know," she said unconvincingly. "Sorry, did you get locked in?"

"What? Oh yeah." Cecil was completely absorbed in the audio. "It's okay, though. Wait, is that laughing? What is that?"

He didn't notice Pippi slip out to the hall, whisper to the guests to keep it down, and slink back. Cecil fiddled with the EVP knobs and removed the headphones.

"It's stopped," he sighed. "But there's something here, no doubt about that. Not sure yet about a portal, but it's something." He beamed at Pippi with a smile she hadn't seen since Lonesome Lily. "I'm so glad I'm here."

"Me too," Pippi said, smiling as her stomach dropped and kept spinning into a never ending spiral. She wanted to add, *But you'll be gone soon. You have to, there's no other way. It's best for them. For you. For me. For us.*

The smell of lunch wafted upstairs and from the intensity of the aroma, most likely it was coming from the guests' campout room, as the inn had recently designed a window-delivery system for their food to avoid Cecil's detection.

"Smells like lunch. I'm starving," Cecil said, turning off his equipment and exiting the linen closet. "Ready?"

Pippi closed the linen closet door. "Let's go."

They descended the staircase as an attic and bedroom door cracked open, allowing a few dozen pairs of eyes to watch their plan unfolding successfully.

Pippi picked up the last of the dishes from Arthur's final midnight tea as the guests retired to bed after giving him a proper send off. After cleaning up, Pippi rolled the tea cart back to the dining room where the inn would take it the rest of the way to the kitchen. She dragged herself to her computer; she'd been ready to collapse into bed hours ago but it was pointless with midnight tea and keeping lookout at the backyard cottage until the lights went out for the night.

She completed Arthur's transfer to The Deverills, England, taking a few moments to click through the pictures of the tiny inn that looked perfect for Arthur's personality, complete with a thick thatched roof and gardens that stretched for yards. Pippi smiled to think of Arthur waking up beneath the quilted covers and looking out at the rainy moorlands he could walk across without an umbrella, getting soaked to the bone, and no one would give it a second thought.

As soon as she clicked *guest transfer complete*, a new notification popped up.

New guest checking in.

"Seriously?" Pippi said out loud.

The front door opened, revealing a man in his late forties, dressed for travel with a long peacoat and tweed golf cap covering a head of thick black hair. He carried a hard, leather suitcase, covered with at least a hundred stickers from different destinations, ranging from Antarctica to Naples, Florida. He set down his suitcase, removed his hat, and smiled, revealing a mouthful of shiny white teeth.

"Greetings," the man said. "John Henry Graham, here."

"Good evening, John. I'm Pippi," Pippi said in her best innkeeper voice. "Your reservation just came through. Welcome to Windia."

John looked around the cozy, dimly lit entry. "Lovely," was all he said.

"So John, I'm sorry, I don't see the inn has your room ready until the morning. This is the first time I've seen this, but I am new," Pippi explained.

"Not a problem," John answered good-naturedly. "I see a fine collection of books over there. Give me a book and a roaring fire and I won't need a thing."

A fire burst to life in the library.

"Ah, delightful," John remarked.

"If you're sure, then make yourself at home." Then Pippi remembered Cecil. And Halloween. "Here's the thing," she added, walking with John to the library. "Um, I will need you to head upstairs at daybreak. We have a...living visitor here at the moment and he pops in and out during the day. The other guests are hunkering down upstairs and can fill you in."

"Oh?" John looked more curious than disappointed.

"This is very temporary, I assure you."

Pippi bid John a goodnight and collapsed into bed, fully dressed, her hand wrapped around the cell phone so she'd feel Stephanie and the boy's 3:00 am phone call coming through. The last thing she remembered was blankets being pulled up to her chin, which she really hoped was the inn and not the spiders downstairs for a midnight snack.

Chapter Fourteen

The guests did a good job of getting John up to speed on the meal situation, allowing Pippi and Cecil to have an interruption-free breakfast of pizza, due to Pippi's return in her dreams to the pizzeria from the night before, only this time they were actually serving pizza instead of quiche.

"Your chef has an interesting menu selection here," Cecil remarked as he took another slice of pepperoni pizza.

Pippi said nothing but smiled and nodded as she chewed her own slice of pizza.

Cecil's hair was slicked back wet, and from the strong smell of his deodorant and cologne, Pippi guessed he had just got out of the shower. Pippi had also had a long shower, taking extra care to blow dry her hair sleek to wear it down, which she hadn't seen the point in doing for awhile now. The inn had picked out another Halloween-themed pair of overalls which Pippi put on with a twinge of embarrassment. She tucked the cell phone into the front pocket and threw a sweatshirt over it, hoping it would look like she was wearing regular pants.

But it didn't work. "Are you wearing overalls?" Cecil asked.

Pippi looked down at her giant Jack O' Lantern face sweatshirt, which looked similar to something she wore when she was five.

"I am, actually," she admitted.

Cecil nodded approvingly. "I like your overalls. I like when someone commits to their style. Take me-" Cecil looked down at his outfit. "I only buy black pants and white shirts. Keeps it simple."

"I've noticed," Pippi smiled. "I like it."

Cecil nodded and smiled back. He took a long drink of ice cold orange juice (another addition from her dream) and cleared his throat.

"I was wondering," he said slowly. "Are you able to sneak away for a few hours today?"

Pippi stopped eating. "Well, um..."

A bell rang in the kitchen.

Cecil looked towards the sound. "What was that?"

This is new. "I think maybe the chef?" Pippi ventured.

The bell rang again. Louder.

"I'll go check it out." Pippi walked over to the kitchen door and cracked it open to peek inside. The inn was busy doing the breakfast dishes and apparently already prepping butternut squash soup for later in the day.

Out of nowhere, a note slapped her in the face. She sputtered and opened the note, which read: *TELL HIM YES. We need time to map out the Halloween tricks downstairs without him around! Signed, Everyone upstairs. P.S. We all feel confident our families won't call for a few hours. So GO.*

Pippi composed her face and tucked the letter away. Her heart fluttered at the chance to go on an outing with Cecil. To further convince him to leave, of course.

"More pizza?" Cecil asked, looking at the spread of a dozen untouched pizzas still on the table.

"No, just that the kitchen is closing soon." Pippi pushed her chair in. "And yes, I can leave for a few hours."

"That's all I need," Cecil said, standing and grabbing his jacket. "I'll drive."

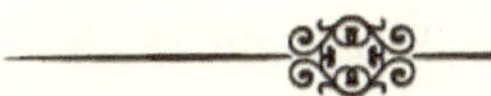

The last time Pippi had left the inn was for the Lonesome Lily experience, but riding in the front seat of the ancient Aerostar was an experience in itself. She learned there was a series of steps to start the van besides simply turning the key in the ignition. First, Cecil checked the oil level and the status of the tires. Second, all the heaters had to be switched to full blast. Lastly, Cecil pushed the brakes three times and rattled the key forcefully, pumping the accelerator rapidly as the van very slowly roared to life, after which the heaters could be turned off. The ride in the van was loud, even with the amount of carpeting that covered the ceiling and the dashboard, and Pippi found herself gripping the door handle most of the way.

After rattling down the bumpy gravel road to the main freeway, Pippi peeked over the edge of the window to see Mo, watching with furrowed brows. Pippi snuck him a quick thumbs up before *oofing* as Cecil dropped a basket of cassette tapes in her lap.

"Your pick, passenger," he said as he hit the accelerator, visibly struggling to turn the steering wheel, and the van, due north.

"No power steering?" Pippi asked, flicking through tapes that were so varied there was no indication of Cecil's actual taste in music.

"That went out awhile ago," Cecil admitted, patting the carpeted dashboard. "But that's okay. She's still a beaut, just a tough old beaut, now."

Pippi selected a compilation of show tunes and placed the cassette into the cassette player. She inspected the pockets of her door, stuffed neatly with paper maps, an emergency kit, and a ziploc of coffee shop punch cards. She opened the bag.

"These are all for free coffees," Pippi gaped.

"Yep," Cecil confirmed.

"Why haven't you used them?"

"I'm saving them for if I really need them. Right now I have the money to buy coffee, so I buy coffee."

"Didn't you quit your job?" Pippi asked, flipping through card after card.

Cecil looked over at Pippi, clearly taken aback. "I have a savings account," he insisted. "I'm not that reckless."

Pippi raised her eyebrows.

Cecil burst out laughing. "Well, maybe I was a little reckless."

"No, I get it, having a savings account makes quitting your job much less reckless," Pippi agreed.

Cecil nodded deeply. "Thank you."

"So you really think this ghost exploring can turn into something?" Pippi asked, pretending to still inspect the coffee cards, which she truly *couldn't* believe he hadn't used yet.

Cecil shrugged. "It's a unique set of skills. People are willing to pay for it. But I won't overcharge," he added quickly. "There's some people out there who really earn that ghost hunter title."

"Okay, tell me, what's the actual difference between you and them?"

Cecil sat up straighter in his seat. "Ghost hunters see the departed as a commodity, they invade their space, rip it apart without a thought of why the spirit might be there. Countless hunters claim to find paranormal activity when there's nothing there, only for the payday. They've got their flashy websites, their 1-800 numbers, their…their…"

"Matching uniforms?" Pippi ventured.

"Yes!" Cecil exclaimed. "Exactly. Matching uniforms! You get it! Now, me, I think of myself as an explorer of the spirit universe. I'm here to observe and collect information. I want to assemble it all in an easy way to understand for my future clients, and hopefully help them find closure while *also* furthering my studies of the paranormal. And I respect space, haven't I respected your inn? I would be in and out, nothing disturbed. A ghost hunter? Like a bull in a china shop."

Pippi listened in silence to Cecil's passionate pitch, so passionate, in fact, now she had to know what was behind it. "What inspired you to get into this?"

"That will be answered today, actually," he teased. "And get that bag out again, would you? Now I'm in the mood for a free coffee. I think I've earned it."

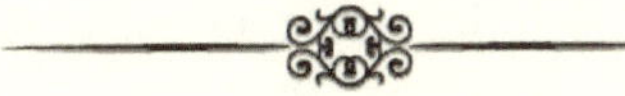

The red Aerostar van veered east into the woods, pulling over for one free coffee and one free chai, eventually stopping at a trailhead identified only by a forest service sign marker. The fir trees stood old and wise and a similarly ancient porta potty was tucked into the overgrowth for the desperate passerby. A car whizzed by, temporarily disturbing the thick silence of the deep wood.

Cecil grabbed his camera and shut the van door, stepping to the edge of an embankment, where the steep downhill trail disappeared into the brush.

He held out his hand. "Ready?"

Whether he meant it to be a callback to Lonesome Lily or not, Pippi fell for it hook, line, and sinker, reaching out for Cecil's hand without hesitation and continued to hold onto it the entire time. Which, by the smile on Cecil's face, was his hope all along.

The trail led them into the deep forest that was damp even without a rain since yesterday. A plush carpet of kelly green moss, spindly ferns, and a beige rainbow of mushrooms that ranged from off-white to chocolate brown covered the ground. There were bright open pockets of young birch trees, their white, crackling bark stark against their neighboring fir brother and sisters. Some areas of the forest were completely impenetrable, guarded by brambles of blackberry bushes that warned any passerby to keep away, their vines of tiny knives sweetened with the wilting berries that remained behind after a late summer harvest. The hiss of a distant creek drowned out the sound of passing cars in the road above them, likened to crashing waves on the sand, just like at home. They said nothing as they walked the rough but clear trail, their crunching footsteps falling in sync as they repositioned their fingers to become perfectly intertwined.

This was clearly a place Cecil had been before. He stopped at a particularly ancient fir tree that stretched tall above the other treetops, whisking away a fallen branch to reveal a sign that read *The Telephone of the Wind. This phone is for those that lost someone they love, to share memories, and to say the goodbye you never got to say.* A weathered black rotary phone was attached firmly to the tree, without a cord in sight.

Cecil stood back and motioned to the phone. "You ever heard of one of these?"

Pippi stepped forward, her voice caught in her throat. The moment she'd seen the phone, every hair on her arm rose to attention in recognition. No, she'd never seen anything like this or heard of a wind phone before yet it was eerily and beautifully in her wheelhouse. She looked at Cecil, contemplating if this was a wild coincidence or pointed confrontation.

Cecil patted the tree. "Last time I was out here was as a kid with my dad." His voice broke off, before he gathered himself to continue on. "He loved this stuff, he loved anything paranormal and probably told me every ghost story out there, maybe when he shouldn't have."

"When did he pass away?" Pippi asked, inspecting the distant cousin to her cell phone.

"When I was nine," Cecil said, patting the tree again. "So the theory is you talk into the phone and the wind carries what you say to the person you lost."

"Beautiful," Pippi whispered to the still forest.

Cecil turned to Pippi. She broke out in an immediate sweat. Reaching into his jacket pocket, Cecil pulled out a folded envelope. He took a few moments to gather his words before speaking.

"I wanted to bring you out here for two reasons," he started. "To show you somewhere special to me and to get you out of the inn. I know something's going on there, you can't deny it, especially after what we heard in the closet. I don't know if you're protecting something or held hostage, but either way, I can help. Here." He handed Pippi the envelope.

Pippi's hands shook as she accepted the envelope, opening it slowly to reveal a handful of photographs. She pulled out the first photo and as she did, the clear ghostly form of Susie the Guardian peeked out at her. It was the photo Pippi had taken that night at Lonesome Lily in an attempt to stop Susie from dragging Cecil into the dark waters. She'd never seen a picture that captured so clearly what she saw and could never explain. Without looking up, she flicked through the rest of the photographs; Stephanie and the boys at the front desk, the dark outlines of the spiders watching from the treetops, and one especially incriminating photo of Pippi enjoying sushi breakfast at a table full of ghosts, taken from the outside looking in.

She handed back the envelope, steadying her breath before asking, "How did you get these?"

Cecil held up the camera hanging from his neck. "My dad's old camera," he said. "Lonesome Lily was the first time I've used it since he died. Then I developed the film, and, well, I guess I owe you a *thank you.*"

Pippi's mind was cluttered with thoughts, freezing when Cecil took her hand. He held up the photos.

"Is this what you see?" he asked.

Other than Hazel and her mother, she'd never told anyone about this. She learned from very early on not to share about the friendly, nearly-invisible people she saw everywhere, dismissed and mocked that only *babies* have imaginary friends. As she grew older, she knew sharing what she saw could even be dangerous; she wasn't sick, she wasn't *imagining it,* she didn't want to sit and explain what was perfectly, while a bit abnormal, *normal* to her. But now she had something real and tangible to protect, this wasn't just people calling her a baby or crazy anymore. This was something much, much bigger.

"Okay," Cecil sighed. "Let me try this. Are you in danger at that inn?"

"No. Absolutely not," Pippi answered at once.

"Well, that's a start. So you're not being held hostage by some ghost monster I haven't found yet?"

Pippi snorted. "No. Absolutely not."

"Great, can check that off the list. Now, there's just-"

"Did you have that kraken picture before you came to the inn?" Pippi interrupted.

Cecil slicked back his hair, reluctant to finally answer, "I did."

"That's what *really* brought you to the inn, isn't it?" she said severely. "I'm so stupid. I'm so, so stupid. She was right." Pippi turned her head before Cecil could see the burning, disappointed tears in her eyes. "I'm just one of your research projects. I really thought-"

"No! No, Pippi, I wanted to see you," Cecil insisted. "Even after I developed the kraken picture, I stayed away because I felt like you wanted me to. The research is important but-"

"Those pictures are nothing. They're fake," Pippi hissed. "You faked them and I'll tell everyone that very thing. And don't you *dare* talk about my inn, to anyone, ever. You faked all of this, just like a ghost hunter would."

"Hey, now-"

"I want to go back to the inn," Pippi declared. She stuffed the hands he'd held just minutes ago into the pockets of her overalls. "Please."

Cecil's shoulders hung, defeated. He kicked the dirt. This had not gone how he'd planned.

"Sure," he agreed miserably. "Can I at least call my dad while I'm here?"

"Have at it," Pippi called over her shoulder, stomping hotly back down the path towards the van. The once beautiful forest now spun around her askew. She thought she saw Hazel's haughty told-you-so eyes in every trunk hollow and dark cluster of ferns. She was halfway to the van when her heart suddenly lurched, which felt extra intense due to how hard her heart was already pounding.

Now she'd made it worse. One of the guests was going to miss a call from a loved one. Her first missed call. She pulled the cell phone from her pocket.

"Wind phone message for John Henry Graham."

Pippi whirled around to look behind her, the cell phone still pressed to her ear.

"Hi Dad, it's me." *It was Cecil.* "Long time, right? I'm at the wind phone and wanted to say you were right. I'm messing everything up. Just like you said I always would."

The ride back to the inn was painfully quiet, even with show tunes blaring at full blast. Cecil kept his eyes on the road, his jaw working and his hands clenching and unclenching the steering wheel. Pippi tucked her knees up to her chest and stayed curled in a ball, turned in the opposite direction of Cecil and staring out the passenger window, hoping to find some sort of answers in the racing landscape.

So the new guest was Cecil's deceased father. What were the odds, and were there even odds involved. If he'd died when Cecil was a kid he was the longest wandering ghost that Pippi had ever heard of.

She was now in a moral quandary. She couldn't tell Cecil about his father without revealing everything about her inn for ghosts to a ghost hunter. Plus, wasn't it a breach of John Henry Graham's guest confidentiality if she told Cecil? But didn't she have a responsibility to help father and son with their connection? Wasn't that part of why she was here? And this was no ordinary son, this was Cecil. *Her Cecil.* Or so she had allowed herself to think for a few brief moments.

And Halloween was practically here. Pippi groaned and pulled her sweatshirt up over her face, imagining all the tricks the guests had up their capable sleeves, tricks that she would crush when she tells them the show is off. Tricks that she should have stopped immediately, that never would have come around if she'd just listened to Hazel in the first place.

Pippi and Cecil split in separate directions without a word exchanged once the Aerostar van arrived back at the inn. It was past lunch but the inn had kept a gluten-free grilled cheese sandwich warm for her, which Pippi consumed in the empty dining room, shooting daggers out towards the backyard cottage.

After eating, Pippi strolled the quiet inn, looking for hints of the guests' plans for All Hallows' Eve. But they were ghosts, they had a natural ability to hide things and hide them well. She peeked up to the second floor, where crime scene tape had been stretched between the railings. Pippi climbed the steps and leaned down to read a sign that stated: *Closed for Halloween prep. No midnight tea tonight! No questions, please.*

Pippi closed her eyes. This was going to be tough. *Real tough.*

A door opened and John slipped out.

"John!" Pippi whispered loudly.

He saw her and waved, beaming. "Well, hello!"

Pippi motioned for him to come over. He looked back at the closed door and shrugged amiably.

"Sorry, they told me not to talk to you," he said.

"No, it's...you got a message while I was out." It's true, she wanted to pepper him with questions but she had a job to do, first.

John approached her. Pippi studied him in a different way, seeing some resemblance now in John and Cecil's chin and hairline.

"It was a short message from your son," she said. "I can get it on the downstairs phone for you."

"You listened to it?" he asked, emotionless.

"I did. I'm sorry, I should have been here."

"No worries. Thanks for letting me know."

"I saved it, if you'd like to listen to it?"

"Not necessary."

"Also, regarding your son..." Pippi had given much thought to this next part. Cecil would be gone tomorrow, if not on his own, then because she was going to tell him to pack up his ghost hunting supplies and get lost. But still, wouldn't a guest want to know their child was nearby?

John held up his hand. "I really don't want to talk about my son. Please."

"But, he's here," she blurted out. "On the premises. In the backyard cottage, in fact."

John said nothing, nodded deeply, and walked away.

"Wait! Can I speak to the others, please? It's about Halloween!"

But if John had heard her, he didn't show it, as he evaporated through the wall into his private room.

Pippi returned downstairs and paced the inn, taking peeks out at the backyard cottage through every window she passed. She wondered once if she should bring Cecil some food but immediately decided against it. He was a big boy, he could figure it out for himself. The inn allowed her to eat dinner in the kitchen, where she sat on the floor and ate a bowl of ramen while the inn did the dishes and kept her company in its wordless way. She dropped a note in the suggestion box and wrote another on her nightstand notepad, both politely and not too desperately pleading with the inn to keep the guests in check. She also wrote a letter and hung it on the upstairs sign for good measure. As she retreated back downstairs, Pippi immediately felt like she'd taken the coward's way out, but she had bigger problems to worry about tonight in bed, making sure to allow enough time to dream so they could all eat breakfast.

Dear Guests:

As you know, tomorrow is Halloween. (Happy All Hollows' Eve-Eve!) I know you've been working very hard on your "tricks" to help get rid of Cecil. And I sincerely appreciate you. But based on events from today, I've decided Cecil will leave tomorrow morning. I will be making sure of it. Please trust me this is for the best. However, I am happy to participate in your Halloween events planned for tomorrow evening! We will make the best of this, I promise!

Thank you for your support and understanding.

Yours truly,

Pippi

Chapter Fifteen

She needed to remember to tell the inn to turn up the heat.

This was the first thing on Pippi's mind as she woke up. Either that, or she needed more quilts on her bed. Because she was freezing cold. And damp. And apparently there was a massive draft in her room as well. Had she fallen asleep with the window open? And had her small lamp that she usually used for a night light burned out? Because it was really, really, really dark.

But she wasn't in her room.

She was outside, somewhere on top of the inn, in fact.

In the middle of the night in her pajamas.

"Wh...wh...wh...?" Pippi sputtered, bracing her body backwards flat against what was apparently the inn's roof. It was raining, slow and steady, adding to the slick sliminess of the shingles. As her eyes adjusted to the darkness, Pippi realized she was indeed on the top attic floor of the inn, balanced precariously on a tiny ledge between the roof and gutters. For a quick moment she could appreciate how beautiful the dark stretching woods looked from this vantage point, but only for a quick moment, before yelling, "How did I get up here?"

"Don't worry, dear, we've got a good hold on you!" Lidia said as she popped her head out through the exterior of the inn.

Pippi covered her mouth to stop from screaming, immediately regretting the sudden movement. Lidia had definitely *ghouled* herself up for the festivities.

"No, no! That's good! Let the scream rip, dear!" Lidia encouraged before popping back inside.

"Wait! Wait!" Pippi gasped. "Come back!"

Stephanie popped her head out next, followed by the boys, who were costumed as some sort of little twin demon pair.

"Oh, thank goodness," Pippi panted, reaching out her hand towards her friend, who looked to be dressed simply as a classic mourning ghost. "Help me inside."

"We got your letter," Stephanie sighed. "So we moved up our plans to Halloween morning instead. This is for your own good."

"This is *not* funny. I'm going to fall and break my neck." Pippi's head was spinning and she was panic-sweating through her pajamas. The rain had steadily and methodically soaked her hair to dripping wet, stringing curly tendrils across her face that Pippi dared let go of the roof for a moment to brush out of her face. "If I fall, no one is getting a decent breakfast again!"

"You'll be fine, we won't let you fall, I promise," Stephanie assured. "Now, scream."

"Scream for *who*?" Pippi shouted.

"For the ghost guy!" Caleb instructed.

"The one you like!" Anthony chimed in.

"And then he can come save you." Stephanie winked.

"No." Pippi shook her head so hard she almost lost her balance. She looked around for a possible escape option. The guests had certainly placed her in a predicament that did not look possible to escape unless Pippi thought the gutters would handle her riding down them like a pole at a fire station. Directly below her stood the dark backyard cottage where Cecil was likely having a peaceful night sleep.

"We had a fight!" Pippi called behind her. "He's not going to come save me, trust me."

Every guest popped their head out now and Pippi had to press her eyes closed at the overwhelming amount of creepy gore. If she wasn't literally hanging on by her fingernails she might feel touched at the amount of effort put into this matchmaking scheme disguised as an attempt to scare Cecil off forever.

"He will."

Everyone turned to look at John, who had completely disguised himself with a full face mask.

John removed the mask to look Pippi in the eye. "He'll come help you, I know it."

"I was going to tell him he had to leave, anyway," Pippi explained. "He has pictures...he practically has us figured out."

"Well," Lidia harrumphed. "All the more reason for our plan to succeed. Now, scream, dear."

Pippi waited a solid fifteen minutes before even considering screaming for help, stubbornly ignoring the prompts from the impatient guests who wanted to get their other plans underway. But at the fifteen minute mark, exhaustion and early hypothermia started to settle in for Pippi with teeth chattering and numb fingers that she *hoped* still had a good hold on the roof.

"Inn? Can you intervene, here?" Pippi whispered.

"The inn is *in* on it, too!" a guest from the other side of the wall chided. "Just trust us, Pippi!"

Fine. She'd shout for help a few times to prove her point, then they'd let her inside again and she'd take a hot shower, go back to bed, and ask the inn to slip a reservation cancellation notice under the backyard cottage door at daybreak. Not that the coward's way out had worked well for her so far.

"Help," Pippi mumbled.

"LOUDER!" everyone inside insisted.

"Help," Pippi mumbled a little louder.

Lidia popped out again. She shook her head and tsked. "We didn't want to do this, but..."

The inn rumbled and started to sway. Leaves and other debris slipped past Pippi, who was quickly losing footing. She crouched down and braced her body against the inn.

"Oh! HELP!" she authentically screamed.

"That's it!" Lidia encouraged, disappearing inside.

Pippi wasn't sure if she was actually yelling *help* or just a primal mix of jumbled, terrified general screams. She was scared, it was like a nightmare that seemed too real but instead of waking up, revealed itself as truth. One thing was for sure, the inn was not letting up and the guests weren't either, so maybe Cecil was her only hope.

The backyard cottage door swung open and Cecil appeared, dressed in pajama pants and no shirt. The inn immediately stopped shaking and froze still, like a child who'd been caught doing something naughty.

"Hello?" Cecil called out, running outside in his bare feet. "Pippi?"

"Up here!" Pippi had to gather all her breath to call out. She was about to cry from embarrassment and relief. He heard her and still came out.

Cecil squinted up into the rain, jumping back a step at the sight of her curled into a ball on the highest eave of the inn.

"Pippi?" he called.

"Cecil!" Pippi reached out across the impossible distance. In an instant, the roof opened and swallowed Pippi inside with one last, "Help me!"

TWENTY MINUTES EARLIER

Cecil laid awake in bed, trying to ignore the gnawing hunger that had not been satisfied by expired trail mix bars and more sticks of gum than he could count. He'd spent the night toiling through fitful sleep, waking to replay his conversation with Pippi at the wind phone, sometimes with the same results, others turning out different depending on how he tweaked it. Other times he'd wake up incredibly frustrated; she wouldn't let him talk, wouldn't let him explain, wouldn't let him elaborate. But would it have mattered? No matter which way it was spun, it always had the same result. Cecil knew Pippi could see ghosts and this inn was definitely haunted and both of those facts were intertwined in a way he hadn't quite put together yet. Most people ran away from ghosts. But Pippi seemed to be *protecting* them?

He sat up in bed and sifted through his bag for a notebook. He'd make an inventory of what equipment was where so he could be in and out and gone as quickly as possible in the morning. Based off the photo captures he'd recorded so far, Cecil took an educated guess that his other equipment had collected a substantial amount of paranormal data. But it didn't matter now. If Pippi was protecting this place then it must be important, and he had a ghost explorer code of conduct to uphold, which included not trespassing where he wasn't wanted. But he hadn't come just for the ghosts, and he knew it.

Cecil stopped list-making. *What was that?*

"Help!" a tiny voice called from outside.

Cecil jumped up and opened the door. It was pitch dark out and silently raining, so quietly that Cecil hadn't even heard it on the window glass.

"Hello?" he called out, stepping out on the cold, wet grass. "Pippi?"

"Up here!"

It was definitely Pippi. Cecil shielded his eyes from the rain and looked up. Pippi was huddled against the roof, clearly shaking.

"Pippi?" he called out again, struggling to convince himself what he was seeing was real. *How did she get up there?*

She reached down for him. "Cecil!"

Then, with one last cry for help, a dark portal opened up and a dozen pairs of hands pulled Pippi inside, sealing up instantly behind her.

"Pippi!" he shouted, reaching up to the empty space.

Cecil raced towards the inn then stopped, slipping and sliding through the mud back to the backyard cottage. Inside, he dropped to his stomach and pulled out the weapon he always kept below his bed but never had the chance to use. He'd fantasized many times about using it, but now presented with an *actual* opportunity made him shake with adrenaline.

The "weapon" was a contraption of his own invention, inspired by technology he'd seen in movies and doodled about for years until finally taking the plunge and piecing it together. The bulk of the weapon was a cylindrical high-frequency emitter with a powerful flashlight mounted on top. The contraption had proved to be rather heavy so Cecil had recycled one of his old guitar straps to use as a harness. The design for the weapon was inspired by Cecil's own theory that spirits were sensitive to high frequencies, so delivering a supercharged blast would send a spirit spinning. In theory. Maybe.

Still barefoot and wielding his Hyper Sonic Blaster (name still a work-in-progress,) Cecil stole across the backyard grass to where the door to the kitchen had once been, but was now gone. Cecil patted his hand on the damp exterior, certain a door had been there at one point, but considering this was clearly a haunted structure, a disappearing door was no surprise. He peeked inside to the pitch black dining room and crept along the side of the inn, across the soggy mulch under the sleeping rose bushes. After a quick look around the corner, the lamp over the front door flickered on and off to reveal an empty porch.

At least that door was still there. If it was locked, Cecil had a crowbar out in the van that could break the stained glass, although it'd be a shame to break it in the first place. But the door was unlocked; Cecil twisted the doorknob, flicking on his flashlight beam, and stepped inside.

He was met first with an absurd amount of cobwebs, thicker and larger than any cobwebs he'd ever seen, stretching from the front entry to the dining room to the upstairs. It was completely dark inside, much different than the welcoming light always on at the front desk. Cecil used the Blaster to slash through the cobwebs, the flashlight beam almost blinding him as it reflected off the silky webbing.

Cecil swirled at the sound of dragging chains and the classic movie ghost *boo* moan.

"Hello? Who's there?" he called out, squinting into the thick white. He jumped back and fell to his bottom as the webbing parted and a ghoul charged towards him, howling *booooo!* The Blaster slipped out of Cecil's hands, causing the flashlight to sputter out and leave him enveloped in complete darkness. He climbed on his belly in the direction he thought the Blaster slid, finding it and quickly flicking on the flashlight again, only to find the ghoul inches from his face.

"Get lost!" Cecil shouted, pulling the trigger on the Blaster for its first time used in action.

"Hey, that hurts!" the ghoul gasped in a completely normal voice and disappeared, dragging its chains along with it.

Pausing to steady his breath and his heartbeat, Cecil laid completely still, straining his ears for any other sounds, but the inn was oppressively quiet as though the building was literally holding its breath. (Which, in fact, it was.) Finally, he rolled to his knees, Blaster outstretched, and pushed his way through the cobwebs down the hall to the dining room.

Passing through the last curtain of thick webbing, Cecil stumbled into the dining room, which was free of cobwebs but filled with eerie blue light that he definitely had not seen from the outside. A shrouded figure sat at the far end of the table, disguised beneath a gauzy veil, huddled over the source of the blue light. As if cued by Cecil's entrance, a mist began to descend from the vaulted ceilings and a record player scratched into action, playing a generic spooky operatic tune.

"Where's Pippi?" Cecil called out, padding across the wood floors towards the mysterious figure.

"Who goes there?" a raspy woman's voice whispered from beneath the shroud.

"Cecil Graham," he answered, inching closer and closer, Blaster at the ready.

"And *who* is Cecil Graham to this Pippi?" the raspy woman demanded.

Cecil paused. "Um, well..."

"Be you her beloved?" the specter pressed. The blue light pulsed from the tabletop.

"Well, no. I'd say no."

"Do you want to be her beloved?"

"What?"

"Do you *want* to be her beloved? It is a simple yes or no question."

Cecil started to lift the edge of the gauzy, near-translucent veil with the tip of the Blaster.

"Hey! Stop that!" the raspy woman demanded in a very regular voice. She cleared her voice and went raspy again. "Well, do you?"

"Pippi...is that you?" Cecil started to reach towards the veil.

"JUST ANSWER THE QUESTION FOR GOODNESS SAKE, YOU KNOW YOU LIKE HER, GOOD GRIEF, MEN THESE DAYS!"

With a giant push of wind that knocked Cecil off his feet, the veiled woman levitated into the air, carrying her pulsing orb that was now twinged with an angry red tint.

"If you really care, seek out the portal...if you dare!" the specter wailed, evaporating up into the ceiling but accidentally dropping her glowing orb in the process, which turned out to be an old globe hollowed out with a bundle of battery-powered twinkle lights stuffed inside. The fog vacated from the room, leaking through the windows that the inn had subtly cracked open for ventilation.

Cecil picked up the globe to inspect it. Cool to the touch, it had the appearance of a real world item that had been fiddled with in an otherworldly way; he could think of no other way to describe it. He started pulling the twinkle lights out of the globe.

"Cecil!" a faraway voice called. It didn't quite sound like Pippi but it was enough to get him back on track. Cecil dropped the globe and ran back out to the hallway, through the path he'd cleared in the cobwebs, and started up the stairs.

"Be gone, human!" two little ghoulish voices shouted from the top of the staircase, rolling fiery pumpkins down the steps, one after another. Cecil dove left and right to dodge them until finally he found a lull in the pumpkin tossing rhythm to fire a hypersonic blast at the two little ghouls, who shrieked and covered their ears, evaporating with a wail that sounded a lot like *Mom!*

Now that the way was clear, Cecil stumbled up the remaining stair steps, crouching down to peek over the final step to survey the second floor. Nothing looked dangerous at first, just a thick, inky black space that *moved.* The hairs on Cecil's neck raised to attention. That darkness was *definitely* moving.

Soundlessly, Cecil pulled the Blaster up to rest on the top stair, positioning his flashlight beam towards the giant dark blob. For a brief, horrifying moment, it almost appeared to be a giant spider in a black turtleneck, but that was impossible. (Then again, there was an enormous amount of spider webs...) Suddenly, he was lifted by the waist of his pajama pants and left hovering in the air, feet dangling. Before he could shout or curse or even scream, the angry face of a female ghoul appeared inches from his nose.

"You hurt my babies' ears!" the ghoul shrieked so loud that Cecil's hair flew backwards.

"I'm sorry!" he blubbered.

"Thank you for apologizing!" the female ghoul shouted again, dropping Cecil unceremoniously to the stairs.

Clinging to his Blaster again, Cecil rolled over and immediately pointed the flashlight back to the second floor, but the dark moving blobs were gone. In fact, the upstairs looked completely normal, a crack of light stretching out from beneath the linen closet door, beckoning him to come closer. He did come closer, limping with a sore tailbone and covered in cobwebs and pumpkin guts. Cecil had done a lot for a girl before, but this topped it all.

Turning the handle to the linen closet door, Cecil was immediately met with the sound and reverberation of a low hum, urging him to open the door completely. He did, revealing a purple swirling portal located under a stack of flannel sheets.

"Cecil!" Pippi's distorted voice called from within the portal.

"What in the..." Cecil murmured, reaching towards the mesmerizing purple swirling mass.

A warm hand rested on Cecil's shoulder and gently pushed him forward into the portal while slipping the Blaster right out of his arms. Cecil turned and saw the silhouetted outline of a man before tumbling into a purple haze and falling face first into a plush green carpet of kelly green grass, wet as if with morning dew and smelling sweet and freshly cut.

"What now?" he mumbled into the grass before lifting his head.

The portal, which had now completely disappeared, had dumped him in what was apparently a giant and perfectly-manicured lawn, walled in by tall shrubberies reaching at least twenty feet in the air. Above him, the sky swirled with varying sizes of clouds shaped like hearts.

"Cecil?" Pippi called out, clear as day.

"Pippi!" Cecil stood stiffly. "Where are you?"

"In the maze!" she shouted from somewhere.

"Are you okay?" Cecil shouted back, hobbling to the giant shrubberies and trying to push through them, but they just pushed him right back.

No response.

"Hey!" he called again. "Are you okay?"

Pippi shouted something unintelligible. Cecil kept walking along the solid wall of shrubberies until he reached a break in the fortress, labeled with a sign that said *Enter here.*

"Hold on, I'm coming for you!" he shouted, ducking inside.

The sky turned dark and stormy the moment he stepped past the threshold into the maze. He was transported immediately back to third grade literature class, where he'd first learned about the Minotaur and his doomed existence in a maze such as this. Why this memory was coming to him right now he wasn't sure but he hoped it wasn't because he was about to come face-to-face with a half man, half bull.

At first, the maze seemed benign to Cecil other than the very threatening sky and the distinct feeling that he was being watched. He felt practically naked without his Blaster, which he allowed himself a brief moment of pride over the fact his working theory proved true. Bringing his attention back to the matter at hand, Cecil quickly felt like he'd walked miles without even a break in the maze; he was just hobbling along a wet grassy pathway walled in by towering shrubbery. But that didn't last long.

It started with a squeaky, chittering sound and rustling in the shrubberies. Then Cecil started to find cobwebs in the shrubbery he passed. Next, a long shadow would pass across the grass and when Cecil looked up, there'd only be dark rolling clouds. He hastened his steps and whatever was following him hastened their steps, too. And there were *a lot* of steps being hastened by the sound of it.

"Pippi!" Cecil yelled into the air as he slipped and stumbled on the wet grass. "I think I'm about to be eaten, here! Anything you can do about that?"

"Leave him alone!" Pippi, who sounded further away than ever, shouted. "I'm serious!"

Was he going in the wrong direction? Would this maze ever end? All signs pointed to the reality that giant spiders were chasing him, but here he was, still running towards Pippi.

Still running towards Pippi.

"I *do* like Pippi!" Cecil shouted, stopping to catch his breath so he could yell louder. "I really, really like Pippi! In a girl-friend-sort-of-way, okay!? There, I said it outloud!"

The chasing footsteps stopped. The sky cleared as if on fast forward and as the sun broke through the dissipating clouds, the towering shrubberies collapsed into manageable hedges, short and stubby enough to look over.

"Over here!" Pippi waved wildly from a good twenty paces away. She was a vision in pink, like a cotton candy cloud, dressed head to toe in frilly taffeta with her hair curled into perfect ringlets and her lips stained a strawberry pink.

Cecil limped over to her, stopping to survey Pippi's fluffy transformation.

"Look at you," Pippi gasped, surveying Cecil's haggard form covered in sweat, rain, mud, cobwebs, pumpkin guts, and wet grass clippings. "What did they do to you? They said they wouldn't hurt you!"

Cecil held up his hand. "So you're admitting you *do* see ghosts?"

"Oh my gosh, yes, I see ghosts!" Pippi threw up her hands, revealing pink fluffy handcuffs around her wrists connected to a long velvety chain.

"What is that?" Cecil stared.

"Oh. Yeah, this." Pippi held up her hands again and shrugged. "You have to kiss me."

"I *have* to kiss you?"

"This was a big matchmaking scheme on the part of the guests. I guess there's nothing to hide now, good grief. Yes, I have ghost guests here, they're on vacation, I can explain it all to you later. They thought if you had to save me it would prove to me and you how much we like each other because if you didn't like me, you'd just let me scream for help and ignore it. But they are insistent that you and I would be great together but we haven't communicated effectively so this is why they had to intervene, for my own good, as they said. But I'm not going to force some man to kiss me if he doesn't want to, they can't leave me here forever, they need me for breakfast, and they know it!"

Cecil laughed and shook his head, releasing a waterfall of grass clippings. "And somehow dolling you up like this would seal the deal, huh?"

Pippi rattled her velvet chain. "I guess so."

"Well, I don't need a pink fluffy dress and or a bunch of ghosts to convince me that I like you - a lot. You've done that pretty well on your own, just with your overalls and you being *you*."

Cecil took Pippi's hands and the handcuffs slipped off.

"And I don't *have* to kiss you," he whispered. "I *want* to."

To the clash of cymbals in the sky and a chorus of cheers and applause from the materialized guests, Pippi and Cecil shared their first sweaty, sticky, pink strawberry-stained kiss. And it was very, very, very good.

Chapter Sixteen

The morning light caused the blanket over Pippi's head to glow like a warm dawn sky. The blanket also muffled the sounds of vacuuming and hammering going on throughout the inn, all to the soundtrack of music and loud singing. They were the sounds of the guests (and inn) literally cleaning up after themselves, a promise they'd made to Pippi once the early morning Halloween shenanigans were complete and Pippi had to walk through the inn to get to bed. She said nothing, covering her mouth with both hands the entire way, her eyes shooting daggers at the guests whose sheepish grins quickly faded.

Pippi didn't know if she was more horrified by the state of the inn or by the visual of what the guests had put Cecil through, who'd she deposited, limp and exhausted, in his backyard cottage bed before retiring back to the inn. Part of her was flattered he'd endured that much to "save" her, another part impressed by his fearlessness, and the final part a bit concerned for his sanity that he hadn't run away, screaming.

There was a gentle knock at the door.

"What?" Pippi yelled. She was currently miffed at the guests and the inn for not having her back, even though they'd had the best of intentions. And they *did* help her score the guy, the guy she was going to chase off for *their* own benefit, so it did all work out in the end. As long as Cecil woke up remembering it all and didn't chalk it up to a dream and body aches.

But it was Cecil who opened the bedroom door, or the inn opened for him.

"I come bearing breakfast," he called through the cracked door, pushing a cart that Pippi could hear and smell before lifting the blanket. She'd miraculously dreamed of a full English breakfast with bacon, eggs, toast, black pudding, and bracing tea. She could also smell Cecil's clean, freshly-showered scent as he limped into her room in clean clothes and wet, slicked-back hair.

Pippi sat up. She was still in her frilly pink dress from last night, providing her a momentary break from linen overalls and her usual oversized pajamas.

"Full disclosure, it was right inside the entryway with a big sign that said *please take this to Pippi and you can have some, too,*" Cecil confessed, running his hands through his hair.

Pippi smoothed out her bedspread and motioned for him to join her. Cecil unloaded the food and they sat in silence for a few moments, inhaling their food.

"So," Pippi said after a long swig of tea. "How did it look out there?"

"Significantly different than last night," Cecil reported. "They're doing a good job."

"*They,*" Pippi repeated carefully, spreading some fig jam on her toast and taking a big bite. "So you remember..."

"Everything," he confirmed, wiping some jam from her mouth.

Pippi smiled. "Okay, good. Then let me have it."

Cecil choked on his tea. "Excuse me?"

"Give me all your burning questions."

"Okay. Let's start with, why did you lie to me?"

"Oof, a heavy hitter," Pippi sighed. "I guess the easy answer is I was protecting the guests."

"But?"

"But I suppose I was really protecting myself," Pippi admitted. "Talking about my ability to see ghosts is a thing I've only discussed with my mom and aunt. And my aunt is currently a fox, by the way."

"A fox. Okay, I guess at this point nothing should surprise me. What's her name?"

"Hazel. She's usually here, but she's pissed off I let you stay so she ran off."

"Oh, there's the Hazel connection. It's all starting to come together now bit by bit."

"She also talks."

"While in her fox form? I'm keeping up."

"And there are giant spiders in the attic, who I am told are friendly but very protective."

"I gathered that one. So, this inn...those spirits live here?"

"Just temporarily. They're on vacation before moving on. And that phone in the entry? Their living loved ones can call whenever they want, when they really need them. I also get a call here." Pippi reached for her cell phone and pulled it off her nightstand charger.

"The phone with no number," Cecil remembered.

"Yeah, sorry about that."

"And the spirits talk back?"

"No. They can't. They just listen."

"Almost like a wind phone."

"Exactly."

"And you facilitate all this?"

"Well, I try to. But as you saw, they still have a mind of their own."

They laughed but Pippi quickly subdued, inspecting the cell phone.

"The truth is, it's the biggest honor I've ever had to be here for them. Other than my dreams, I don't cook or clean, but I can be there for them, for this. And it's the first time I feel like I'm making some sort of difference."

Cecil nodded, clearly processing it all. "You don't cook but...the dreams? Wait, the sushi?"

"Yeah, I dreamed that the night before," Pippi chuckled. "I dream about what we're having for breakfast but when I don't dream, the default breakfast is much less exciting."

"Wow. I feel like I should be writing this down," Cecil said, standing and loading the dirty dishes back onto the cart.

"I think you're caught up for the most part." Pippi shifted in her seat. "My turn to ask some questions?"

"Let me have it."

"How does this impact your research? I don't want all this getting out."

"Of course not. I wouldn't."

"Tell me more."

"Well, how I see it is, if you and the guests *allow* it, I'd have unprecedented access to the supernatural in a way literally no one could ever dream of. So if I can stay, and watch, and record data...maybe I'll learn something I can apply to other clients down the road. Clients I could actually accredit."

"Essentially this would be off-the-record research for your-eyes-only? Is that right?"

"No podcast. No spotlight. Just...exploring."

"Let's bring it up at lunch. I'll add it to the agenda with the other matters I plan to address." Pippi stood, causing an avalanche of pink. "Guess I need to get ready for the day. I've given the guests enough of the silent treatment."

"Before you go...you haven't happened to see a Hyper Sonic Blaster around here, have you?" Cecil asked, pausing at the door with the breakfast cart.

"Hyper what?"

"Never mind, I'll take a look around for it." He started to leave and stopped again. "Do you want me to take the cell phone while you're in the shower?"

"I never even thought about that," Pippi said, looking at the cell phone in her hand. "But no thanks. It stays with me."

Cecil abandoned the breakfast cart and came close to Pippi. He fluffed one of her sleeves and leaned in. "And the overalls? They'll be back today?"

"Everyday," Pippi grinned.

"Good," he grinned back, his lips brushing up to hers.

On cue, the inn popped open Pippi's dresser drawers.

"Stay focused, got it," Cecil said, stealing a quick kiss before returning to the breakfast cart. He winked and shut the door behind him.

Pippi showered and scrubbed hard to wash the glitter and massive amounts of gel from her hair. She never thought she'd be so glad to pull on those linen overalls, which this time was patterned with green and ivory pumpkins against a chocolate brown autumn background, with a speckled oatmeal long sleeve shirt underneath.

She opened her bedroom door and ventured outside, immediately slapped with the smell of pine-scented cleaning solution and roses. The wood floors gleamed brighter than ever before, the rugs looked laundered or at the very least well vacuumed, and the stained glass in the front door (which now depicted a pumpkin with heart eyes) was wiped clean without a streak in sight. The entry was completely void of spider webs (both giant and normal sized) and the front desk had been polished, the once-squeaky drawer oiled to be squeaky no more.

Good, Pippi thought to herself. *They should clean up after themselves, good gracious.* But even considering the absurdity of the early morning events, Pippi felt a twinge of love and warmth for her precious guests, as if they were little children she just couldn't stay mad at.

But still. That couldn't happen again. Seriously.

Later, at lunch, the guests gathered sheepishly in the dining room, all conversation screeching to a halt when Pippi entered. They'd finished clearing up (bettering, in some cases) the inn and turned to Pippi with truly apologetic faces.

"Hello, all," Pippi greeted, taking her seat. "Happy Halloween."

"Hi, Pippi," came a chorus of greetings back. "Happy Halloween."

The dining room fell silent again as the guests picked at their Nicoise salad and French onion soup. They froze as Pippi stood up.

"If I can have your attention, please," she announced.

Wide eyes looked back. Anthony and Caleb whispered into their napkins.

Pippi smiled. "Guys, I'm not mad at you, okay?"

A collective sigh of relief went around the table and the dining room was immediately filled with the hubbub of chatter.

"But!" Pippi added loudly.

The room fell silent again other than a spoon clattering to the table and plopping into the French onion soup.

"But we do need to settle a few things. First, inn, if you would be so kind..."

A dozen pieces of paper fluttered into the dining room and floated down to the table, landing one by one in front of each guest. Pens dropped from the ceiling into their laps.

"What you see here is an addendum to your reservation agreements," Pippi said. "I'll sum it up for you. From now on, if you want to stay here, you cannot kidnap the proprietress for any reason."

The guests looked at each other.

"Just need your signatures, please," Pippi urged.

The guests signed the addendum without argument, having no intention of kidnapping Pippi again. After the guests were done and the inn had filed the addendums away, Pippi did feel she had to add one more thing.

"And one more thing," she added. "Thank you for helping me and Cecil figure things out."

The guests cheered with a pent-up explosion of excitement, both for Pippi and the fact that all their plans had actually worked.

"He's the most handsome creature," Lucy sighed. "And I should know, I was *right* up in there."

"Well, so was I," Lidia sniffed.

"No, you were *not*. Not as close as me," Lucy retorted.

"He's not just cute," Stephanie spoke up. "I mean, that was so gallant, coming to save you. And he apologized about the boys. I love a man who can admit when he's wrong."

"Yeah, what was that thing? It killed my ears," Anthony said after a long slurp of soup.

"Are you talking about the Hyper Sonic Blaster thing?" Pippi asked, sitting down to her own French onion soup at last. "Oh gosh, I totally forgot about Cecil!"

"Gee, thanks," Cecil called from the hallway, where he'd been waiting the entire time for Pippi to give the all-clear.

The guests craned their heads to get a look at Cecil and started loudly whispering.

"Okay, okay, settle down!" Pippi called out. "One more item of business. Is it okay if-"

"YES!" the guests all yelled in unison. All the guests other than John, that is, who sat quietly through the whole lunch meeting. Now, at the inevitable entrance of his son happening soon, John went invisible, the only guest to do so.

Cecil entered the dining room to loud fanfare, taking his seat in Hazel's old spot that was quickly just becoming Cecil's spot.

"Thanks. Thank you," Cecil answered the cheers, adding, "And no hard feelings by the way. You all were very creative. Also, super sorry if the Blaster hurt anyone."

"I just want to be *extra* clear," Pippi continued. "Cecil would be here to also do research. He might ask you questions. Take measurements."

"Recordings," Cecil corrected.

"But," Pippi emphasized. "This would be for his own private research. Not to be published."

The guests seemed the least bit concerned with this new arrangement as they gazed, starry-eyed, at Pippi's new beau. And unbeknownst to them, (and Pippi, at that time,) but having another living person around would remind them of home and help them feel a little closer to their own living loved ones.

Meanwhile, one guest still hadn't said a word.

"John?" Pippi asked the chair that appeared empty to Cecil but in fact held his long deceased father.

John stood, placing what appeared to be a long gun with a flashlight atop the table.

"My Hyper Sonic Blaster!" Cecil exclaimed, standing from his chair just as John left his own.

The other guests watched in tight-lipped silence as John exited the room, passing carefully by his completely oblivious son. Pippi's heart broke a little for both of them; for a son missing what was right in front of him, and for a father knowingly hurting his son.

Cecil picked up the Blaster and inspected it, patting the plastic lovingly.

"This is my Hyper Sonic Blaster," he introduced to Pippi. He held it up to the light to inspect it. "Thank you to whoever cleaned it for me."

No one said a word. The inn broke the silence with a surprise lunchtime dessert, rolling out a giant, ten tier wedding-like cake with little figurines on the top of Pippi in her frilly pink dress and Cecil, all haggard and covered in cobwebs.

"Ouch." Cecil inspected his character. "You kissed this?"

As the guests obsessed over the cake, which was also etched with scenes depicting the events of Halloween morning, Pippi made one more announcement.

"Okay, there's one more thing," she said loudly. "It *is* Halloween. And since we're not getting trick-or-treaters tonight, we're going to do a movie night instead."

A voting booth rolled in from the kitchen, with a privacy curtain decorated with classic Halloween-themed icons, like witches, candles, and carved pumpkins. (Pippi had requested the inn avoid depictions of skeletons, spiders, bats, and ghosts. For obvious reasons.)

"Get your vote in! We'll watch the top three movie selections tonight," Pippi instructed. She smiled at the expectant faces looking back. "And, yes, there will be your favorite treats."

The guests cheered and lined up for the voting booth as the inn cut the cake. Pippi pulled Cecil aside.

"There is someone here that didn't agree to you staying," she said gently.

"Who?" Cecil asked, looking around the room.

"They didn't reveal themselves to you."

"Oh. Okay. Are they sore about last night?"

"That's not the problem."

"I'm getting the feeling you can't talk about it."

"I wish I could."

Cecil looked at the Blaster. "Are they the one who cleaned this?"

Pippi nodded. Cecil's face darkened as he inspected the Blaster even closer.

"Thanks for letting me know," Cecil said finally, kissing Pippi on the cheek and leaving the dining room. He exited through the front door and walked down the gravel drive, past Mo in the bushes, all the way down to the beach, where thoughts could roam free and no feeling is bigger than the sea.

Chapter Seventeen

November ushered itself in on a heavy cloud, as Halloween was typically the unofficial start of the rainy season, wrapped in a cloak of neon red, goldenrod yellow, and burning orange leaves. The first week of November was when those summer clothes could officially be packed away until late spring, cotton sheet sets were swapped out for the flannels, and spicy, sweet chimney smoke curled above the rooftops until the heavy November clouds claimed it for themselves.

The inn upgraded Pippi's overalls to lightly-fleece lined and her rain slicker became considerably warmer although still as communicative. On that day, Pippi's coat pattern was of steamy coffee mugs, brown shopping bags, and tiny, tiny fox faces that Pippi had to get a magnifying glass out to see. But the fox didn't exactly look like Hazel, more like a version that existed in a different reality or multiverse.

But it was enough of a sign to keep Pippi on high alert as she walked the downtown streets of Windia with Cecil. There was a several hour break in the rain forecasted so everyone plus their mother, father, and child seemed to be out and about for a stroll, stopping to admire the storefronts that were already decorated for the holidays to capture every spending second of the prime shopping season.

"They were right, I need to get down here more. It's like I'm on vacation but I live right up the street," Pippi admitted as they passed a chocolatier shop with mouthwatering truffles and hot cocoa bombs in the window. In case of a call, she had done a test run and timed how long it would take her to get back to the car, drive at the lawful speed limit, and get back to the inn in time to summon the guest for their call. It was a solid five to eight minutes, but after a lengthy discussion with the guests who were all in agreement that a five to eight minute wait was *just fine* and that Pippi *really needed to get out more,* she agreed to the outing to Windia.

Cecil smiled to himself but said nothing, especially nothing about how it had been his idea in the first place that the five to eight minute wait was okay. He had also upgraded his winter wardrobe, adding a hoodie layer beneath his trusty leather jacket.

"Let's stop in here," Cecil suggested, motioning to the Windia Mercantile, an old-timey shop that sold everything from ready-made dinners to fishing tackle to movie memorabilia. While Cecil scanned the automobile aisle, Pippi perused a rack of local art turned into greeting cards, featuring the Siuslaw river, downtown Windia, and Lonesome Lily herself, minus Susie the Guardian. Pippi watched Cecil out of the corner of her eye, shaking her head as he referenced the mysterious piece of paper he'd found under his door a few mornings ago. *She* knew who the paper was from, but poor Cecil had no idea who'd left him a note detailing a few suggestions to improve his Hyper Sonic Blaster. John had asked her not to tell so not telling is what Pippi did, although covering for her boyfriend's dead father's ghost seemed like a messy way to start a relationship.

Picking through the used records set in a yellow plastic crate in the front window display, Pippi froze as a familiar reddish-orange flash burst past outside. She craned her neck to look down the street.

"All done," Cecil said, holding up a shopping basket of odds and ends Pippi couldn't even begin to identify.

Pippi said nothing, absently following Cecil to the checkout counter where the shopkeeper was sitting in an oversized, over-stuffed armchair. She was a woman over fifty, with glorious gray hair that frizzed out in every direction due to her hard morning brush sessions before work. She wore a well-worn blue and gray flannel and thick blue jeans that squeaked when she stood.

"We got day-old bread two for one over there," the shopkeeper said as she rang up item after item, placing them in an adorable paper bag with a mermaid holding her own bag that read *Windia Mercantile*.

"Oh, no thank you," Cecil replied.

The shopkeeper paused and looked at Cecil pointedly, which is when he realized it was not a suggestion but an order.

"Be right back," he forfeited and left to grab some old bread.

"Which direction is that coffee shop? I think it's called the Cabin or something like that?" Pippi asked, picking through the local business cards lined up along the counter.

The mercantile shopkeeper slammed down a bottle of glue, who Pippi now realized was wearing a shirt stating *Juniper Powell, owner and operator of the Windia Mercantile since 1977*.

"The Yurt," Juniper seethed.

"The what?" Cecil asked, returning with two loaves of old sourdough.

"Witches," Juniper literally spat. "The place is run by *witches*."

"A coffee shop run by witches?" Cecil winked. "Color me intrigued."

Pippi looked over her shoulder and down at her coat pattern. Hazel's inn-sitting witch friend seemed like a good option for a talking fox who needed somewhere to stay.

"Well!" Juniper huffed, crushing the sourdough bread as she stuffed it into the paper bag. "If you insist on being foolish, at least take one of these."

Juniper plucked a little silver bell from a display box with dozens of other silver bells, each featuring a different design. The display was located beneath a prominent sign that read *No witches allowed!*

She held up the little bell and pointed to the mercantile's front door, where a bell twinkled each time a customer entered or left.

"Keeps the witches away," Juniper declared. "I've got 'em everywhere."

"Sure. I'll take one. Why not," Cecil agreed, opening his wallet.

"Down straight south a few blocks. It's right on the beach. Look for the ridiculous shape," Juniper huffed as she handed Cecil his bag. "And tell her I *don't* say hello."

Once back outside, Cecil pulled the old bread from the bag and tossed it to a group of already very well-fed seagulls who were gathered patiently around a city trash can. Pippi stared down the way at the building that was undeniably The Yurt coffee shop, recognizable by the domed architecture and Juniper had been correct by saying it was right on the beach. A walk to The Yurt risked adding another two minute sprint to Pippi's return trip back to the inn, but all signs pointed that it was worth the risk.

As they approached The Yurt, the mouthwatering tang of freshly-ground coffee wafted through the salty air, which turned out to be an aroma match in heaven. Cecil and Pippi passed a steady stream of customers who were either going to The Yurt or the restaurant next door, at which a dinner crowd was already lining up, gathered under the warmth from outdoor heaters. After shuffling through the sand, Pippi and Cecil climbed the porch steps to The Yurt and opened the door.

The aroma of coffee that had led them there now washed over Pippi and Cecil like a wave that held them under longer than anticipated, leaving them a little lightheaded but delirious and wanting more. The Yurt was decorated with sea treasures, family photos, and talismans and charms that clearly looked *witchy*. They passed tables packed with customers that looked decidedly cozy, laughing and conversing as they drew obvious comfort from the coffee huddled in their hands.

A brown-haired woman wearing a *The Yurt* apron expertly bounced from order taking to order fulfilling without any hint of being overwhelmed. While in line, Pippi searched for any sight of Hazel or reddish-orange furballs.

"What are you looking for?" Cecil whispered in her ear, putting his hand on the small of her back.

"I think there's a chance Aunt Hazel is here," Pippi whispered back. "Her friend operates this place."

"A witch friend?" Cecil joked.

"Yep, exactly," Pippi confirmed as they stepped up to place their order.

"Hi guys, welcome," the woman behind the counter greeted, wiping her hands on her apron with the name *Florence* monogrammed on the top left corner.

"Hi, I'm Pippi," Pippi said. "Are you related to Pearl?"

"Pippi…" Florence repeated. "From the inn?"

"Yeah!" Pippi exclaimed, then lowered her voice. "Well, it's a *special* inn."

Florence nodded and winked. "I *know*. And yes, Pearl is my grandmother. What's she done now?"

"Actually, I'm looking for my aunt, who is friends with Pearl."

"Yes. Hazel." Florence said in a voice that seemed twinged with you-mean-the-fox-that's-starting-to-get-on-my-nerves Hazel? "Well, look no further. You've found her."

Florence motioned with her head down to the floor, where Hazel was stretched out beneath the warm espresso machine in a fluffy dog bed, completely in the way, snoring and twitching in a deep sleep.

"She spends half her time here and half over at the restaurant, where Pearl is the head chef," Florence explained. "I don't mind, really…it's just *here* is not very convenient but convincing her of that, well…"

"I completely understand. I'm hoping I can get her to come back to the inn," Pippi said. "Because this is a little ridiculous."

"Although you have been doing fine on your own," Cecil added.

"Are you the ghost hunter she keeps talking about?" Florence asked, eyeing Cecil.

"Ghost explorer. And don't hurt me, please, I have a bell," Cecil said, only half joking (and half serious) in case this really was a witch. He had experience with the dead paranormal but not the living paranormal.

"Uh, good for you?" Florence snorted.

Cecil produced the bell from his bag.

"Oh, that," Florence laughed. "I can't tell if Mrs. Powell actually thinks those bells do anything or if it's a sales tactic, it worked on you, didn't it?"

"So they don't keep witches away?"

"Well, we just don't go visit her because she doesn't want us to," Florence shrugged. "Plus, she's a tea drinker."

Pippi's heart leapt and it wasn't from the caffeine in the air. "I gotta go!" she exclaimed as she ran out of The Yurt. "Tell my aunt to come see me and she can't hide out any longer because I know where she's at!"

The cell phone rang. Pippi let it ring five times, stopped breathlessly to answer it, then proceeded to tell the recorded voice on the other line *one moment please* as she raced back to the inn, where Stephanie was waiting. It had been days since Stephanie or the boys had received a call, which brought them both relief and sadness. As Cecil took his bag of supplies to his backyard cottage to tinker with his Blaster, Pippi prepped the phone for Stephanie and hung back in the dining room, taking deep breaths to calm her racing heart that also hurt a little. She hurt to know her aunt had been so close by the whole time and never checked in; part of Pippi had just assumed nature had completely taken over and her aunt's spirit was released or on vacation at another inn, not minutes away in Windia, sleeping under an espresso machine.

Heavily influenced by the events of the day, Pippi dreamed of the inside of The Yurt that night, where Florence served oatmeal from her espresso machine and a giant silver bell hung from the domed roof like a chandelier. With a loud *creak* the silver bell rang slow and steady with an ear-deafening *gong*.

"That's for you!" Dream Florence shouted at Dream Pippi, who was waiting patiently in line for her oatmeal.

"What?" Dream Pippi called back.

"It's for *you!*"

Sitting up straight in bed, Pippi reached over instinctively for her cell phone, on which a *Guests at the front desk* notification was flashing. Her heart broke. She knew who would be waiting for her.

Stephanie and the boys lined up along the front desk, dressed in their best outfits. Pippi pulled her bathrobe extra tight as she walked to the computer, her gaze locked on the floor. Selfishly, she didn't want to see their pale and sallow versions hanging on for death, but for them, Pippi looked into each of their eyes and asked, "Checking out?"

"Yes," Stephanie whispered, her frail hands reduced to skin hanging off her bones. She passed Pippi a sealed envelope. "Checking out."

Don't cry. Pippi willed herself to keep it together. Hadn't they heard enough tears on those phone calls? Couldn't she just hold it together long enough to let them check out without one more living person crying out about their tragedy? But Pippi was human, so decorum aside, she raced around the side of the front desk and gave each of them a long, fierce embrace. They were like pillars of air dressed in clothes but when she hugged them, her heart told her they felt everything.

Scrubbing the tears from her face, Pippi pulled up Stephanie's reservation with the two boys listed as minors. That large *check out* button that had been gray many times before now pulsed a burning red.

She hovered the mouse arrow over the *check out* button. "It's been a pleasure having you stay with us," Pippi said. "Goodbye."

With a confirming click, the door to the inn opened smoothly. Stephanie placed a hand on each of the boy's little heads as they melted into the light.

Pippi collapsed to the chair behind the desk and curled into a ball. *This was only getting harder.* Maybe she shouldn't strike up friendships with the guests, maybe it was making it more painful for everyone involved, although Pippi was unsure how much they really felt or understood in that state.

Reaching for the envelope Stephanie had passed her, Pippi decided to just get all the painful and emotional experiences over in one sitting.

The letter read:

Dear Pippi,

Thank you for taking care of us so well during our stay at your inn. I hadn't seen such joy on the boy's faces for a long time. Best Halloween ever.

Maybe you're wondering why we are checking out if we're still getting calls. On my call today I finally heard it in my husband's voice. That he has to let go of us or he can never stop grieving. Somehow, I don't know how, I feel if we move on, he will, too. Does that make sense? I always followed my gut, I have to now, too. What else can a girl, a woman, a partner, a mother, do?

I have wonderful people waiting on me. I feel them there, like on the deck of the train station, looking for our arrival with a big sign. Won't that be wonderful?

The other guests told me it's best to end these letters with some words of wisdom. (Or that's what they've been told.) All I can say is never shy from love because you're afraid of losing it. Maybe you think it will hurt too much when it's gone, but the beautiful change that happens to you when you have it...well, it stays with you forever.

Take care and good luck. Someday, I'll meet you on the train deck.

Love,

Stephanie, Anthony, and Caleb

The ink on the page started to smear from Pippi's tears that she now unleashed with rolling sobs into the fleece sleeve of her bathrobe. The inn lowered the lights so she'd have more privacy and she could hear the tea kettle whistling in the distance. A warm furry head nuzzled under her hand, then jumped into Pippi's lap with one lithe movement, curling into a comforting ball. Pippi pulled the warm ball in closer, disappearing into the smell of salt, soil, and espresso beans.

Fox aunt and innkeeper niece were on their fifth cup of tea by the time the other guests filtered into the dining room for a breakfast buffet of oatmeal that had a slight hint of coffee to it. At times, Pippi wondered if their raised voices were going to wake the guests, elevated in moments of both laughter, aggravation, and some disagreement. But by the time the sun was up they had, for the most part, squashed their troubles and come to an amicable truce.

The guests came to welcome, pet, or ear scratch Hazel as they entered the dining room and saw her, sitting back in her rightful chair that Cecil had been inhabiting for the past few weeks. (The inn had accommodated this change around 5:00 am when it swapped Pippi's chair out for a two-seater sofa.)

"So, this boyfriend of yours, is he always late for breakfast?" Hazel sniffed, lapping at her oatmeal which was topped with a layer of toasted acorns.

"He's not even late," Pippi said with a smile, stirring her own oatmeal loaded up with every gluten-free topping from the buffet bar. She was buzzing from the amount of caffeine she'd consumed and also from the exhilaration that comes from a mended relationship.

As if on cue, Cecil entered and froze upon seeing a fox with narrowed eyes sitting in his seat.

"Cecil!" Pippi exclaimed, running over and giving him a big kiss. "Come sit down. We have a shared loveseat now."

"You're still in your pajamas?" Cecil remarked as Pippi dragged him to the loveseat. "Is everything okay?"

"And why shouldn't she still be in her pajamas?" Hazel huffed. "It's the innkeeper's prerogative."

Cecil visibly gaped.

"Let's dish you up," Pippi said, now dragging Cecil over to the oatmeal buffet.

"That's going to take some getting used to," Cecil gulped, looking over his shoulder at Hazel, who watched him as she licked oatmeal from her chops.

"Don't worry, we had a great talk and everything is okay now and I feel so much better," Pippi explained as she piled Cecil's oatmeal with toppings. "I told her how you saved me when the guests acted up and even though she didn't actually say it, I could tell she was impressed."

Cecil poured himself a large coffee. "If you say so."

And even though Pippi *had* said so, Cecil spent his entire breakfast watching the talking fox aunt out of the corner of his eye from his spot on the loveseat, wondering if he was going to be mauled at any moment.

"Tell me more about being a ghost *explorer*," Hazel asked demurely with a touch of rage. "My niece tells me I've misjudged you."

Cecil swallowed a thick wad of oatmeal. Perspiration glistened on his scalp. "Well, the best way I can describe a ghost explorer is we simply aim to record research for the furtherment of understanding the paranormal. A ghost hunter is interested in banishing spirits and profiting off their disturbance."

"Hmm." Which meant Hazel found his answer satisfactory. "And you've been researching our guests?"

"We asked them."

"They agreed."

"You don't have to convince me," Hazel said with her best fox shrug. "Besides, if the inn-"

Hazel stopped, her mouth hanging open. She stared across the table towards the entrance to the dining room, where John was visible to everyone but Cecil.

"John?" Hazel whispered, visibly wilting.

Pippi looked from Hazel to John and back again.

"You know him?" she asked.

"Who?" Cecil asked, clueless.

"What is that ghost hunter doing here?" Hazel hissed below her breath.

"That's just a guest," Pippi assured. She glanced at Cecil, who was looking around the room for what he'd missed. "A complicated guest, but still, a guest."

"Complicated is right," Hazel said, watching John make the rounds at the oatmeal bar.

"You know him?" Pippi whispered, leaning across Cecil.

"*I was his lover.*"

Hazel made the comment loud enough for everyone to hear at the table, except for John, who was blissfully unaware at the other end of the room. But the sudden silence made him turn and look. No one moved or reacted, still as a painting, until Hazel stood from her seat and raised her head haughtily, breezing into the kitchen, Pippi following close behind.

Typically the inn did not prefer dead (or living) guests (or foxes) in the kitchen, but it was also reeling from Hazel's tidbit of juicy gossip.

"What?" Pippi exclaimed the moment they were in the privacy of the bustling kitchen.

Hazel paced, her little nails clicking on the floor. "It was back in the early 80s, well before your beau was conceived, if that's what you're wondering. He was with some woman and then came across the inn one day on a drive. I told them we were out of rooms, but there was a palpable spark between him and I."

"Ugh. Please don't say palpable," Pippi grimaced.

"Yes, *palpable*, Pippi, don't be inappropriate," Hazel sighed. "Well, he came back, just on his own. I guess he'd sensed what else was palpable here as well."

Hazel jumped on the kitchen counter to look out the window at the foggy backyard. The inn immediately slid a kitchen towel under her.

"He said he was here for me, but really, it was for the ghosts," she reminisced. "Ghost hunting equipment has come a long way I'm sure, but he recorded some of the guests talking and planned to publish what he found. So I destroyed it. He was furious, told me he never cared about me. Then I found out about the magazine."

Pippi audibly gasped. "*John* put the inn in the *Haunted Oregon* magazine?"

"Yes. It was him." Hazel turned to look at Pippi. "And I was the lovestruck fool that let it happen. Nothing came of it, really, but I worried about it for years. Eventually, the publication went out of print."

"Now the freak out over Cecil is starting to add up," Pippi admitted.

"Does Cecil know his father is here?" Hazel asked.

"No." Pippi squirmed. "John won't reveal himself to him and doesn't want to talk about Cecil."

"And you can't violate the guest privacy agreement," Hazel reminded firmly. "You haven't, have you?"

"No, not at all, and it's killing me."

"That's a long time to wander," Hazel whispered. She looked at Pippi. "You never want to lead a life that prevents you from moving on in the end. I suppose that is what's happening to him. Has he had any calls?"

"One. From Cecil."

Hazel thought on this.

"John doesn't know anything about you, unless the other guests told him," Pippi assured. "Also, he hasn't asked about you. Not sure if that makes you feel better or worse."

"Why would he? His behavior was reprehensible. The fact that he had the gall to show his face here again is incredible to me." Hazel pointed a paw at Pippi. "You have to get to the bottom of this."

"I know," Pippi admitted. "I'll work on it."

Back in the dining room, only Cecil and his invisible father remained, seated at opposite ends of the table, one completely unknown to the other. Hazel remained in the kitchen, working out her aggression by batting away the oranges the inn was trying to slice.

"All good?" Cecil asked, standing from the loveseat.

"Oh yeah," Pippi said, pointedly stopping behind John's chair. "Nothing I can't handle."

"Great." Cecil reached into his jacket and pulled out a notebook. "I've got an interview with Lucy. I'll catch you later."

Pippi waited until Cecil left the dining room before circling the table and sitting down across from John. He looked dapper in tweed pants, a crisp white collared shirt, and a shiny gold watch with visible gears that ticked on endlessly.

"Good morning, John." Pippi studied John with new eyes. He was older than the age he would've been with Hazel, locked into his appearance at the time of his passing. He was handsome, but of course she'd think that.

"Good morning, Pippi." John was studying her, too. He was a wise ghost, he was experienced at studying the living, maybe even in those moments where they lowered their guard and thought no one was watching.

"I need to apologize. I feel like I've neglected you since you checked in," Pippi began. "What with Halloween..."

John smiled. "Yes, Halloween. A rollicking good time."

"Did you participate in the fun?"

"I did, yes."

"And what was your part?"

"Oh, I don't think you'd know it."

Pippi half smiled and looked down at her clasped hands. "I know you've been traveling a long time."

John sipped his tea. "I suppose that's relative, when you compare it to the grand scheme of things."

"Are you looking for something?"

"This world fascinated me when I was alive, as well. Now, I can experience it both ways. Who wouldn't want that?"

"Okay, how about this. Tell me something you haven't experienced and I'll see if I can make it happen."

John laughed heartily, standing up. "Okay, I'll think about it. Thank you, Pippi."

"Of course," Pippi said, standing up as well.

"And thank you for honoring my request about my son. I don't wish for him to know I'm here," John added. "The situation is complicated."

"Family always is," Pippi replied, glancing at Hazel, who was glaring at her from the cracked kitchen doorway. "But I'm always here to talk."

"Thank you, dear, but I won't be discussing the nuances of my relationship with my son with his flavor of the month," John chuckled.

"There's always the former proprietress."

John froze. "Who?"

"My aunt Hazel," Pippi said sweetly.

"She's...here?"

"In a different capacity, but yes, she's here."

John nodded slightly. "I'll keep that in mind. Thank you."

He was gone before another word could be said.

"Keep an eye on him," Pippi said to the inn. "And spread the word upstairs."

Chapter Eighteen

The next few weeks were like a complicated game of chess as Hazel tried to avoid John, John tried to avoid Cecil, Cecil tried to avoid Lucy after she gave him *way* too much information in her interview, and Pippi tried to ignore the raging feeling that something was definitely up. Even the spiders seemed to sense it, leaving her a sweet but terribly sticky and somewhat cryptic "note" all over the box of Thanksgiving dishes that read: *We love Pippi Pippi! Old young man is secret keeper. Talks too loud and much.*

Pippi had to agree with the spiders on that. John's booming voice could be heard all over the inn except to poor Cecil, unless he happened to catch the garbled version on his EVP recording. John mostly spoke of his travels and many places he's seen, wooing his fellow guests with talks of dinner atop the Sphinx and spending weeks exploring the Mariana Trench because, why not?

"Oh, but I can't tell you what I found there," he added with a twinkle in his eye. "That's a secret for you to find out."

Pippi watched her guests' faces as John tried to charm them with his tales. But she saw what John was blind to; this was not a real vacation. It was a mourning period wrapped in a pretty red bow. It was a consolation prize for losing the greatest prize of all - to live. To feel the head-spinning thrill of having dinner atop the Sphinx because what if you fall? To feel the burn for oxygen as you sink towards the Mariana Trench, faced with a choice between darkness or life? Pippi would bet her own life that everyone in that inn would pick life, but maybe not John. John would keep sinking to the darkness.

John's presence also seeped its way into Pippi and Cecil's relationship. She was always lying to him, no matter what. She could tell him the truth that her favorite color was purple but it was tainted by the fine print that said *your father is here as a ghost and I can't tell you even though it might bring you peace and closure.*

Or maybe it wouldn't.

Thanksgiving weekend brought the biggest rainstorm of the year so far. Forecasters talked about it for the entire week, warning residents to prepare for power outages and stock up on water, especially since the little town of Windia was one mudslide from having the freeway that connected them with the outside world washed away.

Of course, Pippi and the guests had nothing to worry about at the inn, which never had food delivered yet always had a stock of food on hand and fresh well water that never ran out. Pippi had never once seen a bill for power or trash services, yet the inn had both. If something were to happen to Windia, could Pippi herd the whole town to the inn and take care of them? She once spent an entire afternoon figuring out the logistics of this scenario and settled on it *could* be done with a significant amount of ghost hiding and explaining afterwards, but she was getting very accustomed to that.

In preparation for Thanksgiving day, the inn asked all the guests to submit their favorite Thanksgiving dish from their living days. (Although this request was communicated in the front door's stained glass and took some time to interpret.) There were a few repeat requests (green bean casserole, candied yams, and turkey, of course) but a few suggestions stood out amongst the others, like John's oyster stuffing. Pippi wrinkled her nose at the suggestion but John insisted it was a callback to childhood trips to his grandparents' house in New England for Thanksgiving, so she jotted it down on the submission sheet for the inn.

As predicted, Pippi woke on Thanksgiving morning to the sound of heavy rain on the roof, which must have been very heavy considering there was a second floor and an attic between her and the roof. She peeked out into the backyard, where tiny rivers and streams snaked through the grass, leading to puddle lakes where the surface was disturbed by rain splatters.

"Oh, lucky me," Pippi lamented. She just stepped out of the shower and found her outfit for the day stretched across her bed. The inn had selected a dark brown corduroy jumper dress that fell below Pippi's knees with little cartoon turkeys for the buttons. The undershirt had the same cartoon turkey print on it with a matching dark brown corduroy headband to tie it all together.

"The only thing that would make this better is turkey stockings," she grumbled as she lifted the jumper and found turkey stockings, a size too big, presumably to allow for comfort during the feast.

"I've literally never been so attracted to you," Cecil said when he entered through the front door and found Pippi behind the front desk. He was soaking wet and his leather jacket dripped water across the floor as he joined her.

"I look like a kindergarten teacher from the 1980s," Pippi grumbled, repositioning her headband.

"Hello, teacher," Cecil whispered, grabbing her by the waist and pulling her close.

"Oh my gosh," Pippi blushed. "Is this *actually* turning you on?"

"*You* turn me on, corduroy and all."

They kissed passionately alone in the front entry. Lately they couldn't keep their hands off each other, with arms wrapped around the other's waist on the loveseat at meals or long goodnight kisses that break apart hot. Pippi had to remind herself to stay focused on the guests because she often found herself staring at Cecil, entranced by the way his body moved or his calm demeanor when faced with ghost guests. She liked him. *A lot.* And for the first time, someone she liked *a lot* knew all about her and seemed to like her a lot, too.

He knew everything except for one thing, that is.

The sound of guests milling at the top of the stairs forced the two to come up for air.

"I have a complaint to make to management," he said, stepping back and removing his wet coat, revealing a damp shirt underneath as well. "There's a leak in my cottage."

"Seriously?" Pippi took for granted this old inn (in fact, she didn't know exactly how old the inn was) never seemed to have any issues. The plumbing flowed without issue, and there was never a shortage of hot water (well, she was the only one using the hot water,) never a broken window, never a breezy crack beneath the doorway. The only sign of age Pippi had ever noticed were the creaking floor boards and even that she suspected the inn allowed to add to the charm.

"Yep, it started by waking up to water dripping directly on my face," Cecil explained, looking knowingly up at the inn, who he now understood planned everything. "I'll need to move my darkroom if it gets much worse."

"Your darkroom is out there?" Pippi asked. "Sorry, I could've found you somewhere in the inn."

"It's okay," Cecil shrugged. "It's like having company."

"Can I see?" Pippi had yet to see any of Cecil's photos of the guests, other than the few she'd seen at the wind phone. She just knew the guests ate it up, especially Lidia and Lucy, who often sought out *darling Cecil* to capture their look for the day.

Cecil thought for a moment, then nodded and took her hand. "Sure."

Pippi donned her Thanksgiving-themed water slicker and boots (consisting of tiny illustrated turkeys and ghosts dressed up as pilgrims) and ran with Cecil through the flooded backyard to the cottage. Inside there were signs of Cecil's attempt to contain the leaks, including bowls and buckets scattered throughout the house and a tarp laid over the couch. The little bathroom had been transformed into Cecil's darkroom, which explained why he always came inside to use the inn's bathroom instead of his own.

Pippi peeked inside. The bathroom was awash in dark red, pictures dripping from the ceiling like a slow-motion waterfall of moments caught in time. She'd half-expected to see photos that looked stereotypically *ghostly*, such as standing next to a tombstone, overlooking an ocean ridge thoughtfully, or peeking through a window. Instead, the photos captured small moments, real moments; a smile between friends at breakfast, watching birds play in the puddle from a safe distance, a silent afternoon with a cup of tea and a book beneath the light from the library window. Pippi touched the pictures gently. This was how she saw her guests, too. Cecil managed to capture it. And it made her heart swell for him even more.

Unaware of how much his pictures affected Pippi, Cecil reached for a stack of photos on the counter. He handed them to Pippi in the dark red room.

"This guy is always just out of my camera shot," he said.

Pippi flushed. The photos were clearly discards and also clearly of John, always just out of frame. An arm, a foot, the back of his thick head of hair. She wondered if Cecil would eventually collect enough pieces to assemble an entire father.

"The inn wants me to tell you it's time to eat," Hazel announced flatly from the doorway. She was wearing a fox version of Pippi's rain slicker, adapted for Hazel's current fox form. The hood was tied tightly beneath her white chin.

"Oh, Hazel, look!" Pippi exclaimed, pointing to the darkroom. "Aren't these photos amazing? Look at this one of Lidia."

"Very nice," Hazel sniffed. "Now, food."

Pippi carefully shut the dark bathroom door as Hazel trotted back out into the rain.

"You know," Pippi said, wrapping her arm around Cecil's damp waist as water drip-dropped into the bowls and buckets. "I don't think you can sleep in here tonight."

"I'll be fine," Cecil shrugged.

Pippi squeezed his waist.

"Oh." Cecil perked up. "You're right, I can't sleep in here."

"Very unsafe."

"Very."

"But the inn is completely full."

"Well, I'm not sure what I'll do then."

"And you can't sleep on a couch."

"Bad for the back and all."

"If I'm going to be a good innkeeper, I should take care of all my guests."

"True."

"I guess the only option is for you to stay in my room, then."

"That's certainly the best option."

Pippi smiled. "It's decided then."

"It's decided." Cecil smiled back, leaning down to kiss her. He paused, one eyebrow arched rakishly. "But where will you sleep?"

"FOOD!" Hazel shouted from the yard.

Pippi would learn that the inn did not disappoint when it came to holidays (well, except when it came to cooperating with the Halloween kidnapping, that is.) Somehow in the time between light breakfast and the planned early afternoon feast, the inn had decorated the dining room with sweeping garlands of fir tied together with dark chocolate brown bows. Candles hung from the ceiling but never seemed to drip wax on the table below, which was adorned with white and gold plates of all shapes and sizes and each setting had their own personal salt and pepper shaker. There were punch bowls of spiced cider and mulled wine with a table specifically dedicated to the tiers of fresh pies that either steamed or sweated depending on the type. Piano music drifted through the air in an attempt to drown out the sound of utensils clinking and timers buzzing in the kitchen.

Guests filtered in, summoned by the smell of the food or Hazel literally barking at them to come eat. Some guests dressed for the holiday while others wore comfortable clothes suited for heavy eating. But everyone shared the same excitement for the food memories that were about to be served to them.

Pippi and Cecil sat at their shared loveseat while Hazel took her seat next to them, which included the pillow to raise Hazel to the right height for eating. With everyone settled in their chairs, the inn started to roll out cart after cart of food, stopping at each guest who either nodded *yes* or *no* for a serving. Pippi had already advised what dishes she was interested in so the inn could make a gluten-free version.

"What was your special request?" Pippi asked Cecil as Lucy's sweet potato casserole request rolled by.

"You'll see," Cecil grinned. "I guarantee no one else has heard of it."

A glazed ham and creamed corn later, the oyster stuffing rolled up to Pippi and Cecil, with an extra large portion labeled *John and Cecil Graham.*

Pippi paled. Her stomach, ravenous just seconds before, now dropped towards the bottom of a bottomless abyss. She tried to grab the card but Cecil beat her to it.

"John and Cecil Graham," he read aloud.

The table fell silent. Pippi ventured a glance at John, who had tucked himself away in the corner, out of Cecil's view. He stared at his plate hotly.

"What is this?" Cecil demanded, feeling hot himself. He pulled away from Pippi's grip on his hand and stood up, pacing the dining room, studying familiar faces and their plates of food. He finally stopped next to his invisible father who still couldn't manage eye contact.

"There's no one sitting here, but there's food," Cecil pointed out. "Who's sitting here?" he demanded loudly from the guest next to John, who was inconspicuously sipping on a cup of iced tea.

"Cecil." Pippi stood up. "Let's talk outside."

But Cecil was already on his way outside, ignoring Pippi's pleas to stop as he stalked through the rain back to his cottage. Pippi trailed behind, water slick and rainboots be damned, soaked with mud halfway up her turkey stockings. Inside the cottage, Cecil tore through the bathroom darkroom until he found the pile of discarded photos. He flicked through them until finally throwing the pictures on the floor where they scattered like leaves.

He pointed at the broken glimpses of his father. "He's here, isn't he?" Cecil panted.

Pippi wrung her hands, the words caught in her throat.

"Did you know?" His voice went up an octave with betrayal. Cecil looked at the photos and shook his head. "Of course you knew."

"I'm so sorry," Pippi finally blurted out. "He didn't want you to know...and...my guests..."

"Come before me," Cecil finished.

"No. Not like that. But-"

"But what?"

"But she *does* have an obligation to these guests." Hazel had appeared in the doorway, the rain flattening down her fur severely. "Don't blame Pippi for your father's foolish decisions."

"This is insane!" Cecil pointed towards the inn. "He's been dead for over twenty years! Do you mean to tell me he's...he's..." Cecil couldn't finish the thought.

"He's been wandering this whole time," Pippi whispered.

"I'm going to hurl," Cecil warned himself, running his hand over his mouth.

"Maybe you two can work things out?" Pippi suggested, although she honestly had no idea what exactly needed to be worked out other than it was wrapped in a huge flaming chain of hurt.

Cecil kicked the photos across the floor and grabbed his keys off the nightstand.

"Cecil, no," Pippi said firmly.

"I'm going for a drive," Cecil mumbled.

"It's pouring! There's food! It's Thanksgiving!" she exclaimed.

"Oh, just let him leave," Hazel grumbled. "They're both bad news."

"Stop!" Pippi admonished her aunt.

"Even a talking fox knows about my dad," Cecil muttered.

"I don't like your tone, young man," Hazel visibly bristled. "And I wish I didn't, trust me."

"Please. Stay," Pippi insisted, grabbing for Cecil's hand, which he pulled away.

"I need to think," he sighed sharply.

"But what about tonight? Will you come back?" Pippi whispered. The relief she felt from the truth finally being freed was nothing compared to the grief she felt at the prospect of losing Cecil.

He met her eyes. "I'll come back."

Then he was gone, disappearing into the torrential rain that swallowed him like a misty waterfall.

Pippi wiped away angry tears from her cheeks.

"I'm sorry," Hazel said quietly.

"He'll come back." Pippi tried to convince herself as much as her aunt.

"Oh, I'm sure he will," Hazel sighed. "One thing about these Graham men, they do come back, whether you want them to or not."

Back in the dining room, the guests were all trying their best to enjoy an awkward Thanksgiving dinner in which they tried *not* to snoop out the windows at the scene in the backyard. The inn had already removed Cecil's plate and loaded Pippi's with every gluten-free version of every dish she'd been interested in, covering her plate with a lid to keep it warm. Pippi apologized to the guests, offered a little speech she'd prepared about what she was thankful for (omitting any Cecil references) and then sat down to eat her dinner, which had no flavor in her dry mouth. Hazel said nothing from her seat at the table, although she did have many more negative Graham men comments she *could* have added.

The mood at the table visibly lightened as the evening moved onto pie, at which time Pippi excused herself. John had been absent from the table since Pippi returned, so she grabbed a piece of apple pie topped with warm cheddar cheese and went looking for him. But John wasn't in his room and he wasn't by the fire with a good book. But the stained glass on the front door had arranged into a giant red arrow that pointed towards the porch, so Pippi left the jolly guests behind and went outside.

"Pie?" Pippi offered to John, who was sitting in what was technically the innkeeper's rocking chair but she wouldn't correct him this time.

"Thank you." John accepted the pie, bundled up beyond need with a heavy coat and flannel blanket. He took little bites as though he shouldn't risk more on his stomach.

Pippi leaned against the porch railing, staring at the empty spot on the driveway where the red Aerostar van was usually parked. The early afternoon darkness was already creeping in on the edges of the forest, descending down slowly towards the ocean edge, where the raging Pacific would stop its advance, unable to catch the slippery waves.

"Thank you for honoring my request," John said finally, setting down the pie.

"Well," Pippi sighed. "Not sure where it got us."

"He's smart. He, well..."

"Is like you?" Pippi suggested.

"Yes," John grumbled. "Unfortunately."

Pippi turned to look at John, who suddenly looked like a frail, old man although no change had happened to his appearance. "How about you tell me what's going on?" she suggested.

John sunk further into his jacket.

"I can request more background from my bosses, you know." Pippi, in fact, did not know. She still had no idea who operated the chain of spirit inns and organized the phone calls and no internet search was going to help her, either. She knew because she'd tried.

John snorted. "No, you can't."

"Okay, then," Pippi continued. "Then how about you talk to me as your son's girlfriend?"

John sat with this statement for a few minutes, moved by the urgency of the approaching darkness and the veil of pouring rain, providing the perfect weather conditions for confessions.

"Things were not good between Cecil and I for some time before I died," John admitted with a long exhale. "Which sounds ridiculous now, thinking back to a grown man and a child."

"Ridiculous how?"

"Ridiculous because why would a grown adult allow a relationship to sour with a child?"

John shook his head. Pippi watched his suave and cool persona slip away, revealing a confused father.

"I was hard on him," he continued. "I saw him growing, changing. I was afraid if I didn't hold on tight he'd become a mess and that'd be all on me. And I loved him so much I couldn't bear the thought of him being a mess. That's what I told myself, anyway."

John started to rock rhythmically as if trying to soothe himself. "But it was more than that. I just had to always have my way. He even told me once," John recalled. "What kid is brave enough to tell an adult that?"

"Told you what?"

"That I was hurting him by being *me*."

Pippi looked down at her hands.

John swallowed hard. "I told him I'd been this way my entire life and I didn't plan on changing now." He rocked for a long time. "I told my one and only son that my stubborn ways meant more to me than him."

Pippi turned away to hide the welling tears. John's story struck too close to home. She knew nothing about father-child dynamics, with her own father not even in the picture. But she knew all too well the push and pull of a child growing away from a parent and of that last ditch effort to fix something that felt unfixable.

John cleared his throat. "So Cecil left to live with his mom. Who'd also left me for similar reasons. And then-" He motioned to his ghost body. "This."

"And *this* happened a long time ago," Pippi noted, having quickly composed herself by compartmentalizing. Again.

"Well, in the grand scheme of time," John started with a grand tone, then fell flat. "Yes. It has been a long time. So I found ways to keep myself busy."

"Haunting Cecil?"

"Traveling."

"Inn to inn?"

"Started out like that. I'd always been fascinated by the paranormal, so you can imagine what a dream it was for me to experience the world like that. And then, well, my talents and extensive knowledge were tapped."

"By who?"

John stopped rocking. He stood up stiffly and joined Pippi at the porch railing.

"Do you know the first call I ever received was the message you relayed to me from Cecil?" he said quietly. "I guess that means I still haven't received one, technically," he added with a chuckle.

John reached into his pocket and pulled out a business card, placing it in Pippi's hand. The card was buttery smooth and read *John Henry Graham, Celestial Relations Manager, Ethereal Accommodations for Restful Travel and Hospitality. (E.A.R.T.H.)*

"Don't live a life where no one calls when you're gone, Pippi," he whispered, evaporating back inside.

Pippi stayed up long after midnight tea, which had a deflated tone to it no matter how hard she tried to keep positive. She waited on the porch, her body falling numb under the layers of flannel blankets, her fingers rubbing back and forth over John's business card until they went numb, too. But the rain never stopped and Cecil never came back as the Aerostar van's parking spot became littered with muddy puddles. Pippi drifted off to sleep, Susie's howls blending with the horns of the faraway ships, who she gently guided through the impenetrable fog.

Chapter Nineteen

Pippi dreamed, of all things, coffee that night. Of coffee in all sorts of forms; coffee cakes, coffee crumbles, coffee tarts sprinkled with ground espresso beans, coffee-flavored gelato, and worst of all, peanut butter and coffee sandwiches. And all these coffee delicacies were dispensed in her dream by ghost kraken Susie, who donned a striped baker hat that stretched so high it disappeared into the troposphere. Pippi awoke to the bitter aroma that dominated her dreams, rousing her stiff and aching body from sleep. Hazel sat in her lap atop a mountain of blankets, a harness strapped to her back securely carrying a steaming cup of coffee that Pippi wouldn't touch.

"Good morning," Pippi croaked.

"Nothing good about it for me," Hazel grumbled. "Reduced to a common delivery person."

Pippi carefully dislodged the coffee from the harness, uncovering a chocolate cherry gluten-free cake beneath, which she *would* touch. "Well, you're actually a delivery fox, which is way more unique."

"Oh, how the mighty have fallen," Hazel lamented as she jumped from Pippi's lap to the porch railing.

The rain had run its course overnight, leaving the morning with a trickle that led into the lakes and rivers etched into the ground by the force of the downpour. The thick fog remained, however, thicker than ever before, so thick it appeared touchable, as though it could be wrapped into a cloud scarf or flavorless cotton candy tower. It left a smell too, damp and moody, clinging to whatever person or creature or scene it passed by on its voyage into evaporation.

"What time did Cecil get back?" Pippi asked between bites of cake, removing her cell phone to double check she hadn't missed any calls in her deep outdoor slumber.

Hazel scratched the harness over her head. "Get back? Honey, he never came back."

Pippi jumped up from the rocking chair. "What?" But the Aerostar van's parking spot was still empty, transformed into a lake by the rain, in which birds were currently bathing. She rushed inside, first checking the stained glass for any clues, but it only depicted a thick fog scene with the inn peeking out and shining like a lighthouse beam. After checking for any messages on the front desk, Pippi ran to the dining room. Most of the over-caffeinated guests were all in the backyard jumping in puddles, except for John, who sat at the end of the table, engrossed in the newspaper's crossword puzzle.

"Have you seen Cecil?" Pippi called out.

John looked out the windows to the backyard cottage, which was completely dark.

"No, I haven't," he said, standing up. "I assumed he was with you."

"Something's wrong." Pippi said it more to the inn than to herself or John. She raced to her bedroom, hoping to find Cecil collapsed there in her sheets, but the bed was made with Pippi's fresh outfit for the day already laid out.

Back in the entry, Pippi checked the print on her rain slicker. *It was blank.*

Hazel watched Pippi lose her mind from her perch atop the reception desk.

"What's the inn not telling me? I don't like this," Pippi asked her aunt. She'd broken out in a sweat on the back of her neck and suddenly her Thanksgiving jumper felt like a straight jacket.

Hazel couldn't hide the clear concern in her dark eyes. "It does seem like the inn is protecting you from something."

"He must've dumped me. That's it." Pippi curled up in the chair behind the desk. "And I don't blame him. I lied to him. You can't be with someone that lies to you."

Hazel clearly had more she wanted to say, but settled on, "I'm sorry."

"I felt like he really understood me," Pippi whispered to the chair. "No one ever understands me."

Hazel jumped into her niece's lap, rubbing her soft fur under Pippi's chin. "It'll be alright, lass," she sighed. "This will lessen with time. You'll see."

The front door opened, snapping Pippi and Hazel to attention. Cecil appeared in the doorway, dripping wet, incredibly wet, like he'd just walked through a car wash completely dressed. He was panting, fighting to speak but couldn't quite find the words. His soaking clothes released a stream of brackish water, teeming with fish and tiny crabs and the occasional rock and shell that fell to the floor with soft thuds.

"Cecil?" was all Pippi could manage to say, standing slowly to observe her boyfriend.

Pippi's cell phone dinged. *New guest checking in.*

Cecil finally found his voice, croaking, "Checking in."

"I can't even remember it."

Cecil sat in the overstuffed reception chair, thoroughly soaking it through, his teeth rattling as he brought his lips to the mug full of warm coffee with a few shots of brandy. The other guests, who were also soaking wet from their puddle jumping, crowded the front entry to hear Cecil's story. Pippi crouched next to Cecil to hold his hand, which was cold and slimy like the surface of a river rock that'd been submerged for a long, long time.

"It was raining so hard that the wipers on the van could barely keep up. Oh. My van." Cecil grasped his head. "And then...I don't know. Then I was on the river bank and could see the rear of my van sticking out of the water. And there was...there was...there was..."

Pippi leaned in as the other guests exchanged glances. Cecil looked around the room at the gathered faces.

"Was it...the *Grim Reaper?*" he whispered.

The room broke out in nervous chuckles.

"No, dear," Lucy spoke up. "It was just one of *them.*"

"Who?" Pippi demanded.

"Pippi," Hazel admonished firmly from her seat atop the recep-tion desk. "You know, *them.*"

"No, I *don't* know!" Pippi hissed.

"He said he was going to take me to Processing. I think that's what he called it," Cecil continued, rubbing his head again. He turned and looked at Pippi, grabbing her hand. "But I said I just wanted to get here. So he said he'd set up the reservation and I should tell you I'm checking in."

"I'm so glad you did." Pippi embraced Cecil, who still felt inexplicably soaking wet. She had no idea what was going on, just that he was here. She looked into his face. "I'm so glad you did."

"So, I'm…" Cecil looked into her eyes and swallowed hard. "Pippi, I'm…?"

She nodded, her eyes threatening a downpour of tears. "We'll figure it out," she whispered. "I know we will!"

"This is my fault." It was John, who'd been lurking just out of sight. The guests moved out of the way for him to step forward.

Cecil stood up. "Dad?" He marveled at the sight of his father, levelly meeting a gaze he once had to look up into.

"Hello, son," John said miserably. "I'm so sorry. I never, ever wanted to see you like this."

Cecil circled the desk and embraced John, who wept into his son's chest. There wasn't a dry eye in the inn as the other guests couldn't help but imagine themselves in the same situation but with their own version of Cecil. John released from the embrace and wiped his eyes hard, standing back to survey his grown son who surpassed him now in height by a good three inches.

"You look just like you did," Cecil marveled.

"Yes," John chuckled. He grasped Cecil by the shoulders. "Forever reminded of the mistakes I made at this age."

"Why did you hide from me?" Cecil whispered.

"You said you never wanted to see me again," John said with a bracing sigh. "I took that to my grave. Literally."

Cecil nodded, perhaps remembering the moment he'd said those very words.

"But this-" John motioned to Cecil's dripping wet body. "This..."

"Yes, this," Hazel muttered under her breath, her fur bristling slowly from her tail to the tip of her nose. "Is just another life you've ruined."

"What?" John blinked through the tears at Hazel, a creature he'd previously thought only as a strange and curmudgeonly shadow that glared at him whenever he passed by.

"I said, another life you've ruined," Hazel repeated through barred teeth.

John looked completely bewildered, still in shock over the ghost form of his grown son in front of him.

"This is Hazel," Pippi finally said. "The last proprietress of the inn."

John's eyes widened, leaning in towards her. "Hazel?"

"Careful, she bites," Pippi warned.

John looked from Cecil to Hazel and back again.

"I need to sit down," he panted.

"Oh please," Hazel snapped. "You don't feel lightheaded."

"Force of habit, I suppose," John laughed tightly.

"Will I ever stop dripping?" Cecil asked, holding up an arm from which water trickled.

"Typically you'd go to Processing first, after, well... you know. That's where they get you cleaned up, if needed, and discuss what inn you'd like to stay at," John explained. "A hot shower should clear you up."

"I can't remember anything." Cecil rubbed his head hard, as though trying to awaken the memory of how he died.

"A blessing we all have," Lidia chimed in. "None of us remember how we died."

"I rather prefer it that way," Lucy added, to which the other guests nodded in agreement.

"Why don't you go take that shower," John suggested to his son. "And Pippi and I can talk."

"I better check you in first." Pippi reluctantly woke up the computer and navigated to the reservation screen.

There was all Cecil's information loaded and ready; date of birth, date of death, even food and drink preferences (some of which Pippi knew and some that she didn't.) Under *special notes* was written *Mr. Graham is acquainted with Windia Innkeeper Phillipa Jennings. Mr. Graham requested to bypass Processing and go to the Windia Inn directly. After ascertaining he was of right mind and had a sufficient knowledge of the area, Mr. Graham was advised of check-in instructions.*

After a few minutes of clicking through prompts and check boxes, the inn assigned Cecil a room upstairs.

"Okay, you're all set," Pippi sighed. "Room seven."

"My favorite number," Cecil noted.

"Yeah, we all have that," Lucy shrugged. "I'm room number forty-two. You can probably guess why."

Cecil slowly ascended the stairs to the second floor. He stopped. "The spiders. They won't...?"

"No, they don't bother the guests," Pippi called up to him. "And even if they did, well..."

"Oh yeah," Cecil remembered. "I'm dead."

With the majority of the excitement over with, the guests left to pursue their plans for the remainder of the day, with most returning to the backyard puddles. Only Pippi, John, and Hazel remained.

"Hazel," John began softly, freezing when the fox barred her teeth. "I think it's pretty clear I've been a fool and made a lot of mistakes."

Hazel scoffed loudly.

"But my time here with you was not one of them."

Hazel's sharp teeth retreated.

"That summer," John sighed, closing his eyes. "That summer here with you was magic." He shook his head. "You were right to cut it off with me. I did you wrong."

"And after?" Hazel bristled. "You could have lost me my inn."

"Yes, and after." John accepted his fate as the villain of the day. "But when I heard you'd died, I thought I could come back and revisit some of those good times. But I see my sources were wrong. You are alive and well."

Hazel snorted and stood up to leave. "I'm not quite dead but I'm not quite alive either. But at least I don't have to spend my time apologizing to everyone I've wronged."

John nodded humbly. "You are very right."

Hazel stuck her nose up in the air and began to trot down the hallway.

"Hazel!" John called after her. "*Tu es la chaleur de mon coeur.*"

Hazel turned to look at him and Pippi swore if a fox could glow, then she glowed.

"*Je me souviens de tout,*" she replied softly, then disappeared.

With the two of them now alone, Pippi produced the business card John handed her the night before.

"You mentioned sources?" she asked. "Who are you?"

"Let me ask you this, Pippi," John said. "If there was a chance to bring Cecil back, would you?"

"Back to *life?*"

"Yes."

"Of course I would!"

"Then we have to move swiftly. We need to get Cecil's body."

"Hold on. First, tell me who you are. Or where you work. Or both."

John opened his mouth to speak but Pippi interrupted him. "And don't you dare say *them*."

"I will," John promised. "But we need to retrieve Cecil's body and the van before anyone notices. If anyone else finds out he's...dead...it will complicate the matter significantly."

"I think I'm going to get sick," Pippi warned, her head spinning. It was already too much that her boyfriend had died today and was now one of her ghost guests. But now she has to get his body?

"Steady, Pippi." John paced the floor. "Do you have any particularly strong guests we could tap for this?"

Pippi looked up at the ceiling, where, unbeknownst to her, the spiders were already donning their scuba gear. "I have someone in mind."

Digging through the various manuals and several decade-old telephone books, Pippi found the little notebook where Hazel advised she'd listed important numbers, such as pizza delivery and the movie showtime line. She flipped through the pages until she found the number she needed, which she then realized was taped to the computer monitor as *security.*

Pippi flicked open her cell phone and dialed the number.

"Security."

"Mo?"

"Who's this?"

"It's Pippi."

"Oh, Pippi. Yes, it's Mo. How can I help you, ma'am?"

"I need to send you on a rescue mission."

Pippi could hear a clatter of dishes as Mo audibly fell out of his seat. She imagined him jumping up with a salute.

"Absolutely!" Mo panted. "What's the mission?"

"I need you to retrieve a body. Cecil's body to be exact."

"Say that again?"

"Retrieve Cecil from a river, or lake...some sort of water."

"Uh..."

"I'll send the spiders to help. We need a car out of the water, as well."

"And brought back here," John added quietly.

"And brought back here," Pippi shared.

"Certainly, ma'am. Anything. But..."

"But what?"

"I'll need you to come, too."

"What? No. I can't. I cannot. This is what I pay you for, right?"

"Actually, you don't pay me."

"Seriously? We need to rectify that."

"But ma'am, you don't make any money."

"I don't? Oh yeah. I don't."

"..."

"Sorry. Back to the point, what do you need me for?"

"Well, besides the fact you are our fearless leader, I also cannot operate a motor vehicle and the reason why should be quite obvious."

"Okay, fine. I will drive but that's it. But there's no way you're all fitting in my little car."

Mo chuckled. "Ma'am, the inn has its own vehicle."

"It does? We do?" Pippi asked, looking up as headlight beams flashed through the front windows. She peeked through the curtains as a twenty foot high box van parked in the drive and turned off its ignition.

"Well, who drove that?" Pippi asked before answering her own question.

"We need the cover of night for this mission. I'll find his body and plan out the details," Mo advised. "I'll coordinate with the spiders. Any idea what kind of mood they're in?"

"Uh, no." Pippi's heart jumped. "They have different moods? Like, bad moods?"

"Well, of course. Don't you?" Mo huffed.

"Sure, but...nevermind. Okay, talk soon."

"Yes, ma'am. And ma'am?"

"Yes?"

"Please wear black. You know how, well..."

"Don't worry. The inn has an outfit for everything."

Pippi hung up. She'd been so engrossed with the appearance of the inn's giant van that she hadn't noticed John disappear. Her cell phone beeped, warning of low battery life. She needed to charge the phone and take a shower herself. She looked around the empty front entry and peeked upstairs; all quiet. This was as good a time for a shower as any.

But she granted herself a little longer in the shower, allowing her tears to mix with the warm water draining down her face. She washed her hair, craving the cool feeling on her scalp and blamed her puffy red face on her scalding hot shower. She split her hair into two long braids, which is how she usually styled her hair when she really meant business, such as helping someone move or going on a hike. Or retrieving her dead boyfriend's body, apparently.

Pippi wasn't sure if the inn had a mission outfit always on standby or if it had quickly stitched together a suitable option while Pippi was showering; either way, laid on her bed was a pair of black denim overalls, a black long-sleeved shirt, thick wool socks, black combat boots, a puffy black coat, and a black knit cap with a tiny spider logo.

Pippi smirked. "Oh you, with your little details." She checked the cell phone, which was still perilously low on battery life, and decided if she stayed within hearing distance of the reception phone she was safe to leave it on the charger for now.

The inn was too still, like the quiet before a storm, the deep, dark clouds full of rain casting an ominous shade on what should have otherwise been a normal day. Pippi climbed the stairs to the second floor, which was just as dark and subdued as downstairs. A new door, number seven, was cracked open with a sliver of light stretched out on the hallway carpet and inviting her forward. Overhead, Pippi could make out the muffled voice of Mo, evidently on some sort of speaker phone or intercom with the spiders, who tittered and stomped around as they hyped themselves for the night ahead.

"Cecil?" Pippi whispered at number seven's door.

"Come in."

Pippi didn't make a habit of going into the guests' rooms; it overwhelmed her alive and human brain to make sense of the cavernous (or sometimes cozy) spaces the inn created for each guest, crammed with endless references and Easter eggs that represented small moments in time from each guest's life. It was like invading their mind, digging through their most precious memories and what did Pippi get out of it? This wasn't a place for her. It was for them.

Cecil laid on a little twin bed, his back to the door. The space looked like an eight year old's dream room; video game and baseball posters decorated the walls, piles of laundry on the floor (some clearly dirty, some clearly clean) and a creaky ceiling fan that rotated with a repetitive yet comforting ticking rhythm. Warm yellow light streamed in through the baseball-print curtains that swayed gently in an invisible breeze through the closed window.

Pippi sat on the end of the bed. "Are you okay?"

"Yes," Cecil said after a while. He reached back, and feeling the thick denim of her overalls, turned to look at her.

"What's all this?" he asked. Cecil's own face showed those telltale signs of crying, as well.

Should she tell him? But lies had got them in this mess in the first place.

"We're going to get your body. And the van," she explained, the words tasting strange in her mouth.

Cecil turned back over. "Why? Just leave it."

"John, your dad, said he might have a way to bring you back."

Cecil's head turned slightly. "What?"

"I don't know all the details yet, but-"

"No." Cecil sat up straight in bed. "Don't do anything he says."

"But, I thought...downstairs you seemed..."

"Reconciled?" Cecil suggested. "Hardly. He's my dad. This is all crazy. Insane. But he's still done and said the things he's said and done."

"He's right." John appeared in the doorway, perhaps emboldened by Pippi's presence in the room. He stepped inside and looked around, his hand on his heart.

"Don't say anything." Cecil stood from the bed. He was dressed in clean, dry clothes, no longer leaking water everywhere. The clothes looked like the inn had tried to put its own spin on Cecil's personal wardrobe with black (not *too* tight) pants and a crisp white shirt *with* sleeves.

John put his hands up in surrender. He motioned to a nearby rolling office chair, currently piled with half-folded clothes. "May I sit?" he asked.

Cecil gruffly agreed, pacing the room until Pippi put a hand on his shoulder.

"Tell us what good will come from retrieving Cecil's body," Pippi ventured. "And not just for obvious reasons."

John gently moved the pile of clothing and sat down with a long sigh. "Yes, I will tell you everything," he promised. "Maybe even more than I should."

Pippi handed John's business card to Cecil. "Start with this."

"I am the Celestial Relations Manager for the organization known as Ethereal Accommodations for Restful Travel and Hospitality," John started. "As I told Pippi, I wandered a long time after my death. I'm sure that would come as no surprise to you, son, as I was finally able to explore the ideas and concepts about the paranormal I could never prove in my living existence. As a Celestial Relations Manager, I travel inn to inn, observing, interacting, and reporting back to E.A.R.T.H."

"Like a spy?" Pippi choked, immediately flushing and thinking back to some of the hilarious and borderline inappropriate conversations and anecdotes that inevitably come up at midnight teas.

"A casual observer, if you will," John shrugged. "I've never given anything but a glowing report on any inn I've reviewed. It's just not in my nature to tear anyone down."

At this, Cecil snorted loudly.

"Well, not anymore," John added quietly.

"Who is behind the Ethereal Accommodations for Restful Travel and Hospitality, anyway?" Pippi leaned forward, wondering if she was finally going to get the answer to her burning question.

"Well, they're bigger than I can really explain," John said. He motioned to Cecil. "They are the ones who meet you at death. They are your first experience with death, it's as if you've been born again and they are the ones who point you in the right direction. I was informed it was their idea to start E.A.R.T.H. as a sort of *easing* into the afterlife for everyone involved. I don't know how they handled it before phones, however." John paused and thought that over. "Hmm. That is a conundrum. I'll have to ask about that. But, back to the point, E.A.R.T.H. handles all the calls, all the reservations, and arrange the checkouts to...well, that depends on the person, doesn't it?"

"Is that why you've been wandering so long?" Cecil snapped. "Because you know where you're going after this?"

John tsked. "Now, Cecil. I've been bad, I know, but I haven't been *that* bad."

"So how can you help him?" Pippi asked, annoyed that she still didn't have any real information, but daylight was ticking by fast.

"Yes, so we-"

"What makes you think I'd want your help, anyway?" Cecil interrupted. "If you even can help."

"Because I did this!" John shouted, standing up. "I can't fix many things, but maybe I can fix this."

"I've been fine without you this entire time," Cecil shouted back. "And I'll be fine without you now."

"Cecil," Pippi whispered. "If there's a chance, shouldn't we…?"

Cecil turned to Pippi. "Go get my body if you want to, but don't let him anywhere near it."

Then he was gone, brushing past John to exit the room, which fell dim with the actual fading light of day. The smell of salty chips and books and baseball bats dissipated too, replaced by the aroma of an early dinner being prepared for the evening adventure crew. And John himself began to fade into a true specter, now a shadow on the wall, maybe in a form and place he'd been before, reduced to a sliver of himself, forced to watch his son's life unfold from the hidden corners of the room.

"Go," John whispered. "Please leave me."

Pippi obeyed her guest's wish, lowering her head as she walked by John's unearthly form. She passed the doorway, John's voice a whispering echo in her ear, saying, "Please save my son."

Chapter Twenty

Mo met Pippi on the front porch, dressed in dark green camo, his face smeared with a similar print.

"All set, ma'am," he saluted. "The troops are loaded and we're ready to retrieve the cargo."

"They're in there?" Pippi pulled on her stocking cap as she leerily eyed the large box van, from which tittering and tapping sounds could be heard.

"Yes ma'am, they can really curl up and fit in tight places," Mo assured as he clapped his heels to attention. "Miss Hazel."

Pippi had not noticed Hazel, who was stretched languidly across the innkeeper's rocking chair.

"You're going to need a mighty large offering to make this up to the spiders," she yawned, slowly rolling into a sitting position.

"On the contrary, Miss Hazel, the spiders are over the moon about trying out their new scuba gear," Mo grinned.

Hazel's eyes narrowed to slits.

"Actually, no contrary," Mo gulped, backing up slowly. "Ma'am, I'll wait in the van."

In a blink, Mo scrambled into the box van. The world outside the illumination of the inn consisted of thick darkness; clouds blocked any star or moonlight, and in this area of the country, there were no street lamps and very few porch lights. But there was always the whisper of the ocean, unseeable, saying *I'm here. I'm here, always.*

"What's the good of this?" Hazel asked.

"If there's a chance, I should try," Pippi told her aunt and herself.

"You think you're the first one to try this?" Hazel motioned into the world with her paw.

"My circumstances are a little different."

Hazel shook her head. "I don't know what he told you, but-"

"If it was you, would you do the same?" Pippi interrupted.

Hazel stared at her niece for a long beat, her tail flicking back and forth. She settled back down in the innkeeper's rocking chair.

"You have your phone?" she asked.

Pippi patted her chest. "Always."

"Well, then, good luck."

Pippi had never driven a box van, and certainly not a box van full of giant scuba spiders and a navigator gnome wearing camouflage. Her hand literally white-knuckled the steering wheel as the van's headlights struggled to penetrate the foggy darkness.

"Not much farther now," Mo said, straining to see over the dashboard. "You can drive a little faster, ma'am. You're well below the speed limit."

"It's fine. This is fine." Pippi's teeth were clenched so hard they threatened to crack under pressure.

"Looks like he lost control on that turn up there. It *is* a killer." Mo slapped his hand over his mouth. "I'm sorry."

"It's all right," Pippi assured. "Where do I turn?"

Mo motioned to a near-hidden turn off, disguised by a heavy overhang of rain-drenched fir branches. Pippi slowed to a snail's pace, fighting through the fog to find the entrance, the passengers in the back rolling around as the van rattled down the narrow dirt road. A few bumpy minutes later, the road deposited them at the edge of a wide open valley. Paces away was a small, isolated lake, quiet and unassuming, lapping at the cliff edge where the highway curled above precariously. Pippi's eyes trailed from the highway, down to the cliffside, to the water, where she saw the tip of a bumper protruding out of the gray water.

Mo watched Pippi swallow hard. "Yes, I believe that's him."

"How's this work? This feels so exposed out here." Pippi turned off the headlights as a vehicle roared by on the highway above them.

"I'll show the spiders the way," Mo explained as he unbuckled his seatbelt. "They'll keep out of sight, trust me. We'll retrieve Cecil's car first and hitch it up to the van to tow back."

"And Cecil?"

"Do you really want to know, ma'am?"

"Maybe not."

"Whatever you wish, ma'am."

"And Mo?"

"Yes?"

"I can't watch. But please don't tell Hazel."

"Ma'am. *You're* my innkeeper."

Pippi closed her eyes and leaned her head against the cold steering wheel. The passenger door opened and closed, the back van door rolled open, followed by dozens of little stomping feet that rocked the vehicle as the spiders scuttled by. She dared herself to open her eyes at some point but never did. Then suddenly, the whole van rocked and Pippi heard Mo issuing orders about the hitch along with *Careful, there!* or *Good job, you all.* Then the back van door rolled closed and Mo jumped back in the passenger seat, smelling of mud and damp grass.

"Mission accomplished," he announced.

"Really?" Pippi peeked open one eye. The Aerostar bumper was no longer jutting out of the water. "And you found him?"

"Yes, ma'am. The eagle has landed. Let's go home."

Going home proved to be the most laborious of all the events that evening, resulting in the spiders having to push the box van (towing the Aerostar van) back up the dirt road to the highway, where they limped along the highway without a single encounter, reverting back to spider-pushing the truck up the gravel drive to the inn. Once safely back within arm's reach of the inn's warm light, the spiders unhitched the Aerostar van and stashed it in the woods. Pippi waited in the box van, sweating over her next step and waiting for Mo.

Mo knocked on the window. "All clear, ma'am. The van has been hidden away."

"Okay, thank you," Pippi called through the door, eyes still pressed shut. "Wait. Are the spiders still out there?"

"Yes, ma'am, but I'll-"

"No. Wait."

Pippi took the deepest breath she'd ever taken and opened the van door. The night air was heavy with moisture, chilling Pippi to the bone, especially since she was covered in a cold sweat already. At first, she kept her eyes lowered to the gravel drive and then slowly, ever so slowly, raised them to meet the gaze of Mo and a wall of countless glistening eyes.

"I just wanted to say thank you. Thank you so much for helping me out," Pippi announced loudly, unsure if the towering creatures could hear her way up there, towering creatures who looked a lot less intimidating in their slick scuba gear.

Mo beamed. "You're welcome, ma'am! Our pleasure. Right, team?"

The spiders jumped up and down in agreement. Pippi smiled, her eyes trailing down to the ground, where laid the clear form of her boyfriend's body, wrapped tightly in a protective cocoon of spider silk.

"Oh no. No, no, no, no, no," Pippi gasped, slapping her hands over her eyes. "Unsee, unsee, unsee."

In a burst of wind, the spiders and Cecil's embalmed body were gone.

"Where are they taking him?" Pippi cried out, opening her eyes again and searching the treetops.

"To the tundra, ma'am," Mo explained, as if that was incredibly obvious.

"What? How?"

"The linen closet portal, of course." Mo had a twinge of exasperation to his voice now. "He'll preserve well there until you need the body again."

"What if someone, or something, finds him?"

"No one living goes *there*, trust me."

"Well," Pippi sighed. "It sounds like you have everything covered, Mo."

"That's my job, ma'am." Mo saluted Pippi. "Now, if you don't mind, my stew should be done in the crockpot now.'"

"Oh, yes. Released. Excused. Have a nice dinner."

Then Mo was gone, diving headfirst into the blackberry bushes. Pippi turned back to the inn; she could hear the voices of the guests inside and smell cookies from the inn's *welcome home* snack. Cecil opened the front door, dry and healthy and alive to her eyes. She walked up the steps and joined him, where he surveyed her in full van-and-dead-body-retrieval gear.

"My hero," he whispered, wrapping Pippi in an embrace. She hugged him back, but it wasn't the same. There were incredible things a spirit could do, but it could never replicate the warmth of living life.

"We'll see," Pippi sighed. "I'm going to try."

Hazel sat on the reception desk behind them, her face drawn and tense.

"What?" Pippi asked as she removed her gloves.

"Check the computer," Hazel said.

Pippi circled the desk, pulling out her cell phone to see if she'd missed any calls. Her phone flashed *two notifications.*

"Now what?" Pippi said out loud when she really didn't mean to. The first notification was the notice of a guest checkout for John Henry Graham.

"Oh." Pippi looked at Cecil. "It's your dad."

Cecil's jaws visibly clenched.

Pippi read through the details to herself. This didn't appear to be a standard guest checkout and the *previous guest activity* page was locked other than the activity that pertained to her own inn, clearly stating John's checkout at 4:01 pm on November 24th.

"He's checked out," Pippi explained.

Hazel drew in her breath sharply.

"But," Pippi quickly added. "I'm not sure what that means here. Some of his file is locked. It looks different from when...well, when..."

"His door is gone upstairs," Cecil admitted, reluctant to reveal he'd even looked.

"What else?" Hazel urged.

The next notification immediately scared Pippi, starting with an ominous pop-up threatening *Are you really the innkeeper of the Windia Inn? Click "yes" only if you are the innkeeper of the Windia Inn. All others risk eternal persecution!*

"Golly," Pippi breathed as she shakily clicked *yes.*

Notice from Ethereal Accommodations for Restful Travel and Hospitality. A pop-up consumed the entire computer screen. *An officer of E.A.R.T.H. has filed a complaint against you, Phillipa Hazel Jennings, and the Windia Inn for violations of codes 1.1, 36.22, and 8900.342.*

As follows:

Code 1.1 - Failure to uphold and meet the basic duties of an innkeeper, including but not limited to protecting the privacy and overall experience of the Guest from living involvement.

Code 36.22 - Conspiring with the living about classified E.A.R.T. H. business.

Code 8900.342 - Harboring a ghost hunter on the premises, risking the exposure and expulsion of the Guest.

Phillipa Hazel Jennings and the Windia Inn is hereby issued a one month notice (four weeks from the date of this letter) of the arrival of the Vice President of Astral Affairs and support staff on December 24th to conduct an in-person evaluation of Phillipa Hazel Jennings and the Windia Inn. An unsatisfactory inspection will result in the closure of the Windia Inn and the immediate termination of Phillipa Hazel Jennings, who will be banned from Ethereal Accommodations for Restful Travel and Hospitality for ETERNITY.

Please email innkeepers.feedback@earth.com with any questions or concerns.

Respectfully,

Nancy Lue

Guest Harmony Services Department

E.A.R.T.H.: Your Tranquil Harbor Beyond the Veil

"It was him!" Cecil exclaimed, knocking a large turkey statue (still up from Thanksgiving) off the reception desk on his way to bluster outside, slamming the front door and perilously rattling the stained glass in the process.

"Coward," Hazel whispered, shaking her head and slinking away. "Now, you see. Men never change."

Pippi reread the pop-up notice, which had completely locked her computer screen until she clicked *Yes, I agree.* She had to agree, she had to push forward, she had to *lead.* She became keenly aware of her connection to everything and everyone, a connection that was more a glue than a talking point. Part of her admired John's gumption; after all, hadn't all the things charged in that report been true? But if she could reason with them in person, for herself and Cecil, maybe there was a chance?

Now, just to convince Cecil of that. Pippi found him in the darkest corner of the front porch.

"I'm sorry," he whispered. "Look what coming here has done."

"Yes," Pippi sighed. "Look what it's done. Shouldn't you be the one complaining? Being dead and all."

A smile twitched at the corner of Cecil's mouth. "How are you finding humor in this?"

"Oh, I'm getting a lot of practice."

Pippi took Cecil's hand. She was starting to get used to the new feel of it. Not warm, not cold, but cool, leaving her skin slightly tingly. She wondered if her hand felt like a hot poker in his. They stood like this for a while, breathing in the quiet dark, cut occasionally by the rustling of some forest creature in the woods and, of course, the ocean, which at this point was just a calming white noise. Then Pippi's heart lurched and the cell phone rang a beat later, the reception phone only a half-second behind.

"Duty calls. Literally." Pippi removed the cell phone from her pocket, using its light to illuminate Cecil's face. "We will work this out. I promise." She was assuring more than just her boyfriend. She was assuring a guest. And maybe because she was his innkeeper now and not just his girlfriend, Cecil believed her.

"Hello?" Pippi answered the phone and listened. "One moment, please."

She walked inside to find Lidia, who'd been showing signs of moving on recently, as Pippi would learn often happened at the holidays. But Cecil remained outside, his back against the inn, who assured him to take as long as he needed, it wouldn't leave him for anything.

Chapter Twenty-One

The spiders slept for a solid two days after their scuba mission; Pippi knew they were sleeping since the boxed-up Thanksgiving decorations were left untouched beneath the attic entrance, along with a letter and hefty basket of treats including oversized soup mugs with a value pack of instant chicken noodle soup, the largest Santa hats Pippi could find, and an assortment of jingly catnip balls she thought the spiders would like and immediately regretted buying, prompting a 2:00 am knock on the ceiling to *please keep the jingly ball rolling to a minimum at night.*

Thanksgiving decorations were swapped out because life (and death) had to keep going at the inn, although the date of the inspection was circled in bright red ink on the calendar, which happened to be on Christmas Eve. Pippi thought if she was an employer about to terminate an employee, Christmas Eve was just as good a day as any, if not ideal, due to the overall hopeful cheerfulness and renewal of the season. That, and the fact that the world shut down for the week until the new year, making employers unreachable.

In her note to the spiders, Pippi asked them to check on Cecil's body every other day and alert her of any issues in the tundra. Cecil in his spirit form started out restless (as she would learn all spirits were) testing things like jumping off the roof or walking out to visit Susie or standing atop someone's head while they were drinking coffee until Pearl or Florence shooed him away. But the thrilling anonymity and invincibility of it all wore off quickly, and soon the longing for feeling, connection, excitement, fatigue, *living*, returned, along with thoughts of the place to come.

And it was thoughts of this place that naturally popped into Cecil's mind, a place that promised a return to those feelings again. Even though Pippi tirelessly researched and investigated and dreamed up every possible avenue to *get him back* on her own without E.A.R.T.H. 's interference, the fact remained that Cecil's spirit was instinctively inching towards eternal rest like everyone before him. Other than a quick hug or arm on the shoulder, he withdrew any and all physical affection towards Pippi and maybe she was the only woman in the world who really understood why. He told Pippi he preferred the solace of his own room at night, sleeping deeply even though he didn't need to, drifting off to whispers that beckoned him to this forever home.

In his waking hours, Cecil joined Pippi in her handling of the guests' phone calls. Cecil never got a phone call himself (likely because no one knew he was dead) and the other guests didn't mind his natural curiosity, allowing him to sit in on their calls, which he did so often that Pippi had to request another chair for behind the desk.

"Have you ever tried to talk back?" he would ask them.

"They know we're here," the other guests would explain. "That's all we can do."

Cecil also joined in on Lucy and Lidia's transfer at the end of the first week of December. They wanted to go see the Eiffel Tower together, having formed a deep friendship in their spirit forms. But both they and Pippi knew this would be their last stop, recognizing the gaunt valleys beginning to form under their cheek bones. Maybe they really did want to see the Eiffel Tower or maybe they wanted to save Pippi the trauma of their departure.

"Can I transfer somewhere?" Cecil asked one evening, his coat already on.

"Oh." Pippi's stomach ached. This was natural, she knew, the spirit's need to wander and leave no stone unturned. Safety and roots were for the living.

"Just for one night," he assured. "And I can report back and compare our inn to theirs. Maybe it'll help with the inspection."

It was not in Pippi's job description to turn down a guest. "Okay. Where do you want to go?"

"Hartford. Or as close to there as I can get."

Pippi put on her professional face but said nothing, searching through the inn database until finding an inn in Washington Depot, Connecticut, which would put him within reasonable traveling distance for a ghost.

Cecil watched over her shoulder. "Looks good," he approved. "Thank you."

"Of course." Pippi managed to keep her voice from sounding strained. She felt an overwhelming jealousy at the thought of him being under the care of another innkeeper.

"No one is as beautiful and wonderful as you," Cecil winked.

Pippi blanched. "How'd you hear that?" she asked, drenched in panic at the thought of the guests being able to hear her thoughts.

Cecil laughed until tears were in his eyes, a laugh Pippi had not heard since he was living.

"I can't hear your thoughts," he reassured. "But I can read your face."

Pippi burned red but breathed again. "Okay, okay. You'll wake up in the new inn tomorrow morning. Don't forget to request your transfer back."

"I won't," he promised.

She smiled. "Then, have a good trip."

When Cecil did return two mornings later, Pippi had inadvertently been up all night. But not to worry about whether her ghost boyfriend was coming back; she was up studying every page of the *Handbook for Housekeeping* and completely lost track of time. (And it also didn't help that the inn kept up a steady stream of tea.) Up until then, she'd been using the handbook here and there, like a dictionary to look up the definition of an obscure word. Now, she realized this was a classic textbook, painstakingly contributed to and cherished by all the innkeepers before her.

She was reading by the hearth, cocooned in a fuzzy blanket by the dwindling fire, when Cecil walked in. He glanced out the windows to the thick fog that was slowly burning off from the warmth of the morning sun.

He settled on a seat across from her. "Good morning."

Pippi carefully placed the satin bookmark on the page she was reading about *What to do When the Migrating Warrior Bats Come to Visit Every 101 Years.*

"How was it?" she asked. If she was being honest, she *had* picked up the handbook to distract herself from worrying about Cecil, but quickly became engrossed in the content instead of wondering if her boyfriend was going to like dinner there better.

Cecil nodded and pushed his hands further into his coat. "It went fine."

"Why there?" That had been the real burning question in her mind since he left.

"My mom's in Hartford," he admitted. "I just wanted to see her one more time before..."

"No," Pippi interrupted. "Don't finish that sentence. We will-"

"Figure something out." Cecil nodded to the handbook. "Anything in there about resurrecting the dead?"

Pippi slid her hands over the book. "No," she admitted. "Lots on spirits and innkeepers, though."

"The other inn," Cecil sighed deeply. "It was strange to see the similarities and the differences. Same phone and reservation system, but a different breakfast system."

"Wait. How do they handle breakfast?"

"All guests get a choice between three options which change daily but repeat, for example, Monday is eggs Benedict, omelet, or quiche day. No dreams necessary."

"Well, that sounds wonderful, how do I get that?"

"And my room? *Exactly* like the one here, down to the window placement."

"Wow."

"I talked to some of the guests. It was...sobering."

"How so?"

"These inns are like an anchor. Without it, they just...well, wander. They don't know where to go until it's time to...you know. They can't show themselves to their family or friends. They're lost until moving on."

"A sad way to go. I guess that's why we're here."

"Pippi." Cecil's tone sounded serious, like the tone used by someone about to say something well-rehearsed. "If it comes down to choosing between me and the inn..."

Pippi reached out and grabbed Cecil's hand. "I know," she said. Because she did know. *Some things were bigger than him, or her, or them.*

Ding dong. Ding dong.

Pippi and Cecil stared at each other with big eyes.

Ding dong. Ding dong.

"Is that a doorbell?" Cecil stood up to peer out the window. "There's a car."

Pippi fumbled with her cell phone. There were no notifications, which meant the inn also had no idea what was going on and apparently Mo was sleeping in that morning.

Ding dong. Ding dong. DING DONG!

"Oh, this is ridiculous," Pippi huffed, discarding her blanket and straightening her wrinkled overalls.

Cecil backed up against the wall, ready to go incognito as Pippi went to the front door. The stained glass had gone forebodingly solid black.

Pippi cracked open the door. "Yes?"

Cousin Winifred's blonde head bobbed into view, tucked back with a headband covered with a Christmas cat print. She wore cherry red lipstick and a tight green turtleneck.

"Pippi!" she exclaimed, throwing up her arms. "Surprise!"

"Winifred?" Pippi swung the door open. "And...*Mom?*"

Winifred hooked her arm around the shoulder of Pippi's mother, Rose, who appeared to not only have been coerced into wearing a matching green turtleneck, but, from the look on her face, to come visit Pippi in the first place. Rose crossed her arms over her tiny frame, barely five foot tall, engulfed by an oversized red jacket. Her brown hair was cropped short and firmly withstanding the wind thanks to half a can of hairspray.

"Surprise, again!" Winifred cheered. She leaned forward and lowered her voice to a whisper. "Getting her here has been no small feat, let me tell you."

"Hello, Phillipa," Rose uttered stiffly.

Pippi sighed and smiled. *This was off to a great start.*

Winifred shifted her over-stuffed tote bag to the other arm, which Pippi alarmingly noticed seemed full of exactly what someone would pack for an overnight stay.

"Finding this place, my goodness! You really are tucked away back here!" she panted. "I had the address from an old Christmas card from Hazel, but darling, you need to get this place online! I thought I was driving to my death going up that long road!"

"Well, we kind of like it that way, actually," Pippi said through gritted teeth.

"Oh, right." Winifred placed her finger to her lips. "*It's a secret.*"

Pippi felt a furry creature slip through her legs as Hazel arrived to sit between her niece and the surprise visitors.

"Oh, Hazel! There you are!" Winifred said loudly, looking pointedly at Rose. "Good to see you!"

"Winifred." Hazel nodded to her cousin. She turned to her sister, eyes narrowed to slits. "Rose."

"Hazel." Rose pursed her lips. "You've never looked better."

"Oh, Mom, come on," Pippi groaned.

"What?" Rose feigned surprise. "I can't greet my sister?"

"What do you want?" Hazel asked. "Checking on your daughter that prefers to be here with me?"

"Aunt Hazel!" Pippi gasped.

Immediately, fox sister and human sister descended into an argument that seemed to consist of who could talk over the other the loudest. Subjects of the argument included who their parents liked best, who Pippi was happiest with, who said what and when at the fateful *falling out* that happened at their last meeting, and who sent the most recent Christmas or birthday card.

"Ladies! Ladies!" Winifred tried to break in. "Ladies, please. It's almost Christmas!"

A foghorn blasted from somewhere above the inn, probably set off by the spiders who, if Rose and Hazel weren't careful, would start loading the cannons next.

Once they'd all recovered from the ringing in their ears, Winifred separated the sisters.

"Now. I hope you got that out of your system," she huffed. "Pippi, your mother and I are here to visit."

"I'm sorry, we're full." In fact, they were anything but full and the spiders had fixed the roof on the backyard cottage.

"Told you, let's go," Rose said flatly.

"Oh, dear." Winifred's face fell.

"My daughter clearly doesn't want me here," Rose sniffed.

"It's not that, it's just..." Pippi stopped, trying to find the words that would not set off World War III. "Will you...you know...respect what's going on here?"

"Yes!" Winifred cheered.

Rose pursed her lips again. Pippi's cold heart broke a little as she saw her mother clearly trying to hold back tears.

"If it means I can be with you, then yes," she said finally, reaching out to grab Pippi and give her a tight hug. She leaned back to push the hair out of Pippi's face. "I've missed you."

Winifred clapped her hands together. "Look at that! Healing is already happening. I'll go get the other bags."

Pippi gave her cousin and mother a tour of the inn, keeping her ghost boyfriend and the giant spiders for later. Rose did a moderately good job of putting on a positive face. Hazel followed closely behind, scratching her nails into the wood floors. The inn had quadrupled the size of the backyard cottage for the two living guests, on which now hung a sign reading *backyard chateau*.

Winifred drooled over the crystal chandeliers, Italian marble shower, and the state-of-the-art espresso machine that the inn had rolled out in a clear attempt to impress the innkeeper's family, which apparently also included a talking space heater.

"Welcome, welcome!" the little red space heater announced through the (mouth?) vents, its cheery (eye?) temperature controls upturned in a smile. "Welcome to the chateau, ladies!"

"Oh, Pippi!" Winifred squealed. "This is amazing!"

"Yes. It is," Pippi admitted, wondering why she didn't have a marble shower or a talking space heater.

Rose's penciled eyebrows rose to a sharp arch as the little space heater tottered over.

"Madam, allow me to introduce myself," the heater winked. "I am Emberheart, older than time, once a flame in my creator's hand, now a beacon of warmth for our living visitors, who require a perfect temperature to operate. It is my honor to accommodate you."

Winifred clasped her hands. "Oh, *lovely!*"

The remainder of the day was spent settling Winifred and Rose in for their stay, which they assured would end before the E.A.R.T.H. inspection, promising to lend any help they could to prepare for it.

"Is this a good idea?" Cecil asked, watching Winifred and Rose traverse the mucky backyard on their way back to the chateau. They'd just finished dinner, which consisted of a giant seafood boil that covered the entire table. The other guests had immediately warmed to Winifred and Rose (after realizing it was safe to reveal themselves) finding pleasure in their distinct personalities that clearly reminded them of their own family members with similar distinct personalities. Cecil had passed the family test with flying colors, as Winifred adored his *strong arms* and Rose was shocked to learn someone *so young and hip* knew about the classic British sitcom *Keeping Up Appearances.*

"Is this a good idea?" Pippi repeated, shaking her head at her own decision to get into this predicament. "All I can say is, if the inn is okay with them staying then I am, too."

Cecil took a sip of his dark ale, which had been served alongside the seafood boil. "And what if the inn is doing the same with you?"

Pippi was still pondering Cecil's suggestion hours after dessert, through an awkward evening puzzle with Winifred and Rose, and past midnight tea. She waited until she was at the reception desk, after everyone had retired to bed, alone under the solitary desk light, to really pose that question to herself. Who *was* in charge? Her, the inn, or Ethereal Accommodations for Restful Travel and Hospitality? She flicked through the handbook, looking for some direction. But if the previous innkeepers knew the answer, they didn't share it there.

An alert came through for a new guest transferring in from Nome, Alaska. According to the reservation, Esmeralda Gannon would wake up in room 222. Pippi jotted down her information next to the long to-do list she'd been working on to prepare for the big Christmas Eve visit, which included asking the spiders if she could inspect the attic (she figured a proper innkeeper should see all parts of her inn,) buying more holiday decorations for the front porch, and reviewing the inn's history with Hazel, who took her dinner in her private chambers (which Pippi thought was under the stairs) so as to avoid altercations with her sister in front of the guests.

Pippi turned off the reception light, as something inside told her it would be a quiet night. She paused and surveyed the front entry in its ambient light, thinking of all the dozens, hundreds, thousands of souls that had passed that threshold either to visit or go home forever. In that stillness, Pippi felt fiercely protective of it all. Enraged at the prospect of it being taken away from her for just following her heart, for never turning away a guest, whether living or dead. If E.A.R.T.H. had a problem with that, then they'd have a problem with her.

She flicked back on the light and opened the *Handbook for Housekeeping*, flipping to the blank pages in the back. Searching through the drawer for her best pen, Pippi took a deep breath and wrote her first page, titled *When You Don't Know Who Runs The Inn* followed simply by <u>*YOU DO.*</u>

Chapter Twenty-Two

The next day was abnormally and unseasonably sunny for a December in the Pacific Northwest and the whole inn was buzzing with energy at the prospect of going outside and not getting soaking wet. Cecil organized a field trip expedition down to the beach to practice walking on water out to Susie, while Pippi half-heartedly included Winifred and Rose in her Windia shopping trip after Hazel threatened an act of terrorism if Pippi left her alone with them.

"Oh, goodie, look at you! Embracing the Christmas spirit properly!" Winifred squealed when she saw Pippi in her bright red Christmas-decoration-shopping overalls, which the inn had embroidered with dainty strings of colorful lights and the occasional jolly Santa face.

Pippi looked down at her overalls and over to her mother, who was dressed in slacks, a crisp white shirt that Emberheart had dewrinkled, and a long, wool trench coat.

"Yes?" she queried after catching her mother's eye.

"Nothing," Rose shrugged, slipping on her sunglasses.

Pippi grabbed her bulky coat from the coat rack, which today was covered with a print of shopping bags overflowing with wreaths. "Then let's go. Hazel, we're going!"

"Oh." Winifred grabbed her stomach. "Oh, dear."

"What?" Pippi and Rose said at the same time.

Winifred dramatically wiped invisible sweat from her forehead. "I don't think breakfast is sitting well with me. Too much goulash, I'm afraid."

"Yeah, sorry about that," Pippi said, the aroma of her borscht and goulash dream still lingering in the air.

"You go without me," Winifred insisted.

"No!" Pippi and Rose said at the same time.

"I'm serious, you go," Winifred moaned, her eyes twinkling. "It'll give you two some time to catch up."

It was a setup. Pippi and her mother exchanged miserable looks.

A door upstairs slammed opened, followed by loud stomps. A gloriously booming voice called out, "Hello?"

All eyes directed upstairs as a nearly six foot tall woman appeared, her shockingly white hair perfectly coiffed, a long diamond necklace dripping down to her floor-length red gown. She discarded a white mink stole over the banister and descended the stairs gracefully without even looking down.

"Morning, all! I'm Esmeralda Gannon!" she announced grandly, her heavy diamond bracelets jingling merrily as she waved to Pippi and all the other guests who now crowded the front entry to greet her.

Pippi met Esmeralda at the bottom of the stairs. "Hi Esmeralda, I'm Pippi, the innkeeper. Glad you came to stay."

"Pippi," Esmeralda clasped both of Pippi's hands in her one. "Pleasure."

"Well, there's a few options for you today. This is Cecil, he's hosting a field trip or feel free to relax and grab a bite to eat. There's still some goulash and borscht I can have dished up for you."

"Just a latte and an ocean view sounds perfect to me," Esmeralda assured.

"Sounds good, I'll have my aunt keep you company," Pippi said. "Aunt Hazel!"

"I'll wait out by the car," Rose grumbled, following the ocean expedition group outside.

Hazel poked her spectacled head around the corner. She'd started wearing glasses everyday now, not just for the morning paper. "Is she gone?"

"This is Esmeralda, a new guest. Can you keep her company while I'm gone?" Pippi ordered.

Hazel sat down stiffly. "Of course."

"Can I join?" Winifred asked, enraptured with Esmeralda, her "sick stomach" suddenly gone. "You just seem so *lovely*."

"Of course!" Esmeralda beamed and the two hooked arms and immediately started chatting on their way out the front porch.

Hazel closed her eyes. "Wonderful."

The Christmas music on the radio of Winifred's rental car did a sufficient job of filling the empty silence on the ride into Windia, but Pippi and Rose were on their own after that. Pippi's outfit drew a few looks and snickers but only from the weekend tourists; the real residents of Windia were completely used to it and nodded at her with a knowing wink.

"Do you need anything while we're out?" Pippi finally broke the standoff as they stopped in Four Corners Square to admire an exhibit of the elementary school's drawings of seals dressed up as Santa Claus.

"No. Just here to be with you," Rose replied curtly, adjusting her suit of armor also known as her jacket. She sipped on the tumbler of coffee she'd brought with her from the inn.

"Okay. The Christmas store it is, then," Pippi sighed from the base of their mountain of unresolved issues, leading the way to the year-round Christmas store in Windia known as *A Very Merry Sea-Son*. A giant artificial Christmas tree stood like a sentry at the entrance, lit up 365 days a year and causing passing tourists to ask *Is that a year-round Christmas store or do they just leave their tree up all year?*

The door chime jingled as Pippi and Rose entered the store that smelled of old building and sugar cookies. Mobiles of Santa's sleigh circled through the air and motion-detector music boxes came to life as they perused the store. Pippi loaded her mother with armfuls of fresh fir garland and new strings of lights while she picked up canisters of fake snowballs, Oregon-themed ornaments, and a pair of silver reindeer candle stick holders. She passed a glass cabinet that displayed an array of fancy snow globes and froze.

There was the inn.

"Welcome, ladies! Can I help you find anything?" asked a woman dressed in a nautical-themed Christmas sweater and an elf head-band. She noticed Pippi's attention to the snow globes. "Aren't they beautiful? Most play music, too."

"That one." Pippi pressed her finger hard against the glass. "What is that?"

The shopkeeper leaned in closer, pulling up her Mrs. Clause-es-que spectacles from the chain hanging around her neck.

"That's the inn on the hill," she explained matter-of-factly.

Pippi broke out in a cold sweat. "You know about it?"

"Of course! It's been around here forever," the shopkeeper smiled. "It's not for you and me, though." She winked. "Or at least not for a long, long time, hopefully."

Pippi looked at her mother, who looked equally aghast at the frankness of this conversation.

"Here." The shopkeeper spun around a tower of postcards. She picked out one and handed it to Pippi. "A rather old picture but beautiful nonetheless."

The black and white picture was indeed of Pippi's inn, with the same porch and the same miniature rose bushes leading up the walkway. *1910* was written in the bottom left corner, along with *The Inn on the Hill, Windia, Oregon.*

"I'm the owner," Pippi blurted out, handing back the postcard.

The shopkeeper beamed. "Seriously? It's good to meet you! I'm Mabel Powell, I'm the owner here. Well, you need to start coming to our monthly business association meetings, my dear! It's a great networking opportunity."

"But the inn is for *ghosts*," Rose also blurted out, Pippi nodding along.

Mabel looked at the two, a bit exasperated. "Yes, I know." She pulled out a key from her pocket and opened the glass cabinet, removing the inn snow globe carefully.

"How much?" Pippi asked, reaching into her pockets.

"Oh, no, no. This is a gift." Mabel shooed away Pippi's wallet and left to wrap up the snow globe. "It's the least I can do."

"What do you mean?" Rose asked as she and Pippi followed Mabel to the checkout counter, which was cluttered with local business cards, Christmas candy, and a little wooden mouse propped next to a piece of fake gold that looked like cheese.

"Are you mom?" Mabel inquired, looking between the two women.

"Yes."

"Well, ma'am, your daughter is giving us all a gift. I'm looking forward to a stay there one day," Mabel said, handing over the packaged snow globe. "And you and I can remember this day."

Pippi accepted the gift, blinking back tears. Rose lowered her armful of goods to the counter, looking at her daughter with new eyes. Mabel busied herself ringing up the items, alternately tossing in a candy cane or packet of hot cocoa mix with each *ding* of her scanner.

She smiled. "Cash or credit?"

Mother and daughter walked soberly back to the car, passing the *Annual Windia Polar Dip Plunge* down on the sunny but freezing cold beach. Bags deposited in the trunk, they sat in the quiet car, their warm breath fogging up the windows.

"Look-" Pippi started.

Rose held up her hand, quickly wiping away tiny tears that smeared the corners of her eye makeup.

"I have never, *ever*, understood this place," Rose began. "It took my sister away, took our aunt from our family, and so on. I can't even explain the terror I felt when I realized - when I truly, truly realized

- this was your future, too. You were so little...I was so angry at my sister. How could she even think of making this your future, too?"

Rose cried harder now and Pippi reached out to grab her mother's hand that clenched a handkerchief tightly.

"I thought if I just kept you away. If we just didn't talk about it?" she insisted. "Maybe you'd grow out of it? Or the inn would fall apart? Or both, even?"

"But it hasn't taken me away," Pippi pleaded.

"Oh, it has. It really has," Rose sobbed into her other hand.

"No," Pippi said firmly. "No. Look at me.'"

Rose turned to her daughter, eyes red and swollen.

"I've found myself. I feel more like myself than I ever have before. And Mom, this is going to sound harsh, I know...but you've got to keep up or I'll have to leave you behind."

"What's that supposed to mean?" Rose pulled her hand away.

Pippi motioned down to her Christmas-patterned overalls. "This is me. That inn is *me*." She pointed to the trunk, where the snow globe was waiting to leave. "And for the first time, what I'm doing is important. I won't let it go. So you can either get on this train, or get off."

Pippi started the car engine. *Who was she?* She had never talked to her mother like that before. Her heart pumped hard as she waited for the windows to defog. Her mother's tears promptly dried up, replaced by thin-lipped silence that lasted all the way back to the inn. The car pulled to a stop in the driveway, greeted by Esmeralda who waved from the porch, giant wine glass in hand.

"Pippi," Rose said as her daughter reached for the door handle.

Pippi waited.

"I have an idea for the garland on the front porch, if you'll let me," Rose offered. "You know I took that wreath-making class last year."

Pippi smiled and nodded. "Sounds great." *All aboard.*

Decorating became a group effort the next day, as Cecil had shared more information than he probably should have with his expedition guests and now the whole inn was in on operation *Save the Windia Inn and Pippi's Career, too.*

The morning was crisp and clear again; two days in a row of sun was unheard of for December in the Pacific Northwest. The guests gathered outside the inn, blinking into the bright light, bundled in heavy coats and mittens. Esmeralda stood out amongst the group, not only because of her height but because of her ankle-length red fur coat (faux fur, she insisted) that was trimmed with a high collar of plush white (faux) fur. Her hair was perfectly curled beneath her white (faux, again) fur pillbox hat. She huddled next to Cecil as he opened a tote full of lights.

"Oh, how lovely! Charming! I've never decorated for the holidays before!" she rejoiced. "Now, Cecil, explain to me the mechanics of these wires."

Cecil launched into a detailed and overly complicated explanation of twinkle lights. He and Esmeralda had immediately hit it off over dinner conversation the night before, discussing Cecil's research and exchanging lively theories on the workings of the telephone system.

Hazel joined the group outside, wearing little sunglasses and a wool cap with holes for her ears.

She sniffed the air. "Smells like snow."

Pippi sniffed, too. The only thing she could smell was wood-burning smoke drifting up the hill from the houses down in Windia. But it did seem much cooler than it should have been, even considering it was colder up on the mountain and even considering she was wearing red checkered flannel-lined overalls that made her look a bit like rustic Santa Claus.

"The forecast didn't say anything about snow," Winifred hollered from the front porch, where she was bundled under a blanket with a steaming hot toddy, nursing her "bad back" that kept her from helping. She'd asked Cecil to bring out a little table for Emberheart, who sat next to Winifred and expertly filled any lulls in conversation. "Do you think we need to go home early? I can't drive in the snow, Rose, I really can't. And I don't want to get Pippi in trouble!"

"It'll be fine," Rose insisted from the top of the ladder, where she was already hanging the garland design she'd sketched out the night before. "I want to spend as much time with my daughter as I can. The weather will hold out."

"Thank you, Mom." Pippi clapped for the guests' attention. "Okay, everyone, gather around. I really appreciate you helping out, I'm sorry to have to burden you with this."

"If I may?" Esmeralda stepped forward. "I know I've only been here a short time, but we all adore you."

"And you're not a burden," Cecil added. "You're worth it."

Pippi blushed. "Thank you. Then here's the plan. We're about a week away from the inspection and I'd love to put our best foot forward. I've been studying, the inn will be deep cleaning-"

"And," Esmeralda interrupted. "Cecil and I have a side project planned to impress the visitors, as well."

"Oh?" Pippi raised an eyebrow.

"Purely platonic side project," Cecil added quickly.

"Oh yes, purely platonic," Esmeralda agreed, adding quietly, "*Unfortunately.*"

"Anything to help put Cecil in a good light will help, in addition to his handsome good looks and sweet personality, of course," Pippi cheesed.

"Good grief, you two," Hazel gagged. "We all know you're into each other. Back on topic, please?"

"Another job that needs done is the yardwork, which I have been woefully neglecting, sorry. Really, just look for anything you can see that can be done to *wow* our visitors. And another thing, I haven't forgotten it's almost Christmas. The inn and I will make sure it's still special."

The guests clapped and immediately started swapping theories about what Pippi had in mind. Together, Pippi and the guests made good time on the yardwork and decorating. In the end, the inn looked like a proper establishment ready for holiday reservations. Twinkle lights of all colors dripped down from the eaves next to Rose's garland designs, while light-up statues of various forest creatures had been tucked into the tree line of the surrounding forest.

Clouds rolled in from the east, covering the sun and significantly lowering the temperature. As the guests went inside for a hot chocolate bar, Pippi walked to the back forest, where she'd found a giant sleigh hidden beneath a red tarp after deciphering a not-so-subtle clue left for her on the front door's stained glass window.

She looked up at the dark clouds. The wind blew cold, too; dry mountain air instead of the salty dampness from the sea. Now Pippi knew what Hazel meant. She smelled smoke and pine and frozen soil. Once she reached the tarp, she signaled to the spiders to come down from the roof, where they'd been delicately weaving strands of silky snowflakes and hanging them one by one. After reading more about the history of the inn's spiders, Pippi was long over her fear of them, especially as they were outfitted today, wearing their holiday sweaters like everyone else. The spiders made quick work of dragging the sleigh up to the roof while Pippi directed from the front yard. They just finished as the first drop of freezing rain fell from the dark sky, scattering the spiders back inside.

Cecil met Pippi at the doorway, carrying a towering hot chocolate topped with a *gluten free* flag sticking out of the fluffy whipped cream.

He surveyed the sudden weather change. "Oh, boy."

Pippi accepted the hot chocolate and watched the rain fall and hit the ground with an icy splat. The clouds overhead grew darker and darker and darker.

"It'll be fine," Pippi assured herself. "How much can happen in a week?"

Are those angels singing?

That's what Pippi asked herself mid-dream as she swam through a lake of warm French toast casserole mixture. Above her, the sky was blindingly bright blue with the occasional powdered sugar cloud that wafted by, sprinkling sugar dust along the way. Pippi treaded milky batter and listened closely as egg dripped down her wet hair. On the casserole lake shore stood a whisk butler that waited dutifully with a large beach towel. Pippi spun around as she heard the sound again. *Definitely angelic singing.*

"Hello?" Pippi called out, knowing she should head back to shore but reluctant to leave the warm lake.

"Hi." A giant white swan dropped down from one of the powdered sugar clouds, causing a sloshing wave that knocked Pippi under.

Sputtering batter as she resurfaced, Pippi's eyes stung from the vanilla. "Who are you?" she demanded.

"Wake up and you'll see," the swan said, flapping its giant wings hard as it attempted to lift itself from the soupy lake. It shook any remaining batter from its webbed feet, rising into the blindingly bright blue sky and calling down, "This is disgusting!"

The loud beating of the swan's wings gave way to another kind of beating, this time on her bedroom window. Pippi sat up straight in bed, instinctively wiping batter from her arms, which were perfectly dry and still covered by her flannel pajamas. She fumbled for her cell phone, on which appeared an icon of a white squawking swan that looked suspiciously like the swan from her dream. She'd never once seen this icon before, in fact, she'd never once seen an icon of any sort on her cell phone.

Bang, bang, bang. The swan icon on the phone pulsed as Pippi became aware of a (large) dark and bobbing silhouette outside her window, obscured by the thin bedroom curtains that were there more to diffuse sunlight than to provide privacy.

Pippi pulled the covers up fast to her face. "Inn!? Who is that?"

"Emergency message for the innkeeper!" a muffled voice called through the window. "Open up!"

Leaving the warmth of her blankets behind, Pippi crossed the room to her window, looking around for some sort of weapon, which she then realized was ridiculous. The inn probably had lasers hidden somewhere in the eaves to incinerate anyone it *didn't* want around. It was just before dawn, and the rising sun behind the eastern mountains offered enough light for Pippi to discern the figure outside her window. It was the giant swan from her dream, so giant that it had to bow down its long, elegant neck to remain eye level with Pippi's window.

Pippi pushed open her window, noticing the frost gathered on the track. "Can I help you?" This was no ghost, it was a real-life, breathing, extremely intimidating waterfowl.

"That depends. Are you the innkeeper?" the giant swan asked, its black, glistening eye sizing Pippi up with one look.

"I am," Pippi answered, ready to slam the window shut depending on how her response was received. Maybe this was some sort of E.A.R.T.H. test or trickery but she had to find out, or maybe she'd just add *talking to a swan on inn premises* to her list of offenses.

"Excellent. My name is Dottie, I'm with Swan Warning And Notification Services," the swan advised formally, ruffling dew from her silky feathers. "I have an important message for you."

"Oh, okay." *This was a new one.* "Go ahead."

"First, I need to play you this prerecorded message." Dottie was visibly annoyed as she lifted her left wing. Nestled within the feathers was a tiny device with a blinking light. She poked at it with her beak and rolled her eyes.

"This is a prerecorded message," began the monotone voice on the recording, who also seemed annoyed with these proceedings. "By listening to this message, you, the innkeeper, acknowledge that the message provided by the S.W.A.N.S. representative is accurate and up-to-date to the best of our abilities and that you, the innkeeper, agree that S.W.A.N.S. and all its entities wherein hold no liabilities for damages that may be incurred as a result of said message." The speaker on the message took a deep, exasperated breath, adding quickly, "If you agree, say *I agree*."

"I agree."

Dottie cleared her throat, turning away to hack up something. She took a breath and began to *sing*.

Dear innkeeper, please don't weep,

We must share what we've been advised,

The easterly winds blow cold,

The northern snow uncontrolled,

A storm of great danger wakes from sleep.

Dear innkeeper, please be prepared,

For delays in travel and otherwise,

Defer your outings,

(Don't bother rerouting)

And stay SAFE INSIDE THE INN to be spared.

With the song clearly finished, Dottie stared at Pippi blankly.

"That was lovely," Pippi floundered. "Thank you."

Dottie blinked.

"You have a wonderful voice."

Dottie's eyes narrowed. "You don't know anything about this, do you?"

"Well-"

"Listen, kid," Dottie interrupted, stretching her neck up to full height. "S.W.A.N.S. are called in to relay messages to innkeepers when a catastrophic event is about to happen that may wipe out other communication methods. We've been around since *before* those other communication methods were around, you get me?"

"Got it. So you're a branch of E.A.R.T.H.?"

Dottie scoffed. "An *independent* branch."

"Like the postal service?" Pippi ventured.

Dottie's neck swooped down to Pippi's eye level, her sharp beak inches from Pippi's face. "The postal service *wishes* it was us," she seethed.

Pippi shrank. "Understood."

Dottie snapped back to full height and started to stretch her giant wings. "Look, just stay close to the inn till the snow breaks. No field trips, got it? You'll be fine, kid."

Pippi offered a small wave, reluctant to ruffle the swan's feathers again, and shut closed her bedroom window as Dottie rose gracefully into the air, her massive wings blocking out the sky. With a roll cast, she flew off and disappeared behind the mountains.

Pippi's phone *dinged*.

Thank you for using Swan Warning And Notification Services! On a scale of one to five, how would you rate your recent experience with your S.W.A.N.S. representative, Dottie?

"Nope, not chancing that," Pippi told herself as she swiftly rated Dottie five stars.

Chapter Twenty-Three

Pippi leaned forward in her usual seat at the dining room table, her steaming Earl Grey tea cradled in her hands. She knew breakfast was almost ready (country fried steak and eggs with a side of cantaloupe) by the sound of plates sliding across the kitchen countertops. Soon the guests would be there and she knew they'd be enraptured with the new (but, she would insist, *temporary*) addition to the dining room. The inn had rolled out a television set for Pippi to watch the news, after watching her struggle (unsuccessfully) with trying to work the old fashioned radio in the parlor, which had no internal circuitry and was for decoration only.

It was December 23, one day until inspection. All week it had snowed. And snowed. And *snowed*. Rose and Winifred should have left the day before, but down trees blocked the road southeast to Eugene and a mudslide washed out the route north. The typically-temperate state was wholly unprepared for snow and ice of this magnitude, diverting the few snow plows in service to help metropolitan Portland, leaving the smaller towns on their own.

"Top news this morning; the worst storm in recorded history plummets the Pacific Northwest," announced the newscaster, who sat beside a graphic of a snowplow and a giant icicle. "Unprecedented amounts of snow compounded with freezing temperatures bring the state to a standstill. Flights in and out of Portland are delayed until further notice, with the FAA citing unsafe flying conditions. Providence Medical Center has issued an executive order for staff to remain on the premises. Here at KATU, we've received many calls from frustrated local residents who have been without power for days with no restoration date in sight."

The newscast cut to a graphic of a phone over a purple background with sound waves bouncing up and down. A chyron at the bottom of the screen stated *Esther Oliver, Director of Electrical Services for NorWest Power.*

"We're seeing power outages throughout our entire service area," a staticky woman's voice stated. "The down trees and ice are significantly affecting our cleanup and restoration efforts. If we can't reach the down lines, we can't fix them. At this point we are advising customers to prepare for outages as long as one week, up to two weeks in more rural areas."

The broadcast returned to the newscaster, who did not appear pleased with that information. "Officials are asking residents to stay inside and off the roads until further notice," the newscaster advised. "We'll be back after the break with our chief Meteorologist and his top five tips for beating the freeze. Stay with us."

Pippi paced the room, looking out the window at the rising snow drifts, unaware of the tea sloshing all over her. *Two weeks?* She stopped and surveyed the dining room, soon to be filled with hot food, comforting coffee, and gentle holiday music filtering through the air. The inn, independent of any outside power source or food source, was completely unaffected by the snowy weather, other than it added to the cozy ambiance. After a few afternoons of playing in the snow and covering the lawn with igloos, Pippi and the guests spent most of the week doing about every stuck-in-the-inn activity she could think of, including cards, hide-and-seek, even an attempt at putting together a stage production that they all agreed proved to be too much.

But Pippi had also spent the week watching Windia from her perch atop the hill. Watching as the traffic grew less and less and the snow piled up more and more. The townsfolk made valiant attempts at clearing the road, proving futile against mother nature and her desire to lay her thickest comforter of snow across the landscape, erasing their daytime progress every night. In an attempt at solidarity with the townsfolk, Pippi slept every night without her comforter in her temperature-controlled inn. If the people of Windia were going to be cold, then she was going to be, too. They were, after all, her closest living neighbors. But each time, that thought was followed by the same nagging question, the same one Pippi imagined now written in the frost on the window glass. *If she was going to be warm, shouldn't they, too?*

But the inspection. The inn. Her guests' final moments. Cecil's life. Her mother's approval. She could lose it all if she answered that call in the back of her mind, the one begging her to listen. *But at what cost?*

A knock on the front door summoned Pippi's attention. She left her tea on the table and rushed to the entryway, throwing on her winterized raincoat over her pajamas, which was covered with a pattern of thick red snowflakes. She slipped outside as the guests were starting to exit their rooms for breakfast.

Mo stood on the front porch, dressed in a thick snowsuit topped with a furry-hooded coat and homemade snowshoes made of tiny tennis rackets and what appeared to be chicken wire. He shook the snow from his wiry beard.

"Reporting back, per your request, ma'am," he saluted.

Pippi jumped from one foot to the other to keep warm. She'd stood in that exact same spot last night, checking on Windia one last time before going to bed, covered by a thick sheet of darkness. "How bad is it out there?"

Mo removed his gloves and blew hot air on his fingertips. "Well, ma'am, it's bad. Down trees everywhere. *The worst snowstorm in recorded history*, according to the radio."

"I heard," Pippi whispered, looking around at the blinding white all around her. "This is insane."

"Power is definitely out in Windia. The stores are closed, generators must have run out. The whole town is shut down, as far as I can tell," Mo reported. "It's mighty cold down there, ma'am. Hopin' the power comes back soon."

"The news said two weeks."

"Two weeks?" Mo shook his head. "Great Odin."

"Are you comfortable in your home? Do you need to stay with us?" Pippi asked.

Mo seemed pleased Pippi had even offered. "I appreciate that deeply, ma'am, but I have my little woodstove and plenty of stock. I prepare for things like this, you know." He looked over his shoulder, down towards the dark town of Windia, forced into silence. "It's not me I'm worried about."

"I know." Pippi wriggled her fingers, aware of how hard she'd been clenching them into fists. "If you change your mind, just come on up," she insisted. "And keep me updated, if you can."

Mo saluted. "Yes, ma'am."

"And, Mo?"

"Ma'am?"

Pippi fidgeted with the hem of her jacket. "The roads are completely impassable?"

Mo thought for a second, meeting Pippi's gaze. "Well, for a *car*, ma'am."

"But not a sled?"

"No, that would be fine."

"What about a sled pulled by spiders?"

Mo grinned. "I think that would be the best suited of them all."

"And if I needed sleds suitable for a giant spider to pull...?"

"Then I would suggest the carriages we keep downstairs in the basement, ma'am."

Pippi blinked. "We have a basement? With carriages?"

Mo nodded. "Oh yes, you see, before automobiles, there we carriages, ma'am."

"Where's the basement entrance? Do the spiders manage the basement, too?"

"Oh no, Emberheart's grandpappy oversees the basement and he does so with an iron fist. He's the inn's furnace, didn't you know?"

"I had absolutely no idea. Should I go down and talk to him?"

"Better leave that alone, ma'am." Mo advised gravely. "He might take a bit to warm up to Mistress Hazel's niece. They used to butt heads often about the inn's temperature when she, well...I believe you call it, became *menopausal*. But I can put in a request, if you wish?"

Pippi hesitated. "I'll follow up with you." She looked down towards town. "I need to think."

"Yes, ma'am." Mo bowed, then saluted. "I'll await your instructions."

Mo disappeared into the snow-covered and dormant blackberry bushes. The world was silent except for the occasional cracking tree limb in the distance and, of course, the ocean, unaffected by the freezing temperatures. The door to the inn opened and Esmeralda appeared, draped in a long, heavy, emerald green coat and carrying two steaming mugs. The inn closed the door behind her.

"Oh, thank you, dear," Esmeralda said to the inn. She handed Pippi a mug. "Bracing hot cider. Must keep your constitution up in this kind of weather."

"Thank you." Pippi accepted the mug, which was painted with a black and white image of the inn at the time of construction. She studied it. "Huh. Never seen this before."

"Always learning new things, aren't we?" Esmeralda sighed. "Even now. For example, I learned that spicy chili lime salt is delicious on cantaloupe!"

Pippi smiled. She took a sip of her cider, which really did have a bracing kick.

Esmeralda followed Pippi's line of sight down to Windia. "Heavy is the crown?"

"Yes, it certainly can be," Pippi mumbled, trying to shake it off. "I'm sorry, I've been so distracted lately. How has your stay been here so far?"

Esmeralda fluffed her furry collar. "Wonderful. Simply wonderful. I've especially enjoyed my conversations with Cecil, what a bright young man. Quite the brain on that one," she winked. "One of those taken-too-early-situations, for sure."

"Well, I'm hoping to change that."

"Oh?"

"Yes. And I will."

"I see. Heavy is the crown, indeed."

Pippi's heart skipped a beat as a tree branch fell to the ground and crashed like thunder in the quiet woods. Every inch of her body itched with adrenaline. She jerked when Esmeralda spoke again.

"I say," she began, setting her mug on the porch railing. "I hope you don't mind, but I'm always on the lookout for some obscure reading and picked this up." She pulled out the *Handbook for House-keeping* from the depths of her coat. "Then I realized perhaps this was personal. So sorry."

"Oh," Pippi said. "No harm done, but yes, that has information for the innkeeper."

"It's intriguing. Like the bats? My." Esmeralda released a deep belly laugh. "Good gracious, the things you must deal with!"

"It's fine."

"Is it?"

"More than fine," Pippi admitted. "I can't imagine doing anything else, actually."

The mood fell somber. Esmeralda studied her. She turned to the last page in the handbook.

"Is this you?" she asked.

Pippi wiped the secret tears from her eyes and took the handbook.

When You Don't Know Who Runs The Inn
<u>*YOU DO.*</u>

Esmeralda picked up her cider. "Sometimes we give the best advice to others that we need to hear ourselves."

Pippi traced her own words with her frozen fingertips. She took one last look towards Windia, suspended like a scene in a snow globe, waiting for her to decide between protecting the dead or saving the living. She slammed the handbook shut and held it to her chest.

"Thank you," Pippi said to Esmeralda, meeting her piercing gaze. "I needed that."

Esmeralda took a sip. "We've all been there, dear. Speaking from experience, of course."

Pippi's cider splattered all over the deck as she turned on her heel. The inn quickly opened the door as she stomped inside.

"Attention! Attention, everyone!" Pippi called out as she discarded her jacket. The inn rang a deep bell that resonated through the building. "Can you all join me in reception?" she yelled, which the inn repeated again over the inn's invisible loudspeaker. Pippi took her place behind the reception desk and flicked open her cell phone. "Mo? Operation is a go. I'll be in touch."

Guests filled the reception area, some with plates of food but all still in their pajamas. Winifred (carrying Emberheart, who she finally realized didn't need an outlet to operate,) Rose, and Hazel entered last, a trio (plus Emberheart) that spent a lot of time together considering their constant bickering.

"Pippi?" Cecil's head poked up from the crowd. "What's going on?"

"Are we all here?" Pippi yelled, counting the number of guests in her head until all were accounted for. "Thank you, everyone! I need to speak to you about something very important!"

The entryway fell silent other than the occasional fork clanking against a plate. Hazel hopped up on the reception desk.

"Thank you." Pippi took a deep breath. "First, you've all been wonderful. So wonderful, so helpful, pitching in to prepare for the inspection when you very much did not have to. But I have one more thing to ask of you."

Pippi reached over for the snow globe of the inn, which she had placed next to the inn's phone. She held the cool glass in her hands and caught Esmeralda's gaze. She straightened her shoulders.

"Actually, it's something I need to *tell* you we are doing," she corrected herself. "The town of Windia has been without power since yesterday. I have no idea how long the outage will last. So we're bringing the town...here."

There was a beat of hushed silence, even the forks hung mid air, before the guests started to whisper amongst themselves. Cecil's mouth dropped open until he covered it with his hand, the wheels in his mind visibly turning. Pippi turned slowly to look at Hazel, who stared at her niece with a steely gaze that could have pierced through the wall. All other conversation faded to a dull hubbub.

"Well?" Pippi asked her aunt at last, preparing for the worst. "What do you have to say?"

Hazel didn't blink behind her glasses. She repositioned her paws. "I say," she drew out. "How can I help?"

Pippi tried not to show how relieved she was. "I'll need your help directing efforts here at the inn. We'll need more food, bedding-"

"Done," Hazel interrupted, waving a paw. "In my former life, I was an innkeeper, you know."

Pippi turned back to the guests, who looked to be experiencing a mixture of confusion and fear.

"I know it's not ideal," she said to the group. "And it's probably not right of me to ask for your help. I understand if you want to leave. It won't look good with the inn full of the living. It's not going to look good at all. But I know if this was *your* family down there, you'd believe this was right, too."

The room was silent.

"So that's it," Pippi shrugged. "That's where we're at."

Cecil stepped forward. "I think I speak for all of us when I say, we're behind you, Pippi," he ventured, looking around at the other guests, who nodded in approval.

Pippi's heart swelled. She looked from guest to guest, never feeling so proud. And there she was, at the helm of it all. She'd never felt more *exhilarated*.

"Then let's get started." She clapped her hands together. "Hazel will be in charge while I'm gone and leading efforts in preparing for the townsfolk. Cecil, I need you to gather supplies for the trip; flashlights, blankets, hand warmers, things like that."

"Got it. Are we taking my van?" Cecil asked. "I can't remember how much gas I had. And I might need to shovel the road."

"We're taking spider-drawn carriages," Pippi informed matter-of-factly.

"Excuse me?" Cecil blinked.

"Speaking of, I need to get up there and talk to them," Pippi thought out loud. She flicked open her phone. "One more call first."

The phone rang seven times before a gruff voice picked up. "Hello?"

"Chopper? It's Hazel."

"Who?"

"From the Lonesome Lily trip? The heavy bag?"

"What do you want?" he chided hoarsely. "Trying to go to old Lily in an ice storm, I'm guessing?"

"Not quite," Pippi clipped. "But I do have another job for you."

"Not interested."

She cleared her throat. "Even for Old Herman?"

Silence. Followed by audible sniffing.

"What do you need?" he sighed deeply.

Chapter Twenty-Four

Pippi was outside with Mo inspecting the carriages when Chopper flew overhead on his way down to Windia with his orders. He was to fly over the little town, reaching the houses tucked off private gravel roads and peeking out from beneath trees, announcing over a loudspeaker for all to gather at Four Corners Square for evacuation. He was also to land and speak with Mabel, who Pippi recognized as an organized soul, to inform her of the plan and lead the efforts in town.

The inn had picked out an appropriate outfit for the expedition while still sticking to uniform guidelines; overalls made of insulated, waterproof material in a bright berry color with a matching waterproof parka. It kept Pippi sweaty but otherwise dry as she helped to tether a spider to each carriage, who were also dressed for the trip in sweaters and snow boots. *Lots* of snow boots.

The guests watched through the window, a few peeking through the doorway, moving out of the way for Esmeralda, who joined Pippi's side to marvel at the towering creatures that jittered with nervous anticipation.

"My word," she whispered, daring a gentle touch to one of the spider's spindly legs. "Incredible."

"Yes." Pippi patted the spider, who purred in response. "They are the goodest boys and girls."

Cecil came out next, dressed in, of course, his usual jeans and white shirt, since the cold didn't affect him. He dragged a huge bag step by step down to the carriages.

"Okay, here you go," he panted. "All the supplies I could find."

"I've got it, boy," Mo offered.

"Wait, it's heavy-"

Mo picked up the bag with no trouble and tossed it atop the first carriage in line, which visibly wilted beneath its weight. Cecil stared.

"You need to work out more, boy," Mo flexed. "Always be ready for anything."

"How much longer?" Pippi interrupted, glancing up at the quickly approaching afternoon with evening right on its December heels.

"One more check and let's go," Mo advised, tipping his hat as he went down the line of carriages and inspected each one.

Pippi turned to Cecil. "Thank you for everything. I'll be back."

Cecil shook his head. "Oh, no. I'm going with you."

"Cecil-"

Cecil swung up on the carriage with an agility that Pippi didn't know if was natural or ghost-induced. "Someone has to drive the carriage."

"I don't think they even need driven."

"Sure they do. Besides, I'm a guest," he grinned. "And you can't deny a guest."

"You've got me there," Pippi relented, looking down the line of carriages to Mo, who signaled a thumbs up.

Cecil helped Pippi climb up on the carriage, which seemed surprisingly steady considered the apparent age of the vehicle. The spiders stomped and bristled restlessly, ready to scatter at Pippi's signal. Winifred, Emberheart, Rose, and Hazel gathered on the porch to bid them goodbye, the two living guests averting eye contact with the giant arachnids.

"Good luck, kid," Hazel called out.

"Yes, good luck, dear! We'll be ready for you!" Winifred added.

Rose dabbed her running eye makeup. "I'm so proud of you!"

"Thanks! We'll be back!" Pippi called back. She looked down at Esmeralda, who was looking deeply into the glassy eyes of the spider. "You coming?"

Esmeralda grinned from ear to ear. "May I?"

"Get in," Pippi motioned behind her.

With one last look back, Pippi settled in for the ride. The gravel drive was completely unrecognizable, covered in thick snow and the same was expected of the ride into town, with the addition of down trees and black ice that breeds in the shadows that never see light. In the distance, Pippi could hear the faint hum of Chopper's helicopter circling town.

Pippi turned to Cecil. "Ready to go?"

Apparently, all the spiders heard was *go* because a breath later they were off, careening down the hill at breakneck speed with complete disregard for where the driveway lay buried beneath the snow. Pippi's own squeal mixed with Cecil's curses to hold onto the reins and Esmeralda's wild howls behind her. Pippi held on for dear life and her teeth chattered together as they bump, bump, bumped down the hill, the train of other carriages following as the lead spider dove headfirst, channeling the exhilarating freedom of a horse released to run free.

In what seemed only a few moments, the train of carriages broke through the trees and entered the hibernating town of Windia, the roads impassable and scattered with a few abandoned cars that found out the hard way. They whooshed by a few townsfolk trudging through the snow on foot towards the meeting place, some of whom screamed at the sight of spider-drawn carriages, but for the most part just stared and pointed. Overhead, Chopper's helicopter tracked their journey through town.

"Four Corners Square! We've got to point them to Four Corners Square!" Pippi shouted to Cecil.

"Don't tell me! Tell them!" Cecil shouted back, his hands straining to hold onto the reins he'd wrapped around his forearms in an attempt not to drop them.

"Hey!" Pippi cupped her hands around her mouth. "Hey! Four Corners Square! Four Corners Square, please!"

The spider skidded to a stop, pushing back at the carriage wheels that spun behind them. Cecil grabbed Pippi by the overall straps to keep her from flying off the carriage. With perfect precision their carriage creaked to a gentle stop right in front of Four Corners Square, where the townsfolk of Windia had dutifully gathered for their evacuation and now stood and stared with shocked expressions.

Pippi stood up, stepping over Cecil, trying to find her land legs after the death-defying trip. She offered a little wave to the silent group.

"Hi!" she greeted. "We're here to rescue you!"

Mabel stepped forward, bundled from head to toe, her nose bright red from the relentless cold. She shaded her eyes. "Pippi? From the inn?" she called out. "Is that you?"

"It's me!" Pippi called back. "I've got the inn all ready for you. We have power, food, hot water...you name it."

Mabel raised a gloved hand and pointed at the carriages, which, to her credit, was not shaking. "On...those?"

"Yes," Pippi nodded. "On these."

The town immediately folded together to discuss. Pippi couldn't hear what they were saying but she had a good idea what it was about. Giant spiders, a haunted inn, and a new girl in town who they barely knew asking to take men, women, and children off into the woods. Chopper hovered overhead, undoubtedly waiting to see how this would play out.

Mabel, now the unofficial spokesperson for the near-frozen group, stepped up again. Pippi held her breath. To her surprise, Mabel had tears in her eyes.

"Pippi," she choked. "We're so glad you came for us. Can you take the kids and older folks first?"

Pippi exhaled her held breath in a billowy cloud. "Yes!" she exclaimed, clamoring down from the carriage. "Yes, get in!"

The first train of carriages filled up quickly with stiff elderly and upset kids who stopped crying once they were on the living amusement ride and presented with a hand warmer and blanket. Cecil led the expedition back with Esmeralda taking on a rescued resident liaison role, while Pippi stayed behind, but not before giving the head spider a strict talking-to about taking the trip back easier. Chopper flew off to rescue the townsfolk who couldn't make it to Four Corners Square as the carriage train took load after load of near-frozen residents to the warm inn. As Pippi watched more and more people leave across the snow towards her inn, she imagined it bursting at the seams, the new guests sleeping on the staircase or on the floor of her bedroom. It had to work. It would work, somehow.

Pippi and Mabel were in the last group to leave, just as evening darkness was stretching its clutches through town. Pippi felt frozen through just in her few hours out in the cold, her heart breaking that she hadn't taken action sooner. The spiders were significantly less spry with each trip back and forth, and by the time Pippi and Mabel climbed into the last carriage, the spiders moved at a relaxed jaunt. They left Windia to sleep, watched over by the sea like a knight protecting a princess trapped in a cursed slumber.

Finally safe and sound, Mabel closed her eyes and sat in exhausted silence on the ride to the inn, sipping on her second cup of hot coffee, which was just one of the warm treats that the inn had been sending back for the residents waiting their turn in the cold. Pippi watched Windia fade into a cloud of snow as the carriage bumped down the deserted highway, the darkness chasing them along the way but unable to keep up. The carriage slowed to a crawl as the spider turned up the drive to the inn, where previous carriages had worn a substantial divet in the snow. They labored up the hill quietly until slowly Pippi heard sounds. A hubbub of music, laughs, and warm voices filtered through the otherwise silent forest. Pippi craned her neck to see what was going on.

"Oh my," Mabel whispered, lowering her coffee in awe.

Pippi covered her mouth as the inn finally came into view. It had tripled in size all around, lit up like a lighthouse lamp amidst a sea of stark snow. The whole building shone like a solar flare, near-blinding as the Christmas lights slowly crept like blackberry vines to reach the expanded reaches of the inn. Cecil and Mo worked on releasing the spiders from their carriages, who promptly scurried up the six floors to where the attic was now located. Figures passed by the windows, where residents settled into their warm rooms. Esmeralda walked around outside, offering a welcome and carrying a tray of hot toddies and gooey cookies to residents sitting around blazing fire pits. Hazel, wrapped in a scarf, went from resident to resident followed by Rose carrying a clipboard and Winifred carrying Emberheart, recording names or warming hands. A side building seemed dedicated as a children's area, complete with an indoor gymnasium and swing set on which Pippi could make out the exhilarated, pink faces of the children of Windia playing to their heart's content. But nothing made Pippi happier than seeing her guests step up to comfort the living, offering a pat on the back, a hug, or leading a confused family inside. When her carriage finally pulled to a stop, Pippi needed an extra moment to soak it all in before disembarking.

Cecil unleashed the last spider for a well-deserved break, its stealthy figure unidentifiable in the full-on darkness, even when wearing a Christmas sweater. Cecil leaned over the side of the carriage and looked at Pippi.

"Quite the sight, huh?" he remarked, wiping off his glasses.

"I thought I was past saying I can't believe it but..." Pippi shook her head.

A loud bell rang.

"Dinner, my loves!" Esmeralda hollered. "Please join us inside!"

A stampede of hungry Windians lined up inside politely even though their stomachs were ravenous for a warm meal.

"Shall we?" Cecil extended his hand to Pippi.

Pippi accepted his hand, a hand that never lost the cold dampness that were Cecil's last moments of life. She stepped down from the carriage and held onto his hand longer.

"What is it?" he asked.

"I'm afraid to go inside," she whispered.

"Why?"

"Because, then I'll see what I've done."

"You mean all the lives you saved?"

"What if this is the last night?" she said, her voice barely above a breath. "The last dinner. The last midnight tea."

Cecil looked at the inn, perhaps also just realizing the gravity of what they've done.

"And you," Pippi choked. "Maybe this screwed up any chance we had to-"

Cecil shook his head and wiped the tears from her face. He looked both so real and very unreal beneath the glare of the Christmas lights.

"Bigger than you and me, remember?" he consoled, tears gathering in his own eyes as he studied Pippi's face, as though recording every detail to remember for eternity. "Which right now, seems hard to imagine."

Pippi buried her face in Cecil's chest, desperately missing the warm heartbeat she used to find there. Tomorrow was her chance to get it back, Cecil's sleeping body waiting for its fate, lost in time in the arms of the tundra.

"Pippi." Hazel sat on the top porch step. "The inn is waiting for you to come to dinner."

The bell ran again, deeper and louder, to get Pippi's attention just as the sound of Chopper's helicopter cut through the evening air.

The aircraft sailed towards the inn like a falling star and Pippi and Cecil ran onto the porch so Chopper could land on the driveway. The helicopter blades slowly whirred to a stop and Chopper jumped out, his face completely bundled in a thick scarf. He removed his gloves and slid open the helicopter door with a big swing, as twenty or so chickens spilled out and scrambled onto the porch, immediately pecking and scratching at fallen cookie crumbs.

Chopper pulled down his scarf and big puffs of hot air billowed in front of his face. "I couldn't convince those old folks to leave unless I came back for their chickens," he shouted, as though the helicopter engine was still running.

"Very kind of you," Hazel said. "Old Herman would be proud."

Chopper looked around. "Who said that?"

"I guess you might as well know before you come inside," Pippi said. "My name is Pippi. And this is Hazel."

Hazel flicked her tail. Chopper looked down at the fox and shrugged. "Yeah, so? You also got spider horses. So what? Got some grub around here?"

"After you," Pippi offered.

Pippi followed Chopper inside, trying to ignore the pile of new guest paperwork covering the reception desk. She looked up at the new spiral staircase that reached six stories high and walked down the hallway to the dining room, peeking her head inside before fully entering. The dining room had also tripled in size, along with the table, the chairs, the big windows that lined the walls, and the glittering chandeliers that were now lowered for relaxed ambiance. The guests, a mix of the living and the spirit variety, patiently snacked on rolls as they waited for the proprietress.

As Pippi took her seat, followed closely by Cecil, she felt all eyes on her. The inn took that as its cue to roll out the food carts, which immediately commanded the guests' attention. Butternut squash soup, Beef Wellington, loaded baked potatoes, and roasted asparagus plopped in front of guest after guest, with a few hotdog and macaroni and cheeses thrown in for the kids or the picky adult eaters. But Pippi couldn't focus on her food, or Cecil's playful banter with her aunt, cousin, and mother seated beside them, or even Esmeralda's voice, who treated them all to a dreamy rendition of *Have Yourself a Merry Little Christmas*. All Pippi saw were the faces around the table with warm cheeks and dry clothes, shoulders relaxed, finding comfort in her inn. The spirit guests were so enthralled with their new counterparts, it was hard to tell the difference between the living and the dead. And as she looked from person to person, Pippi's heart ached a little bit more each time, understanding that this was her last time, for all of time.

Then she heard a jingle in the distance, like a small bell hitting the hardwood floors. The guests were too consumed with finishing their meal to notice Pippi get up and leave the table, following the sound as if in a dream. She entered the hallway and was met with the smell of fir dripping with fresh sap, bitter and sweet and sticky. A giant fir tree, as tall as the now six-story inn, stood grandly in the entryway, stretching up to the rooftop, rising through the center of the spiral staircase, as if the stairs themselves were a ribbon on the tree.

Pippi placed her hand on the tree bark, running her fingers over the bubbles of golden sap. A bell fell from the ceiling, causing her to look up, to where the spiders were precariously bringing down the boxes of Christmas tree decorations.

"A Christmas tree!" a young voice shouted behind her.

Pippi turned to find a girl with a macaroni-and-cheese-stained face looking at the tree with wide eyes.

"The biggest Christmas tree *ever!*" she squealed, quickly drawing the attention of the other children in the dining room, which in turn drew the attention of all the parents.

Suddenly, Pippi found herself surrounded by a stampede of excited guests, carefully accepting the totes of decorations from the spiders, who sprung back up to the attic for more totes thanks to their spongy webs. Pippi opened the totes and handed out ornaments of lighthouses and foxes, of gnomes and disco balls, of gluten-free flags and tea carts, of old cameras and stained glass doors, of question-mark rain boots and sea thrones, of smoldering burn piles and linen overalls, of witchy coffee cups and Christmas snow globes, of handbooks and log books, of cell phones and old rotary phones, of suitcases and spirits, and finally, of a key to the inn with her name on it.

Chapter Twenty-Five

Pippi heard the train whistle first, clear and crisp in the still air. The snow silenced everything; every creature, every tree, hibernating until they felt the warmth of the sun again. Beside her, the spider tramped tiny boot marks in the snow, kicking the occasional spray of snow in Pippi's direction in an attempt to lighten the mood. But Pippi wasn't there to play in the snow. She stared down the railroad tracks, unblinking, willing the train to appear, carrying the subjects she'd put on battle armor to face. Or, in her case, corduroy overalls with a Santa Claus print.

"Steady," she told the spider, who had happily volunteered for carriage duty again. They stood at the abandoned Windia train depot, at 9:00 am sharp, to pick up the inspection team from E. A.R.T.H. as they disembarked from Quietus Limited, a train that Pippi could not find on any railroad schedule or internet search, a phantom train, unseen and unheard to everyone else except Pippi and her spider.

The morning notification on her phone advised the arrival time of the inspection team, announcing they'd leave the train station by rental car. Knowing the impossible state of the roads, even worse than the night before, Pippi had a heartbeat of a thought that she'd leave them there, stuck at the train depot, unable to even get their rental car out of the parking lot. Or even *get* a rental car from the abandoned rental company, whose employees were mid-breakfast by now back at her inn.

But maybe these logistics didn't matter to an Ethereal Accommodations for Restful Travel and Hospitality inspection team. Maybe they'd float the whole way there or scorch the earth dry with a single look. So Pippi decided to face the beast head on and carriage ride out to meet them. Maybe it was Pippi's new role as the town rescuer that caused her to do this, or maybe it was the fear of making an even worse first impression by knowingly abandoning them in the ice and snow, or maybe it was just that Pippi couldn't stand waiting one more moment to find out the future for her inn.

"Excuse me, dear innkeeper?" Emberheart's little voice called from inside the carriage. He had bravely offered (and Winifred reluctantly surrendered him) to join Pippi on the trip to the train depot, hoping to put the inspectors in a good mood with his bracing heat.

"Yes, Emberheart?"

"Shall I speak to them when they arrive? I found I've set a few of the new guests spinning when I asked them if they needed my services," Emberheart asked, his voice breaking a bit.

"Why don't you let me handle them?" Pippi suggested, finding that Winifred's sweet countenance was best suited for Emberheart's easily-bruised feelings.

"Very good, very good," Emberheart agreed.

The train popped into existence, rattling down the tracks at breakneck speed, causing the startled spider to curl into a ball, buried under the layers of its fleece Christmas sweater. With a blast of cool steam, the Quietus Limited hissed to a shrill stop at the depot landing, towing a long line of sleek passenger cars with frosted windows. The door on the first passenger car opened and a roll of carpeted stairs unfurled, collapsing to the ground. John, wearing a dapper suit, appeared in the doorway and descended the stairs, shielding his eyes from the blinding reflection off the snow.

His gaze settled on Pippi and her spider-drawn carriage. "Pippi?"

She offered a small wave. "Morning."

Another face stepped into the light, a woman wearing a gray dress suit and matching pillbox hat, her short dark hair curled and tucked neatly beneath. She didn't hesitate a beat to descend the stairs, ignoring John's outstretched hand. One more man appeared afterwards, the door shutting closed and locking behind him. He was a tall, unremarkable figure dressed in a suit similar to John's, carrying a thick book and a crossbody bag he readjusted every thirty seconds. With the disembarked passengers safely on the ground, the carpeted stairs retracted and the train was off in a heartbeat, leaving behind only the echo of a whistle and the smell of red hot steel.

With the train gone, the spider unfurled to full height. Only John seemed concerned, the woman seemed more concerned about the delicate reapplication of her droll red lipstick.

Pippi stepped forward and recited the greeting she'd prepared. "Hello, I'm Pippi Jennings, the proprietress of the Windia Inn. Thank you for coming today and allowing me the opportunity to set the record straight."

The inspection team stared at Pippi blankly.

"Uh," Pippi continued. "We've had a catastrophic storm over the last few days. The roads are impassable so I thought I'd escort you to the inn." She stepped back and motioned to the carriage as the spider curtsied.

With lipstick successfully reapplied, the woman pulled on her gray silk gloves and motioned to the crossbody bag man to follow. She stepped up to Pippi and extended a gloved hand.

"Pleased to meet you, Ms. Jennings. Thank you for meeting us. I'm Mrs. Ball, this is Mr. Hector and Mr. Graham. We're ready when you are." Mrs. Ball looked back at Mr. Hector. She arched her eyebrows and looked down at his notebook, prompting Mr. Hector to click his pen and open his book. She looked back at Pippi. "Don't be alarmed. Just some note taking for prosperity sake."

Pippi offered her hand. "Please do."

Mrs. Ball smirked and accepted Pippi's help into the carriage, Mr. Hector following closely behind. Pippi climbed up into the driver seat, ignoring John as he delicately climbed the rickety stairs and collapsed into his seat.

"There's blankets and a thermos of hot coffee for you," Pippi explained, motioning to the basket that Cecil had helped pack before she left.

Emberheart looked at Pippi expectantly from the floor of the carriage.

"And, of course, our resident heating specialist, Emberheart, came to make your journey as comfortable as possible," Pippi added with a wink.

Emberheart literally glowed and shifted into high heat. Mrs. Ball nodded and motioned for Mr. Hector to make note. The spider, who had been heavily coached on taking the ride *easy*, set off at a brisk but controlled pace, expertly gliding down the hill from the depot to the main highway that led through and out of town. They passed darkened building after abandoned car after powerless streetlight, the ocean waves and creaking carriage wheels creating the only sounds in town.

"Ms. Jennings." Mrs. Ball leaned forward in her seat past Mr. Hector, who was attempting to pour bouncing coffee into a travel mug with Emberheart's calming encouragements. "I was under the impression that Windia was occupied by the living. If you'll pardon my pun, this is a ghost town."

Mrs. Ball looked pointedly at Mr. Hector and John, who responded with forced chuckles.

"Yes, about that." Pippi gripped the reins a little harder. "You see-"

But the spider, already a bit on edge and, of course, jumpy by nature, took the increase in pressure on the reins as a signal to increase the speed and they were off, spinning across the ice, careening up the hill towards the inn, bumpier than ever before as the spider made the split-second decision to explore a new route home. Emberheart flew into Pippi's lap and she held on literally for both their dear lives while the inspection team howled and rolled into each other until the spider finally came to a sliding stop at the inn's doorstep, heaving and shivering with the spider equivalent of adrenaline. Pippi, who had released the reins long ago to keep a good hold on Emberheart and the handrails, looked up to find Cecil and Hazel on the front porch, frozen and aghast, with dozens of other faces watching through the windows, all equally frozen and aghast.

Mrs. Ball raised her head from the floor of the carriage, where she and her companions had collapsed into a heap. Pippi dropped to the ground, her head spinning as she handed Emberheart off to a distressed Winifred. Cecil ran up to release the quivering spider, who flashed up the side of the inn like a giant floating ink dot, eager to tell the others about the successful trip.

Just keep going. "Welcome to the inn," Pippi announced breathlessly, as though the whole trip back from the train station had gone exactly to plan. "If you'll join me, I'll show you around."

"Yes. Of course." Similarly unwilling to appear shaken, Mrs. Ball straightened her jacket as she climbed down from the carriage, taking a triple-take up at the sheer height of the inn in its current state. She righted her hat and snapped for Mr. Hector.

Mr. Hector unfurled his gangly limbs and joined Mrs. Ball. John descended last, pointedly avoiding eye contact with Cecil, who had joined Hazel back on the porch steps.

Pippi led the inspection party around the side of the inn, recently cleared of snow to allow easier access to the children's play building, which was currently hosting a boisterous trampoline dance party.

"Over here, we have our children's area to keep the littles busy," Pippi announced, trying to control the audible tremble in her voice.

"So many children," Mrs. Ball remarked, glaring over at Mr. Hector, who responded with a click of his pen.

Pippi stopped. She turned to face Mrs. Ball with the most confident expression she could muster and hoped it was convincing enough. "Yes. Those are the kids from Windia. I'm hosting the town here until the storm is over."

"Hosting the living?" Mrs. Ball clarified, expressionless.

Just keep going. "Yes. The living."

Mrs. Ball looked up again at the impressive six floor height of the inn with new eyes. She glanced at Mr. Hector, who looked at Pippi with a concerned scowl. John visibly wrung his hands and looked behind him.

"Continuing on," Pippi said loudly, motioning for the group to follow. "It's not much in the snow, but we have a large green back here for activities, and another new addition to our backyard with the chateau."

Winifred stood in the doorway of the backyard chateau. Emberheart, who appeared to have recovered from the carriage ride, sat on a table and warmed a tray of cookies while Winifred offered the group glasses of cold milk. John and Mr. Hector immediately stepped up for the offered snack while Mrs. Ball studied the chateau with arms crossed.

"Welcome," Winifred beamed. "Pleased to make your acquaintance."

"Yes." Mrs. Ball limply shook Winifred's hand. "And you are…?"

"My cousin," Pippi said.

Mrs. Ball leaned in. "And she is…?"

"Living," Pippi replied. "My cousin and mother are staying here."

"This was constructed for them?"

Pippi shuffled her feet. *Just keep going.* "Actually, it was for my boyfriend. When he was alive."

Mrs. Ball looked at John pointedly. "Yes. No need to fill me in there."

After John and Mr. Hector finished their snack (Mrs. Ball declined) Pippi led the inspection party to the kitchen entrance she'd asked the inn to provide when they walked through the rehearsal for this event. As she'd planned, they arrived right in the middle of lunch preparations as the inn plated turkey and cranberry sandwich after turkey and cranberry sandwich with a few smaller plates of chicken nuggets and macaroni and cheese for the picky crowd again.

"This is our kitchen," Pippi motioned around the large room as the inspection party dodged flying loaves of bread and whole roasted turkeys dripping juice across the tiled floors on the way to be deboned. Pippi walked through the kitchen confidently, expertly dodging a floured rolling pin.

"We successfully serve breakfast, lunch, dinner, and dessert, including midnight tea, for our guests here, accommodating any and all food allergies. Our usual patron count is approximately twenty guests, but at the moment, we're around 890."

Mrs. Ball appeared speechless, ducking behind Mr. Hector and tapping on his notebook to record various details she pointed out. The inn opted to leave Mrs. Ball and Mr. Hector alone, but John did not have the same fate, as the inn could apparently *not* forgive and forget, pelting him with wet dough and dribbled hot cranberry sauce on his nice shiny shoes.

John was the first one out the door as the group moved onto the dining room, where lunch service was in full swing. The living guests paid no particular attention to the group other than offering Pippi grateful smiles and hugs, but the spirit guests stopped eating to watch, lips pressed together in tight, thin lines. But as Pippi pointed out the table and the big windows, she thought she could hear them willing her on.

Rose stood suddenly from her lunch, her chair scraping loudly across the floor. Pippi watched as her mother rounded the table to meet the party, cursing under her breath at the deviation from the plan.

"Hello," Rose said loudly, quickly identifying the leader and offering her hand to Mrs. Ball. "I'm Rose, Pippi's mother."

Mrs. Ball considered Rose's hand before finally, limply, shaking it. "Hello."

"I just want to tell you that what my daughter is doing here is simply amazing," Rose huffed. "There's no other word for it. She saved hundreds of lives by bringing them here, and if you shut her down for something like that, well, that's just *wrong*." She looked at Pippi. "And I want you and Pippi to know she has my utmost support."

Pippi smiled and nodded at her mother's attempt to make things better. Mrs. Ball stopped Mr. Hector from note taking. "Thank you for your input," she sniffed.

The final stop on the tour was the front entry, where Pippi demonstrated her check-in process for both the living and the deceased, allowing Mrs. Ball to wordlessly look through her record-keeping, pointing out various figures to Mr. Hector. John continued to hang back, stealing occasional glances at Cecil, who remained on the porch with Hazel.

"My room is around the corner and the guest quarters are upstairs," Pippi explained. "But, in consideration of my guests' privacy, I won't be taking you up there. I'm sure you understand."

Mrs. Ball nodded, somewhat approvingly, Pippi ventured.

"And the portal?" she asked.

Drat. "Yes?"

"Where is your portal?" Mrs. Ball looked up from the phone inspection.

"Upstairs."

Mrs. Ball came to stand in front of Pippi, who was guarding the bottom of the stairs.

"Under lock and key?" Mrs. Ball pressed.

"It's very secure." *Between the oversized comforters and flannel sheets.*

"Show me."

"You've had your time. You can see the inn is in running order."

Mrs. Ball chuckled. "Yes. And full of the living. You can show me what you want, Ms. Jennings, but there are larger issues at play here." She looked at John, who lowered his eyes. "As brought up in Mr. Graham's report."

"Yes, about that. I'd like a chance to respond to my charges."

"This isn't a criminal investigation," Mrs. Ball blustered, straightening her jacket. "There are rules. You either follow them or you break them. Simple as that."

Pippi opened the front door and motioned for Cecil to enter. He joined the group in the entryway, Hazel slinking inside behind him and jumping up on the reception desk, right at eye (scratching) level with Mrs. Ball, who wrinkled her nose in response. Cecil stepped next to Pippi, staring at his father levelly.

"This is Cecil Graham. John Graham's son," Pippi introduced.

"Yes," Mrs. Ball sneered. "The ghost hunter."

"He died unfairly." Pippi told herself she wasn't going to get choked up. She'd rehearsed this part dozens, even hundreds, of times in her mind. Cecil slipped a hand on her shoulder and Pippi took a deep breath to continue on. "Even though he and I were involved in a relationship, I kept to my innkeeper's oath and protected Mr. Graham's identity, as he requested, even when I believed it was the wrong thing to do. And when Cecil found out, he left upset, and-"

"And got into an accident and died," Mrs. Ball finished. "As happens to many poor souls each and every day, since the beginning of time."

"But-"

"If you're about to ask us to bring your dead boyfriend back to life, you will take a highly irregular situation and made it even more irregular. Which I suggest you *don't* do," Mrs. Ball chided. She looked over at John, whose face was expressionless. "Again, sorry for your loss."

Time ticked by painfully slow as the room looked to Pippi for her response. Cecil's hand slipped from Pippi's shoulder. Hazel burned a hole through her niece with her spectacled gaze. John looked at the floor. Mr. Hector took notes. Mrs. Ball smirked and tapped her foot. As for Pippi herself, her racing heartbeat brought a rush of blood to her ears, drowning out the sounds of laughter in the dining room.

This was it. She couldn't have both. Maybe she could save the inn, convince Mrs. Ball that the Cecil situation got out of hand as a new innkeeper, and rescuing the people of Windia was a stupid mistake that would never happen again. She'd learned her lesson. She would play by the rules from now on. This was what the inn was waiting for. This was why she didn't have the key yet. She has to choose the inn above all else, just like Hazel did.

Just like Hazel did. Hazel, who'd been alone her whole life, lost her one true love, lost her niece and sister with only their memories to tend to on the beach. She had an inn of lonely guests, of spiders who could only come out at night, next to a town who feared what lay at the end of the long gravel road up the hill, who never wrote her own page in the *Handbook for Housekeeping*.

But Pippi had.

"I'm not asking," Pippi announced and suddenly the rushing in her ears pounded like a rhythmic drum. "Cecil Graham was a guest at my inn and he was wronged. I want it fixed by tomorrow morning. And I want to speak to your supervisor, Mrs. Ball, about what steps need to be taken to correct errors in E.A.R.T.H.'s policies."

Mrs. Ball's eyes widened a bit but she masked it with a deep laugh. "My, big words for a little innkeeper. Unfortunately, my supervisor is out on another inspection."

"Yes, and it has been simply *lovely*."

All eyes turned as Esmeralda descended the stairs, dressed in a floor-length emerald green satin gown with an exaggerated train that trailed behind her like a silky waterfall. Her long fingers were painted with a deep scarlet red nail polish, one hand wrapped around a martini glass and the other holding a leather briefcase. Mrs. Ball and Mr. Hector stood at attention, their faces noticeably paler, jaws slack, as Esmeralda joined the group, winking at Pippi and Cecil as she walked by.

"Lilith," Esmeralda greeted Mrs. Ball, shoving her empty martini glass in her face. "Take care of this, will you?"

"Certainly," Mrs. Ball mumbled.

"Donnie." Esmeralda inspected Mr. Hector, who visibly quivered. She shoved her briefcase into his chest. "Hold this, please? An put away that silly notebook."

Next, she turned to John. He held his head down, hands clasped together.

"And, as for you..." Esmeralda growled.

John looked up, eyes wide. Then burst out laughing.

"I'm sorry," he gasped between laughs. "I couldn't keep it up!"

Esmeralda embraced John and they rocked back and forth as they exchanged pleasantries, oblivious to the rest of the room. *It's been too long! You look fab! Dearest, you're the best. Oh stop, no, you're the best! I can't thank you enough. No, darling, I can't thank you enough, this has been wonderful for my old bones. Bones! Haha! Oh, I made a funny! I didn't mean to! Ha! You haven't changed. I love you for it. Dearest, you're my champion, don't you ever change.*

Finally, the two apparent friends came up for air, turning to the rest of the room, who had been watching their exchange, frozen in place.

"My son?" John said, motioning at Cecil and beaming. "What did I tell you?"

"Just as brilliant as you said he'd be," Esmeralda sighed, approaching Cecil and wrapping her arm around his stiff shoulders. "If anything, you held back!"

"What's going on?" Cecil asked.

"Son, I'm sorry." John approached Cecil, his face sober. "I truly am. I went about it all wrong before, with you and me. But when you died, I knew I had to right this all. I could at least do that for you."

John turned to Pippi. "I had to make the report to get the attention of E.A.R.T.H. We need official channels here, and they are the only ones who can fix this."

"And then sweetheart Johnnie went straight to the top," Esmeralda grinned, fluffing her hair.

"Yes, I called in a favor," John admitted, causing Mrs. Ball's eyes to flash as she pressed her lips together to keep the words back. "Esmeralda and I go way, way back."

"Don't date me too much, dear," Esmeralda warned cheerily. "And besides, darling, you've done me the favor. Pippi, this inn..." She placed her hand over her heart. "When you saved the town? I thought I would shed a tear, I really did, John, I'm serious."

"Can you bring Cecil back?" Pippi ventured.

"Well, it's a bit more complicated than that." Esmeralda tapped a long finger on her perfectly-powdered chin. "Donnie, briefcase."

Mr. Hector fumbled with the briefcase for a few painful seconds before finally popping it open. Esmeralda pulled out a one page document and held it in the air.

"Cecil, dearest," she cooed. "You've impressed me, young man. Not only with your gentlemanly manners and admittedly rakish good looks, but truly it's the way your mind works that has captivated me. Listening to your ideas, your inner workings, and that gadget you mentioned?"

"The Hyper Sonic Blaster," Cecil interrupted.

"Yes, darling, that thing," Esmeralda patted Cecil on the head. "Now, while ghost hunters are not typically our ideal candidates..."

Mrs. Ball choked on a swallowed comment.

"It is, however, undeniable that your experience gives you a unique perspective on our world. An advantage, even, as you understand the worlds of both the living and the dead. Do you remember our conversation about the phone?"

"Yes," Cecil replied, clearly unsure if this was going in a good direction. "Also, remember, I'm a ghost *explorer*."

"Ooopsie, that's right. Well, ghost explorers wouldn't have that weapon, now would they, dearest? Yes, yes, best to leave that alone for now, hm? Now, the phones." Esmeralda floated over to the old rotary phone and picked up the receiver, on which, of course, there was no dial tone. "Share with the group what you said, will you?"

"Just that it's a shame the guests can't talk back," Cecil shrugged. "Seems like it could make it better." He looked at Pippi. "For everyone."

"Yes! Yes!" Esmeralda replaced the receiver gently back on the hook. "And?"

"And I had a few ideas how to make it happen," Cecil continued with a shrug.

"Yes, that's it! *Ideas!* Beautiful, brilliant ideas! All in that handsome, kissable head." Esmeralda took a breath and offered the official-looking document to Cecil. "That's why I'd love to offer you the job of Mr. Phone Updater for All the Inns."

"That's not a real position!" Mrs. Ball finally blurted out.

Esmeralda shot Mrs. Ball a withering look. "It's a working title, Lilith," she seethed. She flipped the switch back to sweet as she turned back to Cecil. "But I believe this enterprising young man is just what we need to start the job off right."

Cecil stared at the contract, his hands clearly shaking. John came next to his son, offering a supportive hand on the shoulder.

"It's all right, son. I've looked it over," he assured.

"Why should I trust you?" Cecil whispered, clearly fighting back tears.

"Because we have to start somewhere. And I hope this is the first step in earning you back," John said, fighting back his own tears.

"Oh," Esmeralda interjected, sidling up to Pippi. "And because this job will require Cecil's presence in the living world, we will, of course, be restoring Cecil's life."

Mrs. Ball audibly blanched.

Cecil looked at Pippi. "But what about Pippi?" He turned back to Esmeralda. "What happens to her and the inn?"

"Oh!" Esmeralda clasped her hands together. "How I love *love*. This is the future, John, it really is."

"It is. It really is," John agreed.

Esmeralda folded her hands together more seriously. "But Pippi, it's true, you went against E.A.R.T.H. policy when you brought the living here, and no doubt, other policies that we don't even know about. So, unfortunately, I will have to place a sanction on you."

The room fell quiet other than Mrs. Ball, who cleared her throat triumphantly. It was then that the group realized the dining room had emptied out, the hallway crammed with guests who were silently watching the whole scene play out.

Pippi took a breath and braced herself.

"So from here on out," Esmeralda said firmly. "You are *required* to keep doing exactly what you've been doing. You're not going anywhere."

The inn erupted in sound, from the cheering guests, to the pots and pans clanging in the kitchen, to the spiders stomping and jumping in the attic (discussing if it was a good moment to come downstairs,) to Cecil, who wrapped Pippi in an embrace and gave her the first ghost kiss she'd ever received. Pippi wiped the tears from her face, looking through the congratulatory crowd for her aunt, who was nowhere to be seen.

"Oh my goodness, the jubilee!" Esmeralda called out breathlessly.

She handed Cecil a pen, who in turn signed his name on the dotted line, inciting another wave of cheers and this time a kiss from Pippi, who'd just discovered that ghost kisses were not that bad, after all.

The celebration continued on through the day, now that the tension and anticipation were gone, sprinkling like salt on the packed snow and ice outside, melting it slowly hour by hour, until afternoon came and the gravel road was once again visible, pebbles poking out like the first flowers of spring. Excited conversations over dinner revolved around going home for Christmas, to not only their own beds (although Pippi's had been extraordinary) but also to their Christmas presents waiting under the tree. *If there was visible ground, then maybe the line workers could restore power quicker*, they all said. The inn played *I'll be Home for Christmas* as the guests went to bed to dream of the familiar sounds of their own homes.

Pippi was outside on the porch when the lights in Windia flashed back to life. Tomorrow morning would be a mad dash to return the living to their homes, maybe with cinnamon rolls to go and a present from Santa, if he chose to stop at the inn now that the spirit guests had collectively decided to skip midnight tea for fear of discouraging Saint Nicholas.

But tonight was for thinking. For working out the new pathways Pippi hadn't considered. Esmeralda and the rest of the E.A.R.T.H. group returned to their respective homes after the morning announcement, promising to file Cecil's application that night so he woke up living in the morning. The spiders had already retrieved Cecil's body and were unthawing him in the attic before depositing him in Cecil's bedroom for the strange night of sleep Cecil had in front of him.

So tonight was for thinking and watching. Watching for the lights, watching for Hazel, who'd completely disappeared during the morning life-changing hubbub, as Pippi should expect by now from her fox aunt. *Was she proud? Angry? Disappointed? Relieved? Indifferent? Jealous?* Pippi just wanted to see her fox face, which she'd learned to read, even with the thick spectacles that obscured her expression.

The front door cracked open. It was Cecil.

"Just wanted to say goodnight," he whispered, even though the guests were tucked away upstairs and safely out of earshot. He looked past Pippi to Windia. "Oh. The power's back."

"It is. It'll be a busy morning," Pippi whispered back.

"Well, I'll be there to help," Cecil assured.

"Yes, you will," Pippi beamed. "Thanks for saying goodnight."

"Well, there was one more thing," he added, looking down at his hands. "I wanted to say, thank you for waiting for me."

Pippi stood and went to Cecil, wrapping them together in her blanket. They embraced but she knew he couldn't feel her warmth that tried to seep into his cold frame, like the sun trying to penetrate through layers of soil to reach the unreachable earth's core.

"I would wait forever for someone like you," Pippi whispered before they kissed for the last time as a spirit and a living person.

Pippi decided to come inside with Cecil, soundlessly waving him goodbye as he climbed the stairs to his room. She studied the stained glass, which simply depicted a rendering of the six story inn up the hill from the little town of Windia, which now had twinkling lights on in the windows of the little houses. She went to bed still wrapped in the blanket from outside that smelled of damp moss and her gingerbread-scented perfume. She fell into an exhausted slumber and dreamed of the deep woods slowly awakening from the snow, listening and watching for what changed while they were asleep.

Chapter Twenty-Six

Pippi's ears were well-trained to hear the telltale buzz of her cell phone alerting her to a new notification. She was halfway between waking and a dream about Santa plucking spiced gingerbread muffins from blooming poinsettias under the full moon as her arm instinctively reached over to her nightstand to retrieve her cell phone from the charger.

She forced open her blurry eyes to read the displayed message. *Guest at the front desk.*

Pippi slapped herself awake as she tied on her bathrobe. It was still a solid hour until daybreak and from the utter silence upstairs, she assumed everyone else was catching all the sleep they could get. But Pippi understood. Moving on was for the quiet moments and she'd found that the transition between night and dawn was a choice time for her departing guests.

When she rounded the corner into the dimly-lit entryway, the last person Pippi expected to see was Hazel back in her human form, standing straight on two feet, her reddish orange hair tinged with gray at her temples and pulled up into a messy bun, a pair of heeled clogs peeking out from under a hunter green velvet pantsuit. She had no suitcase, just a purse she tucked under her arm. Hazel looked over her shoulder as Pippi shuffled to the desk.

"Aunt Hazel?" Pippi marveled, looking up to meet her aunt's gaze atop her statuesque frame.

"Morning," Hazel said in the same voice used in fox form.

"What happened?"

Hazel shifted her weight. "I'm not sure."

Pippi recognized the start of the transition already. Hazel was beginning to move on, her eyes glazing over until she caught herself and shook it off. Her face looked gaunt and pallid, her knuckles stiff and curled. Pippi rushed to the computer and turned it on, blinking through the hot tears.

"I guess my job here is done," Hazel whispered.

"It is, Auntie," Pippi whispered back, allowing the tears to fall down her face and splatter on the keyboard. She located Hazel's reservation with the flashing red *check out* button, pulsing like a heartbeat.

"Pippi," Hazel ventured, visibly trying to stave off the impending haze. She reached her hands across the desk. "I'm so proud of you."

Pippi rounded the corner of the desk and threw her arms around her aunt, her face inches from Hazel's hair that smelled like the forest. Hazel weakly hugged her then pulled back to study her niece's face. Behind them, the front door unlatched and the two innkeepers looked towards the sound. Releasing her aunt, Pippi returned to her computer and with shaking hands clicked the *check out* button and the front door opened completely. Typically she'd stay behind the desk, head bowed in respect, eyes cast downward to allow the departing guest some privacy. But this time she rejoined her guest, tucking her arm around Hazel, walking with her to the door and towards the blinding, indistinguishable light beyond it that reverberated in her core.

Hazel stopped. Stepping away from Pippi, she reached into her purse and pulled out a slender white envelope.

Pippi accepted the envelope and opened it.

Dear Precious Grown-up Pippi,

I know you like to be called Pippi, so Pippi it shall be. I'll keep this short, because you have an inn to run.

Do you remember the sea throne? You might have been too young to remember, but we built a throne out of driftwood down on the beach on the Fourth of July. We spent all day working on it, just the two of us, we got so sunburned, your mother was furious. After dinner we waited for night and lit our sparklers and you told me they were like dying stars in your hands. That's when I knew.

I've gone down there every Fourth of July since and lit sparklers for us. It was like you were just around the corner. Don't forget you can return to memories if you need them.

The smartest thing I ever did was trust the inn to you. Remember some of the things I told you and forget (or forgive me) for the rest. Don't lose this key, it's the only copy.

Love,

Aunt Hazel

"It's yours," Hazel said. "The inn and I both agree."

Pippi held her breath as she reached into the envelope and felt the cool steel and rough edges. An otherwise plain key for an extraordinary place. *The key to the inn.*

"Thank you." Pippi pressed her fingers around the key hard and held it to her chest. "I'll take good care of it."

"Oh, I know," Hazel smiled, looking at Pippi one more time before stepping through the door and shutting it behind herself.

"It's been a pleasure having you with me," Pippi whispered. "Goodbye."

The stained glass went dark, leaving the entryway in flat silence. Pippi stood in that flat silence for a while, opening her hand to find the key's imprint marked into her skin. She turned and climbed the stairs to the second floor, crossing the thick carpet to Cecil's room. She turned the door handle and peeked inside. Cecil's lanky frame hung off the edge of this twin bed, fast asleep. She crossed the floor to stand next to his bed, dodging baseball trading cards and comic books. She watched the steady rise and fall of his chest, slow and deliberate with deep slumber. Finally, she crawled into bed next to him. Still asleep, he lifted his arm and tucked Pippi in beside him, where she fell asleep again, melting into his familiar warmth.

Chapter Twenty-Seven

"I think it turned out perfect, just as you requested."

Juniper passed a large package wrapped in brown parchment paper across the counter to Pippi. The Windia Mercantile was swarming with tourists visiting town for the unseasonably warm late February day and Pippi had waited a long time in line to pickup her special order.

"Wow, heavy," Pippi remarked, struggling beneath the weight of the package.

"Well, it should be," Juniper huffed. "That's the best cedar you can buy in the fifty states. Maybe even the world. That'll outlast you and your inn...well, maybe just you."

"Got it. Thank you, again," Pippi smiled, dodging tourists as she labored through the store, thanking a gracious customer who held the door for her.

She squinted into the blinding, cloudless light. This spring-like, sunny day was just a tease of what was to come but was still a proper three to four months away. But that didn't stop the residents (and visitors) of Windia from breaking out the sundresses and shorts, snapping photos on the beach with lens flare and hair in their face, smiles upturned to the brilliant sun and soaking in every second to get them through the upcoming rainy gloom forecasted for tomorrow. So just for today, it was spring (maybe even early summer) until nightfall and absolutely no one could convince them otherwise.

The warmer day had encouraged the daffodils to pop above ground seemingly overnight, the first flowers of winter, brave enough to withstand heavy rain and a surprise March snowstorm, bracing against the chill in their yellow raincoats, urging everyone to carry on, *spring really was just around the corner.* It was these daffodils that a half dozen children of Windia were using to tickle the spider that had escorted Pippi to town, as spider-drawn carriage was now her preferred (and environmentally friendly) mode of transportation. The spider in question jumped up and down playfully with the children, creating the occasional glistening web bracelet or set of rings upon request. Tourists watched, mouths agape, from across the street, usually until a Windia resident approached and patted them on the back, explaining the whole situation.

In fact, the spiders had become a regular sight in town, especially after the devastation left from the snow and ice storm. They proved excellent at hauling debris, roof repairs, righting fallen trees, and a plethora of other odd jobs the spiders literally leapt at the chance to do. They were also heavily involved with a downtown revitalization project spearheaded by Mabel, who the spiders had become very attached to, especially since she treated them with candy canes after a day of work.

The spiders were not the only visitors from the inn to grace Windia. Bolstered by the Christmas snowstorm experience, a comfortability had been established between both the living and the spirit guests, who felt safe visiting the place they once considered off limits. As a result, the Windia townsfolk occasionally stop by the inn for breakfast while the spirit guests enjoy trips out shopping *like the good old days* in downtown Windia. (Although they never purchase anything, it's just for the experience.) It was a new sort of relationship between the two groups, comrades from different worlds, both offering a comforting glimpse of what was and what was to come.

On that day, Pippi had invited two new guests to join her on the trip to Windia. She hoisted the heavy package into the carriage and dusted her hands off on her overall shorts. The inn had obviously not wanted Pippi to miss out on the experience of wearing summer clothes like everyone else, also offering her flip flops and short sleeved tee. She climbed up into the carriage to look out for her two guests, beginning to wonder if she'd made a mistake by letting them wander town alone for the first time.

But when Pippi spotted them walking up the hill with two large coffees and even larger smiles, she knew she'd made the right decision. Florence and her tall, dark, and handsome beau Samson walked with the guests, likely showing them the way back to Four Corners Square, where Pippi always parked the carriage.

Florence extended an oversized coffee to Pippi as they approached. "Salted Sea Mussel Macchiato," she explained, hands on her hips. "You *have* to like this."

Pippi took a tiny sip, immediately puckering her lips. "Sorry."

Florence shook her head. "How? *How* can you not like coffee? I've never heard of this."

"Just admit defeat, Flo. Next time just make her a chai," Samson laughed. He'd brought a bowl of whipped cream for the spider, who consumed it in one breathy slurp.

"You're missing out!" Tellie sighed, taking a long drink from her own coffee. Barely five feet tall with long black hair that almost reached her ankles, Tellie was one of the new guests, transferred in from Cape Town where she'd only been for a day or two. The fact that Tellie had stuck around for a week so far gave Pippi hope she was doing something right for her.

Tellie stared at the plastic lid, her eyes drifting off to another place. "I used to have coffee every morning with the crossword. I'd never finish it in time for work, though."

Florence picked up on the shift and hooked her arm through Tellie's. "Well, then you'll have to come by every morning! I'll save the Windia Bee crossword for you."

Tellie brightened. "Yes. Okay, I'll do that. Thanks!"

She climbed into the carriage next to Pippi and returned her focus to the coffee in hand. The other guest on the excursion, a senior man named Clive, was just as preoccupied as Samson was with the spider, who stared back at them, naturally a little wary of men after being employed by powerful women for centuries.

"Simply extraordinary." Clive shook his head and adjusted his straw hat, which in his past life he'd always worn to protect his fragile, paper-thin skin. He was the only one in the party dressed in pants and long-sleeved shirt for the excursion.

Clive was new, very new, to the inn, checking in only a day or two past his birthday. Pippi and the inn had just enough time to transform midnight tea into a lively birthday party the night of his arrival, which turned out to be just what the temporarily-introverted Clive needed to forget where he'd been not so long before.

"Thank you, young man, I greatly enjoyed our exchange." Clive shook Samson's hand enthusiastically before climbing into the carriage. "Wonderful chap!"

"I enjoyed it. Anytime!" Samson replied, wrapping his arm around Florence's waist as they waved goodbye to the spider-drawn carriage.

Every ride back to the inn became a little more polished as the spiders discovered the best route home, which seemed to be determined by the weather for the day. That afternoon's weather called for a trip up the drive in normal fashion, as though they were in a regular car following the navigation system's instructions. Pippi barely had to hold the reins anymore, if anything, it was just for show to instill confidence in her passengers. But something about today made Pippi hold on tight. Maybe it was the precious cargo. Maybe it was the familiar drive. Or maybe it was the day's promise of spring, the yellow daffodils swaying in the wind, reminding her how fast time passes and not a single moment should be taken for granted.

At the inn, which had shrunk back to its more manageable two stories, the guests were taking full advantage of the sunshine just like everyone else back in Windia; a few played croquet and badminton, some simply lounged in the sun, while others decided to help Pippi out by pulling the occasional weed. There was a decent group gathered outside the newly-constructed greenhouse, where the guests tended to seed starts for the first garden at the inn for a long time. The guests had voted for a greenhouse and garden over an indoor pool (there was an ocean and a ghost kraken lifeguard nearby, after all) and Pippi understood why when she saw her guests' faces light up at the new life cradled in their hands.

But most of the guests were interested in playing with the spirit guests that were part of the new program recently adopted at Pippi's inn. Furever Pets came about when Pippi noted that the guests sorely missed the animal companionship provided by fox Hazel, whether that be playtime or contemplative cuddles. After a quick phone call to Esmeralda, Pippi's inn opted into the Furever Pets program for spirit pets transitioning from life to moving on. There were some kinks in the program, starting with the obvious communication barrier, but Pippi quickly found out the spiders understood (most) animal speak, translating the wants and wishes of the new animal guests into (literal) sticky notes. It wasn't pretty or smooth but it worked, and until her new Furever Pets headset came in the mail, Pippi just held the phone up to whichever floppy ear needed it.

As the carriage pulled to a stop, Pippi's heart went aflutter when Cecil emerged from the inn, various tools and instruments hanging from the heavy belt cinched tightly beneath his also-tight white shirt. He stopped to pet a bulldog and wiped a handful of glistening slobber on his pants.

"You get it?" he asked, opening the carriage door.

Pippi couldn't wait for the door to open all the way before falling down into his arms and kissing him long and hard. "I did," she panted.

"Need help hanging it up before I leave?" Cecil also panted. "Or should we go...discuss something real quick?" He raised his eyebrows in Pippi's direction then nodded politely at Tellie and Clive as they descended from the carriage.

"No, no," Pippi laughed. "You go. You can't be late, you're still on probation."

"Dad's already there. I was just waiting to say goodbye. This is the oldest inn we've transitioned yet, supposedly there's a *dungeon*."

"Sounds right up your alley," Pippi teased, thinking of her own version of a dungeon downstairs, which, now that she thought of it, may very well have been a dungeon at one point. The basement finally became known to Pippi after using her key to unlock a door under the stairs, which led to a spiral staircase she was too scared to traverse herself. A quick ride on a spider down to the basement floor and a short moat ride later, Pippi finally introduced herself to Emberheart's grandfather, Brandr, an impressive ancient furnace of little words that kept the inn at the appropriate temperature, all day, every day.

But what Brandr was *not* great at was organization and, as what happened with most basements, his home had become a dumping ground for items the inn didn't know where else to place, like carriages, canning jars, swords, and many, many, many more things including, to Pippi's surprise, her car. The cavernous basement was where Rose, Winifred, and Emberheart (who Winifred had unofficially adopted) were working now, after happily accepting the offer to stay longer at the inn and take on the enormous task of creating an inventory of the cluttered basement's contents. Even though Pippi was in no rush to get the job done it did seem they were making *very* slow progress, but she suspected that was due to the lengthy talks Rose, Winifred, and Emberheart were drawn into with Brandr, who became a furnace of many words if asked the right history question.

After one more kiss goodbye, Cecil went upstairs to the linen closet portal. Pippi had gotten used to Cecil skipping town a day or two a week, as he and his father worked on upgrading all the phones in the Ethereal Accomodations for Restful Travel and Hospitality system. With the distraction of a job needing done, Cecil and John were healing their relationship inn by inn. So far the upgraded phone system was a wild success, not just for E.A.R.T.H. and the innkeepers, but most importantly, for the guests, who could now talk back to their loved one's calls. Their words of comfort traveled the phone line back to the caller, blossoming into a knowing breeze on the face, a break in the clouds at just the right time, a forgotten memory brought back to life, and countless other moments that meant and said everything the living caller needed to hear. Pippi had stopped asking how, all she knew is that it did, and that it changed everything.

Carefully placing the heavy package on the front porch, Pippi tore apart the parchment paper until she unearthed her new sign. Carved into a heavy block of cedar was a familiar fox face, captured perfectly just as Juniper had said. Below Hazel's caricature read *Pippi's Inn for Wandering Spirits, Windia, Oregon.*

A breeze caught Pippi's attention. The sunny afternoon was retreating slowly, submitting to the cold February evenings that had returned to claim its rightful place. She touched the wood, sanded to perfection, tracing her name with her fingertip. Embracing the sign in a full-body hug, Pippi lumbered over to the sign post installed just yesterday in preparation for this moment. The other guests outside jumped in to help and together they looped the sign over the heavy iron hooks that would creak in the wind, a sweet sound that would be heard from anywhere within the inn's property line.

"Do you like foxes?" Tellie asked.

"I do, actually," Pippi smiled. "They just might be my favorite animal, in fact."

Pippi's chest leapt as a call came through. Her eyes still on the sign, she flipped open her cell phone.

"Furever Pets call for...Archie. Ready to connect?"

Pippi looked down at the orange and white tabby cat rubbing against her legs, purring against her exposed skin. Pippi picked up Archie and walked inside.

"Ready to connect."

Chapter Twenty-Eight

The inn was so quiet that Pippi could hear her own breathing, tight in her chest as she stood at the big front windows, watching and waiting. The clock ticked steadily on the library's fireplace mantle. A broom swept the dining room floors. A flock of wild turkeys gobbled and pecked at the grass in the backyard, where the guests had spilled a fair amount of popcorn at last night's outdoor movie night. She looked away for a moment to stare at the warm afternoon light pooled on the window seat cushion, the suspended dust particles glistening like flecks of gold, exposed in that moment of stillness.

The inn was not usually so quiet in the afternoon, even after a day full of summer activities that sent the guests searching for comfy corners where they could take a quick nap before dinner. It was the Fourth of July and in honor of the day and the memories it contained, Pippi had spent the day hosting a celebration down at the beach where she'd left Rose and Cecil to set up the tables for dinner. The day had been perfect and while the rest of the state was battling triple digits, the coast remained the same, a haven forever and always. Special guests Winifred and Emberheart, (who had recently purchased a grill attachment for himself) had planned a dinner for the group of stuffed burgers, brats, and skewers of grilled vegetables. But they were waiting to start until they spotted Pippi's return on the horizon, a basket of fireworks on her arm, her final task of the day complete.

Finally, she heard it. Pippi ran to the entryway at the sound of the helicopter's approach, slipping through the front door on which the stained glass depicted a scene of a large heart floating over a helicopter in the sky with the setting sun in the background. She met the helicopter on the front lawn, shielding her eyes as Chopper expertly landed the craft on the dry summer grass. He opened the heavy glass door and exited, tossing his gloves back inside and shutting the door loudly.

"Ma'am," Chopper nodded. "Afternoon."

Pippi jumped up and down and clapped. "Happy Fourth of July!"

Chopper looked around. Pippi grinned ridiculously, looking over her shoulder towards the front door. She rubbed her hands together.

"I thought you said there was a barbeque," he said flatly.

"Oh, there is. Down at the beach."

"Then what-"

Chopper was interrupted by a long howl that echoed through the inn. He perked up and listened, his wide eyes trailing to Pippi. The howl grew louder and more insistent until finally Pippi turned and ran up the porch steps to fling open the front door. An old hound dog bounded down the steps with the energy of a puppy, barreling straight towards Chopper. They hit the grass together in a heap of howls as Chopper untangled himself long enough to take hold of the spirit dog's face and look him straight in the eye.

"Herman?" he choked.

"It's him! It really is!" Pippi squealed, jumping up and down and clapping. "*It's Old Herman!*"

Chopper struggled to his knees and hugged the dog, who was uncontrollably licking his owner's face.

"How?" was all Chopper could manage, wiping away tears with his leathered hand.

Pippi skipped down the steps. "He was at another inn this *whole* time! Out in Cottage Grove!"

"Cottage Grove?"

"See, a few months ago I joined this program called Furever Pets and even though you never *told* me who Old Herman was, I started thinking about it and took a guess it was a pet, so I put out a notice to other innkeepers to look for a pet that answered to Old Herman, very specifically *Old Herman*, and I immediately got a call from the Cottage Grove inn," Pippi blubbered. "So I transferred him last night!"

"Cottage Grove," Chopper repeated, staring into Old Herman's eyes. "Herman and I used to live there way back when."

"He was waiting for you!" Pippi exclaimed.

Chopper embraced the dog, weeping hard into the dog's brown fuzzy coat. Pippi cried too, but Herman looked more ready to play. Finally, Chopper stood up and blew his nose into an oil-splattered handkerchief. He reached out and gave Pippi a strong hug.

"Thank you, little lady," he mumbled, then released her from the hug.

Pippi straightened her overall shorts. "You're very welcome."

"Can I visit him again?"

Pippi tapped her chin. "Actually, we're kind of full here at the inn, so I was wondering if you'd help me out and keep Herman at your house?"

Chopper tried to hold back more tears. " Yes. Thank you. How long will he...?"

"Don't worry." Pippi placed her hand on Chopper's shoulder. "You'll both know when it's time. I'll be here when you're ready."

With a strike of a match, the sparkler exploded to life. Pippi sat back against her sturdy sea throne and watched the spark travel down the line, burning steady and strong. In the darkness, it was only her and that sparkler, searing through space, setting life on fire without a thought for the inevitable end. Finally, at long last, the spark gave out and transformed to a pillar of pungent smoke, still warm enough to bring the next sparkler to life.

"Hey! Pippi!"

Pippi leaned forward in her sea throne. The guests and Cecil were gathered further down the beach, an army of sparklers swinging fiercely against the wind, tossing sticks into the bonfire as they waited for night to fully descend.

Cecil waved his arms. "C'mon! You're gonna miss it!"

"Coming!" Pippi shouted, wiping away the tears that escaped in the darkness.

She ran through the cool sand to Cecil's side, where he was readying to set off the one big firework they'd allowed themselves for the Fourth of July. It was technically *frowned upon* in Oregon (aka: illegal) to set off any kind of firework that shoots straight up into the sky, but Windia was their own little corner of the world, they told themselves. Surely laws like that don't apply when you live in a place like this.

"I think the time is just right," Cecil said, holding a finger in the air to test the wind. He looked at Pippi. "You okay?"

"Yeah. You know…memories," Pippi sniffed, zipping her jacket closed, which was covered with a patriotic pattern of hot dogs, the United States flag, and a cartoon character that looked somewhat like George Washington.

"Would you rather watch from over there?" he asked, motioning to the sea throne.

Pippi looked over at the bonfire, around which the spirits had taken their seat in anticipation of the show, wrapped in blankets, their exposed faces flickering in the firelight. Emberheart sat between Rose and Winifred, who appeared almost as excited as the Furever Pets who had stretched out across the sand, finally able to watch the wonder of a light show without fear. Mo sat amongst them, guarding the smaller creatures from wandering too close to the fire. John stood by with a bucket of water, which he insisted was necessary even with the Pacific nearby keeping an eye on their shenanigans.

Pippi shook her head. "Nah. This is where I belong."

She turned and raced to her little group, taking a seat next to Rose and resting her head on her mother's shoulder. Pippi smiled as she listened to the guests share stories of summers long past but still very much alive. Then, like a comet, the rocket shot into the sky, erupting into a plume of brilliant fireworks, and together they marveled at the bright light of life, beautiful and complete no matter how brief it may be.

Acknowledgements

I have so many wonderful, supportive people in my life that encourage my writing, it's hard to know where to start. But maybe, in line with the theme of this book, I'll start with the people I've lost. My Grandpa Borchers and Aunt Lee, who told me I should be an author and kept all my old manuscripts. My Grandma Whitmire, who taught me about reaching out with my mind to find comfort when I'm upset. My Grandpa Whitmire, who wrote long before I did, in large, sweeping letters, and in his voice I heard my own.

In this living world, I want to thank my husband Nick, who is my champion, my most-embarrassing-draft reader, and the one I want to make most proud. My daughters Olive and Esper, whose imaginations inspire me every day. My parents Tom and Lori, and brother Ryan, who first loved my writing at ten and haven't stopped believing in me since. To my first readers, including Tess, Savannah, Rachel, Kayla, and Lorna who offer encouragement, valuable feedback, and wonderful friendship. And readers – thank you, too. I have so much fun on social media (I'm talking about you, Booktok!) discussing the ins and outs of giant spider sweaters, the best name for a ghost train, and many more details I think will only matter to me, but seem to connect us all together. And to Taylor Swift. I wrote this entire book to your music. I'm totally serious.

About the Author

Erin Ritch is the founder of No Wyverns Publishing and holds degrees in Broadcasting, Film, and English Literature. In addition to her published novels, her essay work has appeared in Oregon Home Magazine and the Manifest Station. Many of her stories take place in the Pacific Northwest, where there's magic around every corner. Erin lives in rural Oregon with her husband, two daughters, and an Irish Terrier named Arthur Pendragon.

You can learn more about Erin and her work at erinritch.com or by following her on social media at the following accounts:

Tiktok – @AuthorErinRitch
Facebook – @ErinRitchAuthor
Instagram – @NoWyvernsPublishing

ALSO BY ERIN RITCH

Windia Cozy Fantasy
Witchy Coffee

Epic Fantasy
Myth

Paranormal Fantasy
The Reanimation of Robert

Historical Fiction
Memories Wait Alone

Middle Grade Fiction
The Quinn Family Adventures: The Mayan Ruins

Short Stories
No Wyverns Publishing Short Fiction Collection: Volume I

Thank You

I sincerely hope you enjoyed your visit to the Windia Inn! Please consider leaving an honest review so others can discover *Pippi's Inn for Wandering Spirits,* too! Reviews are incredibly valuable to indie authors like myself, so I appreciate you taking the extra time to share your thoughts. Thank you!

www.ingramcontent.com/pod-product-compliance
Lightning Source LLC
Chambersburg PA
CBHW022007310726
48972CB00006B/1560